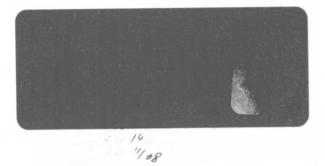

BOOKS BY BILL BRANON

Let Us Prey
Devils Hole
Timesong

SPIDER SNATCH

SPIDER SNATCH

A NOVEL

BILL BRANON

HUNTINGTON PRESS • LAS VEGAS

Huntington Press
3687 South Procyon Avenue
Las Vegas, Nevada 89103
(702) 252-0655 Phone
(702) 252-0675 Fax

Spider Snatch
Copyright © 2000, Bill Branon

Printing History
1st Edition—January 2000

Interior design:
Bethany Coffey & Jason Cox

To the Cunas of Cayos Holandeses ... for your kindness toward a shipwrecked sailor. Never have black ants, pre-chewed fish, and sugar-cane coffee tasted better.

Acknowledgements

The book is stillborn without the tolerance, endurance, and brilliance of editors Deke Castleman and Lynne Loomis.

To Anthony Curtis and his crew at Huntington Press: Bethany Coffey, Jason Cox, Jody Olson, Len Cipkins, Jim Karl, and Michele Bardsley ... deckmates tried and true. Your product speaks for itself. Your enthusiasm and friendship are special. Thanks.

To pre-readers Jon Olson, Brent Lykins, Leona Beltz, Bob Howie, Mike Branon, and Diane Branon for your criticism, support, and insults. Thanks ... I think.

And not least to the players and ghosts: To the old man of Isla Miria with his ivory eye and his three-legged dog; to the elegantly evil El Tigre of San Andreas; to the gentle Cunas—young and old—of the outer islands; to John Mann and the Moodys; to Chuck and Marlene Burns; and to Evvie. And to Lolly who was there.

And to Motu who died on the reef.

This is a singing to the little child.
You have lost your spirit.
Neles beneath the hammock,
Come close to this child!
Here, little spirit, they come
Into the earth to find you!
Ka! Give forth
Smoke through their clothes,
Make the evil spirits cough.
Neles! Go into their houses!
Tear down their houses, look for them!
Uchu, Ka! Go underground now!

      —Cuna chant

Chapter 1

May 23—California

Archibald Simms had a headache. His eyes hurt. His joints hurt. Even his toes hurt.

His skin was as dry as it was white, almost transparent. His diet of back-alley meth and tangerines just wasn't doing the job; it was great for taking off the pounds, but the surgeon general hadn't signed off on it yet. Three weeks ago, his speed queen got herself dusted. The only other garbage in town was in the county landfill, and nobody he knew had figured out how to shoot up coffee grounds or bald tires.

So he decided to ride the black horse. The horse didn't ride cheap.

His hard little stomach temporarily released its grip on the snarl of barbed wire inside, but that tormented digestive muscle was getting ready to cramp all over again. Heroin withdrawal was teaching Simms how to do the zombie twist. He was a quick study.

Simms had to struggle to deliver the prepartum .38 loads into the six dark little wombs of his snub-ugly Saturday night special. But he managed. The monkey on his back had a new pair of ice skates and was going for the gold.

"You've got to be here, Ted."

"I don't 'got' to be anywhere, Evvie. I'll be there when I goddamn get there."

"You said you'd pick up the cream on the way home, Honey. I need it for the salad. The Burns will be here in forty-five minutes."

"Do a tap dance for the Burns. Get 'em drunk. Ed flies better shit-faced than sober, anyhow. Trust me."

"Tell Harry we've got company tonight. Just this once?"

"Harry's got more to worry about than your half-assed dinner party.

DEA's getting its balls toasted in the budget hearings. We need a Waco that works, or there's going to be a lot of narcs selling pencils."

"Maybe this thing with the Burns will get your mind off—"

"Right! And maybe me picking up a fucking bottle of cream, or whatever the fuck it is, instead of finishing this report, will make it easier for the fucking bean counters in D.C. to decide who gets the ax next in this fucking office."

When he started talking again, his voice sounded tired, and she put down the impulse to fire back at his insensitivity.

"Tell the Burns to suck eggs till I get there."

"I'll get the cream. I hate to wake up the baby; she still seems a little bit feverish. I don't think she'll need to be on the medicine much longer. Maybe one more night."

"Wake her up. She'll live."

"Get here when you can, Honey. Love you."

But Honey had already hung up.

In the parking lot of the convenience store, Evvie lifted Cindy out of the safety seat. She didn't want to leave her in the car. Evvie never took chances with her little girl.

Simms was already dead and falling to the pavement when the third round fired by the store clerk clipped off the top of his left ear and penetrated Cindy's temple on the right side of her head. Twenty feet from the door, standing on the outside walk, Evvie had watched the store clerk crouch on one knee and fire a silver pistol point-blank at Simms. Simms' own handgun was only a dark shadow, ineffective, hanging down. Not fired even once.

It happened too quickly to justify the cancellation of a small life.

She'd been carrying Cindy on her right hip when it happened. No place to go. The bright lights. People ducking. Simms backing through the swinging doors with enough momentum to buck them open. Then the fear. The brilliant, sudden fear.

The physical impact of the bullet hitting Cindy was barely noticeable. A tap. A pat. A gentle shove. Not even that. The noise of the killing shot sounded to Evvie as though it had come from somewhere very far away.

It echoed. And echoed. And echoed.

During the one-sided shootout and immediately after, all eyes were on Simms and the store clerk. Witnesses focused on the weapons, distracted by their own fear. Evvie glanced down at her dead child and then, hobbled by shock, looked up at nothing in particular. She shifted Cindy into position across her chest and held her close, like she did when she was nursing. She took three steps back, opened the car door, reached in, and got Cindy's blanket. She didn't get in the car. She wrapped the blanket around her daughter of eighteen months to shield the child's still face from prying eyes.

Evvie turned away from the glare of the lights. She began to walk.

She left the car because she knew that if she drove, she'd have to put Cindy on the seat. She couldn't hold her and drive at the same time. And she had to hold her. She tucked the blanket more tightly around her baby.

She walked through pale patches of streetlight. There was no moon. She turned a corner and waited for a crossing signal to flash, then went across a street and up a hill. She walked on new concrete, the sidewalk of a residential area. She passed a red tricycle with its front wheel turned toward a hedge. A skateboard. The white lines of a hop-scotch game on a driveway. Farther on, a small dog barked. She realized why she was heading west. The hospital. Two miles away between the freeway and the ocean.

Nurses. Doctors. Someone who could help.

The people there would tell her what to do.

She knew that Cindy was gone forever, but it was important to get to the hospital before someone saw, before she had to tell a stranger who was only curious, before she was asked to explain a thing she didn't understand.

After she had covered the first mile, Evvie changed. A corrosive sadness began to eat the protecting numbness. She didn't go into the hospital. She walked past it and continued the extra half-mile to the beach. The same beach where, on the morning of that same day, she and Cindy had drawn faces in the sand with a stick and made eyes for those faces with white stones.

An hour later, a lady named Lolly, walking with her dog, found Evvie sitting on the sand at the edge of the ocean.

Evvie let Lolly look at Cindy.

Whatever words were spoken were the right words ... because Evvie began to cry.

June 20—Connecticut

"Do you think she ever got that extra breast taken off?"

"Not in high school."

"Three-tits Evvie whose daddy drove a Chevy? Top-heavy Evvie?"

"Amy Kravitz! That's crude!"

"I would've had it cut off. The crap she had to put up with. Those rhymes. And the jokes we made. About buying bras, that kind of stuff. My folks said they would've got it cut off if it was me."

"Your folks had bucks. Anyway, it was small. Doc Greenberg called it a vestigial breast. You never saw it? On the left. Below the normal one. Only a couple of inches big. Not something anyone would notice, not if you dressed right."

"And stayed out of the gym shower. And didn't date guys like Eddie."

"I heard a rumor that she just lost a baby. A drive-by shooting or something."

"Really? That's horrible! Poor Evvie."

"Well, if anybody could recover from that, old Happy Face Evvie could. She could've smiled her way through Auschwitz."

"Yeah. So friggin' upbeat. Even with that pervert father of hers and that weirdo mother. Remember that thirty dollars I swiped from the senior fund? My mom didn't pay it back; Evvie did. She told me she had plenty of dough in the bank and it wasn't doing any good just sitting there."

"She did that? For you?"

"Yeah. That was Evvie. Bucky Finney worked at First Federal. He told me she never had more than forty bucks in that account."

"Admit it, Amy. You never really liked her."

"I was down in high school. Screwed up."

"Prom queen? Three colleges in heat? Tony Dixon bare-ass drunk and threatening to jump off the breakwater 'cause you wouldn't give him the time of day? Give me a break!"

"So I was a bitch. But I've got that thirty bucks right here. I was going to pay it back if she showed tonight."

"A high-school tenth reunion's a big thing. She should be here."

"Remember how she used to fold her arms across her chest over that extra tit? I saw her mom slap her once for doing that."

"About all she got out of this place was Best Disposition in the yearbook. At least she got that."

"I thought I had that one wrapped up."

"Amy! You piggy! You got First to Get Married and Best Looking."

"Yeah. I guess disposition was a thing she could do something about."

July 4—Connecticut

In May, the day after Cindy was killed, Evvie had called her mother and asked her to come to California from Connecticut for the service.

Her mother didn't come.

The weeks of mourning passed. Ted fell deeper into the hole that opened up after Cindy's death. He didn't smile. Didn't talk. Never did break down like people break down when a loved one dies. He seemed to absorb the fact of their loss with stone-cold resignation, a reaction she tried to rationalize but could not. Even before the loss of Cindy, Evvie found herself making excuses for Ted. Too many excuses. Now this. She was alone, like being alone was all there was.

God gave Cindy to them, then took her back. The gift had turned into an ulcerated memory.

Over the Fourth of July weekend, she traveled from San Diego back to Connecticut where her mother still lived in the old house a half-mile from the high school. As Evvie drove the town's center street in her rented car, the New England of her youth flooded back. At one corner, she ran a stop sign that wasn't there before. Still, she was struck by the sameness of the place. But her sense of proportion was out of phase with reality: The town was a smaller town; the distances between buildings and corners were shorter; she came to side roads and recollections too quickly; it was too compact, too closed in, smothering, trite.

For a reason she didn't want to understand, she drove past the house three times before turning into the paved driveway. She parked the car on the grass beneath the tall elm tree. She pulled off onto the grass out of habit. She remembered the day her father ran his pickup over her bicycle on purpose to teach her a lesson about the need to keep the driveway clear. She was more careful after that.

Her mother opened the door and gave her a hug and asked if she'd like a cup of tea and said, "There's water on." Evvie said "Yes" and followed her mother to the kitchen through rooms that were exactly like they were ten years ago.

They drank tea.

Said things that meant nothing.

Talked briefly about life and how difficult it could be at times without being too specific, but that "God had a plan." Her mother's words.

Evvie wondered about that plan.

Later, alone because her mother had promised Mrs. Alnutt down the street that she'd bring over a recipe for cinnamon apple pie, Evvie went upstairs to her old room. Not much was different, just smaller. She looked out the window. The elm tree had filled out and blocked the view. She couldn't see the street anymore. She turned away from the window. She walked around the bed and stood in the narrow space between the bed and the wall, where small blue flowers printed in too-straight rows on white wallpaper seemed to muffle little sounds that should have been there. Evvie knelt in the narrow space, then lowered onto her belly and lay down on the worn carpet and rested her head on her arms like she did so many times long ago. That was how she always did her school work, lying on her stomach on the floor between the bed and the wall ... the wall where the floor-level grate covered the heating duct that angled down to the basement; the grate she listened through on Friday nights when the sounds of the men came up from below as they watched the X-rated movies her father put on at one dollar per customer to cover the cost. She often fell asleep there, her head on a library book, a history text, her mother's Bible.

Evvie and her mother ate dinner together in the big kitchen that evening. Not much was said, nothing solved. Shallow memories. Bits of lightweight gossip. What happened to? ... Do you ever? ... And more tea.

Nothing about her father.

Nothing about how he had blown off the top of his head the night the whiskey and time ran out.

Nothing about the young blind girl he raped.

Nothing about the indictment. No talk of the confusing terms used by the defense lawyer at the trial: genetic defect, dissociation disorder, depersonalization. Words that Evvie remembered so clearly despite her young age. Words that she wondered at but which nobody would explain for her. Words that somehow seemed to hold answers, would let her understand.

The looks. The silence.

The shame.

After dinner, Evvie stood alone on the front walk and watched fireworks blossom above the high school. The holiday weekend was one of the reasons her airfare from San Diego to Hartford had been so expensive, that and the fact she had come to New England on an impulse. Airlines made you pay for impulse.

A little after the fireworks ended, a couple came toward Evvie on the walk.

"My God! Is that you, Evvie? Evvie Boxer?"

Evvie took a step backward, but there was no shadow to hide in. "Amy? Amy Kravitz?" said Evvie. "… Amy?"

"Where have you been?! We missed you at the reunion. We were talking about you just two weeks ago. I can't believe it!" Arms around, cheeks almost touching, air hugs. Then at arm's length. Amy's arms.

"Evvie, you look great!" Eyes up and down. Amy still squealed instead of talked. "You haven't gained an ounce!"

Evvie couldn't say the same about Amy. The Prettiest Girl in the Class was a sow. "I'm just visiting Mom … from San Diego. … I live there." Her words sounded stupid, alien, prepubescent. She was fast regressing into another time, another personality, another relationship.

But the regression brought back the old perkiness. She smiled at the guy. "Amy, you son of a gun! Where'd you get this hunk of meat? We knew you'd end up with the best-looking catch on the dock!" *Dock is right,* she thought, and stuck out her hand to the tall, fish-faced simpleton standing at civilian attention next to her schoolmate. *This man is wearing shoes for the first time in his life.* A conclusion more in wonder than humor.

"This is Dittsey Scullion. We're tying the knot next week! Can you imagine? It's his first time!"

Evvie shook her head slowly. *First time? First time ashore? Dittsey? Dittsey Scullion?* The tall sedative of a man took her hand and squeezed her fingers too hard and mumbled something aimed at the top of her head. In the dim light Evvie thought the fellow's eyes were slightly crossed, but she couldn't be sure and she didn't want to stare.

Amy reached over and took Evvie's hand out of his and held it in her own. "Evvie," and she swung Evvie's hand from side to side like they were both five years old, "... can you come? Can you come to the wedding?"

"Gee, I'd love to! I wish I could. But I'm going back in the morning."

They made small talk. When they chatted about the senior prom, Amy started to reach for her wallet, but hesitated, glanced sideways at Dittsey, and stopped. And Amy hesitated a second time when she thought to ask Evvie about the loss of the child. But that moment also passed. Amy preferred to keep center stage.

Twelve hours later, Evvie was headed back to California.

The trip worked. The memories of Cindy had no connection with the New England memories, but California seemed the lesser horror. And her mother, alone with her recipes, was a mixture of doubt and self-willed ignorance far too fragile to disturb.

July 22—California

"The Agency's cutting back. Harry says I'm out."

"Harry can't do that! You carry that place!"

"It's got nothing to do with Harry. He'll be gone himself by December." Ted's voice rose, ranting sounds. "If those pus suckers in Congress think the FBI can do what we're doing ... Shit! Harry and me, we never got a chance to nail one of the big fish, never got a chance. ... Just fucking sidewalk servers and goddamn day trippers ... never one of the big boys. I'd of given my ass to have nailed a big boy. Just one fucking once." Then he descended into that surly place Evvie couldn't reach.

She watched him for a long time. Then, to her surprise, she felt a spark, a tiny flash of hope. "Ted? Let's chuck it. Let's get away and start again."

He didn't look at her. He didn't reply.

"We have enough money to stop for a while. Let's fall in love again."

"You don't love me now?" Hard, aggressive words.

"I love you too much," she said. "I want you back."

A week later, he was out, along with six others. Collect a paycheck to the end of the month. Sayonara.

But something had changed and changed for the better. When she thought nothing else could go wrong, it didn't.

They were munching burgers in the parking lot of a fast-food joint as the sun was going down. "What you said? ..." He looked almost playful, the way he did when they first met. Over the previous few days she had sensed a shift in his mood that she attributed more to her own hope than to reality.

"What did I 'said'?" she asked.

"About doing something crazy."

"About chucking it? Looks like it's been chucked for us."

"That's right."

"You've decided to shoot me?" She reached across the console and stole a French fry. She made him bite off one end before she ate it.

"I'm serious, Evvie."

Her mind came alive. Not because of what he was saying, but because of the way he was saying it. For the first time since the accident, they were alone. No recrimination. No guilt. No small ghost. She waited.

"Still think you can sail?" he asked. "You used to be pretty damned good at it. Or have you forgotten those so-called sailing lessons you gave me?"

She watched the last fry disappear into his grin. She recalled the San Francisco days and the deal they'd made when they first met: If she'd teach him how to sail, he'd teach her some of the Agency hand-to-hand stuff, *Dim Mak, Jeet Kune Do,* kicks, chops, and choke holds. All the stuff a modern girl needed to survive an Oakland commute. The lessons were a transparent excuse to spend time together. Most of all, she liked learning about the things he called "sneaky Petes," improvised, clever gimmicks. Like how to make a time-delay fuse out of a matchbook by tucking a lit cigarette under the matches. Or how to disable an attacker with a pencil poked up under the jaw. Even the ugly, quiet efficiency of an ice pick or a screwdriver driven down through the center top of the skull. And one time, so easily that it surprised her, she put Ted down for five minutes with a sleeper hold. She thought he was faking it, but when he came to he was angry. He gave her a twenty-minute lecture about being more careful.

She put memories away. "Sail?" she asked. "What do you mean 'sail'?"

"I know it sounds off the wall, but Harry knows this guy who wants to get rid of a nice little twenty-eight-foot sailboat. He's not asking much."

Her heart cranked up.

"Well?" He was looking at her.

"Well what?" she answered.

"Give it a shot?"

"Maybe."

"Maybe?"

She was quiet. She only breathed.

"Listen up, sailor girl. I found out this afternoon that I've got an open invite to work a security position on the East Coast. In Newport. Rhode Island. The Agency has a rehire program. It's an open offer. Show up any time between now and the end of the century." He let the words settle into her. Then he said, "We could bum around, cruise a bit, get rid of some of our money, then sail the boat up to Rhode Island. That's if you like the thing and want to buy it."

"Sail up to Newport?" she asked. "Where's the boat? Virginia? Florida?"

"Nope," he said. "Guess again."

The boat could be in hell. She wouldn't care. "I give up."

"Panama."

"Panama City? Florida?"

"Panama … the Canal Zone."

Chapter 2

August—Panama

The hundred-year rain.

An avalanche of rain.

The tropical forest canopy sagged, then groaned like some suddenly overloaded beast. Soft leaves rattled. Spinster twigs snapped. Gangster vines gripped limbs in green desperation. Soil went to muck, muck to quicksand, quicksand to soup. Small things tumbled toward oblivion on churning veins of liquid. Butterflies drowned upside down under branches. Grubs gagged. Spider spit ripped and eight-legged atheists had three seconds to learn to walk on water. Sparks of new life that chirped in abandoned nests were short-circuited to eternity.

Color bled to pastel and then to gray.

White tines of lightning raked the air with helter-skelter, ozone-aromatic violence, and thunder tried to follow, but all sound was murdered by the smothering equatorial torrent. The monsoon pounded the land, a rain so heavy that the only wind was down.

Two men got out of a late-model mud-splattered car and proceeded on a path of wooden planks toward a low white house at the edge of a clearing. The taller of the two held a black umbrella, but not over his own head. Water cascaded off the edges onto his shoulders and down his back. The shorter man, the one he was protecting from the rain, was a dark wiry shape of forty years; a snake skull crowning a body that was a grab bag of razors and wasps covered by tight smooth skin; flat gray eyes that took things and never gave them back; a profile beyond angular, a profile closer to fillet of evil. The protected man held a thin black cigar in his right hand. A lighted cigar. The right arm was normal. The left arm was a grotesque gnarl, a permanently bent right angle of defective bone and withered flesh.

"He comes, Papa! El Codo comes!"

The father turned quickly from the window that framed the two men coming toward the house. He looked at his son. He took the eight-year-old by the hair and snapped back the young head so the eyes were his. "No more El Codo!" he hissed. Urgent words in Spanish. "Never those words! Never! Not with him so near!" He released his grip, and the terrified child ran away to a back room where women hid.

The two men entered. Water turned the wood floor black.

The cigar still burned.

Gray eyes transfixed the father, then flickered to a ragged stuffed chair by the single oil lamp. El Codo, "The Elbow," went to the chair and sat down. "Three days." His words were ice smooth, the tone oddly metallic. "You and the others will be at Punta Mansueto at sunrise in three days."

The flat eyes flashed at the taller man with the umbrella who was still standing by the door. The man laid the umbrella on the floor and produced a folded paper from inside his jacket as he crossed the room. It was a chart that covered the sea approaches to the northeast coast of Panama. The man spread the chart on a table next to the chair.

"We are ready," said the father. "We will be there." His eyes shifted to El Codo. "And you, Señor Arango? Where will we find you?"

El Codo didn't answer the question. He only let the silence hang.

The father lowered his gaze.

More details were discussed. The talk continued in clipped phrases of instruction and acknowledgment. Smoke from the cigar coiled up and hunted the shadows of the low rafters.

Rum was served by the father. The three drank.

The small boy shuffled slowly from the darkness. He cradled a spot of yellow in his two hands. The three men watched him. He came cautiously to the chair of El Codo. With soft Spanish words he held up the baby chick. The child's small arms extended. Eyes afraid, but hopeful. Wanting to share.

"Señor, this is my Bandito. ... My papa brought him from the village."

The gray eyes looked.

"You can hold him."

The cigar went into the large glass ashtray.

The right hand reached out and made a cup of flesh. The boy placed the chick in El Codo's hand.

"He already walks across the yard," offered the boy, "and he eats seeds by himself."

The fingers closed gently on the soft puff of yellow. A thing like a smile moved the smooth flesh of El Codo's mandible. The sign of softness inside hardness drained some of the tension from the father's face. The chick peeked out between careful fingers, its small head flicking from side to side, searching for seed because the day's routine had been changed by the visitors.

The boy stepped back, a tentative, successful look.

El Codo continued to hold the chick and moved it close to his chest. The last few questions were asked and answered.

"I do not want to go back into that swamp," said El Codo. The flat eyes flicked at the window. A twitch of snake grin moved his lips. "But we must go before the road washes out."

The father nodded and, standing behind his son, held the boy pressed against his front with strong hands. On the boy's face silent tears cut twin streaks made gold in the light of the single lamp.

El Codo deposited the crushed chick in the glass ashtray and stubbed out the end of his cigar in a purple extrusion of chick gut.

The 727 carved its way into the edge of a massive thunderhead rising above the jungle. In the passenger cabin, things rattled that weren't supposed to rattle. The pilot corrected to seaward, a dipping turn, unexpected, and the aircraft angled back out over the ocean. The turn made Evvie's stomach float.

Evelyn Boxer North, twenty-nine years of tomboy in blue silk. When she walked, her trim hips viewed from behind looked like they rode some kind of uneven seesaw, one side going too high, the other too low, at each step. In her it was cute; in anyone else, an invite to an osteopath. When she laughed, which was often enough, her laugh ended in a strange little snort, a reason for the osteopath to refer that same "anyone else" to the ENT clinic.

Evvie was almost beautiful. High cheekbones. Bright hazel eyes. Full lips in a perpetual pout, but not a dumb pout, not a put-on. Sexy. Maybe even more than sexy. Short dark hair. A five-foot-three-inch superstructure, sensuous even though the waist didn't pinch in, nothing close to voluptuous, more of the tomboy again. Put together like a Navy destroyer, compact and full of purpose. No man of medicine—osteopath, ENT specialist, or any other—would tinker with such a mix.

Evvie tried to concentrate on the Panama guidebook. She nudged Ted with her elbow. "It says here that the tourist season in Panama runs from December to March. That's the dry season."

Ted leaned forward, looked past her at the storm through window glass streaked with horizontal runs of rain, then settled back. "Okay. So we're four months early." He gulped down the last of his vodka tonic and waved his empty cup at the flight attendant braced in the aisle two seats away. The attendant held a trash bag and was trying to maintain a practiced composure despite the turbulence, an inane smile painted on a high-mileage face. The woman responded to Ted's raised plastic cup by giving him a thumbs-up sign. The move caused her to let go of the supporting seatback, and she performed a dramatic little three-step as the plane lurched sideways.

"I don't like this!" Evvie grabbed Ted's hand. "I wish to hell we were on the ground."

Ted grinned a vodka grin and squeezed her fingers. "Might be a good idea to attach a couple of modifiers to that one, Mrs. North. There's more than one way to get this thing down."

"Thanks for sharing that." Evvie looked out the window again. The plane moved into smoother air and settled down.

She continued to grip his hand as she watched the monsoon boil a few hundred yards away, still too close for her to ignore. The lightning flickered without interruption, like a downed powerline arcing across wet earth in a hurricane. She tried to imagine what it was like in the jungle beneath the storm. The animals. The people. The land itself. She decided that she'd still rather be down there than where she was.

The 727 made a descending turn between towering storm cells. Evvie clamped her teeth together and muttered a few gently obscene prayers as the plane began to shake again.

Ten minutes later she was able to see the ground. It seemed as if the big jet had stopped and was floating, as if the land was alive and lifting up to swallow them. She remembered the map of Panama in the guidebook and studied it again. The continents of North and South America looked like hunks of taffy pulling apart, with Panama the last shred holding them together. A strand that seemed about to snap.

"We'll use the rainy season to get to know the boat." Ted's voice sounded almost giddy, the alcohol shading his words. "We need some practice," he slurred. "It's been a long time."

It's been a long time.

She stared at the ribbons of rainwater trailing from the silver wing. Like sea spray streaming from a sail. She thought back to the days when she and Ted had made love beneath the sun in a small boat on windy San Francisco Bay. How they hurried home, showered together, went to bed, made love again, and joked about sunburn on parts that never got sunburned on proper couples. How Ted took the time a lover takes. How he kissed places a lover kisses. How he never mentioned the small extra breast. How he accepted her the way she was. How he made love to her with no words except a lover's words.

It has been a long time. Too long. They hadn't made love since Cindy's death. Not really. Together that way only when a hand accidentally touched another hand, a leg, a backside during a restless night. Those times were physical. Only physical. And softly sad. In the silence after sex, she'd been thankful that a breaking heart didn't make a sound.

As the plane lined up on the final approach to the runway, she felt an unexpected sense of relief, but not just at the prospect of getting her feet back on solid ground. The day Cindy was taken from them had been as bad a day as they would ever know. There couldn't be anything worse. Love, with time, would heal the scars. Things would get better.

A sudden flare of lightning blazed through the gut of the storm, a brute spark that turned the world from print to negative, all shadows reversed and inside out.

Chapter 3

The plane landed at Tocumen Airport three miles east of Panama City as night shut down the day.

Kent Davis met them on the other side of the customs gate. Davis, a seedy slouching man, stared at them through misted-over eyes that locked on Evvie's eyes after they ran the front of her body from head to toe. He was about fifty years old with short, chopped-off white hair. He had a stubble of beard and wore a white guayabera shirt that was wet and rumpled and seemed to be responsible for the stale oppressive humidity of the air terminal.

"North?" A rough hand was extended toward Ted. Its flesh was stained with brown peeling blotches as though it had been used, instead of a stick, to mix varnish.

"Kent Davis?"

The two men shook hands. When Ted introduced Evvie, Davis didn't acknowledge her except with a glance and a grunt.

"My car's outside," said Davis. "Was that storm pretty bumpy coming in? Ain't rained this fucking hard since I been here." He smirked, coughed, and spit on the floor. "I got you a room at the Hotel Washington on the Atlantic side in Colon. On the water. It's got a casino. You can rent yourself a car at the hotel."

The man had a smell to him. Tarred rope, whiskey, methane, low tide. He was a lean man, once a hard man, and he shifted from one foot to the other when he spoke. But not when he listened. There was something about him other than the smell of boatyards and bars, and Evvie had the impression, though only for a moment, that her husband and Davis had an unspoken sameness, not in appearance but in manner.

They loaded the trunk of the car and got inside. "This is Dulcie," said Davis. He nodded absently at the figure next to him, like he'd introduced them to his pet dog. The woman made a small smile, didn't speak, and only looked through the windshield at the lights and people moving on the concourse. She was unmistakably Central American Indian. Mid-twenties. Smooth brown skin, high cheekbones, a broad forehead, and a nose wide at its base but narrow in its spine. She wore a white blouse and a dark skirt. A generous swell of breast showed below a delicate neck roped by three strands of shell necklace. Her hair was jet black, straight, and short with bangs in an even line above dark eyes. Her teeth white, perfect.

The night ride from the airport to the hotel in Colon fifty miles to the north took an hour and a half. The road wound over hills and past small shacks, some with a single outside lightbulb mounted at the top of a rough pole and swarmed by flying things, some small, most large.

Twice Davis had to brake sharply, once for a cow walking toward them on the road and once for a dog sleeping in the light rain on the still-warm macadam. As they passed the dog, it only raised its head, then lay back down without otherwise moving.

They passed one-room cinderblock buildings with corrugated roofs and small neon signs advertising beer and cigarettes. In front of the cantinas, four or five battered cars parked near a couple of used-up horses tethered to a rail. Passing, they could hear music. Radio music. Brass, maracas, guitar. Shapes moved behind small panes of glass. Through the slightly open windows of the car, air came in carrying the smell of bread baking and of thick vegetation growing furiously in wet earth. Evvie thought she could hear vines twisting.

In the dark stretches between shacks it was as dark as dark gets, and she gripped Ted's hand firmly. Davis drove too fast through the night, mostly in the oncoming traffic lane, when it was empty, in order to avoid the deep sharp-edged potholes that cratered their side of the road like moonscape.

The curving asphalt snaked into the National Rain Forest Reserve. In that section, where no houses, bars, or anything else of civilization was built, Evvie learned that dark could be even darker ... so dark that it weighed something.

What conversation there was concerned the virtues of a sailboat named Coconut. Coconut was a wooden twenty-eight footer that drew five feet, was sloop rigged, and had power in the form of a ten-horse-power outboard motor hung from a transom bracket. Coconut had been sailed to Panama from Australia by a Canal Zone transit pilot. She had sailed "everywhere" in "all conditions" and could "handle herself" in a seaway. The boat had gone through the canal "at least a dozen times."

But in the hypnotic black of the rain forest Evvie's mind wandered. Her tired brain tried to catalog the new sensations and make sense of the old. Her mind struggled to recall the whys and retrace the steps. Davis' voice faded into the night and she closed her eyes.

Memories drifted out of her subconscious. At first, small things. The early morning sunbeam and how it would paint the edge of the countertop in the kitchen of the California house. The soft smell of soap and baby powder that perfumed the back room on laundry days. The sound of Ted's keys being dropped into the wooden box in the back hall when he came home from work. The feel of Cindy's fingers tangled in her hair while she talked on the phone and held her little girl. The crackle of grocery bags as she folded and stored them between the refrigerator and the wall.

Memories grew sharp edges and began to hurt.

… The three dolls and the stuffed bear she gave to the person from the charity. How she couldn't make her fingers let go.

… The ache in her gut that came each time she glanced up and saw another child.

… The expression on Ted's face at the hospital.

… The unholy ice in her husband's eyes during his mood swings, a look her brain understood but her heart couldn't accept. That look made her feel sick, different from the sick feeling she used to get back when she prayed on her knees on the kitchen floor in the middle of the day for her Ted to be safe, back when he was doing dangerous work in dangerous places because that was his job.

She understood why love had gone away. He was being eaten alive by guilt: If only he'd come home, hadn't worked late; if only he'd made the stop at the convenience store instead of her. A guilt unfair to shoulder because that wasn't how life worked. She could have made that day different as easily as he. She should have known he might be late. Could have planned better. Could have changed what happened. It might have been different. She could have gone to the store earlier. Or not forgotten to get the cream the day before. Or even decided on a different salad dressing, a choice so painfully small. It was as much her fault as his, more her fault.

That day.

That terrible day.

She had tried, more in anger than denial, to put away any thoughts of blame. It happened, that's all. It just happened. But how to make him see that? How to make him stop accusing himself?

He was on an island. Alone in an ocean of pain where something inhuman dissolved his soul. She could not reach him.

As for herself, the greatest pain by far, the endless hurt that wouldn't let her alone, was that Cindy's death had been too quick, too sudden.

No time for one last smile.

No time to say goodbye.

"Nothing like wood to give the feel of a real boat." Davis' voice. "You can take all those fucking plastic abortions and melt 'em into snot." The raw obscenity of the words jerked Evvie back to reality. The jungle. The car. Ted. Dulcie.

Davis rolled his window farther down, snorted, and spit something vile into the night. "Wood! It's got to be wood. Wood used to be alive. That's the difference between wood and glass. Fiberglass was never alive."

Window back up.

Ted asked questions about Coconut. How many sails did she have? What type? When was she last pulled and painted? Did she have navigation gear? What kind? But the conversation between the two men had the ring of lines in a play. A sing-song exchange somehow artificial. Evvie wondered.

Davis answered all the last questions without hedging.

Evvie wanted to ask questions too, but the thought of having to talk with Davis was unpleasant. She knew as much as Ted about boats and sailing, probably more, but there'd be time enough for questions. She'd ask Ted. He could ask Davis.

Then Ted asked if Coconut could make a long passage, like maybe one to the States, if the conditions were right? Davis looked briefly at him in the mirror, then looked away and laughed. He reached beneath the front seat, almost leaving the road in the process, and produced a half-empty bottle of gin. He worked the top off the bottle and offered it to Ted over the seatback. Ted drank a small amount and made a strangled cough that brought a smile to Evvie's face. Ted passed the bottle back to Davis.

Then Davis drank with his eyes and the bottom of the gin bottle pointed straight up at the roof of the car. He didn't look at the road for an eternity of seven seconds. Evvie grabbed Ted's forearm hard enough to make him wince, but his eyes stayed locked on the road as tightly as her own.

Davis lowered the bottle. He wiped his mouth on the back of his sleeve and let out a belch surprising in its reserve. Evvie had expected something much worse. "Ted North," said Davis, "that boat can sail around the Horn if she's a mind to. She's tough as nails. More than tough enough for what you have to do."

Evvie tried to figure out what Davis meant. Ted hadn't actually *said* they were going to sail to the States. She had more than a few reservations about making a trip like that, especially in a twenty-eight footer. And there was a growing sense of the unreal in what she was doing ... speeding through dark jungle country with a gin-drinking driver and a stone-silent female Indian, a beauty from another century ... rushing to take delivery on a boat paid for but never seen ... sitting beside a husband who seemed part of a script she hadn't been allowed to read. Why this boat? Why Panama? There were other boats. In Florida. Virginia. Rhode Island. She glanced at Ted and saw a man who needed everything she could pour into his heart if he would let her. But he would let her, now. She was sure of that.

Despite the excitement that came with each new curve in the road, despite the brave hope that their life might work, a weariness took her.

A shape loomed out of the dark. Davis cursed. Her heart pounded. *My God! We almost hit that man!* The rush of anxiety eased off and she came back to earth, passed some sort of emotional midpoint, and drifted closer to fatigue. The ups, the downs. Things were moving too fast. Why so fast? The quick goodbyes; the house gone, bought by the Agency as part of the layoff compensation; their stuff stored until they were settled on the East Coast after the trip. All the things they touched and shared in storage. But not her memories, the good and the ugly; they weren't in storage.

She wished she were in bed somewhere.

Anywhere.

With Ted.

Her eyes closed again.

The motion of the car, the sound of the engine, the drone of male voices ... a lullaby that put her down. Her head found Ted's shoulder. She slept.

When the sun rose the next morning, Evvie was standing on the balcony outside their room. The Hotel Washington faced Limon Bay, a twenty-square-mile holding pen for ship traffic transiting the Canal. The balcony commanded a broad view of the bay and of the four-mile breakwater with its hundred-yard gap in the middle leading to the open sea. Like the hinge point of a Japanese fan, the hotel was at the geographic hub of the exiting and entering activity. Evvie watched the huge vessels move with cautious grace in the limiting space as they performed their slow-motion waltz beneath a brilliant sun.

She watched for two hours.

Ships entering from the sea would slow majestically while small service boats and tugs swarmed their flanks or pecked at their bows, then the gracious steel monsters would veer off-channel to anchor on shining water in the flats. At times a tanker would rupture the silence, its ship's horn trumpeting a warning or sounding some impatient but polite call for attention from pilots or customs people.

Those ships leaving for the ocean, those heading out, would hunt the invisible axis of the channel and, finding it, power down the line for sea, accelerating to gain steerage. Evvie saw them as gentle sea creatures escaping back to the safe embrace of deep water, a place meant for them.

She'd follow an outbound ship as long as her eyes could track it. As the receding shape cleared the breakwater, her heart would cheer. She didn't know why.

Then something strange. Just looking at a leaving ship, she cried. Her self-control was still paper-thin. Ted wasn't the only one shipwrecked on an island of tears. She had her own island. What frightened her was that she wasn't sure she wanted to leave it. If staying on that island was the price she had to pay to keep her lost Cindy, then maybe ...

Evvie went back into the room.

Three miles away along the black line of rock, white water reached up like the talons of some searching thing trying to climb into the bay.

Even at that distance, if a quiet person took the time to listen, she'd hear the intermittent rumble of the sea come through the earth. And if that person touched a wall or leaned against something solid, she'd feel those surfaces move.

Kent Davis, at one o'clock in the afternoon, was perched on a barstool in the Cristobal Yacht Club. He spotted Ted and Evvie squinting in the low light as they walked in from outside. Ted had slept well after the trip, but Evvie, despite her exhaustion, had not. Dreams. Dreams that started after Cindy died. The restless dreams. After watching the ships at sunrise, she managed to fall asleep for two hours around ten a.m., but her body clock was out of sync. She decided to do something about it.

"North!" A wave of a hand holding a drink. Davis shouted again through thirty feet of diesel-smelling air, "Get your ass over here, boy! Help me get this bottle down!"

Evvie leaned toward Ted. "Mr. Davis has a problem."

Ted nodded and smiled. Davis had swiveled sideways on his perch, apparently trying to decide whether he should leave the wobbly barstool to greet his guests.

"Yes, he has a problem," said Ted. "But his problem isn't our problem."

"It's our problem if he sinks our boat before we even get to see it." She liked the way the words "our boat" sounded.

Ted took her by the hand to lead her over to the bar.

"Nope," she said. She took her hand from his. "You talk to him. I'll be in the restaurant eating the biggest meal on the menu."

He looked at her.

"I'm going to find a big bottle of red wine. I'm going to drink it all."

"What's this all about?"

"I read an article on the plane that said the best way to get back on schedule when you're traveling is to eat like a pig. For one day. It shocks the system. Lets you sleep right."

"You drink a bottle of wine and you'll be worthless."

"If I start to sleep all day, I'll be worthless anyway." She twiddled her fingers in the air at Davis and flashed a real-estate-agent smile in his direction. "Bring Davis over later if you want," she said under her breath, "if he can walk that far. I'll be the one behind the crab legs." She pecked Ted on the cheek and walked off.

Chapter 4

The yacht club restaurant was open to the elements on two sides. On the side nearest the water, three steps led down to a catwalk that provided access to the yacht club's mooring piers tucked along the bank of the oil-slicked estuary. The restaurant, and everything in it including the dozen tables, was painted dark green except for the floor, which was bare cement. A number of three-inch-diameter metal poles, also green and seemingly placed at random around the room, supported a wood and sheet-metal roof. The two exposed sides of the place had long roll-down bamboo blinds tucked along the eaves to keep out sun and rain. No window glass. No tablecloths. A smell of saltwater and seaweed. Two scruffy cats prowled beneath the dining tables.

Evvie sat at a table next to the mooring pier steps so she could look at the water. There were no crab legs. She ordered fried won tons, a shrimp cocktail, langosta tails, and a Bloody Mary instead of wine. The waitress was a young Panamanian girl—cute, short, slow, and smelling of jasmine.

The restaurant was almost empty. One couple nursed drinks at a table in the center of the room. And at the table next to hers sat a man.

He was reading what looked to be an instruction manual or gun catalog. On an open page she could see a picture of a rifle. The man had short sandy-colored hair and wrinkles around blue eyes that glittered above a star-shaped scar on his left cheek. He was in his late fifties, perhaps a bit older, a body on the muscular side of thin with strong arms like weathered rope, someone she looked at twice because he was the type who needed more than one look. There was an energy in him, an intensity that her eyes didn't register, but that her brain, a few seconds later, did. Not meanness—that wasn't it—but something close to meanness. Anger, perhaps. That and sadness; not something she could point to, or describe, but it was there. That combination of angry and sad, as though he had been where she had been, had known things she had known, had seen of life what she had seen.

The way the eyelids seemed heavy despite the sharp eyes. Resignation.

The lower lip slightly out. Defiance.

The jaw muscle moving under his skin for no real-world reason. Tension.

Not looking up at small noises; not caring that a fly walked on his forearm; not noticing that she looked at him. Isolation.

She found herself dissecting him. Unable to stop. A delicate compulsion. An obsessive behavior too frequent since Cindy's death, as if her mind were trying to discover how other humans coped, how people survived the tragedy of life. A mind trying hard to save itself.

She averted her eyes.

Not because he looked up since he did not look up. She looked away because she saw in him those things that, in herself, she tried to hide.

An hour later Evvie was angry. *Where the hell are they?* She had eaten until she was past full. Two more Bloody Marys. Fried ice cream and a fortune cookie for dessert. Her irritation simmered. And the stomach-ache didn't help. During the meal she'd assumed that Ted and Davis would join her. When they didn't show up, and after she had read her fortune-cookie future for the fourth time, she went into the bar to look for them. They weren't there. She asked the bartender if he knew where they had gone, but in the tradition of male bartenders he pleaded innocent, an innocence born out of handling drinking husbands and the steely-eyed wives who tried to find them.

She returned to her table in the restaurant and read the fortune once more. And grew more irritated. The idea that the Peking Noodle Company should presume to tell her how to live her life did nothing for her composure, and she crumpled the small slip of paper and dropped it into a pool of melted ice cream at the bottom of her dessert cup. She leaned an elbow on the table. Too hard. The table lurched toward her. Her glass of water slid off the slick surface and landed in her lap.

"Shit!" She jumped up. She corralled the glass, but the damage was done. To say that word aloud in a public place, even though that place was practically empty, was not her style.

She rubbed at her cotton skirt with a cocktail napkin. The napkin wasn't up to the job. She stamped her foot and looked around for the waitress. No waitress.

She glanced at the next table.

The man she had been so aware of earlier, and since ignored, sat there with his own paper napkin blotting the wet pages of his book, no expression, no show of irritation.

"Oh my, I'm sorry," she said.

He continued dabbing at water drops. "It's not important."

She stood there for a few seconds. Neither spoke.

Evvie left the table and went across the restaurant into the kitchen area. The waitress sat with three men, all four of them smoking cigarettes. The group regarded her as if the presence of a customer in the kitchen was not unusual.

Evvie picked up a dish towel that hung on a nail by the sink. "I need this."

"Sure," from the girl.

Evvie returned to the table and handed the towel to the man. He wiped his book a few times, handed the towel back, and watched her fix up the table and her skirt, and finally push the towel around the floor with her foot to get the last of the water.

She sat back down.

"I lost my husband."

"I'm sorry." The man's words were too serious.

"I don't mean I *lost* my husband. I just can't find him."

"Oh." And he frowned at his assumption. "I thought you meant he just passed away."

"He's going to pass away if he doesn't come back pretty soon."

"Is he wearing a blue short-sleeved shirt?"

Evvie looked at him, surprised. "Yes."

"He and Davis left the restaurant thirty minutes ago."

"You know Davis?"

He didn't answer right away. Then he shook his head slowly. "I know of him."

"I didn't see them leave," she said.

"I saw them pass by the service window." He pointed a finger at the far wall.

Evvie looked where he was pointing. It took her several seconds to find the window. It was one foot wide and ten inches high, an opening cut through the restaurant wall to the bar.

"They went down to B dock," he said.

"B dock?"

"That's where Davis keeps the Coconut. Go out the way you came in. Turn left. It's marked."

"Can I see it from here? Can I get there going down those steps?" Evvie nodded at the three stairs leading to the catwalk in front of the restaurant.

"No, you can't see it from here. And yes, you can get there by going down those steps, but there's diesel on the dock. You'll get the stuff on your shoes. It's hard to get off."

Evvie got to her feet and used her hand to smooth her wet skirt. She pushed her chair back under the table edge. "Thanks." She picked up her purse. "Where do I pay? Our waitress seems to have retired."

"You pay her. She pays the barman."

But Evvie didn't even have the check. She stood there perplexed.

"They went out on the boat."

She looked at him. Anger came back. "They went *out?* On the *boat?*" She looked left in the direction he had indicated, where B dock was supposed to be. Then looked back at him. "How do you know they went out? You can't see the dock from here."

"Outboard makes a noise like a chainsaw. It's mounted too high. It should be lowered three inches."

Evvie sighed.

"You might as well sit down. The girl will bring your check."

Evvie yanked her chair away from the table again. Too quickly. She sat down. Too hard. "It's not fair! I wanted to see the boat, too." Angry words.

She realized at once how childish she sounded, then grinned a sheepish grin and shrugged. She knew they both knew she was acting like a three-year-old. The grin turned into a real smile. "I'm sorry. It's been a goofy day. I might as well have another drink. Can I buy you something?"

"I'll fly if you'll buy," he said.

"Done." She fished a U.S. five dollar bill out of her purse and handed it to him. "I assume American money works here?"

"Like gold." He headed for the bar.

No macho problems, she thought. She liked that.

He returned with the drinks. He counted out her change, dropping each coin into her palm one by one. They sat at their own tables, but turned the chairs so they could talk. "You don't miss much, do you?" she asked.

He smiled for the first time. "Neither do you."

Evvie felt her cheeks warm when she realized he'd been aware of her staring at him earlier. She unconsciously folded her arms across her chest, an old habit.

He drank some of his bourbon and answered her question. "Not a lot of professional entertainment in here. Might as well watch the customers."

She put down her drink and stuck out her hand. "My name's Evvie."

He took her hand and shook it. "My name's Arthur."

"Evvie North."

"Arthur Arthur."

Evvie smiled. "You have two first names?" She sensed the question was vaguely offensive, but the Bloody Marys had taken the edge off sensitivity. She uncrossed her arms and sipped her drink.

"Apparently."

An awkward silence followed his one-word reply, and Evvie changed the subject. "I ... we, my husband and me ... we bought a boat."

"Coconut."

"We bought it from Mr. Davis."

Arthur nodded a few times. "It's a good boat. Wood, but wood's okay if it's done right."

"He said Coconut was built in Australia."

"She was."

"He said it was sailed here from Australia."

"No, she wasn't. Coconut came across as deck cargo. On a freighter. But she could have sailed here."

Davis had lied. She wondered how many lies. "We're thinking of sailing it up to Rhode Island."

"Oh?" He just looked at her.

She drank more Bloody Mary.

He shifted in his chair and rested an elbow on his table. "Just the two of you?"

"Sure. What's wrong with that?"

"You must be quite a team."

"We are quite a team." Her words were quicker than they needed to be.

"It didn't sound like it a few minutes ago."

She bristled. Her arms folded across her chest again. She stared back at him and said nothing.

"I'm sorry," he apologized. "That was an impolite thing to say." He took a deeper drink of bourbon. "What I should have said was that making a coastal passage that long is hard to do. It's one thing to two-hand a vessel in the open ocean. There's plenty of room for error. But going to the States from here? You'll be fighting to stay off a lee shore for a thousand miles. You'll be alternating four-hour watches, maybe two if the weather gets you." He drank more bourbon. "Going through the Yucatan?"

She hesitated. Then, "Maybe."

"Maybe?" He set his drink down and rotated the glass slowly in a pool of moisture on the table. "I'd take the Windward Passage if it was me."

"We might take the Windward Passage." She didn't know where or even what the Windward Passage was.

"Then again, you might be a lot better than me," he said.

Time to call it quits. She smiled. "You think I don't know my ass from a hole in the ground, don't you?" She had always wanted to say the phrase "ass from a hole in the ground" to someone she had just met. The drinks were doing the job.

The hint of a smile turned up a corner of his mouth.

Evvie laughed a real laugh, which for her meant a laugh with a snort at the end of it. "Well, you're right, Mr. Arthur Arthur. I'll bet you a buck I can beat you in a boat race on the bay 'cause I'm pretty darn good at that, but the only time I've sailed on an ocean is never." She finished her drink. "So if you think I don't know my Windward Passage from a hole in the ground when it comes to ocean sailing ... well, you're right."

Good drinks, strong.

He didn't say anything for a moment. Evvie watched the hard stuff under his skin soften. What had been a hint of a smile before became a friendly one now. "I don't think you'll have any trouble getting to the States," he said. "If the boat sinks, you'll probably swim the rest of the way."

The drinks, along with his comment, warmed her. The next question came easily. "Is there a Mrs. Arthur Arthur?"

The man looked at the table for a long moment as though he were trying to decide whether to continue the conversation. Then he said, "Not quite. We don't fit yet. We're trying to determine what hurts worse, compromise or giving up." He looked at her. ... "Just like everyone else." He smiled. "She's in Las Vegas letting dry air and love figure it out; I'm down here doing it with humidity and chemical science." He raised his drink as explanation. "Offhand, I'd say we don't have a snowball's chance."

In the empty place that followed his last words, the waitress walked out of the kitchen, came to the tables, and gave each of them a bill. Evvie and Arthur paid, and the girl went away. Arthur nodded toward the estuary. "They're coming back in."

Through the background noise Evvie became aware of an oscillating buzz that was Coconut's outboard.

"You're right. ... It does sound like a chainsaw."

"Just drop the mount," he said.

"Do you have a boat too?"

"Susurro. That means 'whisper' in Spanish. She's a twenty-six footer."

"Susurro. ... That's pretty. That has to be a sailboat's name."

"It is. She's a little double-ender with a cuddy forward. Glass over wood."

"Do you go out much?"

"Sailing? I go out when I can."

"Maybe we could sail together ... the two boats. My husband's name is Ted. We could sail around the bay."

He chewed an ice cube.

The waitress brought the change and went back into the kitchen.

Arthur stood up. He pushed a dollar out of the pile of change for the girl, then pocketed the rest. He closed and picked up the book he

had been reading when Evvie spilled the water. The pages were still damp.
A few drops rolled out of the binding and fell onto his shirt front. He
brushed them away. "Where are you two staying?"

"We're at the Hotel Washington." She looked at the book. "Sorry
about giving your library a bath."

"This? It's just an owner's manual. A friend of mine is into rifles. He
wanted me to look it over."

Cindy playing with her stuffed panda. "Guns, I hate guns. ..." *The
glare of the lights, the dark figure of a man stumbling back through swinging glass doors.* "They scare me."

Arthur watched her face, her eyes, and saw the way she stared at the
book instead of at him when she said the words. He tucked the book
under his arm. "They should scare you," he said. "It depends a lot on
who's holding them. I heard someone say once that the most dangerous
thing in the world is a man with a gun, and the most helpless thing is a
man without one."

She stopped looking at the book.

"Thanks for the drink," he said. "And don't be too hard on your
husband for running out on you. Men and boats, boys and toys ... if
you know what I mean."

"Goodbye," said Evvie. "Thanks for the company."

He turned and left the restaurant.

She waited a few moments, then got up and went out to the dirt
parking lot where she remembered seeing a cab parked in the shade, its
driver asleep behind the wheel. The cab was still there. She took the cab
to the hotel.

"Where the hell *were* you?" Ted's words were sharp. "I thought you
got yourself kidnapped!"

She was standing on the balcony of their hotel room watching the
movement of the ships and the surge of some faraway storm explode
over the breakwater. She kept looking out at the sea. He stood in the
open doorway leading out to the balcony from the bedroom.

She did not answer at once. Finally, she said, "I took a cab."

"You could have left a message at the restaurant, in the bar ... somewhere!"

"I could have." Her words carried an edge, a hardness he wasn't used to.

From the third-floor room, the great distance to the breakwater made the huge plumes of spray from the crashing waves look deceptively small, and that distortion made the action of the water appear to be taking place in slow motion. Arcs of white floated, hung, and slowly collapsed in the twilight. All soundless and unreal.

"Sometimes you can be a real bitch, Evvie."

"Me! Where the hell were you?" Anger built. "You could have walked ten feet to let me know you were taking off. ... I waited two hours. I didn't want to wait anymore!" She didn't turn around.

"Don't you give a *damn* about me?" His words louder, sharper. "A real *bitch*. Sometimes I wonder why I put up with your crap."

An unseen wave, a rogue giant, lifted a tower of brilliant white straight into the sky above the black rocks. The distant column climbed higher than any before it. It seemed to stop at the height of its travel like something painted, its crown of spume tailing to one side in the building wind.

She heard his fist hit the door frame. "Do that again and I'll ..." His sentence unfinished.

"You'll what? Tell me what the fuck is going on, you half-assed son of a bitch?"

The silent surprise behind her poured out of the room like syrup.

Slowly, without turning around, she pulled her blouse out of her skirt top. She backed her feet out of her sandals. Hooking her thumbs into the bands of her skirt and panties, she slipped both garments down and stepped out of them. She stood naked except for her blouse.

She leaned forward slightly, her arms straight and extended, the palms of her hands flat on the hard surface of the waist-high balcony wall, her bare feet on the cool deck, her legs apart. She watched the sea.

She stood that way for half a minute before he came to her.

He pulled her into the bedroom and for the first time since the accident, in a furious silence, they made love. What might have been only physical was, instead, something of the soul. Anger and confusion melted into desperate passion.

They were in a world of two. She and he ... the way it had been in the beginning.

Amilia River, 12 Miles West of the Colombian Border

"He would not listen? I told you Spider would not listen to you."

"But the Colombian was a good man, a good guide. He brought us many miles. His family had many little ones."

"Spider says he was not important. He could not be allowed to go back."

"To die that way ..."

"It is not a thing that matters."

"Will El Codo have the island?"

"El Codo will have the island. El Codo will have the moon if Spider asks for the moon."

"To die that way ..."

Washington, D.C.

"Can I gag once or twice?"

"Gag all you want. Just give him the briefing. If you can't do that, I'll get someone who can."

"What if he wants details? Deep stuff?"

"Give him what you can."

"What I can? What the hell does that cover?"

"It covers anything that won't make Joe Voter spill his coffee when he's reading the morning newspaper."

"There's something left these days that can still spill coffee?"

"Okay, Louis. You know the ground rules. Plausible deniability. We know it. The reporters know it. The big guy in there knows it. Just let him stay inside the lines. That's all I ask. That's all he asks. It's just a game. Just a damn game."

"Harry? How do you sleep at night?"

"Warm milk. Try it."

A Marine guard signaled to them. The two DEA officials rose from their chairs and adjusted their neckties, each motion a mirror image of the other, and stepped toward the door. "Try to remember, Louis ... we make history, not policy."

"There's not enough warm milk in this whole town for this shit."

"So, Mr. President, if we—"

"You're going to get this ... Spider?"

"We're pulling out all the stops on this one. We have to. Thanks to a certain congressman from New York, the press knows we've promised Spider's head on a platter by Christmas. Unfortunately, Spider knows it, too. That's why he's making a run for the Middle East. It's budget time. If Spider Snatch doesn't pan out, the opposition on the Hill will have a field day."

"Spider Snatch?"

"That's the name of the operation, sir."

"So it's a P.R. and bucks game?"

"It's about a lot more than budget dollars and P.R., Mr. President. Since the *de facto* extradition treaties down south and our takedown of Spider's major competition, he's got all the big-money stateside contacts. He owns the border routes. All of them. Canada. Mexico. The Atlantic pipeline. Core distribution from the Far East. He's even crossed over some of our own people. We're talking six to seven billion a year, U.S."

"Seven goddamn billion?"

"Minimum, sir. If he gets to Libya, Iran, or wherever the hell he's going, the whole thing starts over again ... this time in countries where we can't bend the rules. If Spider slips this noose, it's a disaster."

"And a sure as hell political kiss-my-ass-goodbye. What's DEA throwing into the mix?"

"Mr. President, our Delta Force consists of three Black Hawks. We have two F-18s on standby."

"Where?"

"The 18s are at Howard. The Black Hawks are at France Field. Galeta."

"Is CIA in on this?"

"No, sir. We feel confident that—"

"CIA couldn't cover more potential jump-off points? Help you boys out?"

"DEA has the contacts and the assets. CIA doesn't really fit with what ..."

The president smiled. "Before I got here, I had the naive impression that federal enforcement agencies worked together. You hate each other's guts, don't you?"

Neither DEA man replied.

"Sounds like we have a few too many agencies."

Silence.

The president toyed with a rubber block eraser as he flipped through the sheath of background documents. "Do you anticipate any civilians getting caught in the middle? Anything like that ATF goat fuck with Koresh?"

"Sir, we—"

"There's an election next year."

"Yes, sir. But we don't know Spider's jump-off point yet. We haven't any way of—"

"If DEA gives me another Waco or Ruby Ridge, I'll be ... upset." He leaned forward and impaled the pink eraser on a steel note spindle sitting on the desk."

"Yes, sir. We'll do our best."

"Given past history, that's not going to let me sleep very well."

The president stopped turning pages and studied an illustration. "This Spider looks like a goddamn fairy, some geek pencil pusher. You need forty million to nail this?"

"Sir, Spider may look like a ... an accountant ... sir, but he's slaughtered his way to the top. No deals. No quarter. No witnesses. DEA's tracked him into the Darien by following the dead bodies. No one lives who's seen him on this end run of his. No one. He even killed his own people when he moved over the Colombian border. This Spider has no conscience."

"Have you tried to recruit him?"

"Sir?"

"That's a joke."

"Yes, sir."

The president sat back in the swivel chair. "So, that's it? All I need to know?" A smile.

"Yes, sir. That's it. That's all you want ... need to know."

"It'd be nice to know where point X is."

"Yes, sir. That would be nice."

What was left of the president's smile faded to acid as he leaned to one side and flipped a toggle that deactivated the office tape recording systems. "Between you and me, gentlemen?"

"Sir?" in unison.

"If you have to melt down a fucking third-world country on this one ... do it."

"Yes, sir." Two replies, one voice.

The president reset the tape switch. Leaned back. Smiled. "I don't think I'd like to be at point X."

"No, sir. Thank you, sir."

Chapter 5

"She really hauls ass on the wind, don't she?" Davis popped the top on another can of beer and belched.

Evvie fed out the main sheet an extra foot and let Coconut fall off the wind a few degrees to quiet the ripple in the luff. The boat fell into the new groove and accelerated. Davis guzzled half the contents of his tenth can of beer in a single gulp, spilling some on his shirt, then eased the starboard jib sheet to match the set of the mainsail.

"She seems to point higher on starboard than port," Evvie said. "I think the mast is out of plumb ... too much to starboard." Then she had to raise her voice as the bow dipped low, sending water rushing down the rail. "The port shrouds are too loose!" she yelled. Her eyes moved from the flush-mounted compass on the cabin bulkhead up to the port spreader, where the slack top-shroud rippled slightly in the twenty-knot breeze. The boat heeled in a fresh gust, then climbed back on her lines and tore through the light chop of the bay at hull speed. Without looking at Davis, her eyes once more traveling from compass to shroud, she lifted her can of soda from the gimbaled drink holder. She used her left hand to hold the drink and continued to feather the tiller with her right. The vibration of the rudder blade cutting like a sickle through the blue water below chattered through the teak tiller grip into her steering hand. The shivering power sent a tickle all the way up to her right shoulder.

Five straight mornings spent sailing in the protective lee of the bay's breakwater had worked sweet magic. An orgy of ocean wind without the ocean seas. Control, power, rebirth. She had never sailed like this, not even during the best days on San Francisco Bay.

The winds were like the dry-season winds, constant and strong from the east, an aberration in the midst of the rainy season, an aberration that, according to the locals, wouldn't last much longer.

"I don't know what the hell I'm doing out here with you, Mrs. North!" Davis shouted. "You sail this fucking thing better than I can."

Evvie didn't reply. As his supply of beer wore down, his output of foul language surged.

But she devoured his compliment. He meant what he said. She could tell by the tone, the wonder, the disbelief that colored his words. It was as if he thought she might have been sexed wrong, was perhaps really a male in disguise, that maybe there had been some sort of genetic mix-up. She wished Ted had been there to hear those words from Davis. But, of course, if Ted had been along instead of back in Colon, Davis wouldn't have paid her the compliment.

Despite an instinctive wariness, she shouted, "It's a good boat, Mr. Davis!"

"Aye, she's that, Master Hawkins," he rasped.

His imitation of Long John Silver was the only positive feature Evvie had unearthed in the man. She had quickly come to detest him, but not because of his four-letter mouth or his perpetual drunken fog. She'd seen that before. Her own father had taught her to tolerate "crude."

No. She hated him because of Dulcie.

On the previous four days, while he sailed Ted and her around the bay to show them how Coconut handled, Davis had ordered the young Indian girl to stay under a banyan tree next to his car in the yacht club parking lot.

And there Dulcie remained, squatting in the shade next to the car in what to Evvie seemed humiliating obedience made still more humiliating by the way she appeared to quietly accept her guard-dog status. A second-class citizen in both Davis' eyes and those of the Canal Zone. The girl could use the club's boatyard restroom, but she couldn't enter the club. Not her.

Not Dulcie. Not the Indian.

The twentieth century. The U.S. government.

Earlier in the day, as Evvie and Davis were getting ready to take the boat out, Ted had offered to have Dulcie accompany him to the Duty Free Zone in Colon to pick up charts and a satellite navigation system. The girl had looked at Davis, but Davis said no. She would stay by the car. And Ted had gone alone.

"Ready about!" At her command Davis emptied the last of the beer and nodded. "Hard a-lee!" shouted Evvie and pushed the tiller down. Coconut rounded up smartly, her sails rapping the air as she went through the eye of the wind. The boat lay down under a sharp pressure as the mainsail cracked flat. Coconut inhaled the moment in order to savor the delicious energy feeding into her frame, then shook herself and bounded forward in the new direction.

Davis was slow in shifting the jib. He cursed as he crawled around the cockpit sole on his knees, and he skinned his thumb on the latch of a seat locker.

"Fuck!" he swore. "Mother fuck!" But he sheeted in quickly. Then he sat back and sucked at the abraded thumb with its flap of pale tissue peeled up from blotched skin over the knuckle.

He bit off the flap of flesh, spit it across the cockpit into the rushing water, and opened his last beer.

"You and North," he said, not having to shout because he had slid aft closer to her. She could smell beer and sweat despite the strong breeze across the cockpit. "You two get along?" he asked. A half-smirk.

Here it comes. "We get along."

"Think you can spend a month on a boat with him?"

"I think so."

"A man needs to have a woman. Men build things. Bridges, boats, houses. Big things. Things that count. Women don't build things." Another guzzle of beer. "A woman is meant to give a man pleasure, so he can build things."

A gust of wind heeled the boat. Evvie shifted position away from Davis to maneuver Coconut through the puff, and when the boat resumed course, she remained away from him. "What do *you* build, Mr. Davis?"

Davis, oblivious. "A woman's lucky if she gets a man to tend to, to pleasure. There's lots don't get a chance. That's why they're always making themselves up to be pretty, wearing those sexy clothes 'n' all." He looked at Evvie's midsection, then at the crotch of the white shorts she wore. "Like you got on."

She stared at him. He held the beer can in one hand. His other hand rubbed at his testicles through the fabric of his grimy khaki pants. His eyes left her crotch and he grinned at her.

"Is Dulcie one of the lucky ones?" she asked. And looked away, looked up at the luff of the main. The boat powered through the light chop.

Davis tossed his head back and laughed a laugh that ended in a wet cough, a cough that ended with something ugly spit over the side. "Lucky? That gal would be on some island pluckin' fuckin' chickens or selling red rags to tourists weren't for me. She appreciates what she got."

"Women like to build things, Mr. Davis."

"Kent."

"In a way, we build houses, too. Sometimes a house needs decorating. It would be silly to keep it empty, don't you think?"

He drank beer, unimpressed.

"Maybe we decorate it with a flower pot, a man, a dog, a piece of furniture, maybe spread a little manure around the yard to make things look green. A woman needs to build things, too. Don't you think so, Mr. Davis?"

He looked at her with a blank stare. "I guess." He finished the beer, crumpled the can in his hand, and tossed it overboard. He got to his feet and lurched his way out onto the small afterdeck. He stood there holding on to the backstay for support with his back to her and his feet spread. He swayed awkwardly as the boat yawed and shifted.

She stopped looking aft and turned forward to concentrate on sailing the boat. A few moments later, despite the noise of the sailing, she heard a stream of urine drilling into the wake.

"You know, Mr. Davis, we do have a head on board."

"No sense pissing all over the bulkhead!" he said in a loud voice. "The way you got this baby moving, I don't think I'd be able to hit the pisser."

He didn't come back into the cockpit. She turned and looked again. He stood there facing her, three feet away, still swaying on the backstay. He was grinning down at her and his penis, partly erect, stuck out of his fly at her like a white sausage in the sun.

He didn't say anything. Only a mindless leer.

When Evvie got angry, the first person she blamed for the anger was herself. That was how life had shaped her. But not this time. The sleepy confusion so close to fear, the colliding memories of Cindy, the suspicion that she was being hustled by circumstance if not by the people around her—all these finally got Evvie's spunk onto its hind legs and ready to scratch.

"Mr. Davis. What in the world happened to your penis? It's so … small."

The grin straightened out.

"Did you have an accident? Has it always been, you know, like that?"

The penis got smaller.

"I've never seen one quite that … cute."

He blinked a few times, then scrunched his rump backward in his pants. The sausage disappeared into his fly.

"Oh, Mr. Davis. I'm sorry." She shook her head. "It's just that Ted's is so much, you know, bigger. I'm sorry."

She looked forward again. "Come on back in the boat, Mr. Davis. You might fall off."

He climbed back to his station by the jib cam, well forward of where he'd sat before. He toyed with the jib sheet, made some small adjustment in the block, checked the luff, looked over the bow.

She leaned forward and put a hand on his knee. She had to lean forward a long way. "There are things they can do, Mr. Davis. Operations. Injections." She patted his knee three times and sat back. "Maybe it doesn't bother you. That's the sign of a mature man, believe me. Really, it is. After all, it's not the size of the dog in the fight. That sort of thing."

They sailed for another twenty minutes before heading back toward the docks. Evvie chatted about the boat, the weather. Davis nodded, made a few grunts. Not much else.

As they were stowing the sails, Ted came down to the slip with the new navigation gear. He boarded and locked the equipment in the forepeak. After securing the boat, they went to the parking lot where Dulcie waited beneath the banyan tree. Davis declined Ted's offer to buy a round of drinks. Evvie went to Dulcie and gave her an exaggerated hug, which the girl accepted with a puzzled look.

Evvie held Dulcie at arm's length.

"Dulcie, Dulcie, Dulcie," she said. Eye to eye. Sympathy oozing.

Then Evvie took Ted's hand. "Come on, honey. Let's get back to the hotel. I want to tell you all about today. It was fantastic! The boat, the wind, the sun." She turned toward Davis. "And Mr. Davis. Thanks for putting up with me, again. You're such a help." Davis nodded and made a sound at the ground.

"You're so sweet," she continued. "All the help with the boat and everything. You're amazing. Like they say, it's the little things that count."

Ted put an arm around Evvie's shoulders and pulled her close. "Well, folks, I registered the boat while you two were out screwing around on the water. The papers are signed. Coconut has a new papa!"

Evvie reached up and tweaked his nose. "And a new mama."

"And a new mama," he repeated.

Ted smiled at Davis. "How about one more once-around-the-bay, Kent? Then we'll get out of your hair."

"Suits me." Davis was checking out a bird perched on a limb in the banyan tree.

"Tomorrow? Same time? Eight o'clock?"

"Tomorrow sounds okay." Davis nodded at Dulcie, then at the car door. The girl opened it and got into the front seat. "Better make it ten," said Davis. "The wind is gettin' back to normal ... won't pick up early like the last few days."

"Ten o'clock it is," said Ted.

At midnight, Evvie stood on the balcony outside the bedroom. The day wind had become a gentle night breeze. The water below was calm beneath a dark bank of clouds edging over Panama from the ocean, and the great ships lay at anchor like great beasts sleeping. She was tired from the fresh air and from the exhilaration of sailing the bay, a bay that now seemed still and waiting. But she could not sleep.

They had made love earlier, a sweet but distracted interlude sprinkled with comments about the boat and the sailing, and the loving was over quickly, an oddly ambiguous exercise of passion and small talk. She was sure that the unease she felt as she watched the night was because of the incident with Davis. She had not mentioned it to Ted. She'd never do that. Ted's enthusiasm needed protection as much as anyone else's. He was the person she cared about. And he didn't need her words starting something that could lead only to trouble. His first instinct would be to protect her, to give Davis a piece of his mind and perhaps more. Davis wasn't worth it.

And there was something else. The cutting up of Davis had been mean. She stopped him the only way she knew how, other than jumping overboard, but it tore her up inside. She knew how much words could hurt. She knew the damage they could do, how they hung on for so long, sometimes for years, sometimes for a lifetime. Mean words never really went away. A punch in the nose would have been kinder … if it had been an option. Then she recognized the real problem presented by Davis. The second-class status of Dulcie, more accessory than companion, seemed uncomfortably similar to the feelings she was having about her own relationship with Ted. More prop than wife. More front than friend. More pawn than partner.

Evvie left the balcony and crawled into bed. When sleep finally came, it was an uneasy sleep full of words from twenty years ago, words that hurt.

"Momma?"

"What is it, Evelyn?" Her mother, beautiful despite forty disappointing seasons on God's earth, stared out of the oval mirror above her dressing table. She looked at her daughter not directly but through the glass. A Bible lay next to an open makeup kit that held mysterious pads and secret powders in little flat cans. From the adjoining room came the sound of bath water spinning slowly down the drain in the old four-legged tub.

"Momma, what's the most important thing in the world?"

"That's not a good question, Evelyn. It doesn't mean anything."

The daughter was persistent. Nine years living with this one had not been long enough to blunt her spirit. She laughed and touched her mother's shoulder. "Come on, Momma. Tell me what's the most important thing."

"The most important thing is God," and back to tweezing eyebrow hairs.

"Besides God." A rolling of eyes. "I know God's important."

Without looking, her mother answered, "Dignity. Self-respect."

"No, Momma. I mean really important."

Mirror-eyes looked past an upraised hand holding tweezers. "What is it you want me to say, Evelyn? It appears you already have an answer."

"I think having good sex with a man is the most important thing, don't you?" And she was on her behind on the floor with a face stinging from a slap she never saw coming and, if she had, would never have guessed it was headed for her.

Through the locked bedroom door, "Momma? Momma, let me out."

No reply.

"I only meant that people who get married should be happy."

No reply.

"It just seems like such an important thing for men to be happy ... to make your husband happy ... Momma?" Slivers of male laughter escaped the grate.

"Momma? ..."

At ten the next morning they were at the club. Davis was late. He made no apology. Dulcie squatted in the shade. The two men started for the pier.

"Ted?"

He stopped and looked back.

"I'm not going out today," said Evvie. "You two go."

"You got a headache or something?"

"No. I feel great. But you two go."

Ted shrugged and handed her the keys to the rental car. "You're sure?"

"Git!" she said.

Ted and Davis went off toward the boat slips.

Evvie walked over to Dulcie and sat down on the grass next to her. The girl smiled, looked once in the direction the men had taken, then dropped out of her squatting position and sat like Evvie sat.

Other than a few assenting nods, Evvie hadn't seen any indication that the girl understood what was being said. Both she and Ted spoke Spanish, and she considered trying that, but the Indian seemed to respond to Davis' English commands, though it could have been to his pointed fingers, the pushes, and the glares rather than the spoken words.

"You me go store? Buy dress? I have car." Evvie dangled the car keys in the air and took the girl's hand as she spoke.

Dulcie looked at her.

"You me buy dress? You show me stores?" said Evvie.

Dulcie looked at the car keys.

"Store? Keys? You me?" Evvie said the words more slowly.

Dulcie smiled. "I'd like that very much, Mrs. North." Clear articulated English.

"Oh my," said Evvie. She stared at Dulcie for a few seconds. Then

Evvie said, "Me jerk." They both laughed.

"I thank you for your kind offer. Actually me have plenty dress." More laughter. "You're a nice person, Mrs. North."

"Evvie."

"All right ... Evvie. I'd like very much to go for a ride in your car. The places we can get into might be limited by the nineteenth-century social codes of the Canal Zone, but we'll find something to do. That's if you're broadminded enough and don't mind rubbing shoulders with the locals."

"Now that I've made myself look stupid, I don't mind asking. Where did you learn to speak English? It's ..."

"I'm a Cuna Indian, Mrs. North ... Evvie ... as you've probably already guessed from the travel posters. Among the Cunas, it's usually the men who know English, and not many of them. They're the ones who get jobs on ships and in warehouses in the Zone. Nice Cuna girls stay home. Unless they're selling molas in Panama or Colon. English is a third language for me. And I'm pretty damn proud of it. No false humility in this Indian, is there?" A smile. "I was born on the island of Alligandi in the San Blas Islands. My Cuna name is Otelia. Kent calls me 'Dulcie' because a long time ago he read Cervantes' *Don Quixote* ... or someone read it to him." She stood up and brushed off. Evvie did likewise. They headed for the North's rental car. "By the way, Evvie, I like 'Dulcie' so don't start calling me 'Otelia.' ... It's one of the few nice things Kent has come up with."

Evvie wanted very much to ask, "Why Kent?" But this wasn't the right time, if there ever would be a right time, for that kind of question.

They reached the car and got in. Dulcie continued talking while Evvie let the engine idle so the air conditioner could gain some ground on the rainy-season humidity. The spell of good weather was over.

"I learned Spanish and some English at the government school on Alligandi." She looked at Evvie and winked. "Yes, we have a school."

"But the way you sound, the way ... look, I took Spanish. I know there's a difference between just saying the right words and speaking the language."

"When I was a teenager, eighteen, I left the island and came to the Canal Zone. Maybe after a few drinks I'll tell you why." Another smile. "I worked for the civilian liaison office at SouthCom. ... That's the Southern Military Command Headquarters in Balboa on the Pacific side. Not so much 'civilian' as 'Indian.' The Canal Zone is important to your country for a lot of reasons … other than a shortcut to Subic Bay."

Evvie didn't follow the innuendo and didn't care to. She was more interested in Dulcie. The liquid sound of her words was fascinating. She felt the same surprise she'd felt when she first heard the clipped British accent of the Virgin Island blacks, the Carib Masi, on her trip to Bimini with Ted four years ago, a trip supposedly for pleasure but which turned out to be one involving "Agency business," something she realized only when Ted disappeared for two days in the middle of all the fun without anything resembling an adult explanation.

"Part of my job was to work with the Indians—the Cuna, the Choco. The Cuna nation is separate from that of Panama. That translates to a couple of hundred miles of important coastline between the Canal and Colombia. So the U.S. deals with the Indian nations through intermediaries like myself. When you have a job like that, you learn to 'inflect' in both languages, if you know what I mean."

They crossed the tracks separating the yacht club from Colon and drove east on Calle 13. With Dulcie as tour guide, they explored the city by car for an hour before turning north on Avenida Bolivar. The local street scene, painted by Dulcie's words, came alive for Evvie. The small talk during the drive, the things Dulcie pointed out … the endless bars, the Duty Free Zone at the east end, the YMCA, hospital, Club Nautico, the shops along Avenida del Frente … in the space of one hour the city of Colon became a real place for Evvie. At Calle Segunda they turned north toward the Hotel Washington. Evvie decided that since, as she put it, "Indian gal has plenty dress" and "White gal has plenty stupid," it would be best to find a comfortable table in the lounge and use the hotel room to freshen up.

"Do you still work for them? For the Canal Zone?"
Dulcie shook her head. "No, I don't have that job anymore."
They ordered drinks. Piña coladas. The lounge staff recognized Evvie and, whether through social enlightenment or consideration of the day's bar profits, did not raise an eyebrow when she sat down with her Indian.
"Well? …" said Evvie. A second round of piña coladas sat half-empty on the table.

"Well what?"

"Why did you?"

"Why did I what?"

"Leave the island. ... You said after a few drinks you'd tell me."

Dulcie laughed. "I suppose it's funny. It wasn't at the time."

"Tell me."

"My people, the Cuna, are a verbal people. They have no written history to speak of. It's all oral. Passed down by the *Saklakana,* the chiefs. And by the equivalent of your priest, our *Nele* and *Kantule.* Because of this and our isolation from the rest of the world, we conduct our affairs by tradition. The old ways are the only ways. Some of that will eventually disappear ... but it hasn't yet." She sipped her drink and smiled at Evvie. "Promise not to laugh?"

"No. I won't promise."

Dulcie laughed, a rich female sound, slightly animal, slightly out of place. A few heads at the bar turned.

"I was sixteen. The daughter of an important chief. If a Cuna man shows great promise and has learned the chants and the way of the gathering house, he can become a chief, also. It's not a matter of birth. It's a matter of ability, of being able to make decisions, predict events, see the future. The final test of this new chief, this chief-in-training if you will, is a test of his morals. Of his willpower. Can he restrain his urges in the face of great temptation?" More piña colada.

"The sitting chief, one like my father, sends his prettiest daughter into the jungle with this chief-in-training. They stay there for a few days, always together, living off the land, no other people within miles. If the chief-to-be returns to the community with his virtue intact, he's passed the test. He's a big man. He's a *Sakla.* "

Evvie's drink hovered halfway to her lips where it had been for more than a few seconds. "You? ..."

Dulcie spread her arms wide in a stage gesture. "Me."

"Oh my."

"I was one pretty Cuna, a chief's daughter, and a virgin ... a natural."

"Did you? ... I mean, did he? ..."

"He did not. He never tried. And I made some indecent efforts to help the devil test the fellow. Nothing very obvious. Nothing like swinging naked from a vine. But you know ... a test is supposed to be a test."

"So you made him a chief."

"It's more like I didn't make him not a chief."

Evvie got the drink to her lips, sipped a sip, then set it down. She waited for Dulcie to continue.

Dulcie hesitated, then cocked her head to one side and raised one eyebrow. "There was something else involved ... the way I saw it." She leaned forward. "Here I was, the prettiest thing on the coast, more than a little bit willing to make the new chief lose his hat, if you know what I mean. All the other girls waiting. Wondering. Jealous, maybe? The older women guessing. And what happens? Not a darn thing happens." Dulcie looked Evvie in the eye. "How would you feel?" She paused. "I mean, this guy wasn't what you'd call ... how should I put it? ... a movie star."

"I don't get it. Why would you ..."

"Look. Being who I was, what I was ... well ..."

"You were disappointed!" said Evvie.

"Not just disappointed. I was sort of insulted ... maybe even, as Kent would say, and pardon the language, pissed!"

Evvie put a hand to her mouth and tried to muffle the laugh. It didn't work. "You were like bait. Sort of a driver's test with hurt feelings."

Dulcie laughed too.

"And you left?"

"Not right away. I was a student, a good one. English was the way out, the way to the Canal Zone. During the next two years, if you got between me and my language texts ... well ..."

"That's why you speak as well as you do."

"Lack of love triumphs over all."

After a third round of drinks they went up to the room to freshen up and talk some more. Evvie told Dulcie about her own past. About Ted, about San Francisco where she started sailing, and then, about Cindy.

"I'm sorry, Evvie." Dulcie turned away, and Evvie thought she saw the girl's torso shudder. Dulcie turned back and put her arms around Evvie.

"Oh, Dulcie, it was so fast. ... It happened so damned fast. I never even said goodbye."

They drove back to the yacht club.

Dulcie went and stood in the shade of the big tree.

"Why, Dulcie? Why this?" Evvie gestured at the car, at the ground.

"What we did today, Mrs. North? Just between you and me, okay? No Ted. No Kent. Nothing need be said."

"Why, Dulcie? *Why?*"

"Because it's just between you and me." The Cuna Indian squatted down. And was silent.

Ted was excited. It had been a bad day for sailing—rain squalls, no wind, Davis drunk enough to vomit on the side of the boat—but Ted was excited.

Over dinner in the hotel that evening he told Evvie that Davis, despite his late-stage dipsomania, had come up with a great idea. "He said that me and you, Mrs. North, ought to sail to the San Blas! It's a chain of islands about a hundred miles from here. Indians. Coral reefs. Coconut palms. Right out of the South Pacific. Like a Michener book."

"The San Blas?" she asked. It was the second time she had heard the words that day, and she had never heard of the place before. The words reminded her of Dulcie and how their day together had made her feel disjointed and out of sorts. Like the weather.

"Look, we *need* a shakedown cruise on the ocean. All by ourselves. To see what it's really like out there in a small boat. Davis says it's a good test. A damn good test. The weather's all over the place—calms, storms, big waves, a lee shore waiting to beat the hell out of us. What more could we ask for? It's perfect."

She could tell he had a slight case of tongue-in-cheek and was making the trip sound like a death march on purpose. She could tell by the too-wide eyes and the hint of a real smile.

He reached across the table and tapped the back of her hand. "Seriously, Babe, it's not such a bad idea." When he said "Babe," she knew he was selling her something. "At least we can walk back here if we put Coconut in the middle of the jungle. A hundred miles ain't so bad."

It made sense. It would be beyond stupid to have the trip to the States be their first time at sea in Coconut.

"It's how we planned it," he continued. "Use the end of the rainy season to get to know the boat."

"Is Davis going with us?" she asked.

"No way. He'd fall overboard before we got twenty miles."

"Is it hard to get in there? You said there were reefs. Coral reefs."

He leaned back in his chair. His expression turned serious. "To tell you the truth, it looks a little tricky on the charts." Then he brightened. "But we can ask around. Talk to people who've been there. Get some local knowledge."

She thought for a moment. His enthusiasm was getting to her. And the excitement. "Do you think we could tag along with another boat?" she asked. "Maybe someone's going there on a cruise or something."

"I've heard that some of the Canal Zone people go to the islands, some of the people who work the locks, ship pilots, people like that. Even some of the Navy types stationed at the antenna site."

"Antenna site?"

"It's sort of a communications thing. Hush-hush. Something the Navy calls a Security Group Activity. It's over in the jungle on the east side of the bay, about five miles out in the boonies. A place called Galeta Island. It's pretty much in caretaker status, but I hear they go down there once in a while ... to the San Blas ... the ones who have boats."

"We can ask around."

"Got to be honest with you," he said. His tone was subdued. "The rainy season isn't when most people go. Not enough good wind. Too much rain."

"We're not going down there to lie around in the sun. We're going there to check out the boat and see how we do on the ocean." Her energy was up. *She* began to sell *him*.

"Right," he said.

"Let's ask around, anyway. We won't know if we don't ask around."

"Do you think it's an okay idea? Really?" The look on his face was that of a small boy. Evvie had to smile.

"It's an okay idea. Really." She leaned forward. "Besides," she said, "I met someone at the club the other day when you weren't there. Someone who ought to know about a trip like that."

Chapter 6

"Hello, Arthur. What are you doing?"

"Drinking whiskey and figuring how many ways a man can cut another man's throat."

Evvie blinked three times. "May I sit down?"

"Be my guest."

"How many?" She settled into the chair opposite him.

"How many what?" he asked.

"How many ways *can* a man cut another man's throat?"

"Right to left from the front, left to right from the front. Left to right from the back, and right to left from the back."

"That's four."

"Seems like there should be more."

Three empty glasses on a clean tabletop.

Cigarettes like a small white logjam in a seashell ashtray.

"You're not having a good day." She smiled a weak smile.

"No, I'm not having a good day."

"I'm sorry."

He looked at her. His expression was flat. He leaned back in his chair. "I had a problem with the local Guardia jefe. Nothing a few pounds of high explosive can't fix. What can I do for you? Where's your husband?"

"He took the train to Balboa. I just dropped him off. We need some things for the boat." For the first time she noticed an angry red laceration on the left side of his head in the hairline behind the ear. A three-inch slash. No stitches.

"That's right. You're the two who are sailing to the States. Take plenty of charts. No telling where you'll end up this time of year."

The waitress walked out of the kitchen, looked around the room, and spotted the new arrival. She came over to the table. "Get you something?"

"Maybe a soda, a Coke, a Diet Coke."

The girl wrote slowly on a green pad. "We don't have that."

"What do you have?"

"Naranja … orange soda. See here?" She held the green pad in front of Evvie's face. A line of childish letters was scribbled there. "I already wrote it down," she said. "Orange."

"Fine. Bring that. And get this man another whatever." She nodded at Arthur. "He's having a bad day."

"A bad day? Him? All his days are bad," said the girl. "He tries to beat up the whole of the Guardia Nationale … all by himself." The girl shook her head and left the table.

"Why did you beat them up?"

"Why did *I* beat *them* up?" He turned his head. "See this? I beat them up, all right." He faced her again. "I beat on their baseball bats with my head. Did a pretty fair job of it, too. I think I broke two of them."

"That's an ugly cut."

"You ought to see my kneecaps."

"I guess this is a bad time."

"It is if you want to take me dancing."

Evvie laughed her snort laugh. She couldn't help it. The way he said it. The foot-deep dead-pan expression. She noticed him start to smile.

"You laugh funny," he said.

The waitress brought the drinks and went away. Evvie's orange soda was served in a can, no glass, which meant no ice, but the can was cold. Arthur leaned to one side and fished in his pants pocket. He pulled out a small tin and popped it open with a fingernail. A jumble of tablets half-filled the container. He removed one of the pills and put it in his mouth. Tin closed. Tin back in pocket. He picked up the new drink, took a mouthful of bourbon, tipped his head back, and swallowed. He put the drink down.

"For your head?" Evvie asked.

"You might say that."

"Is it painkiller? If it is, you shouldn't take it with alcohol. You should take it with water."

He indicated the empty whiskey glasses on the table. "Water? ... In my belly?"

She scrunched her lips, nodded ... gestures that said: *"Good point."*

More bourbon downed. "Besides, it's not painkiller. It's lithium."

"Lithium? What's lithium for?" She couldn't remember.

"Peace of mind."

"I suppose it's not polite to ask why you and the police had a fight." She picked up her drink and peeked at him over the top of the soda can. "So, why *did* you and the police have a fight?"

He looked at her and shrugged his shoulders. "It was over a paperwork problem. They said I didn't clear in when I came back from a little cruise I took."

"Where did you go?"

"I didn't go anywhere. I just went out a few hundred miles and came straight back. They claim I went to Providencia. I didn't. I just sailed around the place and cruised home. It's crap. They were after my radio. They took it hostage." He smiled. "So now I have to buy it back."

"That doesn't sound like something to fight over."

"It doesn't?"

"Of course not."

He didn't answer right away. Then, "Well?"

"Well what?"

"You walked over here like you had something in mind."

Evvie folded her arms across her front. "I did ... I do ... that is, I wanted to ask you something. Like maybe if you knew someone who might be going to the San Blas in the next week or so, someone we could follow, someone with another boat who—"

"The San Blas." Not a question.

"Yes. Ted ... my husband and I ... we want to take the boat out. On the ocean. So we can learn what it's like sailing somewhere besides the bay. We thought the San Blas would be a good place to—"

"Whose idea?"

"Well, it's both our ideas. Ted was talking to Mr. Davis and he said—"

"Davis?"

"Yes." She looked down at the table. "Actually, I was really hoping that ... maybe you ..."

"Davis." Arthur grunted, a derisive sound. Then he looked at her.

"Okay."

She didn't understand, at first. "Okay? ..."

"I'll do it."

She smiled and uncrossed her arms. "You'll come with us? You will? In Susurro?"

"I'll do it for three hundred and twenty dollars and ten cents."

"Of course. We wouldn't expect you to drop everything and not—"

"The radio."

"Radio?"

"That's what I need to get it back. Three hundred twenty and ten cents. I don't have the money."

"Oh."

"And I don't know anyone who's going there this month ... someone you could freeload off of."

"It would be more than worth it to us."

"I'll get you down there and inside the reef. Getting in is the hard part. You'll be able to get back here on your own. That's not a problem. It's downhill coming back."

"Downhill?"

"With the current. Following seas and wind ... if there is any wind. This time of year everything's flowing from there to here. Getting in is the tough part. The uphill part."

"I ..."

"I'm assuming you're going to want to play around in the islands for a week or so, explore stuff. I can't stick around for that. Don't have time. But I'll get you there."

"That's terrific. It's exactly what we're looking for. Ted—"

"Is Ted any good?"

"Any good? Sailing? Sure! He's darn good. He—"

"I've watched *you* handle the boat. You're not bad. I haven't had the chance to watch him."

"When did you watch me? I don't remember seeing—"

"The day you went out alone with Davis. I was anchored up in the mangrove in the northeast corner. I watched you through the binoculars. You're good. ... It looked to me like you know how to handle everything pretty well."

Evvie felt her skin turn red. "Mr. Davis is a good man. He—"

"Everybody watches the bay. Those who live here. It's like a big city neighborhood. Strangers think they're invisible."

Evvie took a long drink of soda. "The trip, when? ..."

"You name it. Give me one day's notice. We should sit down, the three of us, before we shove off. To talk over a few things in case something goes wrong." He smiled. "I think the Navy calls it contingency planning. You never know, I might get hit by lightning. Then where'd you be?"

Unexpectedly, he leaned forward and transfixed her with a look she couldn't dissect. Something between cold disinterest and meanness.

"Let me tell you something about yourself, North." He leaned more, the distance between them halved. "You don't let people push you around, not too much, anyway. Except your husband. But you push yourself around. You don't see other people's faults. You seem real ready to make excuses for people who don't deserve it. People like Davis. Covering up for them. Like there's something wrong with *you,* not *them.* Why is that, North?"

Evvie, shocked by the lecture from nowhere, blinked a few times. Then she smiled and squinted one eye. "Let me guess," she said. "You're studying to get into psychiatry school?" She nodded at the ugly laceration on the side of his head. "I think it's time for you to take another pill, Mr. Arthur Arthur. You got hit harder than I thought."

"You give too much." He was still serious, but detached. He acted as though he was no longer speaking directly to her. Talking to himself. Thinking out loud.

She finished her soda and set the empty can on the table. She had recovered from his abrupt mood change and was more amused than concerned. She had seen as much of life's unreason as he. Maybe more. She knew what hell was and this wasn't it. "We haven't talked for more than an hour between the other day and today, combined," she said. "What the hell are you doing?"

Her question, her direct tone, the frank open look—these backed him off. The other-world trance melted out of his face. His skin seemed to refill with blood.

I'd be talking gibberish after getting bonked with a baseball bat, too, she thought. *That cut must hurt.*

Arthur didn't press his question. In fact, it seemed he had forgotten it.

And Evvie let her own question die when his look changed. *That cut definitely must hurt.* For some reason, despite his strange mood swings, she felt more comfortable with him than she did with Ted, Kent, or even Dulcie. They all had secrets. Arthur did not. There were personal things she was curious about, but she wanted only to bask in honest give-and-take with another adult. That was enough for now. Even if he was a bit nuts, he was an honest nuts. Personal questions could wait.

"So, you two name the time," he said. "Like I said before, one day's notice is plenty."

"I should hear from Ted tonight ... if he remembers to call. He's really pretty busy, you know. He's got a lot to do. If he gets all the stuff he went for, he should be back tomorrow. I'll tell him you said yes."

Arthur nodded. He seemed about to say something else, but changed his mind. "I'll be here."

She thanked him and got up to leave. "I'll try not to push myself around anymore ... doctor."

"What?"

She looked at him for a moment. "Nothing." She headed for the parking lot.

"That guy I told you about? The one I met at the club? He said he'd sail down to the San Blas Islands with us."

"Is it going to cost?" Ted continued to unload packages from a canvas bag onto the bed in the hotel room.

"Three hundred dollars."

"Three hundred?"

"It's over a hundred miles. It might take a couple of days to get there. And he has to sail back. A hundred dollars a day sounds pretty good to me."

"Does he sound like he knows what he's doing?"

"His name is Arthur. He has a twenty-six-foot boat. Last week he sailed out three hundred miles and back. By himself."

"He's not going to mooch off us while we're down there, is he? I mean, we need some time to kick back without having to entertain him."

"That's funny. Kent Davis asked me the same thing."

"He did?"

"Yeah. I bumped into him as I was leaving the club."

"And?"

"And I told him—"

"Anything else?"

"What is this—an interrogation? He asked the same thing you did ... that's all."

"Well, he *isn't* going to hang around with us, is he?"

"Davis?"

"No! Arthur."

"Oh. He's going back after we're inside the reef, after he gets us to the customs office on Porvenir. Sailing back here to the Canal Zone isn't too much of a problem, he said. We'll know the boat by then, and the current and weather will be in our favor on the return trip."

She peeked over Ted's shoulder as he unpacked the last small item from the canvas bag. The box was no bigger than a pack of cigarettes. "What's that?"

"This? It's just a portable transmitter, a two-way radio. Hand-held job. I figured it'd be smart to have one along."

"Sure is small."

He looked at the box. "Yeah. You can strap it to a wrist, an ankle, a belt. Waterproof too. It wasn't cheap."

"I think it's a good idea, too," she said. "It's a long way to the States."

"The States?"

Punta Mansueto, Panama

"You have everything?"

"Yes."

"Are the small boats lashed down so the storm will not take them?"

"Yes."

"And El Codo ... is he aboard?"

"He is below."

Chapter 7

Evvie picked up the phone.

"Mrs. North? Evvie?"

"Dulcie? Hi! Where are—"

"Are you alone? Is your husband there? In the room?"

"No. He's at the club. He's—"

"Kent said you're sailing to the San Blas with Ted. Is that true?"

"Yes. We're going to—"

"When?"

Evvie listened to the silence. The clipped questions coming over the phone were strained and out of character.

"When, Evvie? When are you leaving?"

"In two days. Wednesday morning."

Dulcie's voice, already low, dropped more. The intensity didn't lessen. "Do you remember that shop on Frente? The one I pointed out to you when we were driving? The one that sold wood carvings from India?"

Through the phone Evvie heard the sound of a door closing. "I remember," she answered. "Across from that big white ship tied up on the other side of the railroad tracks."

"Tuesday night. Ten o'clock. The alley to the right as you face the store."

"Me and Ted? Do you mean we should—"

"You! Just you!" And the line went dead.

Evvie put the phone down.

The urgency in Dulcie's voice was real, and the message itself so unexpected that Evvie didn't know what to think. Until that moment, she'd attributed her feelings of uneasiness to a combination of having to adapt to a new place, to the restless weather patterns of the tropical rainy season, and to the sense of isolation brought about by the pervasive poverty that hovered just beyond the manicured edges of the Canal Zone, my "Third World guilt" as she'd phrased it to Ted after they'd seen children begging, old men fishing hard from the sea wall, and tired women selling trinkets in temporary places between the rain forest and trimmed lawns. Though these things bothered her, they were intrusions she could get her arms around, realities she could see and try to understand. But there was something else. Unseen. Something more than feeling out of place in new surroundings.

She tried to pin it down. The small questions she had no answers for. Questions that were becoming impatient. Aberrations she could feel, but couldn't touch. The discomfort she experienced when Ted forgot time and promises and seemed somewhere else. The nonsense of the man Davis who appeared to be, at best, a seedy caricature out of an old Bogart movie, but who never quite completely collapsed into a harmless joke. Even Arthur, whose eyes betrayed a sullen melancholy close to violence. And the sea, the powerful, restless, muttering ocean that yesterday promised salvation and tonight, after the phone call from Dulcie, seemed to threaten an end to everything she hoped for.

She looked at her watch. Ted wouldn't be back for another hour. She had room service bring up two vodka tonics.

She considered telling Ted about the phone call. Decided yes, then no. Then yes again. She took out her list of things to get for the coming trip and worked on that. Working on the list and drinking vodka started to blur the doubts she was having. Perhaps Dulcie had taken enough humiliation from Davis and wanted to hitch a ride back to the islands. That could be it. That must be it.

Evvie reappraised the list of provisions and increased the amount of food she'd need to buy if Dulcie came along.

And decided not to tell Ted about the call.

She recognized the not unpleasant taste of having a secret. It went well with the new feeling that lingered from defeating the Davis obscenity in the boat and from having stood up to Ted after he abandoned her in the yacht club. She felt a growing kinship with Dulcie, too. Men. Sometimes they were less than grand. She puzzled over these thoughts and tried to decide whether they belonged to her or to the vodka.

"Got something for you." Arthur pushed a book and some papers across the table toward Ted and Evvie.

The club restaurant was empty at ten in the morning. The lunch crowd would begin to filter in about eleven, most to eat, but more than a few who, according to Arthur, were determined to test their Anabuse dosage in the club bar despite knowing that the rest of the afternoon would involve an on-your-knees romance with the office commode.

"What's this?" asked Ted.

Arthur nodded at the book. "That's a brief and colorful history of the Cuna Indians. It helps to know where someone's coming from when you go to visit." Arthur drank some bourbon.

"I've read a little about the Cunas," said Evvie. "They came from the interior, from the other side of the mountains."

"By 'coming from,' I don't mean geographically."

Ted opened the book at random. Evie looked at the upturned page. A drawn illustration showed a Spanish conquistador running a blade through an Indian's chest. A Cuna baby was pictured skewered on a stake next to the Spaniard. A naked Cuna woman lay on the ground.

Ted turned several more pages, then stopped and read a while in silence. "Evvie, listen to this." He began to read from the book. "The Spaniards cut off the fingers of our tribesmen, one finger at a time, until they had cut them all off. They slit up the stomachs of our people. They cut open the belly of a woman, then they killed one of her children and put it into the open wound. They killed all the babies by cutting out the entrails and letting them dry in the sun. They sold the young girls to moneyed Spaniards at thirty pesetas each. One of their customs was to capture a Cuna woman and strip her naked; then they would tie her head and knees down to the ground so her back part was raised. Then the soldiers raped her until she died." Ted grinned and looked across at Arthur. "Nice."

Arthur nodded once at the book. "That's the history of the Cuna. It's not just their version. It's backed up by Spanish writing. Those Indians have been trying to stay out of the way of civilization, if you'll pardon the expression, for five hundred years. French, English, Colombians, Panamanians. Mostly the Spanish. Cuna gold and Cuna gods were the problem. I think some of that history stuff is good to know if you're planning on being there any length of time. It might explain a few things. Can't hurt."

"That's terrible … what happened to them," said Evvie. "You're right; we didn't know."

"What you ought to know also is that they didn't bring all that ugly stuff on themselves. Some tribes did. Not the Cuna. I wouldn't blame the Spanish a hell of a lot if some of their garrisons had been cut up by the Indians, as happened in other parts, but the Cuna never did that." He drank more bourbon and smiled. "The Cuna have gods they believe in. Really believe in. To a fault, maybe. Good ol' God says you treat strangers right. God says you don't kill. That kind of thinking, plus having more gold than guns, makes for hard times. Cunas chant every day about their history. The gold. The gods. The demons they call *Nia*. They really believe that demons rule the night. That's why they stay in after dark. A few missionaries have gone down there to fine-tune the Cuna's beliefs, but for the most part the Indians have politely stuck with their own version."

Ted flipped the book shut. "It's interesting, but why the history lesson?" He glanced at Evvie and grinned. "I don't think we're planning on wiping out any families." Nonchalant, flippant, dismissive.

Arthur stared at him for a long moment.

Evvie felt awkward at Ted's words. Especially the way they triggered the sudden, hard look on Arthur's face.

"Do they still feel that way?" she asked. "I mean do they still treat visitors okay?"

Arthur's stare softened and shifted to Evie. "They do. But don't try to buy what little gold they have, their breastplates, their nose rings. Those things are a token of love to them, passed from mother to daughter. Buy their molas, those little cloth pictures they make, or the wood carvings; don't try to buy the gold. That's an insult. And don't expect to stay overnight; it's forbidden. They've learned that lesson the hard way. Plan to stay on the boat."

"I don't see how they put up with all that murder and rape stuff," said Ted. "Don't they have any guts? Are they simple-minded?"

"In nineteen twenty-five the government of Panama sent a squad of soldiers there. They tried to put the Indians in line, arrest a few chiefs."

"And?"

"Indians twenty-five, Panama zero. The Cunas killed all twenty-five."

"And got away with it?"

"They did. Their gods seem to have repealed the 'generous host' policy, at least for that year. And the Cunas wound up with an independent nation, thanks to some gringos and a few enlightened Panamanians in high places."

"The Canal?" asked Ted.

"That and the fact that most of the gold had disappeared. Take your pick."

Evvie took the book from Ted and held it to her chest. "Can we keep this for a while? To read? We'll give it back."

Arthur signaled for the waitress. "That's why I brought it along."

"When we get there," said Ted, "we'd like to see a few islands, get off the tourist track. Are the charts good enough?"

"No."

Ted pulled his chin into his neck and looked surprised. "No? How the hell do we get around?"

"You eyeball it. Sail during the day. Midday is best. The water's clear. If you see blue water, go. Green water is a sign that it's shallow but sandy. No problem with sand for a boat the size of Coconut. Sail her slow and you'll be able to push off if you ground her. It's brown water you watch out for. Brown shadows. That's coral."

"Why no up-to-date charts?"

"Because there's no financial or military reason to update them. You can get charts anywhere. Hell, you can buy them from the U.S. government. But they're no good. What you get is a slick version of a chart used to sail the Spanish Main updated for coral growth by some bureaucrat with a slide rule who figures coral grows 'X' number of inches a year. That's 'figures,' not 'measures.' Coral doesn't listen to bureaucrats for some reason."

Ted drained his tequila. Arthur did the same to his bourbon.

"There's plenty of used charts on the barrier reef," said Arthur. "Slide rules, too. Every year a few more of the dead-reckoning crowd have to swim for it." He grinned. "The water's pretty, but a lot of the San Blas reef area is shark breeding ground. Sort of puts a little extra kick in your stroke."

"Sharks?" from Evvie.

Arthur handed his empty glass to the waitress, who was spilling the next round on the table. "Don't worry about sharks," he said. "There's enough natural food on the reef. They don't have to munch tourists."

"Never?" asked Evvie.

"Not never. Nothing's never. They kill Indians. Maybe a couple in a good year. Kids mostly. No more than anywhere else."

Ted paid for the drinks.

Arthur raised his glass to Ted in a gesture that thanked him for the round. Then he set his glass down and leaned back in his chair. He winked at Evvie. "How do you rate my behavior today, Mrs. North? Pretty goddamn nice, I'd say."

Evvie nodded. "I was wondering about that."

Arthur patted his pants pocket. "Took two pills. One for each of you. Nearly got me on my ass, though. And makes me chatter like a jaybird."

Ted looked from Arthur to Evvie.

"He got bonked on the head," she explained. "By the police. He takes pills so he won't be such a grouch."

"Bonked on the head?"

"It was about some paperwork," explained Evvie.

"By the police?"

Arthur leaned forward. "Right. The thing about small-time bureaucrats? Don't mess with their paperwork. Kick their dogs, steal their tools, make love to their wives ... but don't mess with that sacred paper."

Ted frowned. "They're not going to grab you away from us, are they?"

Arthur laughed, and Evvie thought she was seeing Arthur drunk for the first time, but she had seen him drink much more without blinking. It had to be the medication. Arthur gave a thumbs-up sign. "Those silly bastards? Grab me? Not them. No way. I told them I had a guide job. I'd get the money to them by next week. I told them not to install my rig in the mayor's boat just yet." He squinted at Ted. "The money's all right, isn't it?"

"Half now, half when we get there."

Evvie was embarrassed again. "Why don't we pay him all of it now, Honey? So he can get his radio."

Before Ted could respond, Arthur broke in. "No, little lady. That's not how it's done. Half now, half in Porvenir. At the dock."

"Don't you need the radio? For the trip?" Evvie asked.

"Not if you've got one. Besides ... if I got in a bind and called for a hand from them, do you think they'd come?" He smiled. "Hell, they'd rather videotape me going under to impress the local whores."

Ted reached into his pocket, took out his wallet, and removed two bills. Both hundred dollar bills. "Two hundred now. The other hundred and twenty in the San Blas, in Porvenir ... after we're through Customs."

Arthur took the money and snapped each bill in the air twice. He looked at each against the light of the mid-morning sun coming through the open east end of the restaurant. Then he made a slow show of inserting the bills into his own wallet.

They spent the next hour going over details. As they talked, Evvie thought about the phone call from Dulcie. Should she ask the men about taking Dulcie if that was what she wanted? Should she ask Arthur privately? Would there be a problem clearing into Customs with her along? But the real-world demands of the trip began to push aside the unreal mystery of Dulcie. Evvie decided that she'd just tell her no. There might be a flare-up with Davis if he found out they were taking her. And, after all, she hadn't promised Dulcie anything. Not yet. But she had implied she'd meet Dulcie on Frente later. She'd do that much. A promise was a promise. To Evvie, a promise was something a person followed up on, whether it involved picking up a bag of sugar for a friend or honoring a marriage vow to a husband. When she said she'd do something ...

What Arthur said next interrupted her thoughts. "So, besides the reef entrance, the only other dicey spot is when we skirt Nombre de Dios. The ocean will be coming at us from the east, right on the nose. Nombre sticks out and bounces the waves back to the east like a natural seawall. That means we'll be in cross seas, maybe big ones. ... It just depends. The waves can go both ways there. East and west."

Ted circled the point on the chart spread on the table between them.

Arthur jabbed a finger at the circle. "Those waves can bounce fifteen miles out. If that's what they're doing, then we go twenty miles out, even thirty if we have to."

He looked up and saw Evvie's face as she stared at his finger. "Hey, Mrs. North."

She raised her eyes, meeting his.

"Don't let it get to you. It's all right, really. It's beautiful. Coconut's well-founded. If sailboats couldn't keep off lee shores, there wouldn't *be* any sailboats."

She surrendered a nervous smile. "How big are the waves?"

Arthur looked thoughtfully up at the ceiling. "I've seen them twenty feet. Heard of thirty."

"Thirty feet?" Her voice was too high.

"Rollers, mostly. Rollers don't bother a small boat any. Just like a ride at the amusement park."

She began to feel better, not good, but better.

Arthur scratched his chin. "Except when you've got a situation like off Nombre. Opposing seas, if they hit together right, can be hell straight up."

She felt instantly worse.

Arthur saw that his words were not having the desired effect. His male reliance on the comforting nature of hard facts was not comforting her at all. He leaned forward again. "Mrs. North?" He held her eyes with his. "I'm not trying to scare you. I'm just trying to tell you why we might have to go out pretty far."

"Well, you are scaring me."

He leaned back again and smiled. "It's natural to get a little anxious heading out there the first time. Even if you've been there before, but have been away too long, it's a little nerve-racking … I guess. But the ocean always looks scary to a sailor from a distance. Once you get going, are out there, the boat gives you all the courage you need. You'll see. Up close the ocean's a piece of cake. One wave at a time."

She shook her head. "Tell that to my butterflies."

"Everyone gets butterflies," he said. "You've just got to get them to fly in formation."

One more round of drinks. A few last details.

"Eight o'clock tomorrow morning, then," said Arthur. "If we're lucky and get an early wind, we might make it in one day. Don't plan on it though. Like as not, we'll have to hole up or heave to for the night. This time of year things are sort of unpredictable. And there's no percentage in running the reef at night." He grinned. "Every damn time the government fills up the sea buoys with kerosene, the Indians paddle out and steal it."

Ted extended his hand across the table. "We'd better get moving. Thanks for the briefing, Arthur."

Arthur took his hand and smiled. "Thanks for the two hundred."

Evvie noticed her husband lurch in his chair as he leaned forward. The drinks. Ted drank, but not like this, not like he had since sitting down with Arthur well over an hour ago. She had dropped out of trying to keep pace with them after the first round. Ted was in one of those unspoken macho drinking contests with Arthur. *They're both doing it. Why do they do this?* She never could quite figure these things. Ted would be useless the rest of the day. Arthur was on a double dose of pills plus the booze. She was glad she hadn't mentioned Dulcie. She held the book close to her chest. She had been sitting that way for the last twenty minutes.

She was aware that Arthur was looking at her. He was showing signs of more than just his pills.

"Mrs. North, are you cold?"

"Cold?"

"Cold. The way you're holding that book."

Evvie quickly put the book down on the table. "Oh, no ... I'm not cold. Just a habit."

Ted laughed. The sound of it was sloppy. "She does that because she's got three tits."

His words hit her with the force of a slap in the face.

Arthur looked slowly at Ted. "What?"

"Three tits. She's got three tits. She tries to cover them up. At least the extra one. It's a birth defect." Ted fished a piece of ice out of his empty drink glass and popped it into his mouth.

Arthur looked into Evvie's eyes. The hardness that had not been there all morning came back like pieces of slate were being shoved under the skin of his face. Then into his neck. She lowered her eyes. She didn't know what to say.

The drinks. Ted said that because of the drinks. Her mind grabbed for other reasons. There were none. Just the drinks.

Ted leaned forward and tapped the cover of the book with his finger. "If she ever writes the story of her life," he slurred, "she can call it 'The Tale of Three Titties.'" He laughed again.

Arthur spoke. "Mrs. North? Evvie? Will you forgive me? I didn't know ..."

Ted chewed ice.

"It's okay," she said. "So I'm not perfect." And she forced a self-conscious smile.

"Nobody's perfect," said Arthur.

"That's for sure," she said, shooting a quick glare at her husband. Then she lowered her eyes. She knew that Arthur was looking at Ted. But she could not look at them.

Arthur got up from the table.

Some dollar bills fluttered down. A tip for the girl.

"Eight tomorrow." Arthur's voice was someone else's voice.

And he was gone.

Chapter 8

The alley went back thirty feet, then angled to the right. The turn was enough to keep anyone standing on the sidewalk from seeing the far end.

Evvie could see boxes piled against the windowless wall of the store. Pieces of wood slat from broken shipping crates and wads of packing paper in clumps made dark shapes in front of her. A few trash cans. She squinted into the dark and saw no one.

She took three steps into the alley and stopped. "Dulcie?"

Nothing moved. Three more steps and then several seconds to listen. Pupils dilated. More details. Something scurried halfway down the space ahead of her. *Rat!* ... *No, a cat. Only a gray cat.*

She wouldn't have dared a rat.

A cat was different. A cat even took away some of the fright. *Nice kitty.*

She clutched her purse against her ribs.

"Dulcie?" Louder.

Nothing. The cat sat on a broken crate and watched Evvie with eyes that gleamed mist-yellow in the backlight of the street.

Evvie screwed up her courage and took six bold strides farther into the alley. "Dulcie! If you're there, say something!"

The gray cat licked a front paw.

Evvie didn't like being stood up. Irritation flooded over her sense of fear. She angrily kicked a pile of packing paper out of her way and walked to the turn in the alley. She stumbled as her ankle got caught up in a clatter of two by fours and crate lath. But she did not fall.

"Goddamn it!" She bent to rub the abrasion on her ankle. It stung and she felt the patina of moisture that told her the skin was broken. As she pressed her fingers on the scraped flesh, she looked up and peered toward the dead end of the alley.

There was no one there.

One more time. "Dulcie?"

Nothing.

Behind her the cat scurried.

She stood, turned, and was hit in the stomach by a hard fist that knocked her off her feet and onto her back. She crashed onto the wooden crate debris. Boards banged, slapped, and skidded.

Two shadows, not big. The closer one, the one who had struck her, was male, short in stature, powerfully built. She could not see the second person, only a silent shape farther back.

The assailant came at her. A knee pressing into the pit of her stomach. A hard palm and fingers covering her eyes, nose, and mouth, pushing her head back into the debris. The weight of him.

In the dark violence, the only image that managed to form in her brain was a slow-motion close-up of one of the long steel packing nails as it punctured the back of her neck. A silver nail sliding into pale flesh. And there were nails. Lots of nails. She had seen them bent and protruding from the boards when she knelt to feel her ankle in the seconds before she was hit.

The image of the nail going in swirled to the top of her consciousness in the turmoil, an incidental thing, removed, an image the brain seized on as it struggled to dilute panic with imagination.

Then the anger.

It came surging, a frenzy of outrage that poured energy into her veins like hot oil.

The fingers of her free hand, the hand not clutching the purse, crabbed across cement and closed over a jagged half-piece of brick. She swung hard where a head should be, and a head was there. The impact was rock solid. Her attacker gasped. The claustrophobic pressure of the hand on her face evaporated.

She had hurt him!

She reloaded her muscles and swung again. As her arm moved forward it was caught in midair, stopped so quickly that she thought something in her elbow snapped.

Then the fist drove into her stomach again. Her lungs emptied. Purse and brick cartwheeled out of her hands. Dim images dimmed more. The world wobbled. Her body refused the call to fight.

She felt herself dragged sideways by the ankles and she was spun around like a sack of grain. One of her legs was tugged roughly onto a length of wood. The wood supported her ankle ten inches above the ground.

The seconds seemed to hang. Her attacker stood up, towered above her. A giant now. She watched him raise his foot.

The foot crashed savagely down onto her shin. Pain speared up her leg into her hip. In that same tick of time, the sound of something cracking. A sharp sickening sound. The sound of breaking bone.

Nausea swept through her chest and stomach.

Vomit tried but did not come.

Then they were gone.

Gone.

She was alone. She lay there for two numb minutes.

A cat face hovered close to her face. Looking down.

She pushed at the cat and sat up. Fear was still there, but not enough to keep eyes and fingers from exploring her leg. How badly was it broken? Did the bones stick out? Was blood flowing?

She tried to focus.

She felt no bone. She felt no blood.

The leg began to throb as sensation moved downward from hip to knee, to her shin, and finally to her toes.

She tried to move toes. Toes moved.

She bent forward more. Felt more. She bent the knee. A broken piece of wood shifted on the alley concrete.

The leg was not broken. The wood had snapped. Not the leg.

She lay back down. Flat on her back, she began to cry. Silent jolting sobs.

The gray cat came again. A rough tongue licked salty tears. Evvie raised her hand and stroked the cat.

Her mind, purged of panic, hunted back in time. Tried to reconstruct and sort the images.

The shape of the man. The force of the blows. The crack of the wood.

Hunted further back.

The other shadow. Watching. Different outline. Shoulders. Waist. Hips.

A woman.

Get up! Move. Clean your dress. Get some water.

She found a piece of packing paper and wiped her face. Coarse paper that scraped her skin. She got to her feet using the side of the building for support. Dizziness took her and she sagged to her knees. Then struggled to her feet again.

She looked for her purse, and found it.

The latch was still closed. The car keys still inside. Nothing had been taken. The robbers hadn't been able to find the purse in the debris.

Then, a new fear. Had these same people attacked and hurt Dulcie, too? *Is that why Dulcie isn't here?* A snaking nausea twisted in her stomach once more and she almost fell. But she did not. She breathed deeply. She straightened her clothes as best she could. She walked a few feet, stopped because of the pain, then made herself walk some more. Back and forth she went in the short space of alley. Wanting to appear okay. Wanting to walk normally. No limp. She gradually worked the hitch out of her stride.

She shuffled to where her car was parked, and no one saw her. She drove west, then crossed the railroad tracks and parked in the yacht club lot near the boatyard restrooms. She washed her face and legs and arms at a sink. Noise from the evening drinkers in the club drifted through the open transom of the restroom, but nobody came in. Nobody came to ask questions. Nobody came to pry.

She drove back to the hotel. Almost eleven-thirty. Ted would be asleep. He was tired from the provisioning and from the drinking in the club that morning, and she knew he wanted to be fresh for the departure the next day. He had asked her not to wake him when she came in from what she told him was a last-minute trip to pick up some things she'd forgotten.

And she did not wake him.

She stood on the balcony at midnight. Too tired to think. Too exhausted to ask questions that needed asking.

Only one thought. *We've got to get out of here; get out of this insane city before it's too late.*

Nothing seemed real. Colon was quicksand beneath her feet. No solid ground. No foothold. It might be hell out on that untried sea, but it seemed a simpler hell.

Across the silent bay beyond the sleeping ships with their solitary riding lights, no column of white rose above the black line of breakwater rock. No rumble came through the earth.

The ocean was calm.

Waiting.

For the first time since their arrival in Panama, she wanted to be close to the sea. To be on the breast of that deep water. To be out there. Even to settle into the still dark depth of it. And to sleep.

Chapter 9

Coconut sliced across the bay at hull speed and lined up on the widening gap in the breakwater. Susurro hissed sweetly twenty yards to port and slightly behind on Coconut's lee quarter. The sun was clean and sharp and a third of the way up the eastern sky.

The day was a jewel. Dry-season winds had ridden through the night on padded hooves and ambushed the rainy season with clear skies and twenty knots of northeast wind.

A blue and gentle ocean, framed by the breakwater heads, stretched away to the north. The wind, despite its thousand-mile fetch, had not had time to build a mean sea.

Gulls faced east and hung like white ornaments, stationary in the steady breeze.

Evvie had the helm. A flannel shirt and floppy sweat pants covered the bruises from the night before, bruises that hurt less than she had expected but still were in need of camouflage. Ted was forward on the jib sheet. Halfway across the bay he had turned to her with a look on his face that told her better than any words that there was still something worth hoping for, that he hadn't quit on her, that they could make it.

It had been a long time since she had seen that look, that little-boy expression that said a day like today was enough.

My God, we're here! We're really out!

Both boats scudded past the twin sea towers and cleared the opening. Pups escaping through a hole in the fence. A pair of white seeds spit by the bay into the ocean. Two slivers of beauty tearing across the seam where green water met blue water.

Bow waves curling.

Sails iron-hard and hauling.

Evvie looked back at Susurro. The double-ender was starboard side up and beautiful. She didn't slice through the sea; she melted through it. Evvie could not see Arthur because Susurro was heeled away, but she knew he was watching, not Coconut's hull but her mast tip, riding shotgun on a compass heading that was too enchanting to change.

She turned and looked forward. Ted seemed dazed by the sea-magic. He turned and looked at her once more.

He cupped his free hand to his mouth. "Can you believe this?" And turned forward again. The wind cut across Evvie's face and pushed more than wind-tears out of the corner of each eye.

The stomach-tickling lazy climb up the face and down the backside of the great rollers began. Like a rider taking a show horse over the jumps, Evvie urged Coconut to rise, then fall, then rise again, each looming seafront an adventure, each broad back a place to frolic and breathe again.

The boat was alive beneath Evvie's senses, an intimate traveler. Coconut talked to Evvie with her rigging, rubbed excitement into her tiller hand, let her know that when trouble came from the sea as trouble would, there was more strength in this hull than graceful spar and sheer showed, that given half a chance she could take the lady to hell and back.

Evvie dissolved into Coconut. She closed her eyes and took each sea on feel alone and let the wind talk to her skin about headings.

She sailed.

They went twenty miles straight out before laying over onto port tack. The coast of Panama was a low line of purple on the western horizon. They powered a few degrees south of east. Susurro was upwind now and half a mile to seaward. Ted took his turn at the helm. For a few minutes they sat together on the windward side of the cockpit. Neither spoke. On the new course the waves marched at their backs from the windward beam. The rise and fall of the hull was longer now as Coconut paralleled the seas. It was just past noon when Evvie went below and made sandwiches and scooped macaroni salad from a plastic bowl. The cabin, heeled at thirty degrees, decided for her that soda would be served in cans, not cups.

They ate in silence, and she fed him with her fingers and held his plate for him when he had to make some small adjustment in the main. She had piled a few potato chips on each paper plate, but the wind blew them all away to leeward and they laughed and watched them spin into the sea.

Once, Ted looked at her as she chewed the last of her sandwich, and she turned and saw something in his look that quickly died away.

"What was that?" she asked.

"What was what?"

"That look. What were you thinking?"

"Nothing."

"Tell me," she said.

He looked up at the sail. Then back at her. "I was thinking how crazy it would be if we just turned this damned thing around and headed for the Gulf of Mexico."

She made a face. "Hey! Don't call my boat a 'damned thing.'"

"No. I mean it. Just go for the States."

"Not enough food."

"We catch our food. That's why we have the fishing gear."

"Not enough water." She smiled and poked his ribs.

"We drink soda." He smiled. "No, you drink the soda. I'll drink the beer."

"No charts."

"We use the stars." He suddenly tired of the game; his face became a mask of sad resignation. He looked over his shoulder at Susurro. Still a half-mile away. Still moving like an arrow. "You'd better get some sleep," he said.

"I don't want to sleep."

"Your friend said we should try. One of us needs to be fresh if there's trouble tonight."

"What I want to do is have sex with you."

He laughed. "I'd like to, but ..."

"Right now," she said.

"Go clean the galley."

She made a small fist and popped him on the shoulder. She gathered the paper plates and empty cans and, bracing against the pitching cockpit seatback, worked her way forward on her rump and started down the cabin steps. She stopped and looked back. "What if I get naked and fool around right here in the hatch? What then?"

He looked up at the mainsail. "Then we probably won't get where we're going."

She went below and tended to small things in the galley. She resealed the open bag of chips with a yellow clip and put the plastic bowl of macaroni salad back on ice in the reefer. She sponged the cutting board clean. The motion of the boat, the intoxicating sense of freedom, and the suddenly sensuous smell of salt air in the small cabin—all these began to build a delicious warmth in her chest. Her mind played with the words she'd said to Ted before she went below. The feeling of warmth moved lower. Coconut yawed sharply to port, and the motion pushed Evvie's hips against a blunt curve of teak that edged the galley counter. The center part of her that was swelling shuddered with a pleasure more electric than muscular. Her knees went liquid. She was startled by what was happening and had to place her palms on the countertop to keep from folding up. She straightened. Then she pressed back against the teak. This time without Coconut's help.

She went to the forward cabin, stripped off her shirt, and lay on her back on the vee-berth.

Get some rest. Sleep. Have to sail tonight. No time for …

After two out-gunned minutes of restraint, she realized that sleep wasn't going to come. Something more urgent was alive in her. The dull ache that nibbled at her shin and the soreness where she had been punched in the stomach, in a strange reversal, began to intensify what she was feeling. The place between her legs that had been soft-swollen a few minutes ago was firm and turgid and laced with lust. Her mind, a sea of thought-confetti. Dizzy. Hot. The sound of water rushing past the hull flooded the tight space. She forced her eyes to focus and she watched as both her hands moved like someone else's hands down her flat stomach and beneath the waistband of the sweat pants. She tried to stop the hands one last time. She forced fingers to lift away from her skin. Not to touch the delectable heat there. The fabric of the sweat pants, tented up by her hands, was past damp. Wet. She wavered twice, then surrendered. She let hands and fingers do what they wanted to do. The first time she lost her breath. The fourth time she frictioned-burned the skin on the backs of her bare heels as her legs pumped frantically against a cotton sheet.

Then she slept.

The rhythm of the boat was sweet in the steady wind, the heel constant, the sound of the ocean against the hull a white-sound lullaby. Coconut rocked and crooned, and Evvie's sleep was deep.

She dreamed. First of Colon and Dulcie, and then of images of the storm as their plane had flown into Panama. Dream-time abruptly shifted. She was nineteen, the day she sat in the library reading about the words she'd heard at her father's trial six years earlier. The defense had brought her to the courtroom in an effort to work on the sympathies of the jury. Not only didn't the ploy work, it backfired. One look at Evvie, coupled with the horrific crime committed by her father, and the jurors were galvanized by the idea of what could happen to Evvie, probably already had happened to her.

Genetic defect. Dissociation disorder. Depersonalization. Words she knew had to be important because no one would tell her what they meant. She memorized them, wrote them down the way they sounded. Words so important that her father had blown off the top of his head on the afternoon he was allowed back home, under escort, to get his affairs in order before going to prison. It happened in the basement, the two marshals distracted for only an instant by a man who knew exactly what he was going to do.

She had seen it begin. Her father bolting through the door leading to the stairs. Junk thrown onto the lower steps to stop the marshals. Shots fired to keep everyone at bay, even her. The sounds of his drinking. Glasses and a whiskey bottle breaking. The slow hours. The people. The cursing and ranting that came up from down there. The long silence. Then the blast of the shotgun. She had tried to run to him then. But they stopped her.

Other dream images flashed by in rapid sequence. Confused shapes in the night. Eyes. Tiny blue flowers in lines on moonlit wallpaper. Nine window panes all reflecting the same single streetlight, like so many wallet-size photos on the sheet of class pictures sent home by the school photographer each year.

In her dream, Evvie hung in the air above the Evvie sitting in the library reading the book that said what the words meant. The floating Evvie felt the same things the sitting Evvie felt. Warm skin. Damp sweat. Embarrassment. Look left, look right. … Is anyone watching? Does anyone see? Guilt. Fear. Sadness at something the book said wasn't evil … sadness because that meant he was sick, not bad. Now the skin gets warmer. Hot. A blowtorch-burn of embarrassment. Mostly that.

"Evvie!"

She opened one eye and tried to remember where she was.

"Evvie! Get up here!"

There was a drill sergeant's urgency in Ted's voice that yanked Evvie to her feet before she was half-awake. She tried to stand, but the heeled decking and a subtle slide to port by Coconut sent her crashing into a table stanchion. She pulled up the pant leg of her sweat pants. The mark on her shin from the alley mugging still looked red, but the stumble hadn't caused any new damage.

"Evvie!"

She rolled down the pant leg and scrambled into the cockpit.

The first thing she saw was Susurro's tall mainsail almost touching theirs. Right on their starboard rail. Ten feet away. The closeness startled her. Water boiling between the two boats jumped and spit, and the sounds of sailing rebounded off each hull and filled the air.

The wind was still fresh but was backing to the north, and the sky was dark. She looked at her watch. Three p.m. Arthur was pointing straight ahead, and Ted stood by the tiller and looked where he pointed.

"That's Manzanillo Point!" yelled Arthur. "Ten miles dead ahead. That landbreak five miles to starboard this side of the point is Portobelo. Nombre is on the far side of Manzanillo Point, another twenty miles from here."

Ted glanced at the folded chart he held in one hand. "Can we get by?"

"It's going to be close. Looks like we'll need to tack a few miles out, a little west of north ..."

A few miles out?

"... then back east. We need sea room. We don't want to get pinned on a lee shore by that."

By that? Evvie saw both Arthur and Ted looking to port, toward the open sea. She turned and looked, too.

The north horizon was black.

Thunderheads boiled over the sea ten miles away. Lightning skipped in the towering cumulus. The squall line was closing the coast, moving toward Panama like a curtain strung from east to west as far as she could see.

Arthur yelled again. "I say we scoot into Portobelo! Hole up this side of the point."

"What's the downside?" Ted shouted back.

"The downside is we might be stuck there for a week! We might not be able to claw our way out and around the point if that storm sets in. She looks like one serious piece of weather."

Ted handed Evvie the chart. A gust of wind almost tore it from her grasp. She threw the chart down the open hatch into the cabin.

Ted turned and watched the approaching storm.

After a few moments he looked back at Arthur. "What do you think? Can we beat it?"

"We can't beat it, but we can go out and meet it ..."

Go out and meet it?

"... get the angle, then run with the bitch. If we can get a few more miles offshore, we should be able to slip by Manzanillo, then hole up on the other side ... Nombre or Escribanos Bay. Storm or no storm, once we're past the point we can coast to Porvenir."

Ted looked at Evvie.

"What do you think?" he asked. She stood close to him now and held his arm.

"We've got two months," she said. "Let's go into Portobelo." The storm was dropping the air temperature. The sudden cold unnerved her.

Ted turned to Arthur. "If we get stuck in Portobelo, do you stay with us? Do you take us the rest of the way?"

Arthur didn't reply at once. Then, "I can't stay in Portobelo for a week. I could come back when the weather clears ... take you down the rest of the way then."

Ted looked north at the storm line. Then up at the sails. Then at Evvie. "We have to ride one out sooner or later," he said. "What do you say, Mrs. North? Take a chance?" He winked at her.

She turned and looked again at the rolling black clouds. It didn't seem to be much of a decision to her. Why try to challenge the storm? Especially that storm? There was time, plenty of time. There was no schedule to meet, no place they had to be. Arthur said back at the club that Portobelo was the best port on the coast: Spanish forts lined with centuries-old cannon; a small fishing town full of history and worth exploring; a natural harbor with good holding ground and protected on three sides by mountains. It simply didn't make sense to push it.

But taking on the storm seemed to make sense to Ted. And that was important, too.

"I think we should go to Portobelo and wait," she said. The words came out before she could stop them. She watched his face change.

"Hey, North!" Arthur's shout. "Make up your mind. We don't have a lot of time."

Ted stared across the churning space between the hulls and did not answer. The boats plunged forward toward the distant barrier of Manzanillo Point.

"North?" yelled Arthur.

Ted blinked out of his stare. "What happens if we're separated out there tonight?"

The response from Arthur was delayed in coming. Evvie was sure she knew what Arthur was thinking.

Finally, "You trust that compass, mister! Trust it like you've never trusted anything before. Keep your masthead light going all night if you've got the battery. Head northeast until daylight. No matter what! Northeast! The storm will be setting you toward the cliffs. Don't forget that. I don't care if we end up fifty miles offshore. We'll find Panama later. It's not going anywhere. Use those safety harnesses. Both of you! Never take them off!"

Arthur's shouted words frightened her. She hadn't known him long, but she knew him well enough to know the tone in his voice. The situation was worse than it looked.

"Ted," she said, "let's go to Portobelo." She tried to use humor. "I'll show you a good time, sailor." She smiled and pinched his cheek.

He knocked her hand away.

"This is no time for your fucking games!" he yelled.

Evvie felt small hopes tumble, illusions she had tried to keep stacked in a neat row.

She sat down against the coaming. She raised her eyes and looked at Susurro. Arthur waited for Ted's answer, but he was watching her. His look was passive. But their eyes held. *He didn't mean that. He's just trying to make up his mind.* Evvie tried to will her thoughts across the air to Arthur. She saw him slowly shake his head. She knew he read her look. It was as though they were sitting back at the club drinking cocktails across a table. She was thankful for the space that separated them. She folded her arms on her chest. She didn't need his accusations.

Evvie took a deep breath and tried again. "We don't have any experience in stuff like this. Let's wait for a little storm."

"You don't want to try it?" His words still sharp. She couldn't tell if he regretted slapping her hand away. "You're sure?"

In the strange forward-reverse of married-couple arguments, she almost said, "Okay." But ...

Damn it, I'm scared. "I really don't think we should."

He stood braced against the boat's heel, both hands on the tiller in the freshening breeze. He did not look down at Evvie. "Arthur!" he yelled. "I'm not going to Portobelo!" And he put the tiller down and tacked for the squall line.

Both boats beat away from land once more. Coconut's sudden turn toward the sea had opened up a lead on Susurro, but the sleek double-ender closed the gap quickly. Once again the mainsails of the two boats overlapped. Susurro rode the lee quarter again, this time on Coconut's port side. This time only six feet away.

Arthur held station and simply watched Ted and Evvie sail. Except for the times the boats almost touched, Ted did not look at Arthur. Evvie did. She saw Arthur smile when a cresting sea broke across Coconut's foredeck and carried away one of the spinnaker pole tie-downs. The thick spar banged hard against the port side of the cabin, then dragged an end in the water, sending a torrent down the scuppers. Ted gave the helm to Evvie and went forward to relash the pole.

While Ted was forward Arthur talked to Evvie. He didn't have to shout, only use a loud voice; the storm they rushed to meet was close now, and the wind was suddenly falling off as one weather system replaced the other.

"Mrs. North ..."

She nodded.

"Keep all sail on until you see me shorten up. We want to make as much as we can to seaward, take every inch she'll let us have." He looked up at the shelf of black cloud that had advanced over the boats.

"Okay."

"When you see me shorten, then get your storm jib up. Roll up that main. Double reef."

Evvie knew that Ted could hear what Arthur was saying as well as she could, but he kept working on the loose pole forward.

"It's going to be windy, noisy, and wet tonight. But we won't have trouble with the waves. Some, not much. There hasn't been time for this system to build a sea."

She watched him raise a bottle of whiskey from somewhere down by his feet. He drank straight from the bottle. He capped the bottle and looked at it, then looked at her. He held the bottle up. "Don't let this bother you … it's my dinner." He wiggled the bottle a few times and smiled. "It's going to be a long night. This"—he nodded at the storm— "just makes it more exciting. You've got your husband for company. Lucky him. I know you won't begrudge me a little warmth, too."

She concentrated on the sails.

Thirty minutes later the sea had turned to jello. The wind only whispered. The afternoon's bluster was gone. Telltales and trailing edges that whipped before fluttered now. Only the slow-moving remnants of ocean rollers stayed to gently lift and lower the hulls. The water gleamed oily, green. Tall black clouds churned with no sound above the mast tops. The setting sun astern and to the southwest lit the underbelly of overhead storm line with a charcoal cherry-red glow. Looking up, Evvie felt like a bug in a barbecue pan.

Susurro had borne off to port, and sails were reefed on both boats. Now they closed ranks again. In the eerie calm Evvie could hear the trickle of Susurro's bow wave as she approached Coconut. Both hulls ghosted forward on glistening glass. A quiet settled over the sea, and tiny clicks in the rigging poked at the silence. A small fish broke the surface eighty feet away. All three heads turned at the sound of the splash.

"This is unreal." Ted's first words in forty minutes. Soft words.

Arthur spoke. His voice was as calm as the sea. "It's that," he replied.

Evvie could feel the closeness in the tone of the voices. It seemed as if all three had put away the prickly hostilities of the day. They made small talk about the boats and the coming night. Words drifted like milkweed seed through the silence. She remembered the time she and Ted had gone camping with two other couples and how, in the morning stillness of the redwood forest, low voices spoke in other tents. Soft. Close.

This was the same.

The flanks of the storm front seemed to wrap the northern horizon around them like two dark arms laying claim to a meal.

Evvie heard it first.

A hissing sound.

She couldn't be sure if it came from sky or sea. Whatever it was grew louder with each moment. Then she realized that the sound came from the direction of the storm line. She stood to look over the bow. The base of the front was on the water, and the bruise-colored roll cloud was reflected by the sea surface. There was no way to see where ocean ended and air began. The temperature dropped more. The hissing started to rattle. Arthur was on his feet and fitting his arms into a white foul-weather jacket. Lightning flared in sheets through the liver sky, but no thunder sounded. Only that strange sound came across the sea.

"That noise ..." she said.

"Rain," said Arthur.

"I've heard rain before," said Evvie.

"Not like this you haven't. Get your gear on. Take the storm on the bow quarter for a half-hour if you can, no longer. Then make your north-east tack. And remember that masthead light." He eased the sheet, and Susurro veered away. She watched him turn and wave. "See you in the morning!" he shouted. He gave them a thumbs-up sign.

Evvie snapped the last hank on her rain gear. She hooked her harness into a stanchion ring and clicked it shut. Coconut luffed, then filled, then luffed again, skittish like a wild horse in the noose for the first time. Ted finished hooking in, then took the helm from Evvie. Fifty yards ahead, the water surface jumped like hailstones on a china plate. When the clattering wall of rain was twenty yards from the bow, Coconut's restless sails exploded flat to port with a whip-cracking bang ... but did not tear apart. The small boat, with no way on and caught by the great gust of wind, lay down on her beam ends with the boom tip submerged.

For a few seconds.

Only for a few seconds.

Like a prizefighter bouncing up from a lucky punch, she rose from the sea and sliced into the wind's hard belly, her main and storm jib tight as tin. She leaped forward. Seawater streamed from the after end of each sail. Ted had been pitched over the tiller handle into the lee safety lines. His harness kept him in the boat, but for a split second the tiller was free. Any longer than that and Coconut would have slued into the wind, lost way, and taken another knockdown. Instinctively, Evvie caught the teak handle as soon as Ted let it go. And Coconut was able to keep her feet, to fight her way to windward.

They barely had time to breathe, let alone talk. The storm seemed to suck their lungs empty. Only a few frantic words were shouted in those terrible first minutes.

"My God, Ted! Your head!"

"It's all right."

"You're cut! You're bleeding!"

"I'm all right. I'll be okay. Keep steering, Evvie! Just keep steering her!"

Ted unhooked his harness. He managed to stumble his way into the cabin.

Thirty minutes later, at the edge of night, Evvie tacked the boat northeast.

By herself.

When Coconut settled onto the northeast heading, her motion eased a bit. The little boat seemed to take deeper breaths, more powerful strides. No longer was the storm's fury full on the bow. Evvie's world improved ... from horror to mere terror.

But the ocean turned savage in the dark. Black water hissed past the hull. The backs of maverick waves heaved up like the spines of enraged beasts alive beneath the sea surface. Wind-lashed rain became glass slivers. Evvie's hands locked in a two-fisted death grip on the tiller. Her legs shivered. Fear. Cold. The top two hanks on her foul-weather coat came unlatched in the furious wind. Rain and sea ran a river down the inside front of her clothing ... and washed the urine away.

Never had she imagined such power could exist in one place. Her mind hunted ... and found something ... a memory of Chichester saying in a book, after sailing around the world alone, that the place he feared most was the Western Caribbean.

At the time she read that quote, she was sure he had made a mistake.

At eight o'clock she vomited three times in quick succession. The detritus washed down the cockpit drains into the sea. In seconds there was no trace of her sickness.

At ten o'clock her grip on the tiller quit. Her fingers stopped listening to her brain. She tied the mainsheet tail around the handle, wrapped the line around her wrist, and steered with one arm.

The storm kept coming. She swore at Coconut when she realized that the boat was trying to sneak off to the east, trying to veer away from the pressures that the northeast heading brought against the port bow.

Ten minutes after midnight the small red light inside the compass dome failed. No warning flicker. No flare of burned-out filament. It just instantly went away. She panicked. Her angel, her hope, her only reality … and suddenly it was gone. The last reference point in the world was gone. Sailor panic. Aviator panic. Unique. Total.

Oh, God! The light is gone! The light is gone!

Fear cut her heart. She inhaled sharply in the blackness, and choked on the rivers of water streaming down her face.

She felt the boat start to slide off the wind. Coconut was taking quick advantage of the helmsman's sightless world.

She screamed words: "You bastard light! Come back!" She smashed at the compass dome with the flat of her hand. That momentary distraction moved the tiller, and the little boat slued violently to starboard.

"Son of a bitch! You come back!" She smacked the glass again.

The light came back on. No flicker. No sputter. It glowed bright and red and steady. White numbers rocked beneath red liquid where they were supposed to be.

She pushed the tiller slightly to starboard. The boat nosed up.

It was then she remembered the masthead light.

I forgot to turn it on! He's lost us! Arthur's lost us!

The failure of the compass light had plunged her into total darkness, and that darkness made her remember. Now she bent down and pried open the switch cover set into the cockpit side wall. When the cover snapped open, the panel lit up. She flipped on the masthead light. And the running lights. The deck glowed red to port and green to starboard. The pitching topside structures gave her a moment of relief, a world that made sense, teak and brass surfaces that she had polished and worked on and were still there. Two minutes later she bent to the switches and shut off the running lights.

While seeing the deck glow red and green, she had also seen the sea. She chose the dark. As terrible as it was, she chose the dark.

But she left the masthead light switched on for Arthur. It illuminated the sea only when Coconut heeled far over in the press of a big wave. And when Coconut did that, Evvie closed her eyes.

At two a.m. she became frightened of something else. She had not seen or heard anything from Ted since he had been hurt. She stared forward at the closed hatch barely visible in the red glow of the binnacle.

No sign. No sound.

Are you hurt? Do you need me?

She tried to think how she could leave the helm and get to the hatch, if only for the seconds it would take to crack it and look inside. In Limon Bay she had learned that Coconut could heave to on backed jib and rudder, but that could not work here. The wide pressure variation between the wave crests and the wave troughs would be too much for the boat to handle. A sea anchor would work, but she could not rig it alone.

She could think of nothing to do. She kept on sailing.

Two forty-five a.m. She stared at the compass light. Intense concentration and fatigue began to hypnotize her. Her mind wandered while her senses and body continued to work the boat. An image came to her of Ted lying on the cabin sole, of Ted bleeding and hurt and alone in the dark. Then a quick image of Cindy. Ted again. The razoring realization that Ted was all she had left.

Please, Ted. Let me know you're all right.

She looked over her shoulder to port. Giant shapes moved at her. Then another revelation: Except for the sheet lightning that flickered through the clouds, there had been no air-to-sea lightning bolts. No crash of thunder. She wondered if there was something different about this storm, and that thought began to scare her, too.

Goddamn you, Ted! I can't do this by myself much longer!

She sat up straight and blinked away weariness. The mind-words slapped her conscience.

Goddamn you to hell, Ted! She could not stop them now. *You bastard! This was your idea. You should be here!*

First-time thoughts.

"You bastard!" First-time words. "You lousy bastard!" Shouted words.

Something deserted her soul in that moment.

She could not tell if it was a good thing … or a bad thing.

So she concentrated on making Coconut sail northeast.

Three twelve a.m. An eerie calm stopped the rain. And the dark. It seemed as if her boat had sailed into a large neon-lit dome. The still air doubled its weight. Then tripled it. Evvie seemed to be inhaling water, but the rain had stopped. She was in a place where the storm had been hollowed out by something more powerful than itself.

Wild waves lay down. Continuous sheet lightning strobed the ceiling of the dark canopy. All around her electricity lit sea and cloud and boat with a constant unreal green. It was day inside night. Silence was the sound.

Sails fluttered. Water dripped from rigging. The rudder lazed about in liquid nonchalance and hunted for something to push against.

She saw it.

A dark tentacle reaching down from the black center of the dome.

One hundred yards off the port bow. Half a mile high.

It twisted and writhed like something alive and reached two-thirds of the way to the ocean's surface. Her eyes followed its thick line. Directly below the spiraling arm the sea began to foam. Then turn. Then turn faster.

She heard a sound like that of steam escaping through a narrow space. The sound grew louder. First a sizzle, then a rumble that was quickly overtaken by a gurgling roar … like something large and drowning.

The water, where it turned under the great black screw, began to hump up. Four feet. Eight feet. Fifteen.

The lump of sea spun faster. It stretched toward the mother coil, fell back partway, then stretched higher than before.

Two arms reached, one for the other. Adam trying to touch God's finger.

The air vibrated.

The rumble became a screech.

Dark clumps and strings of translucent green water spun off the lower column as it gyrated higher.

Coconut began to pivot slowly in the gently moving air, and Evvie, her eyes never leaving the vortex, shifted position to the other side of the cockpit ... dazed ... fascinated ... unable to stop looking.

She watched as a delicate tunnel of mist, the vapor tube, bridged the vertical gap between the two spirals. The tube quickly filled with water.

It was complete.

The giant waterspout turned instantly black in its core. Green lightning bathed its whirling flanks, and sparkles like silver scales dressed the entire length of the monster from hell to heaven.

Chapter 10

The churning vortex towered over the small boat. It hovered and pulsed, trying to determine where in the domed space it would go next. Evvie was paralyzed by a pervasive sense of helplessness that took every emotion from her except that of stupefying awe.

The maelstrom drifted back two hundred yards. And stopped in a new place. The roar weakened only because of the greater distance.

She became aware of another shape, a presence drifting close beside her. Something white. Slow. Twenty feet away. Then ten. But she did not turn. Could not turn. She only stared, a frog before the weaving serpent, unable to acknowledge any other thing, not even terror.

"My God, look at that." Arthur's voice. Quiet. Near to her.

Her lips moved. Her head did not. Not even her eyes. She made one soft word: "Arthur."

"Where in hell is Ted?" An urgent tone in Arthur's voice this time.

"Look at it, Arthur."

"Ted ... where the hell is he?" Some of the urgency gone, worry now. Even an edge of fear in his words. "Evvie ... where?"

"Look at it."

The hulls touched. He wrapped a line around a winch drum on Coconut's coaming. Evvie knew a shadow moved past her to the cabin hatch, but she did not focus on it. She looked only at the majestic violence that tied sea to sky.

"Look at it," she said again.

The shadow disappeared through the hatch. She was alone with the beautiful monster that was probably God.

The shadow came at her.

She saw his hand coming. After it rebounded from her face she wondered how a hand that moved so slowly could hurt so much.

"Evvie!"

She looked at Arthur. For the first time since it had formed she tore her eyes away from the column of water.

"Goddamn it, Evvie! ... Snap out of it!" Strong hands shook her by the shoulders.

"Did you see it, Arthur?"

His face close in front of hers. "We don't have much time. He's drunk. He's got an ugly crease in his skull."

"He fell down."

More shoulder shaking. "If you don't come back to earth, I'll have to put you both in Susurro." Another stinging slap rocked her head back. "We don't have any more time, Evvie! We've got to get the boats apart or we'll lose everything."

Then she saw his eyes shift and look up at something behind her.

His strong arms tried to lift her up.

She grabbed the tiller handle with both hands and yelled at him, "No! I can do it! It can't have Coconut!" Loud but not hysterical words. He let go of her.

She saw Arthur turn toward the waterspout and followed his look. "It's collapsing," he said.

She stared over his shoulder. The great vortex had split apart. The lower section tumbled back into the sea. The upper section spun a thin winding whip of water as it dissolved back toward the mother cloud. A gust of wind banged Susurro into Coconut. Cold green lightning flickered out, came back, flickered again. The light level was cut in half.

Hard eyes, close, bore into hers. "You'll do it?"

"I'll do it." Her words were back ... her words again. "Get off my boat." She tried to smile, but her mouth only twisted.

She saw him do what she could not. A smile.

He shook his head. "I'll be damned, lady. Whoever the hell put you together did a job!"

And he was gone, taking the line with him and kicking Coconut away from Susurro all in one smooth motion.

In seconds the world went black and sails exploded flat.

But Evvie was ready.

The boat climbed up from horizontal for the second time in twelve hours, her two small triangles of sail taut and drawing. Coconut powered forward into the wall of rain.

Coconut swung on her anchor beneath a hazy afternoon sun. Susurro came alongside, nudging Coconut, and Arthur tied the boats together with a short bow line to a cleat on Coconut's stern quarter.

Five minutes earlier he had dropped Ted off on the end of the Porvenir Customs pier three hundred yards from where Coconut was anchored. Ted had disappeared into a squat concrete building that flew the flag of Panama on a short pole out front.

Arthur climbed into the cockpit and sat across from Evvie, who was rinsing Ted's vomit-stained shirt in a bucket of seawater.

"We stay here until the captain clears you into the San Blas. You can go ashore after the paperwork is taken care of."

Evvie could not miss the sarcasm in Arthur's voice when he said the word "captain."

"He drank the whiskey to get rid of the pain," she said.

Arthur ignored the remark. He reached over and took the bucket from beneath the shirt she was wringing out and, holding the end of the bucket line, tossed it overboard. He hauled it back into the cockpit with a fresh load of salt water and shoved it under the dripping shirt.

"Tired?" His question was gentle.

She looked at him. "Me? I'm not tired at all." And she smiled at him. "I'm too damned exhausted to be tired."

He watched her rinse the shirt some more. He lit a cigarette.

She nodded at the pack. "How did you keep those dry last night? Our boat's soaked clear through. Everything. Even the toilet paper is sopped."

"I have my ways. If I'm going to die, I intend to get that last cigarette."

She pushed Ted's shirt down into the bucket again. "How did you find us? I didn't turn the masthead light on till after midnight. I screwed up."

"I found you because you were right smack damn where you were supposed to be." He dragged deeply on the cigarette and blew smoke slowly into the air with his head tilted back.

"I never saw *your* mast light at all," she said. "Not that I could have in that weather."

"That was more than 'weather.' Besides, I didn't have it on."

"You didn't?"

"The last thing I wanted out there was to have you come looking for a friend and run me down. We'd all be on the bottom looking up."

"I did pretty good." She grinned and stretched the shirt over the coaming to dry.

"Yeah. You did damned good." He put his feet across the cockpit onto the opposite seat close to where she sat and stretched his legs. She dropped her hand under his shin and pinched him hard. "That's for belting me in the face."

He laughed. "Sorry about that."

"Thanks anyway." Evvie stretched her legs across to his side of the cockpit so she could sit like he was sitting. "I don't know what happened to me last night. That waterspout. Whatever it was. I guess I froze up, didn't I?"

"You didn't freeze up. You just got yourself hypnotized." Arthur puffed on his cigarette. Then he shrugged. "People who haven't been where you were last night don't know what it's like. Your muscles chew up eighty percent of your energy just fighting the motion. No sleep. No food. Cold. Wet. Scared to hell ..." He paused. "And no help." He smiled. "You learn to cheat after the first time. You learn how to save your energy, use shortcuts. You'll be okay, sailor."

"How far out were we?" she asked.

"When we sailed into that waterspout?"

"Yes."

"Twenty-five miles."

"Long swim."

"True. That was a blow. Twelve and a Chinaman."

"What's that mean?" she asked.

"In the old days, clipper ships dragged the ship's log by hand. Story has it one night a Chinaman, the cook, had to do the honors in a Cape Horn storm. The log hit twelve knots and jammed. That's as far as it went in those days. Yanked the Chinaman right off the stern. Never found him. When you're sailing faster than twelve knots, that's what they call it ... twelve and a Chinaman."

She laughed her funny laugh, then folded her arms across her chest. "I'd hate to tell you how many times I thought about turning around."

He shook his head. "I don't think you turn easy." He flicked his cigarette butt over the side. Then he looked out to sea. "Anyway, just think how easy it'll be getting back. With all that crap pushing you west you won't even need sails. Even the captain should be able to handle that."

They said nothing for several uncomfortable seconds.

"Last night? ... In the storm? ... I ..."

He waited.

"It was like being pushed back to the beginning."

"The beginning of what?"

"I don't know. Maybe the beginning of me."

Arthur tapped the bottom of his pack of cigarettes. He removed one, lit up, and put the pack in his pants pocket.

Her voice seemed far away and soft. "I felt so small. The storm. It made me feel so ... so ..."

"Helpless? Afraid?"

"Something like that. More alone than afraid, I guess. Really alone. There was something else, too. Like I was ... like I didn't have a lot of time. A lot of time to be alive."

He nodded. "I get like that sometimes when I'm sailing far out. By myself. But it doesn't take a storm."

"I was two different people. I was looking down from a long way off and I was looking at myself. I felt sorry for that little girl, that woman, whatever she was. She was all alone. I wanted to take care of her and I didn't care about anybody else. It was me. They both were me. I've never ever felt like that."

He waited.

When she spoke next, she looked away from him. "I keep secrets, Arthur. And I think I shouldn't keep so many secrets."

The way she said the words made Arthur stare at her.

"Four months ago my baby was shot by a stray bullet. She died in my arms. I hurt. I hurt a lot. But only for a couple of months. I know what that sounds like, but I learned a long time ago how to put pain in a box and bury it. I learned how when I was a kid. Nobody does it better than me."

"I'm sorry, Evvie. I—"

"Shut up, Arthur. Just shut up." She looked at him. "You're going to hear my secrets, whether you want to or not. My baby was killed. My mother's crazy ... soft crazy, but crazy. My daddy, the town pervert, raped and killed a little blind girl when I was thirteen and then blew his head off with a shotgun. I was there. I'm not exactly sure of all that's happened to me, but I know it's not all good. I'm scared to death I've got what he had. Something between schizophrenia and sleepwalking. In *my* life, having a third tit qualifies as a lucky break. Try to guess what *that's* like for a young girl whose momma believes God has a plan."

She took a deep breath. "And just so you don't think I've been exorcised in the last couple of months, my husband got laid off from his half-ass job with the DEA right after our baby was killed. Now he treats me like yesterday's news. We don't make love. We fuck ... every other full moon. He wants to sail this boat to Rhode Island, but for some reason I can't figure out, I'm totally out of the loop. Ted's buddy Davis thinks it's okay to wave his dick in my face when he feels like it, and I got mugged two nights ago in a alley in Colon. My first night out on the ocean, I sail into an F-5 tornado. I've got two friends in the whole world—you and Dulcie. Dulcie seems to have more secrets than I do, and you fight cops and eat pills so you don't run around killing everybody."

Arthur, despite the quick hurt he felt for her, smiled. He puffed on his cigarette. He blew a smoke ring and shrugged. "Deal with it."

It was her turn to smile. "Deal with it? Okay. That helps. Any other suggestions?"

"Feel better?"

"Yes. I feel better. I do feel better. Now I don't have any secrets. Not from you, anyway." She didn't know if she was going to laugh or cry.

He moved his head to one side and looked past her. "Here comes the pitch." She turned and saw a brown dugout canoe with two Cuna women, their wooden paddles resting across the gunwales, gliding toward Coconut.

"These Indians," Arthur said, "they're shy as deer except when they're out to sell you molas. Hold on to your wallet."

As the cayuco came alongside, the woman in the rear dipped her paddle into the sea and feathered the small boat to a stop inches from the sailboat's port quarter.

Each woman wore an ankle-length print skirt and a bandana-like red scarf as head cover. They were barefoot. Their blouses were single panels of colorful cotton material reverse appliquéd in layers of red, yellow, green, and orange, and were cut so that the underlayers showed through finger-sized slots to form patterns on black-outlined shapes of fish, birds, turtles, and on one blouse a small boat.

Both women wore a gold nose ring; large earrings, discs of thin gold, sparkled in the sun; on the bridge of each nose and running from between the eyes to the nose-tip, a painted black line. They wore large necklaces of silver and gold coins that covered the top third of each blouse, and tight strings of white anklet beads showed at the lower edges of the skirts.

Their shiny black hair was cut straight across the forehead.

The woman in the front of the cayuco lifted up a single mola panel about sixteen inches square and sewn like the panels that formed the front and back of the blouse she wore. She draped the mola over her left arm. Another mola was lifted from a pile on the floor of the cayuco and was laid over the first mola, partially covering it. Then a third.

Indian eyes looked at Evvie. The eyes did not plead. The eyes did not blink. The eyes did not intimidate. They simply stared and implied that Evvie should buy. There was no seller-buyer inequity in the look, no humble disparity implying that the customer was king. The eyes said that seller and buyer were at least equal, that if there were any caste system at play, it wasn't the Indian who was inferior.

The look surprised Evvie. She almost interpreted it as hostile, then realized it was not.

She was looking at pride in a place she did not expect to find pride. She was more than surprised.

The eyes. These were poor people. These were people a century behind time. These were ... These were women. Evvie saw a strength beyond confidence. In a subtle span of seconds, she felt something in her own world turn upside down. It was a small moment not so small.

The Cuna holding up the three molas nodded once at Evvie. *Let's get on with it,* said the gesture. *I want you to buy. But you don't have to buy. We both know that. Decide.*

The woman with the paddle gently stirred the water. The boats stayed in place as though they were joined by an invisible iron rod.

Evvie pointed to the mola on top of the stack lying in the cayuco. On it was a picture of a small boat with a sail. The boat was a caricature of Coconut in yellow and orange and outlined in black.

She was handed the mola.

"How much?" she asked in Spanish.

The woman spread her palms, fingers and thumbs splayed up. Ten.

"Ten dollars?"

The woman nodded.

"No," said Evvie. She held up three fingers.

The woman shook her head curtly. And held up eight fingers.

Evvie offered five. Seven back. Six from Evvie.

The Cuna hesitated. Then shook her head.

Evvie turned to Arthur.

He made an "X" with his forefingers. Evvie turned to the woman and did the same. A nod. Evvie paid six dollars and fifty cents, all in U.S. quarters, the San Blas preferred currency, and took the mola.

A friendly smile from the woman. She picked up another mola and nodded at Evvie. Evvie shook her head. Another smile and one returned. The cayuco went away.

"You're tough, lady. Do you know it takes weeks to make one of those things?"

"So what? Do you know how much it cost us to get down here?" She held the mola up to the sun and looked at both sides.

"You've got a point," he said. "Look at the back. Are the stitches even?"

Evvie looked. "No."

"Good. You got yourself a deal. Regular stitches means it was done on a machine. Not the real McCoy."

"Arthur? I've got a stupid question."

"Shoot."

"Do you believe in God?"

"This is turning out to be a hell of a conversation. Where the hell did that come from?"

"Do you?"

He pursed his lips. "I believe in justice ... an eye for an eye ... that sort of thing."

"I didn't ask you that."

"Tough. It's the best I can do." He squinted at her. "Why? Did you get religion last night?"

Her expression was flat. "No. I think I lost it."

"You want one of my pills?" He was grinning at her.

She returned from somewhere far away and smiled back. "You don't use those things out here, do you?"

"No, I don't."

"Why not?"

"I don't have to. No people bugging me."

"Thanks a lot."

"Now, I've got a question for *you*," he said.

She looked at him. "Shoot."

"Why don't you and the captain have a radio?"

"We do."

"I looked around in there last night. I didn't see one."

"Ted has one, portable, real small."

"Where is it?"

"He carries it on his belt … or somewhere."

"And what if *you* need to use it?"

"Me?"

"Yes, you."

"I guess I'd just have to ask him for it." She paused. "You don't have one at all."

"I will as soon as Captain Ted pays me what I've got coming. … Then I can pay off those blackmailing bastards back in Colon."

She folded the mola and held it on her lap. "I think you're about to get your wish … and your radio." Her eyes were on the Customs house.

Arthur turned around. He signaled Ted, who was standing on the edge of the pier, to let him know he was on his way. Then he turned back to Evvie.

"There's something I want to say," he said.

She looked at him.

"You're a grade-A lady, Mrs. North. Don't you forget that. What you did last night was more than tough. But—"

Evvie held up her hand. "Wait a minute. We're not going to psychiatry school again, are we?"

He looked through her smile. "What your husband said that day at the club, about your having that … defect … as he calls it. Has he ever done that to you before? … Embarrassed you in front of someone like that?"

Evvie lowered her eyes.

"I didn't think so," said Arthur.

He stood up. He untied Susurro's bow line and hauled her up to Coconut, but he kept looking at Evvie. "When he said that, I ..." He stopped talking and climbed out of the cockpit onto Coconut's starboard rail. "Mrs. North? Evvie? ..."

She didn't look up.

"I'm your friend," he said. "Especially now. I don't want you to forget that." The voice was soft, but full of steel. "And as long as we're telling secrets ..." A smile, then his face grew serious. "There's someone I love, someone I'm trying to love who's a long way from here. She's the one I want. Not you. Not that way. I'm not some yacht-club ass-grabber. You know that. I know that. No reason to flop all over the deck trying to say something that doesn't need saying."

He stepped onto Susurro, but still held on to Coconut's backstay. "I never could pull the trigger on getting married. Not because I didn't know what I was getting into, but because I didn't know what she might be getting into. It seems to me that marriage is like going into a birdcage ... for the woman. She goes through that gate and three things can happen. Two of them bad. One is that the cage is just what she thinks it is, all buddy-buddy and pretty and clean. She works her ass off to keep things right and things stay right. Or two, she gets in there and finds out she's locked in the cage with a monster. That's bad enough, but there's something even worse. Number three. Number three is when she finds out that she's the only one in the cage." He released the backstay. Susurro began to fall away. "Sometimes friends can help. If things don't go right ... give a howl."

He shook out Susurro's mainsail.

He looked back one more time.

Evvie wondered if they would ever talk again.

A strange last word between friends, she thought. *"Howl."*

Chapter 11

When Arthur dropped Ted off, it was done in a sizzling pass. Susurro never broke speed. She hissed by without the simple courtesy of slowing down, and Ted had to jump from Susurro onto Coconut's afterdeck and grab the backstay to keep from tumbling into the cockpit. Evvie reached up to help Ted climb over the rudder head.

Arthur never looked back as he headed Susurro out the San Blas Channel for the open ocean.

"Are we all set?" she asked.

He handed her a sheath of documents and glared at Susurro for a few seconds. "All set. Christ, do I have a splitting headache!"

"Go lie down. I'll fix something to eat."

They sat across from each other in the cabin and ate sandwiches on the gimbaled cabin table.

She smiled at him. "We made it! We're here."

"I sure as hell don't remember much about last night," he said. "I guess you had a pretty rough time, too."

"That's why there's two of us. I guess we're still a team."

He shoved his empty water glass across the table. She refilled it from the freshwater spigot and handed it back. "What next, Skipper? What's on the schedule?" she asked.

"The Customs guy gave me some info on the Cunas. And the islands. It's in with the boat papers. Right now I just want to get some more sleep. We'll stay here for a while, maybe a few hours. I have to hook up the satellite positioning rig. This is a good place to do it, a good reference point. We know what it should read being right here next to Porvenir. We can test it more when we sail around the islands, make sure everything's working."

"I met some Cunas, two ladies. I bought a mola from them. It's amazing how Dulcie has so many of the same features."

"The Cunas are a pure race." He smiled. "Know why? For five centuries any Cuna woman who had a child by an outsider was killed. The baby, too. That kind of birth control keeps the strain pure."

Wrong words. His talking about killing babies made them both go silent. "I ..." he started. But he did not continue. She saw tears and realized the hurt was still there and still deep. Maybe too deep.

He began to cry.

She was surprised by his sudden breakdown. She thought the pain of losing Cindy had started to scar over for him. At least a little bit. It had not. It was going to take longer than just four months ... much longer.

She went around the table and sat next to him. She put her arms around him and pulled his head down and rocked him as he sobbed.

The storm? The drinking? The injury when he fell? Or something else?
She held him and wondered. He cried for a long time.

Then she made him lie down on the cabin bench. She covered him with a blanket and he closed his eyes.

On her knees, on the cabin sole, she watched the muscles of his face twist in sleep. Then a sad question came: Who had lost the most ... he or she?

She went outside into the cockpit. The breeze was clean and gentle. Waves tossed and tumbled to the north. But Coconut was safe behind the barrier reef. Not even the ocean swell reached the anchorage. She could see small islands far away, and looking through the binoculars she could make out the silhouettes of coconut palms and huts on three of them. A lone Indian in a cayuco paddled toward the mainland. A distant, small figure. The paddle dipped then sparkled in the late afternoon sun. Down, up. Down, up. Over and over. Steady. Ancient. Mysteriously beautiful and oddly unsettling at the same time. It said she was in a different world, a world she'd seen mirrored in the eyes of the Cuna woman who sold her the mola. The beauty around her was more than she'd thought it would be, but her sense of unrest was also more. She tried to reconcile the trade-off, life needing to balance the books. Pleasure never far from pain. Beauty from ugliness. Happiness, sorrow.

Giving to, taking away.

Everything came with strings attached. A price. Positive defined by negative. No free ride.

Coconut eased off the wind and approached a plank pier crowded with Indians, mostly children. Evvie could see the excitement in the brown faces, the wide smiles, the good-natured shoving to be in the front row.

The night they'd spent anchored off Porvenir in Coconut had been a blessing ... physically. Though Ted tossed and moaned all night, at least he managed to sleep. And the beating she had taken from the storm, coupled with the fact that she had stayed awake past midnight listening to him, finally put her down too. She surrendered to a deep, dreamless sleep more coma than slumber. Ted installed the navigation system at daybreak, and Evvie never changed position in the forepeak vee-berth until he woke her with a kiss at nine a.m.

"Drop the jib!" shouted Ted.

Evvie let go the halyard and scrambled onto the foredeck. She gathered in white dacron with both hands. The late-morning sun was bright, the day clear.

"Ready the bow line!" She made ready to heave the coiled line into the clutter of chattering faces.

Ted sailed Coconut past the end of the dock, toward the beach, then rounded up into the wind. The main luffed and Coconut slowed. The boat nudged against the pier just as all her forward momentum wore off.

Evvie didn't have to heave the line. She only handed it over to a small boy.

She turned and looked at Ted. "Nice landing, sailor!" She clenched a fist and pumped it once.

He returned the gesture with a smile.

For the next hour they performed the ritual of the tourist. Escorted by a jumble of Cuna youngsters, they walked dirt paths between tightly packed rows of cane-walled palm-thatched huts. Every house was fronted by chest-high hangings of brightly colored molas attended by Cuna women. Some of the molas were fastened top and bottom to a pair of parallel cane poles that were part of the hut's bracing architecture. Others hung in slanting rows, pinned to brown ropes that ran from one house to the next. A few, the special ones, were offered up on Cuna arms, draped and held in the manner of the woman in the cayuco at Porvenir.

No one blocked their way, but only moved forward a single step to draw attention to the particular display as they passed.

On a tilting, gray, driftwood table an old man lined up small wooden carvings of gods and idols, the *uchus,* the spirit dolls that went down into the eight rings of the underworld to cure sickness, carry messages to the dead, and bring back magic for *neles,* the priests, to use.

Ted picked up a carving, one with four heads. Animal, not human. He asked in Spanish, "How much?" The old man gently took the figure back and said he couldn't sell it. It was *uchu uksi,* the armadillo spirit, not a thing that could be sold. Evvie found a Cuna woman nearby who spoke more Spanish than the old man. The woman explained that the armadillo spirit was special because it could dig so fast through the earth. And the four heads allowed it to see many dangers, an important advantage when an emergency demanded a quick trip to the spirit world and back. There was no doubt; the *uchu uksi* was much too important to sell.

Ted was offered another carving, a small cayuco, and bought that one for two dollars.

Evvie found a dozen molas she liked and bargained hard for each one. Ted watched her haggle like a professional tourist, and he shook his head and smiled and paid for the pieces.

At one corner a teenage boy stood surrounded by twenty younger children and, with a serious expression full of business, he offered up two bottles of orange soda, one in each hand. His crowd of supporters chattered and waited. Ted took one of the bottles. It was wet, but not cold. Ted looked at Evvie. "Would the lady care for a drink? We have orange and we have orange."

She peered into all the expectant faces. "How much?" she asked the boy.

He held up two fingers.

"Por dos?" She raised one finger and pointed to each bottle in turn. The young man considered the offer. Then he nodded. A clatter of approval rose from the assembled.

With a courtly flourish, the young entrepreneur took a machete from the hand of his seven-year-old assistant. Using the blade tip, he smartly nicked off the cap of each soda bottle. Ted handed over eight quarters. The crowd watched them drink every drop. The empty bottles were handed back. The tour proceeded.

Evvie bought a necklace of beads and teeth from an older Indian woman. She asked what the teeth were. Were they shark's teeth? "No," said her translator, stepping forward from the crowd. "They are alligator, *taim,* from the mainland."

In the doorway of a large hut where fires burned inside and a pepper smell drifted out, Evvie saw a young woman looking out. Taller than the others.

Dulcie!

Evvie's hand went to her stomach and touched the still-sore muscles bruised in the alley attack.

She stared at the girl, examined her more closely. The dark eyes were slightly different. More apart. The arms not so long. Standing in the shadow, in the smoke, just for a minute ... but it was not Dulcie.

They walked a bit more, and Ted joked with Evvie about how elegant the women looked while the men, who stood back, were as plain as their wives and daughters were colorful. "These guys all dress alike—white shirt, dark pants, straw cowboy hat. Looks like the women own the bank. What else is new?" He was at ease again, his old self.

But Evvie suddenly felt unhinged. Despite the distractions of walking through the village, smiling and talking and holding hands with the small Indian girls who came out of shadows to walk beside her, she felt uneasy. One minute he was the Ted she knew, the Ted she married; and then he was someone else, someone who cried too long and drank too much and said things he didn't mean, things he couldn't possibly mean to say.

All at once the tight streets and packed houses seemed to close in, to press at her. The paths of the small island were a maze that led around and around. The people ... the women ... the crowding, pushing children ... the silent men watching ... too many people ...

The smoke, the harsh pepper smoke ...

Hands that touched ... too many hands ...

And the eyes, eyes carved into wooden *uchu* faces, eyes on molas staring out ... fish, turtles, birds, snakes, alligators, gods ... eyes that wanted something ... wanted their money, maybe even their lives ...

"Ted? Let's go back. It's time to go back."

They turned and were escorted back to the boat. They stowed the items they had purchased. They raised sail and headed out.

Children waved.

As Ted sailed the boat away from the pier, Evvie stood on the bow near the foot of the jib as far forward as she could get. She had never felt claustrophobic in her life. She tried to put her feelings of panic aside, but panic stayed. She wondered if maybe the storm experience had something to do with what she was feeling, if perhaps the water spout and the fear of being so alone had somehow changed her sense of space and time and self.

She held tightly to the jibstay and looked down through thirty feet of clear water at the gradually deepening sea floor moving beneath the bow. Weed and rock shapes contrasted with brilliant patches of white and pink and orange and fluorescent purple. Darker patches of brown, black, and green ... coral. Delicate spreading nets of lace ... sea fans. Suddenly, she wanted to be down there inside the colors with the small fish that flashed silver in the beautiful silence, her own body weightless and drifting. How pleasant it would be. How simple. How still.

Her eyes focused on her own reflection. The underwater Evvie studied the other Evvie. The image shimmered as it moved across the background of deep shapes.

Coconut beat into a light chop and angled northeast away from the island toward a string of small cays stretching out into the middle of San Blas Gulf. Evvie snapped out of her watery reverie, worked her way back over the cabin top to the cockpit, and sat next to Ted. She pecked him on the cheek, then picked up the folded chart and saw that he had drawn another plotline in pencil. She read the names of the islands along the line. Gunboat Island and Los Grullos Cay to port. Moron Island to starboard. The course veered north after passing Los Grullos Cay, tracked along the edge of the San Blas channel, then ended near an island called Icacos that was ten miles offshore. The chart showed one last chain of islands beyond Icacos right on the barrier reef, the Holandes Cays, the outermost limit of the archipelago. Beyond the Holandes was the deep Caribbean. To the east of the Holandes, two hundred miles of Cuna island nation curved toward Colombia. To the south, on the mainland, one of the most primitive jungles in the world, the infamous Darian Gap.

Ted reached over and tapped a spot on the map. "See that island?" he said. "That one called Icacos? That looks like a good spot for us to hole up tonight. It looks like it's uninhabited. There's none of those little house squares on the chart. Just palm trees. The south side should be protected from the wind and the seas coming off the Holandes Channel. We can anchor there and get some peace and quiet."

Evvie looked at the chart. "I wonder why there aren't any Indian houses marked on that island. It's big enough."

"Probably too far out. The Indians have to paddle to the mainland for water and supplies almost every day. And most of the coconut farms are on the mainland. The fellow at Customs told me that's why the islands near the mainland are more desirable. They don't have to paddle so far. He said the poorest Cunas live farther out. Or the sick ones. Some of the crazy ones."

She looked at the margin of the chart and saw a string of numbers written in Ted's handwriting, which she recognized as longitude and latitude position numbers. "What are these for?"

He looked where she was pointing. "Those? Just some reference points. Islands, reefs, channels. I'm practicing to be a navigator. So I can be as good a sailor as you are." He blasted her with one of his smiles.

She put down the chart and moved close to him. She put her hand on his shoulder and gently began to massage the muscles there.

"Ted?"

He turned his head to look at her.

"What do you know about Kent Davis? And Dulcie?"

His eyebrows went up. Another smile. "I think they probably do it."

"I don't mean that." She pinched his shoulder hard. "Why do you think they're together? I mean it doesn't seem …"

He glanced up at the sails. He made a small adjustment to the course and did not look at her. "Things here aren't like they are back in the States," he said. "This is a different part of the world."

"The Canal Zone is part of the States, sort of."

He gave a small laugh. "The Zone? Maybe part of the pre-Civil War States. Look at the housing. Look at the social stuff. It's probably okay to keep slaves here."

Evvie thought for a while. She decided to tell him. She made an effort to act casual. "Dulcie wanted to ask me something before we left." She felt him tense.

"Dulcie? You talked with Dulcie?"

"She called me on the phone a few days before we took off."

"Called you on the phone?"

"She was worried about something. She sounded afraid."

He didn't reply.

"I thought maybe she was having trouble with Davis."

Ted leaned forward and eased the mainsheet out in its cam a few inches. Evvie's hand fell from where it rested on his shoulder. When he leaned back he was farther aft, and Evvie could not put her hand where it was before.

"Did you know she speaks English?"

"She does?"

"She sure does," said Evvie. "Better than I do."

His eyes were still on the sail.

"Did you know? That she could speak English?"

"No," he said. "I didn't know that."

"She told me she worked for the Army, I think it was. She was a go-between for the Cunas and some government office over in Balboa. Sort of like a translator."

"What did you find out? Was it something about Davis? A lover's quarrel? Maybe something juicy? Like Davis is into wearing dresses when he gets excited?"

Evvie smiled and shook her head. "She didn't tell me on the phone. She wanted to meet me before we left for the San Blas."

"Oh? ... And?"

"Something happened."

Now he was looking at her again.

"I went to meet her. I thought—"

"When?" he interrupted.

"Two nights after the phone call. She—"

"Where?"

"Down in Colon. Near some stores we went to that day you and Davis went sailing and I stayed back."

"You went into Colon with Dulcie?"

"Yes. She asked me not to say anything."

"And?"

"And I went to meet her and almost got myself robbed."

"Robbed?"

"In an alley. Near where I was supposed to meet her. Before she got there. A guy knocked me down. But it was dark. I guess he got scared when he couldn't find my purse. He took off."

"Did he say anything?"

"No."

"Did you recognize him? Someone from the hotel? From the yacht club?"

"No."

"What else? Do you remember anything else?"

"There were two of them. I think one was a woman."

He was silent.

"I didn't get hurt," said Evvie.

"Hurt?"

"Just in case you're wondering."

The water was deep behind Icacos Island. Ted had to put out every inch of anchor line to keep them off the underwater coral shelf that rimmed the backside of the cay. They used the outboard motor to back down and set the anchor that dragged and bumped off deep chunks of broken coral head. Evvie felt the hook suddenly grab as it wedged into a hard crevice more than one hundred fifty feet below. The bow jerked down, then recovered in the easy current sweeping around the channel side of the island. Ted had rigged an anchor trip line to a Styrofoam float so they could retrieve the ground tackle when it came time to leave. The Styrofoam bobbed on the blue water fifty feet in front of Coconut's nose. The anchor line ran down at a steep angle, too steep for anything less than a coral purchase.

They used the motor to back in a wide circle to test the set. The anchor held fast and they secured the motor and sails.

"I guess that's one reason no one lives here," Ted said. He mopped sweat from his face with a towel. "That's one hell of a drop-off."

"Looks like the anchor's not going to pull out of this one by accident, sailor." Evvie took the towel from him and began to dry his bare back.

He draped his arms up and over the furled sail on the boom as she rubbed him. "Not unless we get a rough night and that damned coral cuts the line," he said.

"We've got twenty feet of chain leader. It'd have to get pretty darn rough to saw through that, Captain North." Evvie mussed his hair. She flipped the towel through the open hatch into the cabin, then stood behind him. She encircled his waist with her arms. "Ummm." She squeezed him. "This is nice," she purred.

He took a deep breath and straightened up. "Yes, it is."

She ran her hand inside the front of his pants and gently tweaked the hair that came out of him there. She pushed her sex against his rump. She ran her hand lower down. "Hey," she said softly. "Let's get naked and go for a swim."

"There's still another hour of daylight left. We don't want to scare the natives." But he let her touch him.

She worked at the top buttons on his pants with her free hand. "Are you going to put the ladder over the side or do I have to do it myself?" she asked.

The sun was low on the mountains to the west. The sea glittered blue and silver. Twilight painted orange highlights into the crests of tiny waves. Evvie stood on the starboard cockpit seat, steadied herself with her left hand on the lower shroud, and faced the sun. Naked. Legs slightly apart. Sleek and trim and hardened by exercise, her body gleamed in the bronze energy of day's end. The last of a cool sea breeze played around the curves of her, kissed her shoulders, lifted into and out of her hair, moved over her arms, wrapped between her legs ... and a shudder of pleasure rippled through her in the freedom of her nakedness and in response to the fondling breeze. A sensual surrender hardened and softened her in different parts in the same moment.

She arched through the air and dove headfirst into the waiting sea with only a small splash at her ankles to mark her passage through its surface.

Cold. Deep. She coasted far down into the blue depth, then kicked easily toward the surface ... her arms locked and straight out in front of her body ... her fingers meshed ... her eyes closed ... her heart banging from the cold … her skin a deliciously clean peel of sensation.

Only the sweet cold water and her.

Nothing else.

Then he was swimming naked beside her. They sprinted around the Styrofoam trip buoy and raced back to Coconut. He would have beaten her by three feet if she hadn't grabbed his ankle, pulled him down, and swum over his shoulders to the boarding ladder. There she turned her back to the ladder and with her arms over her head, her fingers wrapped around the ladder rails behind her, he took her.

There in the water.

Hanging from the side of Coconut.

Her legs locked around his waist.

Coconut's rigging slapped and rapped in time with their motion.

The Cuna sun slipped into the Darien Gap.

At thirty minutes to midnight, Evvie was dreaming. She dreamed of faces drawn in sand with a stick, faces with two white stones for eyes like the ones she and Cindy made. That dream faded away and was replaced by a dream in which Evvie floated toward a beautiful birdcage made of golden wires. The cage was open. The door was hinged to a frame standing in space, a shining frame with its door ajar. She drifted closer to the opening. She felt fear, and the fear made her shift in her sleep. Just as the cage seemed about to suck her inside, she came half-awake. She reached an arm across to Ted's side of the vee-berth. Her arm fell on an empty place.

She brought her arm back, pulled the pillow close to the side of her face, and began to sleep again.

Voices. She heard voices.

But she was so tired. Small waves whispered at the waterline. The muted clickings of sea shrimp tapped through the hull. Furled sails rustled in the tie downs. The bone-deep pleasure of muscles at peace after the stress of the storm crept over her like a warm blanket.

She felt herself letting go.

And sleep came back.

Chapter 12

Evvie was up at dawn and prepared a breakfast to match her optimism.

The galley filled with the aroma of eggs, bacon, sausage, and strong coffee. For the first time since leaving Colon she had the energy and opportunity to treat her shipmate the way she wanted to treat him. She rigged the cockpit sun canopy from the mainsail boom and set the outside dining table on its stanchion. With the wind funnel strung on the foredeck, a cool ocean breeze ran down into the forward vee-berth where Ted still slept; the breeze moved through the cabin and out the open hatch to the cockpit, and Evvie hummed a soft melody as she set the breakfast table in air spiced with the smell of salt spray and hot bacon.

She kissed him awake and greeted him with a steaming cup of coffee and a back rub.

They ate breakfast outside in the cockpit and flipped toast crusts to three gulls who picked off the morsels in flight with quarrelsome dexterity.

Ted seemed refreshed but preoccupied, his furrowed brow at odds with his relaxed pose.

Evvie stretched her leg toward him under the table, and her toes explored his foot. "I had a funny dream last night."

"I had a few dreams myself," he replied. He sipped his coffee. "What did you dream about? It didn't have anything to do with swimming and boarding ladders, did it?"

She winked at him. "Maybe I dreamed about that. But that was beautiful dreaming, not 'funny' dreaming."

"So, what qualifies as 'funny' dreaming?"

"I dreamed there were people on the boat last night. That they came aboard and were talking with you in the cockpit while I was asleep. I dreamed I was supposed to get up and make avocado dip, but I was too sleepy to move."

He looked at her, then back at his coffee. He didn't reply.

She grinned and raised her cup to him. "Sorry, Captain. I promise I'll get up next time and be a better hostess."

"Okay ... next time," he said.

"But you weren't in bed. I reached for you, but you weren't there." Sleepy images turned in her mind. Then, the more she thought about the dream, the more she seemed to remember.

He laughed and shook his head. "I did go out and sit in the cockpit for a while. Around midnight. I couldn't sleep."

"No Indian girlfriends, I hope? No bare-breasted beauties paddling out to get a piece of my man?"

"Even if one did, she would've been out of luck. You don't leave much in the barn, lady."

Evvie picked up the last piece of her bacon and reached across the table. She placed the crispy strip of meat between his teeth and held it while he nibbled until it was gone.

He held out his cup and she refilled it with coffee. As she did so, bits of the words she thought she had heard in the night gained more definition in her mind. Like the brain doing a crossword puzzle the second time around. Like a dreamer picking up more details of a dream in the telling.

Only *his* words.

Only *he* had been speaking.

If he was awake out there and talking to himself, talking out a problem, why didn't he tell her about it? She was about to press the issue, but then decided not to ask anything more. The beauty of where they were, and how they were, was so full of hope, so full of magic ... and she didn't know how fragile that magic might be.

They stayed two more days and nights in the Icacos anchorage. They swam ashore both days with canvas sneakers looped around their necks so they could walk across the coral and explore the island. They snorkeled together on the reef wearing swim fins and cotton sweat suits to protect knees and elbows from sharp edges. They collected shells and small stones and put them in a plastic box. They ate like royalty, drank wine, and sat together both nights beneath the stars.

On the third night, in an early morning hour, she reached again for him and he was not there. This time she got up. She went through the cabin toward the closed hatch leading to the cockpit.

She leaned forward and peered out through the narrow gap between hatch and cabin top.

Ted sat naked with his feet up on the cockpit seat, facing aft, his back to her. His right hand held something close to his ear. Something small and black and square. Despite the thick slow-moving clouds, the moon gave enough light.

It was the transmitter, the small radio he had shown her back in Colon.

He was talking.

The sound of the words was the sound she had heard that first night.

Low sounds. Clipped phrases. Numbers. Days of the week. She couldn't make out more than a few phrases even though he was no more than a few feet away.

What he was doing was strange, but not so strange that she couldn't figure it out. He was testing the radio, making sure of its range, making sure it worked if they should need it.

Then doubt flickered. *Why not test it during the day? Why test it only at night?* She knew enough about how radios worked from her early sailing days to know that transmitting at night was easier than transmitting during daylight hours. If he was going to test the radio, why not do it when conditions were toughest?

She thought about opening the hatch, climbing out into the cockpit, pretending she couldn't sleep either, and simply asking him what he was doing.

But she did not do that.

Because something happened that turned simple curiosity into disbelief.

Ted stopped talking, swung his bare feet back onto the cockpit sole, and pulled up his testicles. He placed the small radio against the skin on the underside of his scrotum and turned the radio in small increments. He let go of his testicles and pried open one end of the transceiver. He fumbled inside the cigarette-sized packet for a moment, then withdrew a capsule that was the size of a small tube of lipstick. He unwound a wire from around the outside of the capsule. He draped a few feet of the wire around his neck. He put the bigger packet down on the cockpit seat and started to talk once more, but this time he only talked.

He did not wait for answers. He only talked. Only transmitted.

Then he reassembled the packet. He talked some more. This time a conversation; this time he waited for answers ... and got them.

Evvie realized that only when the packet was fully assembled could it both send and receive. The smaller capsule that Ted had taken out of the packet could not receive. It could only send. It was the transmitter part.

Ted said a few more words, then stopped talking and clicked the radio off.

What happened next caused Evvie to stop thinking.

She could only watch.

Ted snapped opened the packet once more. He extracted the transmitter capsule again, rewound the aerial wire tightly around its small bulk, and secured it somehow. He placed the packet, now empty of the transmitter, on the cockpit seat. Then he picked up what looked like a tiny tube of toothpaste, metallic gray in color. Holding the transmitter capsule in one hand and the tube in the other, he raised the tube to his mouth and, using his teeth to hold the cap, twisted it off. He applied liquid from the tube to the transmitter capsule. He recapped the tube. He spread his legs apart. He reached down and pulled up his testicles again to expose the underside of his scrotum.

Evvie watched, only three feet away.

She lay alone in the vee-berth and stared up at the pattern of small air holes in the fabric of the overhead liner. She pulled her blanket tightly around her even though the night was warm. Moonlight coming into the forward cabin through the overhead hatch illuminated the space with pale yellow light. The varnished trim pieces glowed a lustrous orange. The boat tugged gently, first right, then left, as a fitful wind tested the ground tackle.

She heard the scratch of the cockpit hatch being moved, and she felt Coconut's hull dip toward the bow as Ted worked his way forward through the cabin toward her.

The bed linens rustled when he slid under the covers. She felt the warmth of his body travel the short distance between her and him.

She listened to his breathing change from shallow to deep as he fell asleep.

The image of him in the cockpit. Knees apart. His testicles pulled hard up against his abdomen.

She had watched him glue the small transmitter capsule into the place where the underside of his scrotum met his groin. Saw him press and hold the capsule with his fingers while the glue set.

The glue dried quickly. A matter of seconds.

He had gotten to his feet then. Moved his legs. Probed with his fingers. Then he had turned around in the moonlight and walked a step forward to stop only inches from her face, turned again and took two steps to the back of the cockpit where the tiller was tied at a sharp angle pointing at the sky.

He stepped onto and off of the cockpit seat a number of times. He squatted, stood, squatted, and stood again.

She lay in the vee-berth and listened to his steady breathing as he slept beside her.

She tried to find an explanation. One was obvious. What she had seen reminded her very much of their Bimini trip, the one where he had used what she thought was a pleasure trip to conduct some hush-hush agency work. But maybe there was an innocent reason. She fell asleep trying to find it.

The next morning he told her he had an idea and he wanted her opinion. She listened as she mixed a batch of pancake batter and tried to sort out what she had seen the night before. A part of her brain felt numb, but she had come up with an explanation that seemed plausible: He could have hidden the transmitter there in case of trouble. This was a dangerous part of the world. They both knew that. Pirates. Drug runners. Political problems. He didn't want to alarm her. He was just taking precautions in case they ran into some sort of confrontation.

DEA guys did those kinds of things. Force of habit. A sneaky mix of training and paranoia.

He was just being careful and resourceful and kind.

Nothing else made sense. That had to be it. To tell him that she had seen what he had done would have popped his balloon.

"How's this for a plan?" He was sitting on the cabin settee as she worked in the galley. A small-scale chart of the Western Caribbean was spread open and covered his lap.

She turned and looked down at him. He was studying the chart and pointing with a pencil.

"Look." He turned the chart around. "We go out the Holandes Channel. That's right here." He pointed to a space between two islands. "We sail straight out, maybe go east for a bit. We sail two-hour watches, just like we'll have to do heading for the States. I sail two hours while you sleep. Then we switch. We give it one, maybe two days. Nonstop. No shore leave. A real test. What do you think?" The power smile.

"Out there again?" she asked.

"Sure, out there."

The vision of the monster column of water twisted to life in her brain. But if she knew anything at all in the confusion of the morning, it was that she had to go out there and go out there soon. The fearsome memory had to be dissolved before it took control.

Otherwise the dream was dead.

Coconut took the blue rollers that marched at her from the northeast on her port bow. White clouds mixed with gray clouds, but the sky had been that way since before noon, and the winds were fair. Two hours ago, the islands of the San Blas had dropped below the southwestern horizon. Only the black tops of the tallest mainland mountains showed above the backsides of great waves that lifted Coconut and passed beneath her keel.

Evvie sailed the boat alone while Ted rested below.

The first taste of the powerful ocean when they left the protected Gulf of San Blas had made her sick, and it was made worse by the uneasy swoon that comes with feeling too small.

Ted had teased her. "Set the shark watch, mates!" he yelled at her rump as she hung over the rail to unload breakfast in a not-so-ladylike series of spasms. He laughed. She called him a bastard. Then they both laughed while she wiped sea spray from her face with a towel.

The first moments of being sick had embarrassed her and made her angry.

After anger came strength.

The strength turned into confidence. And joy. Or something like it.

She was more than relieved to find fear gone. She knew in her heart and from Arthur's words in the Porvenir anchorage that she wouldn't see, in this life, another storm like she'd experienced off Nombre de Dios. She reasoned that she had seen the worst. And she had pulled it off—even if it did take a few smacks in the face from Arthur to get her going.

Something else, too.

Ted had showed her how the satellite navigation system worked. Before they had pulled anchor back in the gulf, he'd turned on the system and let her read the numbers and compare them to those on the chart. The figures came right down on top of Icacos Island. She was impressed.

"That's pretty neat. Where'd you learn all this stuff?"

"There's nothing to learn," he replied. "It's all done for you. All you have to do is be able to count to a hundred."

"I suppose you guy-types like the old ways better? Sextants, dead reckoning, pencils, and rulers?"

"Not this guy-type."

Then he told her for the first time how much he appreciated what she had done the night of the storm when he was hurt and drunk. Arthur had set him straight in "real colorful language" while transporting him back to Coconut from the Customs House on Porvenir.

To hear Ted say those things about what she had done, to know that he knew. Even tossing breakfast had been worth hearing those words.

A large roller began to crest in front of her. She came back to reality and put the helm down to take away the wave's power.

Evvie's little ship plowed on while Ted slept his off-watch sleep.

With the satellite system they could go anywhere, night or day. No more threat of cruel coral just below the surface. No stumbling around far off the coast at night waiting for daylight. No jutting point of land with no name that looked like every other jutting point of land. Not now. The SatNav gear made a big difference. It pinpointed within a few yards their position on the charts.

The depth sounder on Coconut had proven to be undependable. They hadn't discovered how it gave false echoes in deep water until they left Limon Bay. Navigating with the depth sounder was out of the question. The satellite system filled that hole nicely.

But she wished there were some way to fill the hole dug by unanswered questions; some way to understand what she had seen last night when she watched Ted in the cockpit; some way to completely explain the incident in the alley and the odd relationship between Dulcie and Kent; and some way to explain the perception that Arthur seemed to be afraid for her without being able to pin down, either for himself or for her, just why. She wished that someone could explain all the little things that didn't add up, including the strange panic she'd experienced in the Cuna village when she suddenly felt like a fly in a spider web.

She was startled by a sudden movement above her head. A small sparrow fluttered into the foot of the mainsail near the boom, struggled for a moment in the turbulence, then gained a purchase on the sail track. It grasped the edge of the track with its tiny claws. It balanced there, wings extended, then found equilibrium in the wind and motion, tucked its feathers, and rested.

Evvie could see it was exhausted. The tiny eyes were misted. Spittle bubbled at the corner of the small beak. The head was down. The bird didn't try to fly away when Evvie moved the tiller or adjusted the sail. The nearest upwind land was two hundred miles to the east with nothing in between. Had it come from there? All that way? With no water? No rest? Pushed by storm or instinct so far from home?

She wanted to move, to get it water, some bread. But she couldn't. There was no way to help except to hold Coconut steady over the waves.

Ten minutes passed. The small head came up. The eyes seemed to clear. The feathers were ruffled and refolded. The bird watched her now, its tiny head cocked in her direction, small eyes brighter.

I'm all right, little bird. Are you?

She looked at the resting sparrow and knew it would have drowned in the sea if she and Coconut hadn't been there. That small spirit seemed to know it too. The tiny head bobbed. Wings fluttered. It jumped into the air and circled the masthead once, then headed southwest for the saving jungle of the Darien, a place of water, food, and rest ... and hawks and snakes.

It would make the land.

At least that small spirit would get there, now.

Both joy and sadness came to Evvie, sadness at the departure, joy in the salvation.

She had been unable to explain her rapid mood changes since crossing the San Blas reef into deep water that morning. It seemed as though she were suspended in time on the face of an other-world sea. Then, in a vivid moment at the top of a great and gentle wave, she spied a freighter far away on the northern horizon.

She remembered how the beautiful sadness came when she stood on the balcony back in Colon watching the ships leaving Limon Bay.

Suddenly that sadness came again. She didn't know why. Cindy? Ted? The storm? The bird? Without knowing why, she turned her face southeast in the direction of Colombia, so near, the land of Gabriel García Márquez. As they had years earlier, the haunting dream-like descriptives of the great writer began to wrap like vines around her frail assumptions, testing, probing, twisting reality.

When Ted came on deck a few minutes later to take his turn at the helm, he saw tears that seawind had no time to blow away. He asked her if anything was wrong. She said nothing was wrong.

Her forced smile hurt the muscles of her face.

She kissed him hard, a quiet desperation, and Coconut took advantage of what they were doing by heading up and tossing water from a breaking wavetop high over the deck. The cold spray made her yelp, and she laughed. Ted smiled.

Evvie went below to sleep her off-watch sleep.

And dreamed of the day Cindy took her first bath in the big tub and splashed water on her and on Ted and giggled.

Chapter 13

After the first night, Ted decided that four-hour turns at the helm would work better than two. They tried that sequence through the second day, then settled on three-hour watches, which allowed them a few moments together to talk, tend to the rigging, put some kind of meal together, and still let the person being relieved get some meaningful sleep.

The routine was efficient, but Evvie wanted more time to sit with Ted between watches. He insisted they keep to the schedule.

She noticed each time she came on deck that he was checking the navigation readings with increasing frequency. Once, as she sat with him and shared a glass of wine, she asked how deep the water was. He showed her the chart. She looked where his finger pointed and read the number 2034. "Two thousand feet?" she asked.

"Two thousand meters," he replied.

She looked over the side.

"Right," he said. "We're a mile above the earth."

They had reversed course and were heading back toward the San Blas. Coconut was closing the islands quickly in the hours before sunrise. Evvie had seen the dark shapes of the Darien mountains on the port bow when Ted had relieved her at three a.m.

Now Evvie rested in a tangle of blanket in the forward berth. She drifted in a twilight of sleep. She was wrapped in one of his T-shirts. The rushing waves grumbled at the hull. Coconut skidded in long fish-tailing sweeps as the little boat surfed through the night toward land, and Evvie braced herself against the vee-berth bulkhead to dampen the uncomfortable rolling motion.

She tried to force sleep, but sleep wouldn't come.

Shortly after Ted had taken the helm, she realized that he'd altered course slightly. The feel of the surfing runs had changed, longer stomach-churning runs that lasted almost thirty seconds. Evvie shifted across the berth and braced herself in a new position. The tension of trying to balance body and mind slowly wore her down. Weariness settled into her, and she finally began to sleep. Fitful. Shallow.

She dreamed a short dream. She was on a roller coaster at an amusement park. A single car. She was going up toward the top of a steep rise. The roller coaster wheels clattered on rough steel track. The car would slow as it reached the top of the incline. Then, just before cresting the incline, the car would pause and begin to roll backward down the track. Faster and faster. She tried to twist her head around. Tried to see where she was falling. Then the bottom. The roller coaster car would shudder to a stop, and the forward climb would begin again. Over and over. Never quite reaching the top.

In her dream, a deep far-away rumble began, hardly a sound she could be sure was there. But it was there. The rumble grew louder, more guttural. She no longer sat in the roller coaster car. Instead, she lay on her back, naked, on a sloping stretch of damp sand, a wide beach. She was held down by a great, invisible weight. She could move only her head. She could do no more than look down the length of her nakedness past her toes toward a pitch black sea. The sand and her body began to resonate with each muttering growl as unseen brutes thundered somewhere in a distant void.

She struggled in her nightmare.

Instantly, in a flash of fear, she woke to the real world. A confining tangle of blanket. The vee-berth. Coconut. Evvie was being tipped aft off the berth toward the cabin. She grabbed two fistfuls of mattress and held on. For a terrifying moment it seemed that Coconut was trying to stand on her stern. Pointing up. Evvie fought against the falling. Then her world smashed back down to horizontal, and rapidly past horizontal. The boat was almost on its nose and pointing straight down. Evvie slid toward the bow into the narrow angle of the forepeak.

Wide awake now.

No dream now.

Reality's nightmare now.

"Ted!" Her scream dissolved into blackness. "Ted!"

Then Coconut's bow rose again. This time more quickly, more steeply.

Evvie wedged herself back against the forepeak locker at the foot of the berth. Her fingers were claws driven into and through the bulkhead vinyl liner. She knew that if there were light to see by she would be looking vertically down through the length of the cabin at the cockpit hatch.

Oh God, dear God!

Coconut was pointing straight up. Everything not tied down inside the boat let go. The clattering crash was furious.

Coconut hung for a full second with her bow to the sky. The little boat seemed to inhale.

Something said goodbye.

And down she came.

A cruel foam-bearded head of coral the size of a car exploded through the bow hull and blasted into the center of Evvie's spine. The incredible force bent her forward. If the berthing mattress hadn't been pinned between her and the coral, her back would have been broken.

Evie's world slued to one side, crushed under a wall of water as the boat ground against more coral. The flesh of her right leg tore open from knee to ankle on something sharp.

Salt water filled her mouth.

Her forehead bumped hard against something.

Numbing darkness took her. The fearful roar faded.

And Evvie no longer cared.

Gray light high in a bleak and barren sky. It oozed into her through eyelids swollen by salt and caked with sand. Then her leg. On fire. Someone touching her there.

Evvie's eyes flickered open.

A young Cuna girl. Fourteen, fifteen years old. The girl's head covered by a red scarf. Bending to bathe the torn leg with a wet rag. The rag moved against the cut, and a lightning bolt of pain lanced up toward Evvie's groin. She fainted. Then pain brought back consciousness in seconds.

Her gut muscles cramped, and her eyes went wide. The muscles began to unlock. Her eyes focused; she raised her head and looked along her body. She was still wearing one of Ted's T-shirts. It covered her down to mid-thigh. She wore nothing else.

The girl touched the slashed leg again, but with a softer touch. Wet yellow leaves were laid on the wound. Evvie watched the girl wrap a red rag around the leg and knot it.

Evvie's head fell back onto cold sand.

She looked straight up.

Faces.

Men.

Not Indian faces.

Cruel faces. Hard faces.

Her hands went to her sides and tried to pull the T-shirt farther down over her hips.

"Where is Ted?" Her words, squeaked out through bruised lips, seemed to come from someone else.

The faces leered.

The circle of stares parted against the background of gray sky to make room for one more face. Staring down at her, set deep in that face, was a pair of lifeless eyes that made her feel as though she were looking at a snake. This one held a stump of thin black cigar in one hand. His good hand. The other hand and arm were twisted, deformed things.

No one spoke.

Except her. "Ted," she said.

She could focus clearly now. The next thing she saw, felt as much as saw, was the Cuna girl being shoved away, kicked by a dark boot.

An iron hand across the circle from the serpent face reached down and grabbed Evvie's wrist. She tried to smile, tried to see the extended hand as something meant to help her.

The hand jerked her onto her feet with quick brutal force. Pain tightened like piano wire being twisted around her injured leg. She wobbled, her knees buckled, but the iron hand made her stay on her feet.

"Fuck this one," said a man. Spanish words. "We fuck this one now." Other men laughed. But the meanest face, the one above the withered arm, didn't laugh. It looked at her and drew smoke into its mouth from the black cigar. The eyes of this one gazed at her like she was a piece of trash washed onto the beach.

The free hand of the man holding her wrist reached for the neckline of her shirt. Fingers grabbed the cloth there. And yanked down hard. The T-shirt tore to her waist.

Laughter turned to quick silence.

Then, "Three tits," from one of the men. Wonder in his voice.

"She has three tits!" said another.

Two men laughed.

"Animal." A small man.

"She is like a dog." A fat man.

"Look at her."

"Three tits."

Then her own voice, "Ted?"

More laughing. A hand with dirty fingers reached out and pinched the smallest nipple. Evvie winced in pain and pulled away. The dirty fingers found her again and pinched so hard she could not move. Until a different hand reached out of a cloud of blue smoke, the hand with the thin cigar. It lightly brushed the back of the fingers that pinched her, and the fingers released her nipple as though they had been cut away by a straight razor.

Eyes of a reptile looked at her breasts, then at her face. At her breasts once more.

That one spoke. "Come." A vulgar parody of a smile worked a curve into the face. "Come with me." Spanish words.

The hand that locked her wrist let go. The circle of men opened. Only the snake face was near her now. "Come," once more. The head nodded at her. "Do not be afraid. They will not hurt you."

Its good right hand took her left hand.

It pulled her forward, and she took one step. Then they walked slowly across sloping white sand. None of the other men followed. She was led toward a hut made of cane stalks and covered by a palm-thatched roof. As they walked beneath coconut palms, she saw Indians near a row of palm trees. Cunas. A dozen of them. Mostly women and children.

Evvie stopped and looked around before entering the hut. "Ted. Where's my husband?" Her words, Spanish. She'd learned the language with Ted after the Agency assigned him to monitor Mexican drug-cartel traffic. She spoke the language well. But for her throat to make any words at all seemed, to her, a miracle. Fear, mixed with confusion and pain, made the sound alien, not her own.

The thing she walked with nodded toward a palm tree near the beach. At the base of the tree was a man. Naked. Sitting. Chained with his back to the trunk.

"That is called Ted?"

Since Evvie only stared, the thing did not wait for an answer. "He is all right. He is only drying in the sun." Something like a laugh escaped from thin lips that peeled like burning paper away from brown-stained teeth.

She was made to sit in a woven cane chair that was dragged across the dirt floor so that it was near a hammock strung between two lodge poles. The one with the thin black cigar sat sideways in the hammock, both feet on the ground, the head and torso in shadow except for a shaft of weak light that spilled across the eyes.

They were alone in the hut.

Evvie tried to draw the torn shirt around her shoulders.

The hand of the one that looked at her came up, and the head slowly moved from side to side. "You will take that off." The words were not mean words, but the command, given quietly, was full of brilliant edges—precise serrated sounds.

Evvie's body stood up. Hands that didn't seem to be hers, even though they were attached to her arms, removed the remnants of Ted's shirt. The torn cloth dropped onto the dirt floor. She remained standing.

A pair of eyes worked all the places of her body.

"Turn around."

She turned around and faced the far wall.

Long seconds passed. She stared straight ahead at tan strips of cane laced together with brown twine. She felt her back burn even more than the cut on her leg as eyes did to her what she never thought eyes could do. Deep inside her belly she felt fear trying to turn to rage. But rage was too afraid.

She smelled the smell of wet, dead, cane stalks; of palm thatch; of the flat musky earth that pressed against the soles of her bare feet. A breeze came from somewhere, ran over her skin, and seemed to dissolve the pain out of her leg.

Ted? Where are we, Ted?

"You may sit down."

She turned the rest of the way around and sat down.

A long moment passed. The gray eyes kept looking at her and ...
God help me ... she looked right back.

Their stares locked, wedded across six feet of space. She sat with her
knees together, her arms resting on each side of the chair where arms
were supposed to rest. She did not attempt to cover her breasts. She did
not fold her hands in her lap to cover herself there. Her mind felt dull
and slow in one part, unspeakably alive in another.

The skin on her forehead seemed hot and she remembered being
bumped there when Coconut wrecked on the reef, but she did not reach
up to touch the abrasion. She thought of the leaves the Cuna girl had
placed on her cut leg, leaves that were still wrapped under the damp rag.

*They must be some kind of drug. That and the bump on my head ...
those things caused this insanity. What's happening to me?*

She inhaled slowly and tried to will the pounding in her chest to
stop. She took another deep breath. The air carried a stale smell of burned
wood. The fire pit would be near the center of the hut, but she had not
seen it and did not shift her eyes to look for it.

She wished she hurt somewhere, anywhere—her head, her leg—any
place that would block out what was happening. But she did not hurt
... she did not hurt at all.

Please make this stop. Please.

And still it looked at her.

Two minutes.

Looked at her. Five minutes.

Ten.

The cane surface of the armrests pricked at the skin on the underside of her forearms. The seatback seemed alive in the way its cross-
weave of narrow strips cut into her bare skin.

She grew lightheaded. She struggled against the urge to cry. Crying
seemed dangerously inappropriate. She breathed deeply once more. The
smell of burnt wood and wet cane swept her lungs and pried open all her
pores.

Her heart pounded too hard.

She knew those eyes could see the veins in her neck, could see the
blood surging there, could see that much without even moving from her
eyes.

The thin cigar drifted up. The tip glowed as smoke was drawn into the face. Blue smoke came out with words.

"What is your name?"

She did not look down. She swallowed once and wondered what her voice would sound like, if it would sound at all.

"Evvie." Her voice. Her own sound. Firm. No tremble, no rasp in the single word.

"You are not afraid. That is good."

Not afraid? Not afraid?

"Why are you here? Where have you come from?"

"I ... my husband and I ... we were sailing. In our new boat." *Not afraid?* "I don't know what happened. I was asleep."

"Your new boat? It is not so new anymore."

She blinked once and turned her head toward the partly open door, then looked back at the face. "Coconut ... Is she? ..."

"You speak Spanish very well. Where do you come from?"

"I ... we come from the States. From California."

"And your husband? He speaks Spanish too?"

"Yes. A little."

"You do not sail from the States. The boat has Canal Zone numbers."

"We bought it here. In Panama."

A long silence and more blue smoke came out past thin sharp lips.

Not afraid?

"I am Carlos."

What do you want me to do? Shake hands? She nodded once.

"Why do you not have that cut off?" Eyes on her breasts, the head nodding toward her breasts, the black cigar moving up and pointing at her breasts.

"I don't know," she replied.

The gaunt head moved slowly from side to side, dismissing her response. "Why?" A question that would be answered.

"It's part of me. It's the way I am."

The head nodded three times.

She dared a request. "Can I ... may I have something to put on?"

After several seconds the shape on the hammock edge leaned down to one side and rested the thin cigar in a white seashell on the dirt floor. The hammock lines squeaked as the thing stood up. It stared at her for a long moment, then went to a wooden table by the cane wall to her right. She couldn't see what was on the table and didn't turn her head.

"This. This will be for you."

Then she turned her head. The deformed hand held a sleeveless ankle-length dress above the tabletop. It was made of the rose-colored cloth the Cuna women wore, a dress they would wear under the intricate mola blouses. The dress was spread on the table and smoothed with the good hand.

"But I must fix it." That same good hand reached into a shadow on the wall where the blade of a machete gleamed.

The blade drifted up, then descended in a smooth powerful arc. It impacted the wood of the tabletop with a solid thud. The machete was put back into the shadow.

The good hand held out the dress to her, the lower half, the half from the waist down.

"You wear this."

She turned to look at the table where the upper half lay.

"You wear this. Only this."

She put on the half-dress. They sat across from one another again.

"What does your husband? ..." A squinting look, a pause that was a question.

"Ted," she answered. Evvie smoothed the fabric over her legs with one hand; the other hand held the waist of the dress in a bunched knot against her midsection. "His name is Ted."

"Ah, yes. Ted. That was it. Ted. And what does Ted do? What is Ted's business?"

Her heart flipped. Her mind scrambled. "He's retired."

"Retired?"

"He worked for ... the post office. The post office in California."

"Ah ... the post office." Gray eyes that didn't move scoured her face and soul.

She shifted in her chair. "How will we get back?"

"Get back?"

"To the Canal Zone."

"You said you were asleep. And ... Ted ... he was sailing the boat?"

"Yes."

Ten seconds passed. "Many boats hit the reef. Some come from far away."

"Where is *your* boat?" she asked. "What kind of boat do you have? Can you get us back to the Canal Zone? We can pay you."

"There is one boat on the reef that came all the way from South Africa. The name is on a piece of metal at the bottom of the reef."

She did not say anything.

"The people on the boat drowned. They did not know they were so close. It is a story the Indians told us."

"What do you do here? Are you doing something with the Indians? Are you trading for coconuts? I read that the Indians in the San Blas trade coconuts. Or sell them."

"Coconuts?" More blue smoke. "We do not trade for coconuts."

She was running out of words. The courage that had come with talking began to ebb. Fear started to rise once more, and a burning substance heaved up into the back of her throat. A hot slippery liquid bathed the teeth there. "My husband is tied to that tree. ... Why is he tied up?"

"Husbands do brave things before they think ... some husbands."

"We will not do anything. How can we do anything?"

"You will sleep in here. This is my house. You will sleep on the floor by my hammock."

Panic prickled and crawled. "You have to let Ted go. He can't stay like that. You must let him go."

"There is wine and water behind the table. You may walk around this island. You may talk with the Cunas. Most of them speak Spanish. They will tell you where to wash and piss. You wear only what you wear now. If you try to leave the island, I will give your husband to my men. There are two that would have him. The others will take his skin away in pieces after that."

Her fingers began to shake. Her jaw trembled.

"Do not worry." A slit smile. "The men will not hurt you. They will only look at you. I want them to look at you. You will keep yourself clean."

"But I ..."

"You are free to go. Do not go near ... Ted. You and I will talk tonight. In here. When we sleep."

"Can't I just ..."

"Go out. The day is early. Go out now."

Chapter 14

"I am Olonaya."

"I am Evvie."

"Evvie." The young Cuna woman repeated the name. "I am sorry, Evvie." The words were Spanish; the accent was not. The Indian stared for a long moment at the small vestigial breast.

"Sorry?"

"This is my island. It is our way that strangers should find happiness when they come to our island. There is no happiness here. I am sorry." Olonaya looked at the ground. Evvie saw tears rim the eyes before the eyes fluttered shut.

"How old are you, Olonaya?" Her own voice was strained and weak. She was exhausted. Fear had sapped what energy remained to her after the boat wreck and the horror of the man who had taken her into the hut. She wanted to lie on the sand and sleep.

"I am twenty. I am the wife of Nagolo. He carries the stick of the *suarribgana*. He is young to carry the stick, only of twenty-two years, but he is a good man."

"*Suarri?* ... "

"*Suarribgana.* You would say 'policeman.' ... He is that. But there is nothing he can do. They are too many. They have the guns. And they have El Codo."

"El Codo? That is? ... "

"The one with the twisted arm. The one who took you into his house. El Codo is what the men call him when he is not near. But they do not let him hear."

"Where are we? What happened to us?"

"We are the people of Karatuppu. Your map papers call our island Cayo Holandes. We are farthest of all Cuna from the land. We have little."

They stood together near a coconut palm at the edge of the sand. Two hundred yards away, across a stretch of coral plateau covered by shallow green water, waves curled and broke against the edge of the barrier reef.

Olonaya brushed a cheek with the back of her hand as though to wipe away a tear that wasn't there, and gave a brave smile. "Come," she said. "We will walk around my island. It is not so big."

They turned and headed south along the beach away from the cluster of five thatched-roof houses that stood beneath the coconut palms in the center of the island.

"They came four days ago. We do not know why they are here." Fine white sand squeaked under their bare feet as they walked. "They came in two motor boats before dawn."

"Where are the boats? Are they still here?"

"The boats are under the trees not far from the place you were found. The boats are covered with nets that are colored green and brown."

Evvie asked a question she did not want to ask. "Our boat? Is it gone?"

"It broke in many pieces on the coral between the islands. The men gathered all the pieces that were not too big. They covered the pieces with sand while you were with El Codo. There was a part they could not bury. The biggest part. It was inside the reef under the water. The men went into the water and tied brown canvas over it to hide it."

Something cut into Evvie's heart, a pain she was ready for, but not as ready as she'd thought. Coconut was gone.

"Why did you try to make your boat come between the islands?"

"Islands? There are two islands?"

"This and Piryatuppu. Piryatuppu is a small island across the water."

"How far across the water?"

"Fifty meters. A person must go into the water. It is not for the cayuco. It is not a place for us. No one goes to the island. Only one special priest of the Cuna nation goes there ... the one who has not seen evil."

"Why does the priest go there?"

"He takes prayer sticks to the night spirit. It is the island of Purkwet Kala. Purkwet Kala is the god who calls to the dead. He is the god who lives in the hollow stone."

"That island can't be as dangerous as this island. Not now."

"Piryatuppu is the last island before all the water of the San Blas goes out to the great sea. The water goes fast. Many sharks. On Piryatuppu, mist comes from the sand and eats the eyes. Many dangers are there. These men who hurt us will someday leave my island. But Piryatuppu will always be the place of Purkwet Kala."

Evvie needed facts, not folklore. "What is the shape of these islands?"

Olonaya squatted. Evvie kneeled down beside her. With her finger, the Cuna drew on the sand. She drew a shape like a bow tie, separated in the middle, one side half the size of the other.

"The small one is Piryatuppu. The big one is Karatuppu."

"How far is it to the mainland?"

"It is twenty-five kilometers in the cayuco to bring the water."

Fifteen miles. "You go there to get water?"

"One of our men goes there once in three days. Sometimes he cannot go if the storm comes."

Evvie stood up. Olonaya stood also. They continued to walk. After going less than half a mile, they reached the south end of Karatuppu, then turned west around a stand of palms and proceeded north up the other side of the island.

"El Codo and the men, have they hurt you?" asked Evvie.

Olonaya did not reply at once. She folded her arms across the front of her mola blouse and kept walking.

Evvie stopped her by reaching out and putting a hand on her shoulder.

Olonaya looked toward the sea. Tears moved on brown cheeks.

"Olonaya?"

"There are thirteen of us. Four children and two girls of fourteen years. Three men ... my husband, his brother, and my grandfather. Myself and three other women ... my mother and Inlota and the old one who is called Alecta who is the grandmother of Inlota."

Olonaya began to cry. Evvie put her arms around her and held her close.

Olonaya wept softly against Evvie's shoulder. The words were muffled, but Evvie understood what Olonaya said: "All the women. All. Even Inlota's grandmother. Even her."

"The girls? … The fourteen-year-old girls?"

"El Codo took one of them into his hut. She will not speak. We do not know. She will not speak about what happened there."

"And the other girl?"

"She is a moon child … a white one with the pale eyes."

"Albino?"

"Yes, that is what she is."

"Has anything happened to her?"

"No. El Codo said to his men that she will not be touched."

The women fell silent. The slow, steady cadence of surf assaulting the barrier reef far across the lagoon subdivided time, a natural metronome, absolute, indifferent, the reiteration of understated power.

"Olonaya?"

Olonaya did not acknowledge what she knew would be asked next.

"Olonaya, what will happen to me? What will he do to me?"

Olonaya watched the sea.

Evvie's eyes filled with sting, and something in her chest grew hooks. *I've lost it all. Everything. My Cindy. Coconut. Now this.*

Olonaya spoke. What she said led Evvie away from panic. "Our tears will not give the little ones more days. The little ones do not eat tears. They do not wear tears. Tears do not hold back the storm."

They began to walk again.

"Have any of the Cuna men been hurt?"

"They have not been hurt. El Codo makes them go to the mainland in the way of the Cuna. To get the water. To get supplies. They must not tell of what happens here … or the children will be killed. That is what El Codo said."

Evvie felt her stomach flip. But she was aware of something else. In a fraction of one day it seemed as if she and Olonaya had known each other forever. The common enemy, the horror that dissolved time. "Why are they here?" she asked. "You must have heard them speak. They must have said something about why they are here."

Olonaya slowly shook her head. "I do not know. They seem to be waiting for something. We hear El Codo talk in the night into the radio. Not many words he says. Only some hours and some minutes. We do not hear more."

"How many are there? How many men?"

"There are seven. And El Codo. Eight."

"Do you know where they come from? By the way they speak words?"

"They are most from Colombia. They sound like the men who come from Colombia on the coconut boats."

Evvie's brain connected the dots: Colombia ... drugs ... DEA ... Ted ... radio ... El Codo. But she was exhausted and confused. Her conscious mind was busy with fear, not abstractions. But the seed was struck. The brain had done its job.

"Colombia?"

"Except for the one ... the one with the wires."

"Wires? What do you mean 'wires'?"

"The white man who is from your land. He is not old like the others. Maybe he is thirty years. He has pictures of fence wires painted onto his skin, on the skin of his arms up near the shoulders. Blue and black wires that go around the arms. He does not do what the others do ... to the women. He is always by himself. Or he is with El Codo."

"What is his name? What do they call him?"

"He is called Mark. ... El Codo calls that one Mark."

"This is Nagolo. This is my husband."

Evvie reached out and shook the hand of a short powerfully built young Cuna man. He wore black pants, a white shirt unbuttoned down the front, and a green baseball cap with no logo. Barefoot, like the rest of the men. He had a wary, guarded look, but that look quickly dissolved into one of soft, almost tearful, desperation. "On your boat? ... Was there a gun on your boat?" he asked.

"No. There is no gun," said Evvie.

The man's jaw tightened. "I must stop them." The voice growled. No softness now. "I must do something."

Olonaya quickly moved to his side and held his arm. "No, my husband! We must wait. They will go away." She looked at Evvie. "Tell him we must wait! Please tell him!"

Rage hardened the features of Nagolo's face.

"Please tell him!"

Evvie looked from her to him and back to her. A weakness almost cut her knees away, and she recognized the corrosive helplessness she had known when she looked down at Cindy on that night ... too quiet in a shadow of blanket ... too pale in cold, hard light ... too small in a mother's arms. Arms that could do nothing but hold.

"I don't know what to say," said Evvie. "I don't know what to do."

Shapes moved in the tree line, and other Indians came forward from the shadows to stand in front of her. And all of them, even the children, wearing that horribly unfair look. A look ... *Damn you! God damn you all!* ... that said: You must help. You are the one who must help us. ... *I can't help you! I can't help myself!* ... You must tell us what to do. ...

All the faces looking.

Evvie folded her arms across her chest and took a step backward toward the water.

Away from the faces.

An involuntary step.

But the unwilled act of recoiling made her ashamed. She stepped forward again and stood in front of Nagolo.

She looked hard into his eyes.

"They are men," she said. Her words cut like sharp shell. "They are only men." She reached out and grasped Nagolo's arm. "Not yet. Wait. Listen to Olonaya. Wait."

Evvie turned abruptly and walked alone toward the place where Coconut had been gutted on the reef. She wanted to see where they had wrecked during the dark hours of that morning.

She wanted to understand an accident that made no sense. The satellite navigation system was working. The weather had been good. But that "something" hovered just beyond her conscious mind. A question not quite framed.

Not yet.

She looked out toward the ocean. The apparently unbroken line of surf plunged and exploded spray skyward above the unseen coral ledge beneath the surface. But when she looked more closely, she could see a churning piece of deep water, perhaps fifty feet wide, that betrayed a break in the continuity of the reef. She followed the break shoreward as it cut through the coral flats toward the place where she was standing, the place where they'd found her on the sand. She was able to trace the course of the winding channel by the darker color of the water. It snaked toward her and passed between the two islands, between the north tip of Karatuppu and the smaller Piryatuppu to the west.

There was no sign of Coconut on the beach. The boat was somewhere in that small channel. Or at its entrance. Otherwise she and Ted would still be out there where the big waves crashed on the coral ledge. They must have been swept along the channel. Coconut must have hit right at the entrance.

Blind luck.

If luck could be that blind.

She turned and looked across the channel at Piryatuppu.

It was no more than ten feet above sea level and empty of huts. The water between Karatuppu and Piryatuppu looked deeper on the Gulf end of the pass, and she remembered how the chart numbers gave the depth of the San Blas Gulf as more than two hundred feet in places.

She heard a sound in the trees behind her and turned. Three of El Codo's men smoked cigarettes and watched her. They stood close together and talked in low tones. She heard the name El Codo. One of them grabbed the crotch of his pants and jerked the loose material in her direction. All three laughed.

She was instantly enraged. She could taste her own saliva. Tart, metallic, foreign. Exhaustion, grief, and hopelessness had their chance to gang up on fear. She walked toward the men. They looked surprised. One turned his head and glanced at his companions, unsure, then looked back at Evvie.

She walked faster toward them.

The man who seemed afraid turned and quickly walked away and disappeared into the thin line of palm trees. The other two waited where they were, their expressions blank.

She came up to them and stopped three feet away. She looked into cruel faces.

She nodded at the crotch of the one who had made the gesture with his hand on his pants. "You're trying to tell me something. What are you trying to tell me? Do you have a problem down there?"

She could smell them. A thick blue fly landed on the neck of the man who had made the gesture. He made no move to brush it away. The fly's body angled up as it bit into flesh. Still no move to brush it away. The man's eyes shifted, and he blinked and looked past her toward the sea at some unseen thing.

Neither man spoke. Neither answered her question.

Evvie took a step forward, halved the distance. More than halved the distance. "Should I ask El Codo what that means?" She pointed directly at the man's crotch. Her finger hovered an inch away from a dried stain on the wrinkled material.

His companion backed a step. Two more steps.

"That's what you just said his name was, didn't you? 'El Codo'? I will ask him that, too. I will ask him what it means when you say 'El Codo,' and I will ask him what you mean when you do that thing with your pants. I would like to know what it means. Should I ask him that?"

Eyes that had looked past her before now looked at the ground.

"I would not want you to do that," said the man. A deep voice, not a loud voice.

"I beg your pardon? I must still have water in my ears."

"Don't do that. Don't ask El ..." Eyes on her eyes. A softer voice. "Don't ask Carlos."

"You stink." She wrinkled her nose. "You stink like a pig."

Suddenly, a cruel sneer. A threatening angry glare. "El Codo is a man. And a man can die, whore. Any man."

The pig's companion backed away, frightened, then turned and moved toward the tree shadows. Once, he looked back over his shoulder. Then he was gone.

"El Codo is going to die?" she asked. "You're going to kill El Codo?" She put her hands on her hips. "El Codo should hear about this. He will be impressed." She thrust her chest out. For the first time in her life she felt she had breasts that were badges. Campaign medals. Battle decorations. She breathed in as deeply as she could.

The acid glare of the man standing in front of her threw a net of such quick hate over her that she started to feel fear. Then she thought of Olonaya. And Nagolo's desperate eyes. And the others. But she couldn't stop now. She was in too far. She would see it through.

"A man should not smell like a pig. What do the ones you sleep with think about the way you smell? Your mother? Your sister? Your daughter? How do they sleep with you and put up with your stink?"

She watched his hands turn to fists.

"Even a pig should bathe." She pointed to the channel between the two islands. "Bathe, pig!" She jabbed at him with her finger and pointed to the pass once more. "Into the water, pig."

The man didn't move. What she saw in those eyes was a look past evil.

"One last time, pig. Into the water!"

Still the man did not move.

She stepped around him and headed in the direction of El Codo's hut. "I will see if El Codo will help get you cleaned up."

Evvie had gone nine steps when she heard the splash.

She turned and saw the man neck deep in the channel and glaring at her.

Evvie ate rice and beans with the Cuna family at noon. They gave her water to drink and offered her strong sweet coffee as thick as honey. They showed her a small hut on sticks that was built out over the water on the west side of the island. She would relieve herself there as the Indians did. She was shown where the fresh water was kept in covered containers behind the largest hut, the *Onmakketneka*, the gathering house.

Olonaya removed the red bandana and dried leaves from the gash on Evvie's leg. It was healing fast. Some dark poultice and a new red rag went over the wound. There was no pain.

Nagolo strung a hammock in the gathering house where Evvie could rest. Other hammocks were tied to lodge poles in the large one-room structure. Olonaya explained that the *Onmakketneka* was the only one of the five huts on the island that El Codo allowed the Indians to use. The individual living huts toward the east side of the island had been taken over by the Colombian invaders.

"You may sleep here at night with us." Olonaya's upturned face carried an expression of hope.

Evvie looked at Olonaya, then looked away. "El Codo says I am to sleep in his hut."

"I am sorry, Evvie. I am so sorry."

"Do not worry about me. I am a woman. I am not a girl."

Nagolo stepped forward. "Please ask your god to forgive us. This is not our way. Our gods do not listen. I would give my life to make these men go away."

"I know that. You are not to blame. No one here is to blame." She felt bone weary. The incident with the pig-man had drained her spirit. The strength she used on the man was the last of her strength. The energy that was left to her fueled nothing more than a desire to curl up and sleep. She forced a weak smile. "Perhaps one of you could get near my husband? To see if he is all right? You do not have to try to talk with him—just see if he is all right."

Nagolo spoke. "Does he speak the Spanish, too?"

"Yes," said Evvie.

"I will try," said Nagolo.

"No." A voice from the shadow. Evvie turned to look.

A girl of fourteen stepped forward, the one Olonaya called a child of the moon. "I am Ile. I will try to speak with him."

They all looked at the albino girl. She stood tall in the dim light of the hut, but like some pale ghost, she seemed fragile, almost transparent. Evvie saw the way the skin on her forehead and on the backs of her hands had been peeled away where the tropical sun had worked like acid on the delicate flesh.

Olonaya stepped to the side of the girl and put an arm around her waist, then turned to face Evvie. "Yes. Ile would be the one. El Codo has said she is not to be harmed. She could do it." Olonaya looked at her husband. "I think she could do it. Please, Nagolo? I think it is better for Ile to try. Not you."

In the last half-hour of daylight, after she had slept in the hammock in the gathering house, Evvie walked on the west beach away from the others. Near the turn at the south end of the island, she saw the figure of a man sitting on the sand. He threw pebbles and small bits of shell into the shallow water of the coral plateau.

Evvie watched him for a long time without moving.

Finally he stood up. He turned toward her, started to walk, saw her, and stopped.

Across fifty feet of sand they looked at each other.

He was tall, over six feet. His body was a young man's body. Supple and strong. Tanned. Muscles sharply cut. He wore black pants and a white tank top. Dark hair curled in a short twist onto smooth skin above the right eyebrow. Hard, well-defined arms. Both upper arms were encircled by winding strands of barbed wire, tattoos in blue and black.

She saw something else even from that distance. Cut into his left cheek was a horizontal scar. Five inches long, it ran from the side of his nose to the lobe of his left ear. It passed under the eye by one inch.

She remained where she was.

He crossed the space and stopped in front of her.

Neither spoke. He looked at her, she at him. More exactly, she looked at his eyes. Only at his eyes. Everything about him was young and alive. But not the eyes. Not those.

He looked her up and down with those strange tired eyes. His gaze paused for the smallest part of a moment when he looked at her breasts, then traveled to her face and stayed there.

"You're the woman who was on the boat." Words spoken in English.

"Your name is Mark." Her own English words sounded alien in the first seconds.

"That's right."

"My name is Evvie."

"Hello, Evvie."

"Hello, Mark."

"Tough trip." His words were sarcastic. His look was sad, resigned.

"It *is* a tough trip," she replied.

Still he did not move. "You're a beautiful woman."

"No. I'm not a beautiful woman."

"Yes, you are."

"He's going to kill us, isn't he?"

"He might."

"Why?" she asked.

The barbed wire shrugged.

"What reason can there be for all this? Is it just a sick power trip? Are you all psychopaths? Why are you here?"

"Travel broadens the mind."

Evvie chewed hard at the inside tissue of her right cheek. "That's a flip stupid-ass answer."

"Yes it is. I'm sorry."

"And if I hear the fucking word 'sorry' one more time today, I'm going to walk into the fucking ocean and swim to fucking England."

Something flickered for a brief moment in his tired eyes, and a small smile came.

"I don't usually say that word," she said.

"Yeah? Well, don't worry. ... You've pretty well got it down."

She turned and faced the sea. He turned, too. Side by side they watched a wading seagull lift a small silver fish from the shallows, tip an orange beak to the sky, and gulp it down.

"You're not like the others," she said. "Why are you with them? You don't come from where they come from. They speak Spanish. They're butchers. They rape old women."

"Hey ... I speak Spanish."

His words were not a simpleton's words. They revealed a real, if misplaced, sense of humor. The man apparently had a brain. He looked like he would understand, might help ... but he was making small talk, making jokes in the middle of her nightmare. He had a brain but no soul. The beautiful stranger who had no life in his eyes had no soul. A deep sadness settled over her.

Then he did an unexpected thing.

He put an arm around her shoulder and eased her down so they sat side by side on the sand. Long moments passed and the young man only sat next to her and watched the sea.

Three minutes later the sun across the Gulf touched a mountaintop.

"You can't help us, can you?" she asked.

"No. I can't help you."

Evvie was silent for a long time. The fishing gull flew away toward the ocean. The shallow water lost its green to gold. And then turned black.

"Did you escape from some prison? Is it a drug thing you're doing?"

He did not answer.

"I've heard of mix-ups like this. In movies. In the newspaper. Nothing's been real for me the last twenty-four hours. Please tell me. At least do that. Please tell me what's happening so I don't go insane."

He breathed in deeply. The words that came next came on the wings of a long sad sigh. "It's just as dangerous for us as it is for you," he said.

She tried to understand how that could be. Those words were senseless words, but the way he said them was not.

He spoke without looking at her. "We're all small people, right now. All of us. Even El ... even Carlos is small."

Carlos. He called El Codo Carlos. There was nothing left in her. She would have fallen asleep—she was that tired—but triggered by his words, a vision of snake began to slither through her mind.

146

"I have to go to him tonight," she said.

She thought she heard his breathing pause, then resume its same steady rhythm.

"You might be all right," he said. "For a little while."

His words, so matter of fact, so detached, cracked through her hope like rock through crystal.

"Undress."

She removed the covering skirt.

"Come, sit by me."

She moved across the dirt floor toward the hammock. A single candle burned on the packed earth next to a blanket. El Codo lay naked in the hammock and stared up.

"Did you wash yourself in the sea?"

"Yes."

"Did you piss for the night?"

"Yes."

"Good. The men do what I tell them, but they are still men. I do not want you to walk in the night."

She sat down on the blanket spread on the ground next to the hammock. A hand could have reached out and touched her. It did not.

"Did you like him?"

"Did I like who? I don't—"

"He is called Mark. He saved my life. That is why he has the scar. Did you see it? On his face?" A thin smile. "Of course you saw it." The snake skull nodded at the blanket. "Lie down."

She lay on her side and curled into a fetal position, her backside toward the hammock. The flickering candle cast shadows that danced in orange skirts on pale cane walls. The sea rumbled on the reef. A current of musty air wormed across the floor of the hut. Air that smelled of things dead and rotting on damp sand.

"He has no place to go. He thinks they look for him back in the States because of the cocaine. I think they do not. It was too long ago. But I take care of him. He is a son to me. So I take care of him."

She closed her eyes. And waited.

"I think this will be over soon. I think you will be able to go back."

She didn't believe him. She could never go back.

Hammock ropes squeaked as weight shifted.

Please, God.

The tip of a finger touched her shoulder like the tongue of a viper touches warm meat.

Chapter 15

She trembled.

"You shiver. Are you cold?"

She didn't reply.

The ropes squeaked again. She heard a bare foot hit the ground next to her head. An inch away. The other foot made the same sound down by the flare of her naked hips. The legs of the one sitting on the hammock were spread wide apart.

A tip of finger again, this time a slug working along the crest of her body from shoulder to knee as she lay on her side.

She heard wax sputter as the candle was moved. The light that came through her closed eyelids was darker with the candle now behind her. Her senses went past electric. Everything mattered.

A callused foot touched the raised curve of her up-facing hip. The foot pressed gently forward, and she rolled face down for it.

"Closer." The voice was strangled, alien.

She did as she was told, moved sideways on her belly until her shoulder and her hip touched the feet of El Codo. She closed her eyes and tried to melt through the blanket into the earth.

A hand touched the skin high on the back of her thighs. Cold fingers moved into the space between her legs. The fingers pulled slightly, rubbed slowly, fingers that told the legs to spread apart.

The legs spread apart.

If there is a God . . .

The fingers, satisfied by what had been asked, and done, left her skin. Only toes touched her now at thigh and shoulder.

I am a woman. I am not a girl.

Almost too soft to hear, a rhythmic sound began. Flesh folding on flesh. Flesh stretching and compressing in concert with the whispered cadence of the hammock ropes, a faint, debasing, corrupting sound.

Take me from this place.

The toes wriggled forward like hard insects into the seam between the blanket and her body, roaches squirming into a tight place. She felt the insects move in concert with the other sounds as the beast masturbated above her back in the flickering light of the single candle.

It breathed faster. The quiet tempo of perverse violence increased.

She was afraid to move.

In the hammock, El Codo slept a deep sleep. He made noises like a swimming animal. Grunts. Hisses. Wheezing exhalations of air that flopped the tongue like something wet in mud.

The semen on her back dried slowly, and her skin was gradually pulled tight by the foul contracting pools. She wanted to scream until her chest split. She wanted to sprint for the ocean. She wanted to roll on serrated acres of dead coral until the drying scum was lacerated away.

But she only breathed.

And prayed for the day.

When El Codo awoke he rubbed his eyes and looked down at the floor. She was not there. He swung around and sat on the edge of the hammock. On the floor in the farthest corner she sat wrapped in her blanket and stared at him with hollow eyes.

"You did not sleep?"

"You let my husband go!"

"It was a good night to sleep. Cool. Quiet."

"Let him go! Now!" Her voice hammered the words. Her hands were fists. Strands of hair trembled on her forehead. But she had not put on the half-dress. It lay on the floor where she had dropped it the night before.

El Codo regarded her with cold disinterest. Then he stood up. His naked body, hard and efficient and centered by a half-erect male part, appeared more gray than brown in the light coming in from the overcast day beyond the cane walls.

He is a corpse standing.

El Codo walked across the hut and stood in front of her. The end of the penis swelled more; it swayed one inch from her forehead. She looked past it, kept her eyes on El Codo's eyes.

"So. You want me to let him go?"

She made no sign, no sound.

"How badly do you want me to let him go?" His erection was complete.

She only stared into his face.

Then El Codo stepped back. "Let's stop this business." He squatted in front of her. "I treat you very well. I give you a place to sleep. I tell the men to stay away. You have clothes to wear. Food. Drink. I do not kill your husband. I do not understand."

"I can't give myself knowing he's out there like that."

"Give? You do not need to give. I do not need you to give anything. There is no giving; there is only taking. Why did you not sleep?"

"I heard the noise the Cuna woman made. Two of your men. In the night. Three hours. Why don't you leave these people alone?"

El Codo gazed at her with a dead expression. "Leave them alone?"

No. God, no.

"It is only who is strongest. That is all. It is no more than that."

"You bring them pain."

"Pain? But there is no pain. I have never felt pain. ..."

Dear, dear God.

"There are only small pleasures. There is no pain."

In that moment an image crystallized in her brain. She was balanced on a sliver-thin high wire above a deep chasm where something irrational and vicious waited ... a monster who saw courage as something to attack and helplessness as an invitation to degradation.

Attack the strong, degrade the weak, its only choice.

More than choice. Its profane obligation.

Why? Especially when the thing itself is defective. That arm.

And then she knew.

El Codo's own defect was the reason. Because she also was defective, he saw himself in her. Not compassion for her, but for himself. ... That twist of ego was his motivation.

No subtlety now, no gray area, no room for error. She had to keep her balance. No left or right, no easy logic, no hiding. She had to walk that shining wire. El Codo was evil, the purest kind of evil. An evil equally as intolerant of strength as it was unmoved by abject frailty.

Knowing could be her weapon. Her spear was a small spear, but it was all she had. She seized it.

She got to her feet. From his squatting position, he stood also. She faced him.

"I'm afraid of you," she said. But her words were oddly, deliberately, clear and strong.

She walked past him, went to where her half-dress lay, picked it up, and put it on. "Do you have a rope?" she asked. She stood with her back to him. "Something to keep this damned thing up?"

She fumbled with the cut material at her waist. She waited. She tried to knot the fabric. She succeeded in making a knot. Then she undid it. Waited. Made the knot again. Slow seconds uncoiled.

A hand reached past her left side. The hand held a piece of plaited reed rope.

"Thank you." She tied the rope around her waist and turned to face him. Ready to play the game. She cupped that smallest breast with her right hand. She jiggled it. "I guess I'll never be a movie star, will I? Not with this." Her hand moved away from the breast. "But at least I can keep my damned dress up." She smiled and indicated his bad arm with a movement of her head. "Carlos, we might not be movie star material, but I'll bet the two of us are worth any ten of them." She nodded once at the door to the outside.

He looked at her.

She reached across the space between them, not too slowly, not too quickly. Before touching his withered arm, she began to talk. "Now, we need to talk about ... *touch the arm* ... that guy out there ... *hold the arm* ... tied to that tree like some kind of ... *turn him* ... animal ... *start for the door.* ..."

She stood next to El Codo while two men unlocked and unwound the chains around Ted's waist. He was still naked. Even though he'd been chained for only one day, the sun had turned his white parts fiery red. Ted had been given water, but he was too weak to stand and had to be helped to his feet. He was led into the shade of a small bohio.

Evvie watched as her husband was forced to sit down. Ted did not look at her.

One of El Codo's men lifted a galvanized anchor from the ground next to the bohio. Evvie recognized the anchor. The fluke tips were painted white. The anchor was from Coconut. The man shook it a few times to get the sand off the ring end. He went to Ted, knelt down, and fastened the anchor around Ted's neck with a short length of chain and a lock. The man stood up and rubbed his hands together, then wiped them on his shirt. He looked at El Codo.

El Codo nodded.

"Carlos, the anchor? ... Why? ..."

Ted sat naked supporting the twenty-pound anchor in front of his chest with both hands.

El Codo lit another cigar. Smoke puffed out. "Husbands. So emotional. We don't want him swimming off into the sunset like some ... movie hero, do we?" Blue smoke curled up. "You will stay away from him, of course."

"Of course," she said.

He gestured toward the north end of the island. "Come."

El Codo and Evvie walked barefoot along the water's edge. A father with his daughter. A professor with his student. A Malibu couple on a Sunday morning beach stroll. El Codo gave a friendly wave of his cigar to a man standing under a tree, then to a man working on one of the skiffs.

Evvie saw the shape before he pointed it out.

Staked spread-eagle at wrists and ankles, face up and naked on the sand, was Ile. The young albino girl was beginning to fry in the sunlight even though it was only ten a.m.

No! Not her. Not Ile!

They stopped walking and looked down. Tear drops ran streaks on each side of Ile's face as the sun worked on eyes that couldn't hide beneath eyelids devoid of pigment.

El Codo shook his head. "In the night she was caught talking to your Ted." El Codo slowly shook his head more. "I told them. I told them all. It would be better if they listened." He turned to Evvie. "Well, what will you do today? Have you plans to walk with Mark? Talk some? I know he would like to talk with you. In English. About the States."

Evvie wondered if she could pull it off ... just walk up to El Codo's man who whittled a stick in a chair beneath the trees, take the knife from him, and cut Ile free. "I—"

"It is not often he gets to talk with a pretty gringo woman."

She still stared at Ile. Perhaps she could stick the knife in El Codo. But then the other men ...

"You know, if your husband would fall in love with one of these nice Indians"—the cigar pointed at Ile—"perhaps you could be together with Mark. I think he would like to have you. How would that be?"

She raised her eyes from the Cuna girl in the ropes. She looked at El Codo. She had heard only his last few words. "How would what be?"

"Come." He steered her toward the trees, and he waved and nodded when he passed the whittling man. The chips stopped falling. The knife hung in the air. The whittling man's face was a mask of disbelief. El Codo, the citizen, looking like he owned a flower shop in Cartegena ... him, strolling with his lady.

"You've got to get her out of the sun! She'll be dead by sundown!"

"How do you figure I do that?" Mark continued to skip flat stones across the water.

"For Christ's sake! Tell him you want to fuck her! Tell him that!"

Mark's arm stopped in its backswing. He looked at Evvie. "For someone who doesn't use that word, you sure use one that sounds like it."

"Have you seen her?"

"I don't look at things like that. It's bad for the conscience." He launched a flat rock toward the lagoon.

"What in hell has happened to you?"

"Enough."

"Haven't you ever been burned by fire? Don't you know what that feels like? This isn't some kind of macho game. You don't have to play it. Don't let the last thing that separates you from them get—"

"You ever coach football? You'd make a great coach."

"Listen, damn you! El Co ... Carlos says you've got a problem back in the States. You must have had enough of this jungle stuff by now. My father's a lawyer, a big-shot criminal lawyer in Los Angeles." Lying. "We just might get out of this. All of us. If you're looking at some five-year-old possession charge, my father can clean that paper in a New York minute. Give me a reason to go to bat for you! Please! Damn it, this could be your last—"

"Jesus, coach. Don't throw a wedgie!"

"I don't have a wedgie to throw, goddamn it!"

He looked at what she was wearing. He laughed. Despite having one foot in hell, she laughed, too.

Mark took Ile into one of the huts before noon.

Olonaya sat next to Evvie on the west beach, and both women faced the Gulf channel. They watched what was happening out of the corners of their eyes. Ile could barely move on her own, but Mark did not help her. When they reached one of the huts, an empty hut, he stopped and pushed Ile hard. The girl stumbled into the hut. Mark turned in the direction of El Codo, who was talking with another man next to the beached motor launches. Mark grabbed the crotch of his pants with one hand and made the same gesture that the pig-man had made at Evvie, only Mark directed it at the hut. He grinned at El Codo. And went inside.

The man with El Codo laughed.

It might have been the distance, but it seemed to Evvie that El Codo smiled.

She looked out at the water, then turned and looked at Olonaya. The Cuna woman was looking at the water, too. Tears, like sliced pearls sliding on smooth teak, sparkled on brown skin.

Without turning her head, Olonaya slid her hand across the sand and touched Evvie's fingers with her own.

Brown fingers wrapped into white fingers and held on.

Evvie stood on the west beach and watched the children splashing in the shallow water. Even Bibi, the two-year-old baby girl of Nagolo and Olonaya, laughed and frolicked with the others.

A naked Cuna boy, six years old with shiny black hair, came down to the beach from the gathering house. He carried a tattered, rolled-up comic book in his right hand. He grabbed the top edge of Evvie's skirt with his free hand and yanked hard to get her attention. The unexpected move caused her to grab the rope belt to keep her skirt from being jerked off her hips. "Hey!" yelped Evvie.

"My name is Niki. Ile is my sister." Bold eyes sparkled over a wide smile. The words were Spanish, the tone cheerful, the face full of impish energy. Other than the baseball caps some of the Cuna men wore, teaching their children Spanish seemed to Evvie to be the only concession the Indians were willing to make to the twentieth century.

Evvie hitched up her skirt. In the middle of her own smile, she realized how far away a smile had been. She knelt down on the sand so that her eyes were level with his. "Well, how do you do, Mr. Niki?"

"Niki. Not Mr. Niki."

"Okay. Niki."

A thin brown arm went around Evvie's neck, and the boy positioned himself close by her side. He bent his head forward and looked past her, then looked back the other way to be sure they weren't going to be interrupted. A conspiracy was afoot.

"We can get them," he said.

"Get who?"

"The bad men."

Evvie couldn't resolve the incongruity of the horror that was Karatuppu with the pint-sized naked conspirator at her side, and she didn't know whether to laugh or cry.

His arm came away from her neck and he squatted down, pulling her lower with small fingers firmly on her arm. Not gently. Not even looking at her. Male. Impatient. In command. She pursed her lips to hide a grin as she settled down and sat next to him. He unrolled the frayed comic book and laid it flat on the sand. He opened the book to its middle and pressed the pages smooth.

Word balloons in English. Faded colors. Dog ears, creases, rips. Fifties superheroes bulked up and zooming across pulp. The Green Hornet, Captain Marvel, Wonder Woman, and some lantern-jawed freak in Army fatigues popping his buttons and swinging on a rope. Standard U.S. drugstore issue printed back when cub scouts were the toughest gang in town.

"Where did you get it?"

The boy didn't answer her question. He slowly turned pages, deep in concentration. He found what he was looking for. Being careful with the worn paper, he pressed the open pages flat once more.

A small brown fingertip tapped gently up and down on a panel showing Wonder Woman and the button-popping figure in fatigues dismantling a sleazy group of opponents with a magic rope and flying fists.

Bam! Biff! Kazow!

"We can get them," he said.

Evvie raised her eyebrows and nodded. And had to smile again. "Maybe we can."

The boy closed the comic book and rolled it up. He looked around and behind. Nobody was near. He stood up and pulled Evvie to her feet. He brushed sand off her skirt. "I got this from a boy who came to the island with his family to trade for molas," he said. "I gave him a spirit boat and he gave me this."

Evvie realized that, to Niki, the comic book was a part of the world of gleaming planes that split the high San Blas sky and of the great steel ships that moved like living mountains on the Cuna horizon. A world where justice came on lightning bolts and bad guys always lost. Evvie wanted to pick Niki up and hug him, but the thought of further encouraging him to do something that would get him backhanded into eternity stopped her.

She didn't know what to say.

So he said it. "Goodbye." He turned and walked off toward the others.

One by one, the Cunas came to Evvie. A few said words, but eyes said more. Some only touched her.

Then Nagolo came and sat by her. His words said plainly what the other Cunas said with looks. "Those like Ile are children of the moon. They are descended from the first chief who came down from heaven. We call the white-skinned Cuna *ibepundor.* To us, they are special. They are from the gods. They are different, like you are different." He extended both hands, palms up, fingers together, toward her breasts. The gesture was made openly in reverence. "Are you a god? Are you *Mu?* We talk of these things by the night fire. Have you been sent to help us?"

"Don't do this to me, Nagolo. I'm no god," she said. "If I were a god, these men would be inside sharks."

"You came from the storm. You threw El Codo's big man, the dirty one, into the sea with words. You walk with El Codo and he does not hurt you. You sleep in his hut and you do not scream. You make the young white man save Ile."

Evvie turned quickly on Nagolo. "If you think like that, you won't fight when the time comes to fight. Don't hope for miracles. It's worse than being afraid. Hope kills courage." Evvie was startled by her own words. She wondered why she'd said them, where they came from.

"Then what you do is only something from a human heart?" asked Nagolo.

"A heart like yours. A heart like Olonaya's."

Nagolo knelt beside her and stared. Evvie felt uncomfortable.

"But if you have magic," he said, "you do not need to be near these men to help us. You could help us from the safety of the sea. Your magic could come from another island where you would not be hurt. Am I right?"

"You are wrong. I am no god."

"Well, I think you must be a god. But if you are not ..." He seemed lost in thought for a moment.

She waited.

"... then we must help you. Because you have saved Ile."

"What can you do? How can you help me?" Her heart beat harder.

"A cayuco. In the night. I cannot escape or Codo kills my people. But you could try. Do you know how to work the cayuco?"

Evvie had stepped into a cayuco only once. Back in Colon, Davis, half-drunk, persuaded two Cuna fishermen to let Ted and her try to paddle one in Gatun Lake. They turned it over in five seconds. They wouldn't get fifty feet into the Holandes Channel. She pictured Ted with the anchor chained around his neck. She shivered at the image of him sinking beneath dark water. And El Codo had the black motor boats. Fast pursuit boats. Plus the twenty-four-hour guard who was posted by the launches to prevent a mass exodus by the Cunas.

She saw no chance that she and Ted could escape in the cayucos. None at all.

"No, Nagolo ... the cayuco will not work for us."

Bibi, Nagolo's child, pushed between them and flopped onto her father's leg. Nagolo tickled the little girl's nose. Evvie reached out and lifted Bibi, then turned the child around and sat the small brown body on her lap so they both faced the sea. She wrapped her arms around Bibi and held her. She closed her eyes and thought of all the times she had held Cindy that way on a beach far away.

Evvie walked between dark trees. It was after nine at night, thirty minutes past the time she was to be in El Codo's hut. She'd gone to his door, but he had been with one of his men and had curtly waved her away with a flick of his wrist. She had seen maps on a table, papers, a black radio with its antenna extended.

In the light of a quarter moon the island reminded her of a large empty room beneath the canopy of coconut palms. Clumps of brush and vine grew in only a few places, mostly at the south end of the island and behind some of the huts. The earth under her bare feet was smooth, burnished by the comings and goings of many generations of Cuna families. Karatuppu, like all the other Cuna islands, was no more than six feet above sea level at any point. More billiard table than island. Coconut palms formed a solid roof over all but the collar of beach.

She passed the Cuna gathering hut, looked in, and saw brown faces lit by the fire burning at the ends of three logs pushed together like the spokes of a wheel. As the fire burned, the logs would be pushed forward to feed the flame through the night.

As she walked south toward the deserted end of the island, she wondered what the Cunas would be talking about if there were no El Codo on the island, no brutal Colombians, no Evvie and Ted. Perhaps they would talk about the children. About other islands. Food that was needed. Maybe the latest gossip. Like families everywhere, anywhere. And religion. They'd talk about religion more than most. She knew Cunas feared the dark. She'd read in Arthur's book how the Indian night belonged to devils ... the Nia who rose out of the earth seeking vengeance; the Massar Turpa; and the most feared of all, Purkwet Kala, the flying skeleton that soared through black shadows with a basket strapped to his back, a basket that carried the monster Kanir Sikwi whose gruesome screams were the portent of immediate death. When Olonaya had described the devil spirit on Piryatuppu with respect and fear in her eyes, Evvie realized how deeply the Cunas believed in their primitive fairy tales.

That evening, an hour earlier, while she ate rice and fish with the Indians, the rough laughter of El Codo's men drinking rum and mescal at the north end of the island haunted the night. The Indians tried to talk with her about the children and small things, but the noise of the men brought fear. The dark hours would be sleepless ones. Codo's men might come to the gathering house. Women might be taken out. Cuna men beaten. Each noise in the night made eyes look at eyes. Each silence trembled, waiting.

She'd seen Mark and Ile leave their hut at twilight. He had started to walk her to the gathering house, then stopped. Their hands touched. And Ile had continued alone beneath the trees.

As Evvie neared the island's south end, the canopy of palms thinned. Low clumps of brush began to take shape. She came to the water. Small waves from the gulf rippled toward the shore over the shallows, and she pictured the Cuna children playing and splashing earlier in the day, the children laughing in the sun, unaware of the building horror under the trees. In her mind she saw the smiles, the beautiful eyes, the water running down small brown bodies. The freedom of not knowing.

The image of arms and legs and bare backsides pulled up another image. Ted! In the cockpit! The transmitter ... the transmitter!

Does he have it? Did he hide it on the island?

She lowered herself to the sand and sat facing the water. Her heart raced. Mind searched memory.

If you have the transmitter, why haven't you used it? We're in trouble. All of us. Bad trouble. What the hell are you waiting for?

She recalled what Ted had told her when he still worked for the Drug Enforcement Agency, how drug traffickers used Central American countries as transit points for shipments coming out of Cartegena. And then Olonaya's words about the men being Colombian.

The pieces of the puzzle teetered, were about to fall into place, when her thoughts were disrupted by a sharp out-of-place stench. Pig smell. Whisky smell. Filth.

She spun around on the sand and froze on hands and knees. She stared at dark shadows.

A large male shape loomed above the brush thirty feet away. He had come silently. So silently that, if not for the smell, he could have come close enough to grab her.

She crouched like a cornered cat.

"Whore." The rasping voice of the man she'd put in the channel. "Codo's slut whore." The words were full of hate and slurred by drink. "Codo's freak slut."

He ripped off his shirt and slipped out of his pants without undoing belt or button. He wore nothing else. "It's time, whore. It's time for you."

A menacing silhouette. No detail showing. Only the massive outline of him.

Evvie scuttled six feet to her right like a crab. Toes and fingertips carried most of her weight now.

The dark shape moved to that side also, keeping between her and the center of the island. Cutting her off.

Evvie backed toward the water.

"Bitch!" A rasping snarl. "I've seen your husband naked in the sun. He is not a man. He is a boy. I am Toro. I will show you what a whore should know. I will fill you, whore! Fill you up and kill you. I will kill El Codo's slut whore!"

Her feet touched water. She glanced left, then right. Neither side offered an advantage. Both strips of beach were narrow and curved away from her around her attacker. He had the center.

He took two quick steps toward her. Though the man was fat and drunk, his agility surprised her. She backed farther. Water covered her hands. Both her legs were submerged to mid-thigh. The red rag dressing that covered the slice on her leg sucked up salt water. Stinging pain shot up her thigh. Without taking her eyes off him, she undid the rope around her waist with her right hand. She pushed the ankle-length half-dress down past her knees and kicked out of it. If she had to run, if she had to fight, she could not do so wearing the restricting skirt. With the same hand she unknotted the red rag. The dressing unwound itself in the water. She knew from the hand-to-hand stuff she'd learned from Ted in California that she couldn't give the opponent anything to hold on to, not even that.

Completely naked, her body a pale smoke in the tropic night, she waited.

He charged.

Each closing step doubled the size of him. She dug her toes and fingers into hard sand. She coiled back on her haunches. He'd expect her to scramble sideways to the right or left. He would guess which way. If he guessed correctly, he'd pin her. She'd be finished.

Fifty-fifty seemed like bad odds.

His leading foot splashed into water, six feet in front of her face. She uncoiled straight at his center.

The top of her skull thudded into the flesh of his gut below the navel, and the impact drove her head back. She thought she had broken her neck. Yellow light flashed through her brain, and she had to shake her head to make the light go away. She was down on her belly in the shallows with only her head and shoulders above water. She tried to focus her eyes.

He was flat on his rear end in foot-deep water in front of her. One of his arms was behind him, propping him up. The other was folded across his stomach. He was making an odd, desperate, wheezing sound as if a full-grown man were trying to inhale through an infant's nostrils.

She shook her head again to clear her brain. The yellow light dissolved into a spiral of white stars somewhere behind her eyes. Both her arms were numb.

They were close enough so that, when he vomited, rancid spittle sprayed her face. He gasped for air and retched again.

She staggered to her feet. The feeling in her arms was back. Only her fingers tingled. She took a few uncertain steps, then started to run. She veered left and covered fifty yards before she realized that the soft sand was cutting her speed by half.

Running in a nightmare.

Moving like she was underwater.

Struggling in slow motion.

The water! Hard sand there!

She angled toward the saving shadow where small waves sparkled.

But the downward slope mixed up her stride, and she began to stumble. She tried to make her feet behave, but the deep sand only shifted more. Her arms splayed out in front of her, and she pitched headfirst onto her face.

Her mouth filled with grit.

She scrambled on all fours for the water.

Her hands splashed. She tried to regain her footing. She leaned forward like a sprinter coming out of the blocks. Too much fear. Too much lean. She stumbled and fell again. This time the taste of salt.

She gasped for air.

Then spit sand and seawater.

Back on her feet. Hard sand at last. Ten accelerating strides. Solid, hard, wet, beautiful sand. Long leg muscles fed the speed.

She was hit from the side by a wrecking ball.

The world went black as her head was driven underwater by a massive slippery weight.

Her next breath filled her throat with liquid.

Her left arm was twisted behind her back in a vice of fat fingers. She took a hammering blow to her rib cage. Left side. High. Close to the armpit. Another smashing punch rammed her in the same place.

The two hits froze her breathing muscles. Her face pressed against suffocating shell and sand beneath the water's surface. She tried to make her jaw chew air. It chewed grit and ocean instead.

A black cotton ball began to expand inside her brain.

The cotton ball grew larger until all the muscles in her body quit. One by one they quit.

She was being dragged by one leg across the sand. Her eyes fluttered open. Against the night sky she saw the outline of the fat monster that pulled her up the slope of the beach.

Sand became dirt, then sticks, brambles, and the hard turns of roots scratched and tore her back.

The dragging stopped.

The brutal thing seized her other leg, and the legs were scissored in a sharp twist that flipped her over onto her stomach.

Her legs were let go. She lay face down in a tangle of brush.

She tried to breathe. Raw bits of air began to find her lungs.

But she couldn't make her muscles work, and when her legs were spread apart, she could not bring them back together.

Death seemed a quiet hoped-for answer to the nightmare.

Some animal obscenity pressed at the flesh of her sex and started to force an entry.

Then the blunt heat that had pushed partway into her was gone.

Silence.

A wet cloth dropped onto the skin of her neck. It wiped at scratches she was only beginning to feel. A strong hand turned her over. She was eased up into a sitting position, her back resting against the chest of someone sitting behind her. The cloth that had touched her neck touched her face. Rough strokes brushed caked sand from her eyes and lips.

Her eyes opened. She couldn't see who helped her, who cleaned her

face with the cloth, but ten feet beyond her toes she could see the outline of a body propped against a bush, the beast who had attacked her.

She squinted.

Her eyes adapted to the low light.

The skull was not shaped right.

The fat freak who had assualted her had half a head. It was sliced
vertically down the middle. She saw that the vertical cut had been
transected by a horizontal cut. The half of the head that was missing was
hacked away like a watermelon might be sliced apart at a picnic. She
knew that the vertical cut had been made first because the machete that
made the cuts still gleamed in the light of the quarter moon, still rested
horizontally where it had stopped after traveling partway into the half of
the neck that remained.

El Codo bent forward to light the candle on the floor of his hut. "I
do not like to kill my own men," he said. "It is expensive. I told you not
to walk in the night. Now I am missing a man I need. Have you eaten?"

El Codo's unholy detachment still shocked her, but she was too exhausted to react. Rape ... Murder ... Food. One and the same. "I ate
with Olonaya."

"Yes. I know that one."

"How did ..."

"What did you have?" he asked.

"Have?"

"To eat. What did you have to eat?"

"I had fish to eat."

"Fish?"

"Yes."

"Do you know how they make the fish? The women chew it first.
Then they spit it into a bowl. Did you know that?"

"Yes."

"You must have a big hunger to eat fish like that."

She nodded.

"A very big hunger," he said.

She nodded once more.

"You can sleep now. Sleep next to me. Like before."

"Yes."

Chapter 16

Arthur finished whipping the end of one of Susurro's mooring lines. He melted the cut end of the nylon rope in the flame of his cigarette lighter and used the blade of a screwdriver to mash the hot strands together to form a flat surface. He rolled the cut end in his hand and checked the work. Then he coiled the line and flipped it forward onto the starboard seat.

He leaned back against Susurro's cockpit coaming and lit a cigarette. A strong smell of spilled diesel fuel drifted over the yacht-club finger piers. The water's surface glistened with the metallic sheen of floating petroleum.

His eyes policed Susurro's deck, her dock lines, her rigging. Everything was in its proper place. He passed a few minutes looking at the boat tied in the slip next to his. Then his eyes moved past it, and he saw a solitary figure standing in the sun by the paint shed above the access ramp. The Cuna woman. The one who waited each day for Davis when the man was in the bar or out sailing. The Indian called Dulcie. Staring at him.

She raised one hand in front of her chest. The hand moved a bit, a subtle move that told him to come.

The two of them squatted in the shadow of the boat barn at the east end of the yard. A place where no one walked.

"I can tell you one thing," Dulcie repeated. "Evvie's in trouble. A lot of trouble."

Arthur studied Dulcie's face, her hands, and he saw fear shaking the material of the blouse she wore where the fabric hung down from her left wrist. What she had just finished telling him was almost beyond belief, but she was frightened, close to breaking down, and he knew she told the truth.

"How much time before? ..."

"Not much," said Dulcie. "It could be too late, already. At least for her."

"Can you tell me any more?"

"Only that what I'm doing is all that I can do. It has to be you. Someone like you. There is no one else. Not the police. Not the government. No one."

"Davis?"

"Not him. Especially not him."

"Couldn't you have done something? Warned her somehow?"

"I tried to stop her. To have her hurt. So she could not go."

"Only tried?"

The Indian drew up. Anger flashed in her eyes.

"I'm sorry," said Arthur.

"I'm sorry, too."

Arthur slowly shook his head. "Looks like nobody plays by the rules anymore."

Two hours later, a small white sailboat passed between the twin towers of Limon Bay. It sailed out to sea beneath a lowering sky. One man sat by the tiller.

Sussuro traveled due north for twelve miles.

Then tacked and headed east.

Karatuppu ran with rain. It smothered the island. Relentless curtains of water swept in from the sea from dawn to twilight and into the night. The hard-packed dirt under the palms was soaked and slick. Small lakes formed in each depression. Yellow fronds broke loose from older trees and littered the shallow pools like huge lost feathers. Branches of waterlogged thatch sagged along the horizontal lodge poles of the Cuna houses. El Codo's two boats had been turned upside down in the tree line, and their metal skins shed rivers of rainwater from chines and stern boards. The earth beneath the canopy of leaves was deserted.

At the north end of the island a grimy stream of rain mixed with ash from a fire pit meandered past empty rum bottles down to the channel. Old footprints in the sand became unfocused hollows, their outlines muted by the rain. They filled with water that floated a gray-brown scum of tiny things that sand surrendered when sand got wet.

At the south end of the island gulls walked around a dripping bush and pecked and fought for tidbits from a meaty treasure they discovered there. The fat one's body had been buried in a trench at midnight, but the two men who buried the body had missed finding the wayward half of head.

Gulls squabbled in the rain and jumped away from gulls that had no morsel.

On the channel side of the island and floating at the water's edge, four Cuna cayucos tied to a fallen palm tree gradually filled with rain and sank to the level of their toprails. On the painted edge of one of the swamped canoes a stranded population of brown ants hurried east and west in a desperate search for salvation.

A rolling mist blanketed the mainland far to the south, and banks of rain moved toward the mist. Waves lay down despite a restive wind.

Everywhere on Karatuppu the sound of water dripping from the coconut palm trees.

Onto bushes. Into puddles. Even inside the huts.

Evvie sat next to Olonaya and held Bibi while the Cuna woman sewed colors into a mola.

"There were eight men," said Olonaya. "Now there are seven."

Evvie's lost dress had been replaced by a pair of men's sweat pants. El Codo had taken the pants from the duffel of the dead man. The bottom edges were rolled up, and the extra material at the waist was bunched in a knot that made Evvie look like a small child playing dress-up in a father's clothes. She wore only the sweat pants, her intimate parts pressing where his parts had pressed. She gently rocked the child and stared with no expression into the flickering flame at the hub of the fire logs.

It was early evening. Evvie had spent the entire day in the gathering house. She had gone out only three times, twice to relieve herself in the shack over the water and once to bathe the cuts on her body with salt water near the rain-filled cayucos. The rest of the time she'd held the baby and watched Olonaya and listened to the rain.

Evvie drifted in a mire of confused exhaustion. The image of her attacker, his skull split down the middle, floated in and out of her consciousness. The aftermath of terror dripped inside her like a slow narcotic. The hollows in her spirit were awash with muted memories: of running in slow motion; the panic of being held under water; the suffocating sand; the acid residue of bone-deep pain after the physical beating; helplessness; the debasing evil of El Codo and his men. She was almost out of energy, almost out of will.

But not quite.

Dazed and enervated, she knew, somewhere deep inside, that she was still herself, still Evvie. The resilience of the human spirit, pushed to the edge, had not stepped over that edge. The flame, though small, still burned. Had she been confronted again, even with a terror as hideous as that of the past night, she would have snapped out of her trance and would have fought. But there in the gathering house, beside the fire, holding Bibi in her arms, there was no terror. Only the memory of terror.

A black night wrapped around Karatuppu. Nagolo came in from the storm. He'd been gone for more than an hour. He handed three fresh fish to the young Cuna girl who had dressed Evvie's leg with the red rag, then he sat down next to Olonaya.

Evvie tried to make herself listen to Nagolo talk of fishing. And the weather. She heard Olonaya mention Cuna gods and how they might protect the family from the men, but there was nothing in their words to make her think that Nagolo and Olonaya reached a conclusion that had not been reached before.

Whenever the Cunas talked in her presence, they talked in Spanish, a courtesy Evvie had noticed from the start, a kind decent thing that made her know she was a part of them.

As she held Bibi and stared into the fire, she heard Olonaya and Nagolo switch to the Cuna dialect. No Spanish words. None at all.

Minutes passed. The tone of Olonaya's words changed. When Evvie looked closer, she saw that Olonaya wept. Tears dropped from brown skin onto the mola and disappeared into the fabric. But Evvie drifted in yesterday's nightmare, and so she only watched.

Bibi stirred. The feel of the baby in her arms began to call Evvie back.

She saw that Nagolo was on his knees, his hands on his wife's shoulders. Then Nagolo got up and walked to the door of the gathering house. He looked out at the rain. After a few minutes, he came back and sat next to Evvie.

Olonaya put down her sewing and lifted Bibi out of Evvie's arms.

Nagolo spoke in a low voice. "What happened last night must not happen to you again," he said.

Nagolo. A nice man. She turned away to look at Bibi.

"Look at me, Evvie." She turned back to him.

His words were stern. Like he was talking to a child. "This will get worse if we do not fix it," he said. "We must do more than watch the evil come. Each night the men get more like animals." He looked at Olonaya, then back at Evvie. "The spirit light is leaving your eyes. That must not happen. That must not be seen by El Codo."

"El Codo," Evvie repeated.

Nagolo looked into the fire. "I think there is a way."

She smiled a vacant smile. "Way?"

"The rain will stay for many hours. I will take you from this island in my cayuco. Tonight. Now. I will bring your husband. He is not watched. He sleeps by himself on the other shore. The rain will keep the others inside."

She tried to concentrate on what he said. His words were like a cool wind moving in her mind, a wind that started to blow all the bits of fear and confusion in one direction like dead leaves being pushed across a winter surface. Reason flickered. She began to focus.

A gust from the sea breathed on embers in the fire pit. The embers glowed brightly.

"Right now? Tonight?" Her mind began to accept possibilities. "You can take us away from this place?"

"I will try."

"And Ted? We can take Ted with us?"

"I will bring him to the beach. The rain will protect us. My cayuco is fast."

Evvie remembered the Cuna fear of the night. The Indians fought terror just to walk their islands after dark. To go out onto the sea? ... "You are very brave, Nagolo."

"You have spirit magic. You have strong *uchus* to help you. You have made El Codo kill the man for you. You will protect us. I am not afraid."

Evvie turned to look at Olonaya. A cold realization came. She turned to Nagolo. "The others ... Olonaya and Bibi," she said. "They'll be—"

"I will come back. I will make the cayuco hurry. I will take you to a safe place."

"El Codo will know. I must sleep in his hut tonight. In three hours. If I'm not there he'll search. He'll know you—"

"I will come back and let the wind take the cayuco out to the ocean. El Codo will not know that I helped you."

"Nagolo, you—"

"Before we go I will tell one of them that I am going to get fish from the shallow waters behind the long reef. We do that many times. We do not need the cayuco to fish there. They know the rain brings the fish to that place. I think they will believe that. I think they will believe also that you went in the cayuco only with your husband."

"This is too dangerous."

"It is more dangerous if we do nothing."

"I need to think."

"No more thinking. The rain is now. The wind comes from the sea. The cayuco will go fast."

She turned to look at Olonaya, who was holding Bibi. Olonaya was staring into the fire.

Evvie pulled one of Olonaya's scarfs tightly around her head and neck. She waited just inside the open door of the gathering house.

"Now," said Olonaya. "Now. Walk slowly. Goodbye, Evvie."

Evvie hugged Olonaya and kissed Bibi, then stepped through the curtain of water pouring from the eaves.

She walked through pools of rain toward the shack built over the water. If anyone should be watching, she was going there to answer nature's call. She moved carefully beneath dripping palms in the darkness. She couldn't see more than ten feet ahead. She tried to will away the shivers that raced down her arms and back.

She reached the shack, did not go in, and crouched on hard sand at the shoreline. The warm water of the coral plateau lapped over her feet and ankles.

Five minutes. Ten minutes.

She heard quick splashes. Feet pounded through shallow water. The sound came toward her from the right. A curl of white took shape in the rain, the bow wave of a dugout canoe moving quickly parallel to the beach. Then she saw Nagolo bent low and pushing the wooden boat at a run like someone shoving a sled through snow.

"Get in! Get in the front!"

She scrambled over the side into the bow. She kneeled in cold rain-water and steadied herself in the narrow dugout by holding on to the top edge of each side. The cayuco pivoted toward the channel.

Nagolo, still out of the boat, pushed hard from behind. Fifty yards out. A hundred.

The sound made by his legs became heavier, and she knew they were in deep water. Suddenly the cayuco tilted hard to port as Nagolo rolled into the stern. Even before the boat righted itself Evvie heard the heavy wooden paddle break the surface. She had to brace herself against the powerful surge of Nagolo's first stroke.

"Where is Ted?" She asked the question without turning her head. They plunged through heavy rain toward the channel. She was hypno-tized by the black void in front of her. She couldn't take her eyes off it, couldn't turn to look at Nagolo.

"There is a paddle behind you! In the middle of the boat."

She let go of the starboard gunwale and reached back with her right hand. Her fingers touched wood floating on rainwater that slopped in the bilge. She worked the paddle forward, then picked it up and began to use it. Her first strokes were awkward and out of sync with his. When her blade hit the water, it lurched backward; the force driving the boat forward was more than she could generate to keep pace. She concen-trated hard. She took her eyes off the emptiness over the bow. In less than a minute her stroke matched his, if not in power, at least in rhythm. The boat cut across the drop-off at the edge of the plateau into a heavy chop of two-foot waves. They were into the deep Holandes Channel.

After two minutes, the rhythm was automatic.

"Nagolo! Where's Ted?"

No answer.

"Nagolo! Are we going to pick him up? Are we going to pick him up on the other side of the island?" She stopped paddling and twisted around to look at him.

Nagolo kept driving his paddle into the sea with powerful strokes. "He would not come!"

Not come?

Cold rain wasn't cold anymore. The mental fog she thought was gone drifted back in.

Nagolo spoke again: "He said it wouldn't work. He said we'd be caught."

Not come?

She managed to speak. "We have to go back."

Nagolo continued to paddle, each hard stroke taking her farther away from Ted. "He told me not to do it!" Nagolo had to shout over a sudden rush of rain and wind. "I told him we had to try. He said he would not let us go."

Evvie slowly turned forward and stared over the bow.

More shouted words came to her from the stern. "I told him what they did to you! And still he said to stay."

"We must go back." Her soft words were not heard.

They had altered course slightly to south of west and were a half-mile offshore when Ted's howling shriek, carried to them on the wind, froze Nagolo's stroke.

Then came again.

"Evvieee! …" The long wavering cry pierced the darkness like a banshee wail.

"Evvieee!"

She felt the boat surge as Nagolo's paddle slashed into the water again. She was with him by the third stroke. Together they drove the cayuco faster than before. Nagolo turned the boat back to the west, directly away from Karatuppu. Evvie was up on her knees. She attacked the black water with long deep sweeps of her paddle. She worked as hard as she had ever worked in her life. Cold water sloshed violently in the bilge. The small boat shuddered every three seconds in response to the powerful pulse of their effort. The cayuco took the channel waves broad on its starboard side, not on the stern quarter as before, because the only thing that mattered was to gain as much distance from the island as possible. Whatever destination Nagolo had in mind was no longer important. She remembered from the charts on Coconut that, by going west from the Holandes, they would miss the other islands. And they would miss them to seaward. They were angled toward the open ocean.

The rain began to ease.

She could see farther ahead. Twenty feet. Then forty. Fifty feet. She could make out the white tops of waves breaking in darkness even farther than that.

Don't stop raining. Rain! Hard!

The fabric of the sweat pants had worn through at the knees. Saltwater was mixing with rainwater in the bilge, and she could feel the sting of the brine as she knelt and worked the oar. But pain was nothing now—knees, back, arms. She knew only the rhythm of the paddling.

Behind them to the east they heard the whine of an outboard motor. A few moments later the sound changed and became a buzzing harmony as it was joined by a second outboard. El Codo had launched both boats.

How far? How far away are they?

She wanted to ask Nagolo these questions and more, but the answers wouldn't have made any difference. The only real answer was escape.

"In front of you. There's a can on a line in front of you."

She shipped her paddle and leaned forward. She found the can under the bilge water.

"I have it!" she shouted. She didn't need to be told what to do. She began to bail with furious energy. She worked quickly. Despite the physical effort of bailing the boat, she felt relief as her long muscles recovered from the stress of working the paddle.

The rain became a drizzle.

Far to the southeast, between them and the mainland, the sound of the boat engines began to fade.

We're going to make it!

She began paddling again. She could see two hundred yards. The clouds still boiled on all sides, but overhead they had parted and some stars appeared.

Don't let the storm stop.

She guessed they were in the middle of the channel when he spoke to her again. This time he spoke softly because the rain was gone. The sound of their voices would carry.

"We must sink the boat. Don't let your paddle float away."

Sink the boat?

"Nagolo, we don't have to. ... I can't hear them anymore. They've gone the other way."

They both rested. The cayuco slowed. In the absence of the rain and the noise of paddling, a silence fell like damp velvet on their world.

Only the rustle of small waves capping and the clink of the bailing can floating in the bilge intruded on the quiet.

"We must go into the water," he said. "We must hide in the sea."

"Listen, Nagolo. They've gone. I can't hear them."

The sound of the outboards had faded away under the curtain of rain still falling to the south. The cayuco coasted to a stop.

"They have gone south to cut us off. They know we are here. We cannot reach another island. There was not enough time."

"What will they do?"

"They will turn soon and come up the channel in a way that crosses from side to side. They will not use the lights until they turn. That way they will not be seen by anyone from the land."

"But the channel is so big. It's at least three miles wide."

"They will come. They will find us if we are like this. We must go into the water."

Evvie looked over the side. Black water. Over a hundred feet deep. They weren't past the perimeter of the barrier reef, but they were on the ocean side of all the islands.

She thought of sharks. She knew they cruised the dark depths along the reef and forayed at night into the deeper channels, channels like the one they were in now, the channel that emptied the western end of the Gulf of San Blas and carried all the things sharks ate.

The current going out. The breeding ground. The outer reefs where ocean rollers threw tons of water at the moon.

No life jackets. No way to signal for help.

And then she thought of El Codo.

"How do we do it?" she asked. "How do we get into the water?"

He went over the side first, then took her paddle and held it along with his own while he steadied the boat for her. Evvie rolled into the sea.

He tied the paddles to the short line at the bow, and they pushed the starboard gunwale under. The cedar cayuco filled with water and floated with its rails awash.

"Now you climb back in," he said. "I will steady the boat."

"Why get back in? It's full of water."

"Your knees. You are bleeding. It would be best for us if you stay in the boat."

She knew the reason. Though small waves broke into and out of the flooded cayuco, most of the water would remain inside. There wasn't much bleeding, but it didn't take much to draw the sharks.

Evvie pulled herself over the gunwale and knelt in the center of the swamped cayuco.

Ten minutes passed before they saw the first spotlight on the water. It gleamed a long way off, perhaps four miles away. It moved slowly, then disappeared and reappeared to the left. Nagolo saw the second light two minutes later. The boats were criss-crossing the channel in a grid pattern. The slow lateral progress of the lights made Evvie think the boats weren't getting closer, but she knew they were.

Nagolo's hand reached out of the water and touched her arm. In the thin light of the quarter moon she could see he held out a necklace, a string of cowry shells he had taken from around his neck.

"Here," he said. "Put these on."

She took the necklace and looked at it. "These are the shells Olonaya wears," she said.

"Wear them. They are to protect you." His words were calm, too calm. In the low light, Evvie stared at the smooth folded shape of one shell on the string.

"The shells are of the earth mother, *Mu,*" he said. "They are shaped like the place on a woman where the child comes out to enter the world. They are worn in time of danger. In the storms. In the sickness. They are worn when the baby comes. They have strong magic."

Evvie put the necklace on. He needed as much luck as she needed, more if they were caught, but she knew that a gift like this was given to be received. "Thank you, Nagolo."

To the south the lights moved back and forth across the channel. They looked no closer than before.

More minutes passed in silence beneath a clearing sky. "Why haven't I seen any guns, Nagolo? Don't they have guns?"

"El Codo keeps the guns, now. Some of the others still have the knives. I think the guns are kept away because of the drinking and the fighting."

"Where does he keep the guns?"

"I do not know."

She was out of the swamped boat and back in the water again where it was warmer. The noise of something powerful churned the surface to their left. Evvie was surprised when the sound didn't make her afraid. A feeding shark was nothing compared to El Codo.

Like condemned prisoners waiting, they began to talk of small things. There was nothing else to do.

"The men haven't taken the gold rings the women wear," she said. "Or the bracelets. Why haven't they taken the gold?"

"It is not so valuable in money. They know that. But they would take the gold if El Codo did not tell them to leave it alone. Maybe they will take the gold when they go away."

Evvie didn't say anything, and Nagolo spoke again.

"If they take the gold now, there would be much anger. He knows the gold is a spirit thing for us. It is the love of a mother for a daughter. Perhaps then he would have to kill us all. I think he knows that we must go each time to the mainland to get wood and water. If we do not do that, there are those who would come to see what is wrong."

"Why do you go to the jungle for water? You can catch the rain."

"The gods gave us the long rivers many years ago when we were children of the mountains. The rivers gave us many things in that time. Food. Drink. A way to escape the white ones who came with death from the west. To forget such a gift is not our way."

The moving lights were closer, three miles away. The faint sound of the motors traveled over the water like the hum of mosquitoes on a summer night.

"How did you meet her?"

"We met first at the *inna* feast in Ciedras Village. It is the feast when a Cuna girl becomes a woman. It is a time of big celebration. Much *chicha* to drink. Too much. And many hours of tobacco."

"Was it Olonaya's time? Was it her *inna?*"

"No. It was after that." She saw him smile. White teeth flashed like the tops of small waves breaking on dark water. "She was beautiful then like she is now. I went from her hammock four times before I went to collect wood for her father. It is the custom of the Cuna that the man is brought to the hammock by the family of the wife. Then he runs away.

The leaving is what the man does to prove he does not want her, that he is strong. It is the custom to run away at least two times. But never more than four times. If he runs away more than four times, there is no marriage. The bringing of the wood to the father shows that the man agrees to marry. I did not want to let the village know how much I loved her. I tried to be cold in my blood. That is why I went away four times. But she knew."

Two miles away.

"The girl Ile. Will she be all right?"

"The white man, the young one, he did not make her have him. He is not like the others. What you did for Ile, it was a good thing."

"The sun. Was she burned?"

"She can see shadows. Some of those with the white skin do not burn too much in the sun. It is in their spirit. Ile did not burn much in the sun. Only her eyes. They will see again in three days." Nagolo paused, then asked, "The young man. The one called Mark. Will he help us?"

"I don't know."

One-half mile. She could feel engine vibrations on her skin.

"I think you will be strong," he said. "Just pray to your spirits."

"I'm so afraid of those men."

"I do not think you are so afraid or you would not fight them like you do. I think you are more angry than afraid."

She watched the lights move far apart to opposite sides of the channel.

"I will do this," said Nagolo. "I will push the boat toward them. You swim away. I will tell them that you are under the water, that you have drowned."

She looked at him. He didn't look at her, but kept his eyes on the light to the left, the light nearest Karatuppu.

"You will take one of the paddles," he said. "It will let you float on the sea. I think the morning current will move you to an island over there." He pointed to the southwest.

"No. We stay together."

He was silent as he watched the lights begin to converge again. He let go of the boat and swam around Evvie to the bow. He untied the two paddles from the end of the mooring line and pushed one of the paddles toward her.

"We will try to trick them," he said. "Come."

Nagolo started to stroke toward the point where the boats would cross. He used one hand to hold the paddle in front of him and swam with his free arm. She did the same and followed. As they moved away from the cayuco, she heard the gurgling noise the waves made when they broke over the abandoned boat wallowing low in the water. She stopped and looked back. She had not been aware of the noise before. Nor had she been aware of how the small waves breaking over the sides of the cayuco framed it in white. She realized why Nagolo had decided to leave the swamped boat.

He waited for her to catch up. "Swim next to my side," he said. "We must be together on the waves. We will be harder to see that way. It will not be so easy to find us if we are hidden at the same time."

After swimming for another five minutes, Evvie realized what Nagolo was trying to do. If they could get close enough without being seen, they would be able to swim south between the searching boats. The escape had to be timed perfectly. They had to get through after the two boats crossed each other and were heading in opposite directions out to the sides of the channel once more. She and Nagolo had to make it through the gap before the boats turned and converged again.

"We're too close," she whispered. She was sure that they were going to be at the mid-point before the boats got there.

Nagolo slowed, but still moved forward. "We have to be close," he said.

Her heart pounded. It wasn't the deep water, the dark, the fear of a shark slamming into her belly and pulling her under. It was the skin-crawling thought of El Codo and his men and what would happen if she and Nagolo were caught. She knew that she had been treated with surprising restraint by the monster. She'd heard the remarks and seen the astonished looks of El Codo's own men as they watched him parade her around the island. But always beneath that bemused look of his was the icy indifference, the mile-deep evil, the promise that when indifference moved, it would move toward violence.

Nagolo stopped swimming. The waves had subsided. The water was almost flat. They were in some sort of upwelling above an underwater mount on the bottom of the channel. She'd seen these smooth spots when she and Ted had sailed Coconut through the same pass five days earlier, five days that seemed a lifetime away.

They waited.

The upwelling tried to pull them apart. Nagolo reached over and held her hand to keep them together.

They were spun around again and again in the strangely calm but twisting water as the lights rapidly closed. The drumming of the motors tattooed her torso.

She noticed a spreading pattern of ripples on the water around the blade of her paddle, and wondered what caused it, then realized that it was caused by her trembling.

She and Nagolo, side by side and holding tightly together, lowered a few last inches into the sea to the level of their nostrils. They held on to the floating paddles with fingertips and moved only their legs to keep position. Nagolo moved closer until the sides of their heads touched at the temple, then he freed the hand that held hers and moved it to press her head against his to break up their silhouettes, to make a shape less recognizable to those searching for human shapes.

The boats were two hundred yards apart and closing.

The upwelling slowly pushed Evvie and Nagolo toward the point where the boats would cross.

But they could not swim now … only drift and pray and try not to gag on water that tried to get through nostrils into throats.

One hundred yards separated the boats.

Bright spotlights played back and forth over the black surface and seemed to illuminate the water well past the edge of concealment.

We're too close!

They were less than a hundred feet from the place the boats would meet.

She heard male voices.

Words passed between the two boats.

Propellers thumped water.

Her heart ricocheted inside her chest.

Nagolo's hand moved from where it pressed her head against his and found the string of cowry shells around her neck. He grasped a length of necklace, and the hand moved back up to press again, and Evvie felt the hard pressure of the shells against her ear.

The water around them seemed lit by the sun.

But no one saw.

The boats crossed.

Evvie dared a silent breath.

Nagolo let the strand of necklace fall from his hand. Under the water, Evvie felt the small shells settle on the skin of her neck ... tiny weights, tickling pressures, small sensations magnified a hundred times by fear.

Slowly they began to swim forward, barely feathering more than toes and fingers, barely stirring the surface as the boat lights receded on either side.

Darkness settled on the water.

They moved three feet apart and began to stroke again with one arm underwater, still using the paddles as floats. Bright beams bobbled and probed the night and moved away toward the edges of the channel.

They swam past what Evvie judged to be the spot where the boats had crossed. She and Nagolo one-armed their way through the water. After the blinding lights of the boats, and in the soft rain that had begun to fall, their world was only ink and hope.

But hope built with every stroke.

Dear God ... we've done it.

She dared a whisper. "Nagolo! We made it!"

"I think you are right. They will have to think we headed for the ocean. They will keep going out."

"I don't see how they missed us."

"Do not speak more," he said. "Not even now." But she saw white teeth behind a smile.

Her right arm started to cramp, and she shifted the paddle to that side so she could use her left arm to swim. The cramp tied an ugly knot in her right biceps, but she hardly noticed it.

They were one hundred yards past the crossing point when the sky lit up.

In a wash of brilliant white light, the flare floated down from the sky, a deadly beautiful blossom trailing delicate spirals of falling sparks that fluttered like flower petals.

In the bow of one of the Indian cayucos, guarding the center of the channel, sitting in front of two of his men whose paddles shimmered in the light of the flare ... El Codo.

Chapter 17

El Codo sat motionless in the bow of the cayuco. His face, savage even in shadow, framed a pair of serpent eyes that glittered in the light of the dying flare. He didn't look at Evvie and Nagolo as they floated together holding the paddles. He only stared past them at the black sea beyond, an out-of-century gargoyle, a sea-going incubus silent and inanimate as he waited for the two motor launches to return to the center of the channel.

The flare sputtered out just before hitting the surface. A flashlight held by one of El Codo's men snapped on and transfixed the couple in the water. The two motorboats hurried in from the darkness.

El Codo transferred from the cayuco to the motor launch that picked Evvie and Nagolo out of the water, the boat that would bring the escapees back to Karatuppu. The second motor launch remained in the center of the channel in case the flare had been seen … in case someone came to look.

But no one came to look.

On the trip back to the island, nobody said a word. Not El Codo. Not Evvie. Not Nagolo. And, even more ominous, not any of the men in the launch. Codo's crew didn't curse or talk or joke. They only tended the boat and didn't look at the two people they had captured.

Once ashore, they were taken to the Cuna gathering house and were told to stay there … not by El Codo, but by one of the men who pulled them out of the sea.

The same man told Evvie in a matter-of-fact tone that she would sleep in the Cuna gathering house. "El Codo says no more you sleep in his hut. From now, you sleep with the Indians. Only there."

On the east beach, El Codo stood in the early morning drizzle and watched the day begin. From the doorway of the gathering house they saw him standing alone, shrouded in the haze that drifted in from the sea. When the sun flared on the horizon, he turned and walked back into his hut.

Two men came to replace the two who guarded the gathering house. But the pair who'd guarded the house through the night didn't go away. The four guards stood together and waited. They did not talk.

A fifth man went into El Codo's hut. After several minutes the man came out and walked toward the north end of the island. He carried a machete.

Evvie saw Mark move inside a shadow near the center of the island. Mark stopped and remained where he was, looking toward the gathering house from a distance.

Children began to stir. Ile and the other fourteen-year-old girl tended the young ones. They helped them dress and gave them morning food and kept them quiet. Inlota's grandmother sat on a blanket near a wall. Her eyes were closed and she rocked back and forth. She made soft chanting sounds, ancient Cuna phrases that lifted and settled back like gentle waves on smooth sand.

The man with the machete came back toward the gathering house from the north end of the island. As he walked, the trunk shadows of Karatuppu's slender palm trees slipped over and off his body as though he were moving in a cage. He carried a straight wooden pole that was six feet long and sharpened to a fresh point at both ends.

The man stopped in front of the hut. He hacked at the ground with the machete until the hardpan surface broke. Earth was dug out to make a thin hole.

One end of the stake was rammed into the hole. Another man dragged two fire logs from the covered pile beside the hut and rolled them against the base of the pole to keep it upright.

The five men stood shoulder to shoulder forming a ragged row behind the stake. Mark remained in the shadow of a palm tree a hundred feet away.

Ted North was not there.

El Codo was not there.

Inside the gathering house the Indians and Evvie waited and talked in whispers. Three children played with Bibi in a hammock near the fire pit.

Then El Codo came out of his hut.

He held a black cigar in his good hand. He stopped to look once more at the sunrise. Smoke, as delicate as morning mist, coiled off the tip of his cigar. No wind moved from the sea, and the narrow blue line of smoke trailed up toward the palm-top canopy.

The rain had stopped. Everything flat that faced the sky wore beads of water. The plump drops, like thousands of watching eyes, mirrored a universe of curves. On those shiny convex surfaces, lines became arcs, arcs became circles. Straight was twisted; twisted was twisted more.

Waves on the distant reef had settled down in the early hours as a new storm began to spin pressures at the sea in a different place.

The men and women in the gathering house stopped their whisperings as El Codo approached. The grandmother's chant ended. The silence of the adults stopped the noise of the children. A blue rubber ball touched by a child's foot rolled slowly across the dirt floor and turned a slow circle in a shallow depression, rocked gently a few times, and was still.

El Codo stopped next to a tall man standing at one end of the row of men. He said something to the man, clipped words, and the tall one trotted away to the south and was gone for several moments. When he returned, Ted walked by his side. Ted was naked except for the grotesque necktie of anchor and chain fastened beneath his chin. He supported the weight of the anchor with both hands.

El Codo smiled and gestured with the cigar.

Ted went to the place indicated by the cigar and stood there.

El Codo nodded to the man with the machete, and the two of them walked forward past the pointed stake into the gathering house. The Indians who clustered around the doorway parted for them like a school of fish parting for a pair of barracuda.

El Codo stopped in the middle of the hut. He looked around. He said something to his man. The man nodded, stepped forward, and using the flat side of the machete blade, herded the four children out of the hut. A four-year-old girl held Bibi's hand and guided her wobbling steps.

Evvie drifted in the nightmare.

The children ... at least the children won't have to see this.

Her terror flickered into rage and rage dissolved to terror again. Back and forth. Panic rolled in her stomach like a live eel. Her knees tried to fold. Her throat ached like it was packed with ice.

El Codo stood alone. No person moved or made a sound.

She watched El Codo's eyes stop on Nagolo.

Olonaya stood next to her husband. As El Codo looked at them, Olonaya stepped even closer and squeezed Nagolo's hand. She trembled enough to make gold bracelets click.

El Codo's stare shifted to Evvie. His expression was flat, cold. Evvie felt El Codo's eyes work the skin of her face like beetles crawling. If she had a knife and if she could move her hands, she was sure she would peel the flesh from her skull to get rid of that feeling.

El Codo shook his head slowly, twice.

She saw no curiosity in those eyes. No interest. Not even the snake working the toad.

The eyes went back to Nagolo.

The man with the machete came back into the hut with three other men. All four men stayed just inside the door and lined up side by side so no one could go out.

Except El Codo. He went out.

Is it over?

Blood pounded inside her chest. She took a deep breath and tried to keep her heart from flailing itself to pieces.

Oh, God! That's all! Scare us. Only scare us!

She drew another breath and dared a forward step. Then another. She stood facing the line of men who blocked her way, stopped only inches short of stained shirts and whisky smell. She looked out into the clearing.

Her knees let go. She sank to the ground without a sound. Her hands covered her mouth as though trying to keep outside things out and inside things in.

Two images.

First, three children standing and staring, their eyes glazed by an outrage raw and wrong.

The second, Bibi.

The little body had been driven onto the upright stake, back first, thrust down over the sharp point almost to the middle of the wooden pole that seemed to be growing out of the child's stomach. Small arms splayed apart, the palms facing up, the gesture a child would make when it wanted to be picked up and held.

Behind Bibi, El Codo was standing between Ted and the one guard who had been left outside.

The guard was bent over. Vomiting.

Ted stood naked, holding up the anchor, his face drained of color.

El Codo calmly wiped both his good hand and his bad hand with a piece of rag.

Chapter 18

The four men blocking the door backed out through the entrance and went to stand on the far side of the stake where El Codo stood.

The Indians slowly filed past Evvie as she knelt on the dirt. The only sound she heard was Olonaya's sharp gasp when she saw Bibi. All the Cunas, even the children, appeared to be in shock, and each adult only stopped and stared after going a few feet into the clearing.

Evvie got to her feet. She walked toward the stake. She put her arms under Bibi and lifted her up. The pole began to lift also, and Evvie had to press her knee against it to keep it from rising out of the ground.

The lifeless body came off the stake easily … like a small bundle of cloud.

Holding the baby next to her naked chest, she turned toward Nagolo. "Give me something," she said.

Beside her, a brown Cuna hand held out a broad red scarf. Evvie wrapped the scarf around Bibi to cover the terrible wound. She stepped forward and handed Nagolo his child.

He took the body without a sound.

His eyes never left Evvie's eyes.

She turned to face Ted, who was standing next to El Codo.

The kernal planted by Olonaya on that first day, when she told Evvie that the invaders were Colombian, went from seed to blossom in the instant. Colombians … drugs … DEA … the small radio … Coconut wrecked … and Ted's refusal to escape—the last critical piece. What had been buried by exhaustion then, now unearthed by horror, was clear. The whole trip was a setup. A DEA setup. And Ted was at the heart of the betrayal.

Hope hadn't been enough. Hope was in the wire. El Codo had just proved that fact past doubt. The dirty moment had come. A war had to be fought.

The breath seemed to go out of her. An aura, a premonition, a lightness came. Her hands felt different, itched. Her fingers, weightless. Something somewhere collapsed and fury took its place. Reality seemed to shift as she experienced the disconcerting but oddly exhilarating sensation of leaving her body. Rage mixed with vertigo, and in that single atom of time, she wanted very much to talk to a combat vet ... to an old cop ... to God.

Then, as quickly, she put God away.

She walked slowly across the clearing and stopped in front of Ted. She looked into his face one last time for answers.

She found nothing there. He averted his eyes.

She took one step backward, stopped, and with all her strength kicked him as hard as she could in his naked crotch. Ted's testicles were precisely crushed between the inside bones of his pelvis and the top of her bare foot. The kick was delivered with a force equal to the outrage she felt at seeing Bibi impaled on the stake.

Ted would have collapsed to the ground except for a male hand that buried in his hair and held him upright at the moment of impact. El Codo's hand.

Evvie looked at testicles that oozed purple serum in tiny bubbles. A trickle of blood ran down the inside of Ted's right leg. When air finally got back into his lungs, Ted emitted a whining moan that ended in a whimper, an undignified sound in the company of those who stood beneath the morning and fought greater pain in silence.

Evvie turned and went to Olonaya. She put her arms around the Indian, then gently led her into the gathering house.

In a dark corner Olonaya crumbled. Evvie knelt on cool dirt and cradled Olonaya's head in her lap. "Speak to Nagolo," said Olonaya. "Do not let him be killed. Not now."

"I will speak to Nagolo."

A strangled screech tried to escape Olonaya's throat, but couldn't get out.

Then another, stillborn, stopped like the first.

Evvie bent close to Olonaya's ear. "Go ahead, Olonaya. They will understand."

The third screech took wing and stopped whispers in the morning.

But that was the only wail. Prayers needed to be said. Children had to be talked out of trances. And Bibi had to be made ready for her journey to the spirit world.

The day would be spent in mourning.

Water was heated and scented and Bibi was bathed. Then she was dressed in her finest cloth blouse and sarong. Nagolo strung a small hammock between two lodge poles. Women trimmed Bibi's shiny black hair. Olonaya painted colors on her daughter's face.

Inlota's grandmother sang a slow lament.

The rain came back and closed out the world beyond the cane walls.

After the women finished grooming the little one, Nagolo lifted his baby and placed her in the death hammock. The base half of a calabash shell was placed over Bibi's head. … "To keep the evil-spirit birds from pecking at her," Ile explained to Evvie. A pot of cocoa-bean incense was lit. The incense was placed on the floor near the death hammock. The old woman chanted on.

The others gathered around the little hammock and said soft words. More hammocks were strung so all, including Evvie, could sit close and see how beautiful Bibi was.

Big hammocks made the small hammock seem smaller.

Even the children came forward and told how they splashed in the water with Bibi, how they found shells together, how they made her laugh, how her laugh made others laugh.

Olonaya nodded to Evvie, and Evvie said her words to Bibi.

Four painted sticks were brought from a cloth-wrapped box and placed in the strings of the death hammock. Ile told Evvie they were the *massar* sticks that held the spirits that would protect Bibi on her journey. The sticks carried the prayers of the mourners. Bibi would have their love with her in eternity.

Evvie fought the images of her dead Cindy, but memories came anyway, and she cried in the middle of the day.

Olonaya sat next to Evvie in the hammock and held her hand. "I think you mourn not only for Bibi."

"I lost a baby, too. My little girl."

"Was she beautiful and brave like her mother?"

"She was my Cindy."

"Has time not helped your spirit?"

"It was helping ... until this morning."

Olonaya looked into Evvie's face. After long moments Olonaya squeezed Evvie's hand. "Did you not say goodbye?"

"We had a funeral, a priest."

"But did you say goodbye?"

Evvie looked at the small body in the hammock. "No, I guess I didn't say goodbye. Not like this. It happened so fast."

"The dying happened so fast?"

"Yes. Like what happened to Bibi. So fast. So wrong."

"Many times death comes too fast. But that is a sadness the heart can come to understand. I think you hurt because you did not say goodbye. I think that is what happened. You forgot to say goodbye."

"I can never say goodbye. That time is gone forever. I guess that's what hurts so much."

"The time to say goodbye is not gone."

Evvie looked at her.

"Wait," said Olonaya.

In the late afternoon a grave was dug in the dirt floor beneath Olonaya's hammock. It was made so that Bibi would face the rising sun. In the wall at the head of the grave, a small chamber was prepared. A second chamber was carved at the opposite end. Olonaya placed small dishes and cups into the first chamber. Nagolo put together a covered basket containing money, pieces of gold jewelry, and some of Bibi's favorite toys. The basket was put into the second chamber.

At twilight, Bibi's hammock was untied from the lodge poles, and together Olonaya and Nagolo wrapped the sides around their child. The closed hammock was placed in the grave. Bibi was covered with a cloth. More *massar* sticks were placed next to her. Braided cords were laid on top of the child. Other things were put in: a woven fan with Cuna symbols painted on it; bits of wrapped food, chicken, rice, sugar cane; and a miniature boat called the *ulu ikko,* equipped with tiny paddles to take Bibi to the upper world.

Olonaya came to Evvie. "It is time. Come."

She took Evvie by the arm.

Five people stood, one behind the other, in a silent line. Each in turn knelt down and gave Bibi spoken messages to carry to someone gone, someone loved, someone in heaven. More small gifts were put into the grave. Pieces of cloth. Some packages of food. A piece of jewelry. Bundles with secret things inside. All with instructions to Bibi about who should get what and what should be said.

The dead would know the living cared.

The last in line was Niki, who knelt, put in a rubber ball, and told Bibi to throw it with his father.

"Now you," said Olonaya. "Say your words to your daughter."

The rest stood back.

Evvie knelt. For a long time she said nothing. Words would not come.

Only tears.

Then she asked Bibi to go to Cindy. "Please tell her I miss her. Tell her I love her, Bibi. Tell her … tell her that her mother who loves her very much says goodbye."

She wanted to send a gift. Some final, healing offering.

But she had no gift.

Her hand moved up and tangled in the cowry shell necklace that Nagolo had given to her when they were in the sea.

She placed the necklace next to Bibi.

Chapter 19

The death hammock was roofed over with cedar planks laid on ledges cut deep in the grave. Soil was shoveled onto the cedar planks until the grave was filled to the level of the gathering house floor. When that was done, Evvie went to a dark corner, curled up on a blanket, and slept for three hours, a kind of sleep she hadn't known since Cindy's death. A sleep too deep for dreams. A sleep so free of pain and memories that the old woman, Alecta, had to shake Evvie's shoulder hard.

"What? What do you …"

"You said to wake you." Deep in an ancient skull, in skin like carved oak, Alecta's misted-over eyes hovered above Evvie's face. To come awake, from a place so profound, six inches beneath that forbidding front should have frightened Evvie. It did not.

The old woman's words were more Cuna than Spanish and thickly accented, but Evvie understood.

"Alecta. Yes." Evvie looked past the face. The ends of the fire logs were apart, and only embers glowed at the center of the pit. Everyone else in the gathering house was asleep. She wrapped a Cuna blanket around her shoulders in the manner of the old woman and together they left the hut.

They walked without speaking to the edge of the west beach. They stopped in the dark shadow of a thick palm. There was no sign of El Codo's men, although a fire flickered on the opposite side of Karatuppu near the motor launches.

"They aren't drinking," said Evvie.

"There is only one on Karatuppu who would drink this night."

Both women drew the covering blankets tighter.

"Why do you ask of Piryatuppu?" Alecta's words. A hint of hostility.

"I have to know what's over there. It may be the only place for us to go if something happens."

Alecta turned slowly and looked north toward the smaller island. "No one goes to that place. It is for Purkwet Kala."

Again, Olonaya's words and the description in the book Arthur had given them in Colon came back to her. Purkwet Kala, the demon of darkness, and riding on his back the bird monster Kanir Sikwi, whose screech brought death. Evvie was suddenly impatient with Cuna myth. It was beginning to interfere with reality. "Olonaya says a priest goes there."

"He is a protected one."

"What do you mean?"

"He is of the moon. A white-skinned one. He has not known pain. For all his years he has been made safe. He is given all things. Food. Long-river water. The chewing leaf. He has not known woman. He has no feeling of the loss of children. He does not learn the spear. Only the prayers."

"Why does he go to Piryatuppu? How many times?"

"He makes offering at the stone of Purkwet Kala so my people are safe in the night from the call of Kanir Sikwi. The priest goes four times in the year. He will not go there for many weeks."

"If I go to Piryatuppu, what will ..."

The old woman abruptly turned and started back to the gathering hut.

"Please, Alecta. Please!" She stopped the old one by putting a hand on her shoulder. "Please don't walk away. If you tell me what is there, maybe I won't have to go to Piryatuppu. Tell me what's there."

Alecta didn't turn around. She kept her back to Evvie. She said nothing right away. Finally, she began to talk.

"Only trees and the stone of Purkwet Kala are there. In the middle of the island. In the ground. The altar of Purkwet Kala is in the ground."

"Why is ..."

Evvie's words stopped as Alecta turned to face her.

"You cannot go to Piryatuppu because there are three reasons."

Evvie waited.

"It is the place of Purkwet Kala. You have known evil. And the spirit air. Those are the three."

"Spirit air?"

"The Nia breathe out near Purkwet Kala. The special one who goes with the prayers makes his face go into ash wood. But even for him it is too much evil. The special one does not stay long near Purkwet Kala."

"About the other reason. The evil. I'm not evil."

"Only to know evil. The Christian man who talks at Aligandi does not speak the truth when he says that weak ones will have the earth. It is not like that. Death makes death. Evil makes evil. Only to be near evil is enough to be evil."

"If I go to ..."

"I have said my words to you. I think you are not right to be here with my people. I do not think you are good like the others think. You bring death. I say no more words."

Evvie stood alone in shadows.

The next day was spent with Olonaya. And the children. Stories were told. People held other people in their arms. Cuna men stared at the ground or painted new prayer sticks. Or cried alone at the edge of the sea.

"Yes, Ile?"

"You must go to him. He is outside. He is waiting."

Evvie cringed.

"It is not El Codo who waits. It is the one who came and took me away from the sun."

The gall that had floated up into Evvie's throat went back down. "Mark? Mark's waiting?"

"Yes. The one who wears the wires on his skin." Ile pointed at the ragged sweat pants. "But the man El Codo says you must be pretty." Evvie frowned. She didn't understand.

"I have a mola dress." Ile smiled. "It will fit you. You are smaller now than when you came."

Evvie smiled, too. "Tell him I will come ... if he will wait."

"I will tell him."

When Ile returned, she went to a corner of the hut and retrieved a book of matches and two candles from a box wrapped in wax paper. She set the candles on the ground next to Evvie. She lit the candles and held a blanket so that Evvie could have light and privacy while she dressed.

When Ile finally lowered the blanket, Evvie stood straight in the flickering orange glow of the candles; her deeply tanned skin, set against the bright patterns of the colorful mola blouse, gleamed like gold if gold could gleam.

Ile stepped back. "Oh, my. You are so beautiful. So very beautiful." Tears sparkled in Ile's eyes.

"Thank you, Ile," Evvie said. "Don't throw these away," and she kicked the ragged sweat pants into a corner. "This beautiful dress will probably get tailored by a machete."

"To see you like this for one night is worth more than any dress. You will keep it. It is my gift."

Evvie and Mark walked on the beach toward the deserted south end of the island. The hour before midnight was warm. The air was heavy. Thick clouds rolled over Karatuppu toward the mainland.

They walked side by side several feet apart. Mark's words had slammed into her brain like hot shrapnel.

"I'm sorry," said Mark.

"Why be sorry? We do what he says. All of us. The Indians, his men, Ted, me, you, all of us. It's just more of the same, isn't it? Nothing matters except what he wants."

Mark didn't reply. They kept walking without speaking. They passed the place where she had been dragged up the beach into the brush. A subtle smell of something rotting hung in the air. Evvie shivered.

They rounded the south tip of Karatuppu and stopped on the east beach facing the ocean.

"Where?" she asked.

"My hootch, I guess."

She thought of making a remark about his hut being a busy place, but the words were hollow in her mind. "You didn't make Ile do it. Olonaya told me. Do you know how much that meant? What you did? The way you helped her?"

"This can't be like that. Carlos said that he'll spread you apart and look. See for himself when you come out. See if I appreciated his present. That's you. You're my present."

There was sadness, a resignation in his voice, and for an instant she felt almost as sorry for him as she did for the Cunas.

She watched white foam blossom and fade on the invisible reef. "There's not much left here," she said. "Will he kill us for trying to escape? Me and Nagolo? When you're through with me?"

"I don't know. I've seen him like this before. When he's curious about something, he keeps it around until ..."

"Why hasn't someone ..."

"Killed him?"

"Yes."

Mark didn't answer at once. His silence finally ended in a sigh. "Carlos knows everything that's going on, everything that's happening on the island, even what the goddamn weather's going to do. Like he has a sixth sense. That's why he's lasted this long. Killing Carlos would be like hunting rattlesnakes barefoot." He looked at the sea. "Besides, there's something else."

She waited for him to say more.

"The real boss is a guy called Araña. The Spider. He's worse than Carlos."

Evvie wondered why Mark was standing there on the beach making up stories. *Worse than El Codo? Worse than that?*

His game made her angry. She folded her arms across the front of the mola blouse. "There's nothing worse than El Codo," she said. "Nothing!"

"If that were true, there wouldn't be any more Carlos. He wouldn't make it through another night. His own men would kill him. But Spider is coming. The men know that. So nobody touches Carlos."

"Araña? ... The Spider?"

"The Spider is why we're here, not Carlos."

She stared at him and realized that he was telling the truth. The sad, handsome face revealed that Mark wasn't playing games.

Worse than El Codo? "How much time?" she asked. "How much time did he give you to fuck me?"

Mark ignored the anger. "Morning. When we're through he wants me to tell him. Then he'll want to see—"

She covered his lips with her hand and stopped the words.

Eighty miles to the west, three Black Hawk helicopters dripped rain on concrete. France Field had been abandoned to the jungle years earlier when the Galeta Island Navy Station, a security group activity, was down-graded to caretaker status. Orphan tufts of wire grass sprouted through cracks in the runway. Brown vines like serpents extended from the jungle to explore voids in broken cinderblock. Lizards raced from under broad green leaves to gulp down bugs eating bugs, then scurried back into wet shadows to watch again. Beetles the size of apple halves lurched to pri-mal directives. *Bufus Giganticus,* the giant rain forest toad that ate those beetles, waited with bulbous blinking eyes and studied the night's entrées. A fer-de-lance slithered toward a mound of toad, paused as instinct cal-culated probability, then retreated.

DEA Agent Rawlings picked his nose and flicked something into the night. "Fucking place gives me the creeps."

His fellow agent, a flat-faced man named Gompers, sucked a ciga-rette and wiped sweat from his cheek with the sleeve of his black jacket. He made no comment on Rawlings' observation. He'd heard it before.

Rawlings shook his head. "Look at the size of those fucking frogs."

Gompers put his left arm through the sling of his M-16 rifle, shoul-dered the weapon, and looked at his watch. "Midnight. A new day in paradise."

Rawlings drew his .45 pistol and sighted through the drizzling rain at one of the huge toads thirty feet away. "Look at that one. I never seen such big motherfuckers."

"What's the late skinny?"

Rawlings holstered the pistol. "Same old bullshit. Hurry up and fucking wait. Nothing new from any of the pickets."

"What's your guess? Where's it going down?"

"Want to bet on it, Gompers? Ten bucks. My money's on Cape Tiburon on the Colombian border."

"I say he's sitting right here in some hotel in the middle of Colon."

"Nice and dry and flossing his teeth with warm pussy."

"Of course. Some thirteen-year-old daughter of a guy whose throat he just slit. Why do you think Tiburon?"

"Close to home. He can slide back into Colombia if the shit hits the fan."

"Spider must be one hell of a piece of work."

"Last of the big fuckers. Escobar's gone. Abrego. Samper. Maybe Carillo. Only one left is Spider. The biggest one."

"How about some place in the middle? Nombre? The San Blas?"

"Don't think so. Too much slop in the Darien. We got the air. He can't fly. It'd take a fucking week for him to get through there on foot."

Gompers wiped his forehead again. "Hell, it's been more than a week already." He threw his cigarette onto the runway. It sputtered in a puddle of rainwater. A hungry toad shifted position and stared at the puddle. "What kind of feed do we have in Tiburon?" he asked.

"Mormon kid. Working with a missionary."

"Nice. We're using missionaries."

"It's good cover. And we got every Agency big dog hanging around Panama City planting stories and praying to his little pink woody that he makes the front page without getting frogs run up his ass like a couple of dumb shits I know."

"Who's in the San Blas?"

"Some deep-cover guy. DEA. Took his fucking wife in there with him on a sailboat to make it look good. Like a couple of damned tourists. Can you beat that? He must be as sweet as she is stupid."

Evvie followed Mark to the hut, but stopped at the entrance. The rain had started again. "Do you have any soap?"

"I've got half a bar left."

She looked into the shadows. It was after midnight; no one moved under the trees. "Can I have it?"

Mark went into his hut. He came back out and handed her the soap and a brown towel. "I've got two razor blades left and a can of wet Band-Aids and a toothbrush with no toothpaste. And three aspirin. But the aspirin's swelled up and sort of fuzzy."

"Does this stuff work in saltwater?"

"No."

She turned and walked toward the ocean.

He stayed in front of the hut in the rain and watched for things in the night.

Ten minutes later she returned carrying Ile's dress and holding the brown towel against the front of her body. She was naked.

"Well?"

"I lost the soap in the water."

"Easy come, easy—"

She interrupted him. "Don't joke. Don't make me hate you."

They went into the hut.

"Should I light the lamp?" he asked.

"No."

He took the dress and blouse from her. As her eyes began to adapt to the low light, she could see him on the other side of the hut carefully spreading Ile's dress on a wooden table. She looked around the rest of the room and saw a single hammock strung between two support poles.

He came back and gently took the towel out of her hands. He stepped behind her and began to dry raindrops from her shoulders. He moved the towel softly on her bare back. The brown towel was damp, but it soaked up the beads of water. Then he reached around and let her take the towel, and she dried her front and legs.

"I don't sleep in the hammock," he said. "I sleep there." He pointed at a pad of blankets on a low pallet across the room near the table.

She walked over to the pallet, sat on its edge, and smoothed the blankets with her hands. Then she lay down on her side so she faced the cane wall. She brought her knees up and pushed her hands between them and was quiet.

He knelt behind her. He covered her with a dry blanket he brought from somewhere in the hut. "I keep this one wrapped in plastic," he said, "to keep it from getting wet."

Warmth built quickly under the dry material. She squeezed her knees together on her hands to stop the shaking.

She heard him take off his clothes. He moved beneath the blanket and lay next to her.

They did not touch.

"Would you like to sleep?"

"Yes," she said.

He moved closer, and she knew he was on his back when the outside of his hip touched the curve of her backside.

The dry warmth melted into her.

They lay that way for a long time. Her heart slowed as her skin warmed. She felt strangely safe. The constant wariness that wired every waking minute on Karatuppu began to slip away. She was still afraid, but suddenly very tired. Tired won. She slept.

She dreamed that she was walking naked down a pier toward a large pleasure boat like the ones she had seen at the clubs around San Francisco Bay, a gleaming luxury yacht, and it belonged to her. She stood for a long time on the pier looking at the wonderful white boat. In her dream it was the only thing she owned. She untied the stern line. She walked forward on the pier and untied the bow line.

She was crying.

A space gradually opened between the dock and the boat, and she could see black water.

Her heart ached more.

The yacht drifted farther away.

And farther. The boat disappeared. The dream ended.

She woke up. She had rolled over onto her back. She lay close by Mark's side.

"Evvie?"

She stared into darkness. She didn't want to answer him. "Yes?"

"You were crying. Were you dreaming?"

"Yes."

"What about?"

She told him her dream.

He listened to her without asking questions.

When she finished, she lay quietly for several minutes.

They were silent for a long time. "The dream?" she said. "I think it was about losing everything I ever had ... or thought I had."

He waited and did not say anything.

"Nothing matters, now." She took his hand and placed it gently over her lips. A small kiss.

He rolled onto his side. He caressed the side of her neck. Then he leaned forward and kissed where that hand had been. Kissed the turn of her shoulder. Kissed her neck once more, then found the cool contours of an ear, kissed the ear. Slow touching. Soft kisses. Over and over. Long minutes of tenderness.

"Mark? I tried to make it all work." In the darkness her hand searched for his upturned flank, found the hard angle of his naked hip, and rested there.

She shivered as a finger touched her nipple. Her reaction startled them both. He pulled back and waited for the tension in her to ease. Then touched her there again. A touch as light as falling cotton.

Somehow, in the hell that was Karatuppu, they began to build a place where hell couldn't be.

He kissed her cheek and shoulder. He caressed her upper body slowly until her fingers moved on the skin of his hip. He bent to her breast and kissed the nipple he had hardened.

His fingers traveled down the flat plain of her belly. That slow electric trip on flesh took five silken minutes, and when his hand moved onto the swelling where soft hair tangled, she jolted hard as though he'd touched raw nerve.

Retreat. Advance. Each advance a bit farther down than the one before.

Suddenly he heard her breath draw in deeply, then release in a shudder of surrender. In the next moment, she encircled the strength standing out from his groin, her fingers clamping like rawhide strips.

Mark's hand melted the rest of the way down over her sex, and nature opened her like nature opened flowers. Her fingers gripped him more tightly in return.

Her mind began to surf away from Karatuppu nightmares on waves of pleasure. No more El Codo. No fear. No failed husband. She discovered how nerves she thought could do no more could do much more. With unexpected fury, like silent summer lightning, her passion exploded into the pressuring palm of his hand.

If the hut had been anything less than dark, she'd have curled into a ball of embarrassment and crawled under blankets.

Almost immediately Mark began again. Still gentle, but with more hunger. She was instantly ready. The wet sounds his hand made there mingled with the sound of the rain that ran on Karatuppu. In seconds, she pitched over the edge once more. Then she growled and pulled him on top of her.

When he entered her, she gasped and pulled him past pain. She opened the skin on his back with fingernails. She bit his lips and tasted his blood. Restraint delaminated like an onion peeled. She wanted to wrap her legs around his hips and turn herself inside out for him, if such a freakish thing were possible. She rolled him over so she was on top and went at him until she climaxed with a spine-bending shudder. Mark ejaculated with a childish squeal.

In the unlit room, still riding the ripples of after-sex, she smiled.

Enjoy it, you son of a bitch. It might be your last.

And then they slept.

They woke, dressed, and stepped out into morning.

El Codo stood by a tree. Cold eyes. Thin cigar.

He looked at Evvie. He looked at Mark.

El Codo turned and walked away. He did not have to see more.

Mark walked her back to the gathering house. As they reached it, a man standing outside one of the small huts yelled and waved for Mark to come. The man was agitated. She heard the word "radio" three times. Something important was happening. Mark hurried to the hut and went inside.

During the next half-hour, Evvie moved toward the north end of the island. It wasn't a safe place to go, but she wanted to find Ted, to watch him for a while. Where was the small transmitter? Did he have it?

None of El Codo's men was doing anything unusual. Everything seemed the same. Finally, through the trees, she saw Ted sitting in the shade of the bohio by the boats. He seemed to be asleep with his head on his knees. The anchor hung from his neck, its flukes resting on the ground between his ankles.

She watched him for several more minutes. He shifted position and seemed to doze off again. She squatted down and waited. Nothing happened. She couldn't tell if he was really sleeping. She went back to the gathering house.

In the first hour of afternoon she returned to the same spot. She watched for ten minutes. And went away.

At twilight she returned. After she watched for a while, one of El Codo's men appeared. He made Ted kneel in front of him. Ted didn't protest. The man made Ted do what she had never seen one man do to another.

But what she saw didn't affect her. It seemed unimportant, like so much junk mail. In those odd, dead seconds, she floated on the wonder of not caring.

She didn't watch until the act was finished. She went back to the gathering house.

She sat by herself in a dark corner and closed her eyes. She did not sleep. She only wanted to make the others stay away from her so she could think.

If Ted brought the transmitter ashore, they haven't found it or he'd have been killed.

She knew it wasn't still attached to the skin under his scrotum. Not with what they were doing to him. If it was there, they'd have found it.

The tree! That first day when he was chained to that tree!

He must have buried it there so he could get to it later. While he was chained to the tree he wasn't watched. That would have been his only chance to get rid of it.

What if he moved it somewhere else after they unchained him?

She realized it was a possibility, but moving it while he was unchained would have been dangerous. That's when they did watch him. Someone would see. Ted wouldn't take the chance.

She tried to think of a safe time to search the sand around the palm. Early morning, when the sea fog came in from the ocean before sunrise.

An hour later Mark came up behind her as she sat on the south beach.

"You missed all the excitement," he said.

"What happened?"

"One of the Cunas, the kid called Niki, bombed one of El Codo's boys."

She scrambled to her feet.

Mark saw the fear in her eyes and grinned. "Don't worry," he said. "The kid's all right. Somehow he looped a string over a palm branch. Probably tied a rock to it and threw it over. Then he hauls up a coconut, hides in the bushes, and lets it go when one of the Colombians walks under it. Wouldn't have been so bad, but one of the guy's pals sees it coming and yells. Doofus looks up and takes the coconut right between the running lights." Mark laughed.

"What happened to Niki?" Concern thinned her voice. "Did they catch him?"

"The kid takes off for the main hut like a shot. He's got this goddamned red scarf tied around his neck like a cape."

"Mark! Answer me! Did they do anything to him?"

"Hell, no. Everyone's laughing their ass off. Carlos pops out. They tell him what happened. Doofus wants to skin the kid, but Carlos says no. I swear to Christ I think Carlos thought it was funny, too. Maybe he just admired the kid's cojones."

He saw the fear drain out of her expression. "Sleep with me tonight," he asked.

"I want to," she replied. "But we can't. His hate-trip doesn't include me having a good time."

"Who says you're going to have a good time?" He reached out to take her hand, but she slapped it away and moved back.

"No. He knows everything. He sees everything." She hesitated several moments, her eyes down, then looked up at him. "What you ... what we did last night?" she asked. "Did you want to? I mean on your own ... if El Codo hadn't ..."

"Carlos says he owes me. If he's got a friend, I guess I'm it. But he said he'd cut my dick off and shove it down my throat if I didn't rape you."

"That's nice to know," she said.

"You ought to know something else. I wanted you very much."

She nodded. "Yes, you did."

"That's a pretty cocky way to talk, for a lady."

"You're pretty cocky too. I spent an hour this morning learning how to walk again."

He cut off the small talk by squatting on his heels at the water's edge and looking away from her. "Listen to me," he said.

She remained standing six feet away. She listened.

"I'm not going to bullshit you. I'm what you see, nothing more. I'm no plant, no narc, no big-deal cocaine wheeler-dealer. I'm a small frog who's in over his head and can't get out. I can't get you out, either."

His words were just above a whisper, but she heard every one. What he said was important, but not for the reasons he would think. *Come on, Mark. Fall in love. You can do it.*

"Carlos doesn't keep me around just because I stuck my face between him and a knife one night." He reached down and picked up a broken piece of coral. "He and I both know radios, two-way equipment. I used to fly loads into the States out of Sonora. Marijuana. That's why I'm sitting on my ass on this beach. If you make a living moving grass, you learn the squawk talk, the radio talk. I know English better than he does. At least the insider stuff, air shorthand, fed-code, the gringo radio chit-chat they don't teach in Medellin English class. That's the real reason I'm here. I'm an ear that's pointed north toward the States." His words had grown angry. He stood up and threw the piece of coral out into the water.

Evvie was startled by how far the piece of coral flew. *Male reflex. If nothing works, throw something. Talk, Mark. Keep talking.*

"When there's nothing hot coming in, I pass the time surfing the bands on the high-power gear in the hootch next to the boats. That's where the long-range radio equipment is. Keeps me from going nuts."

"I thought the only radio was the portable one he carries."

"That's short-range gear. Under twenty miles." He paused as if trying to decide whether to say more. "Someone's watching. Someone big. Someone who's willing to write off everybody on this pretty little island. I've heard things that I haven't told Carlos. High-band stuff. Air to ground. Nothing but coordinates, timed runs, altitudes. But I know the radio profile in this part of the world. That's my job." He picked up another piece of coral. "The stuff I'm picking up is weird, way out of whack."

"Aren't there oddball bases all over the Canal Zone? You told me that."

"But there's nothing down here that's used for measured runs. The only time I hear flight coordinates this far east is when the weather puts incoming aircraft out here. And that's a one-time passover."

"It's happening all the time?"

"Every day ... and night. I keep hearing two guys over and over again. That means the same unit is doing all the covering."

The DEA—they're trying to catch a Spider. "You're sure?"

"There's more. Twice in the last five days while I was listening on the long-range equipment, there was interference. The long gear is real sensitive. Whatever it was that was blowing on my signal was close. Almost on top of me. It didn't click more than a couple of times, too quick for the scanners to find it, but it had to be coming from here, from Karatuppu. It wasn't our portable. It's on standby. I'd have heard the squawk."

Ted. The transmitter.

He looked straight into her eyes. "You wouldn't know anything about that, would you? Maybe you and your husband didn't just drop in out of the blue."

She stared back, just as hard. "You haven't been paying attention, have you? You haven't seen what they've done to me?"

"Sorry." He nodded. Then he looked away and made a smile that wasn't a very good smile. "So why haven't I told Carlos about what I've been picking up on the radio? Because if Carlos spooks, you can bet your pretty little butt there won't be any seats reserved for us on the last train out … let alone your damned Indians. And if we did ask for help, we wouldn't get it. No one *wants* to help us. They want Spider alive. Both sides. They need to keep this game going to get him. Bad guys *and* good guys. We're not going to make it. Not you, not me, not the Cunas." His voice rose. Angry. Frustrated. "I'm not even sure Carlos is going to make it. We just don't goddamned count. None of us." He shook his head. "This ain't no back-alley goat-fuck. Not now."

His gaze hardened. "This wouldn't be such a mother-fucking problem if it wasn't for your goddamned bitching being here."

Evvie waited for a few moments. "That's an unusual way for someone to say they like someone."

"We can make a run for it in one of the outboards. But you won't leave your fucking Indians, will you? Hell, I could still make it out myself!"

"But you won't leave 'fucking me,' will you?"

"Right! You've got that mother-fucking right!"

Small waves chased over the coral plateau and gurgled onto sand at their feet.

"Carlos has a big job in front of him." His words were controlled again. "Unless this Karatuppu bullshit is just a show, a decoy to throw off half the feds on this side of the planet, Spider's in the Darien, right over there." He nodded south toward the mainland. "Spider's not your average kingpin. If he hooks up with what's out there … trawler, sub, chopper, whatever"—he nodded in the other direction, north toward the sea—"then eighty percent of the drug routes into the U.S. shift from South America to Christ knows where. Maybe the Middle East." He swung his arm south to west to north, level with the horizon. "There's a dozen decoys out there from Brazil to Miami, all designed to spread the feds real thin. But I'll lay you ten to one we're it. Too much talent on Karatuppu not to be. Carlos is special." He smirked like a death warrant was a joke. "Spider is taking the scorched-earth concept to a new level. He's capping everyone. So we're in a vise. No way out. In four days we're dead meat. All of us."

He turned and started to walk away. Then stopped. "By the way," he said, still with his back to her. "I think I love you." And he was gone.

Bingo!

For the first time that day, Evvie smiled.

She had stolen Mark from El Codo.

Chapter 20

The shoreline on either side of the narrow channel between the two islands reflected the light of the half-moon. Dark water moved toward the sea, but slowly, slack tide, a safe time to swim the pass.

Piryatuppu to the northwest was a serrated outline above the pale sand. Evvie retied the knot at the top of her ragged sweat pants. In her teeth, she held the book of matches she had filched from Ile's candle box in the gathering house.

She turned one more time to check the tree line behind her. Karatuppu's beach was clear. No one watched her. She waded into the channel separating the two islands. The bottom dropped away quickly, and she was in water up to her neck before she had gone twenty feet. She began to breaststroke her way across. The current was stronger in the deep center of the pass and the tidal flow pushed her seaward. She altered her crossing angle to compensate for the drift.

She swam hard.

Her feet touched bottom. She crawled up onto Piryatuppu's beach and rested on the sand to get her breath back. She examined the book of matches. It was dry. She wedged the packet into the knot at her waist.

One last check of the Karatuppu beach. Empty.

She got to her feet. A sparse stand of unharvested coconut palms loomed above her. She walked up the slope, careful not to move too fast. Karatuppu eyes would be drawn to movement.

She entered the tree line, then stopped and listened. She heard no sound except the distant rumble of waves on the ocean reef. She began to walk counterclockwise around the island, staying in the trees at the edge of the upper beach. Her plan was to circle the perimeter, to check out the beach approaches and shoreline, before exploring the center of the island.

She proceeded around the island to a point opposite the spot where she had crawled out of the water, but was stopped from going farther by a jumble of black lava boulders. The rocks were spread across the beach from the trees and blocked her way.

On tiptoe, she peered over the five-foot-high barrier of stone. In the light of the half-moon she saw a small protected beach and a short landing pier made of bleached sticks and driftwood. Beyond the small pier, more boulders. She decided that the pier was put there so the priest who came could moor and unload his cayuco. She realized that the small beach might provide a place for her and the Cunas to hide, and she filed that fact away.

She turned and looked up at the tree line.

Evvie wasn't afraid of night and shadow. Or of Indian superstition. Not after what she'd been through. If the Cunas wanted to believe in demons, that was their business. Not her. Still, despite knowing that Piryatuppu was uninhabited and that she was out of sight of anyone on the other island, she had the feeling that she was not alone.

She turned and walked up the slope in order to skirt the barrier of rock. She approached the tree line.

Once out of moonlight and into the palms, she was able to see what the interior looked like. The island was similar to Karatuppu except that there appeared to be a flat plain in the center, a large clearing, circular, about two hundred feet in diameter, where white sand lay like snow under the half-moon. Nothing broke the surface outline or protruded to indicate an altar.

Then the first tendril of nausea came. Only a hint. The air teased her sense of smell. Beach kelp? Fish rotting in shallow water? An aberrant whiff of jungle fire far away?

None of those.

She put her hand against a palm trunk for support. Not that she needed support to keep from falling. More to touch something. Something solid.

The nausea passed.

She walked twenty steps farther. The smell came back. This time it made her dizzy. No debilitating swoon, but enough to force her to stop once more and lean against a tree.

The smell receded along with the dizziness.

She started for the clearing again, but was stopped by a memory. *"The spirit air ..."*

The old woman had spoken of the priest and the spirit air and how the priest had to do something ... *"make his face go into ash wood"* ... so he could deliver his prayers.

Then Evvie sat down.

So, that part had not been a fairy tale. She recalled her father saying that "all religion contained a grain of truth in a silo of shit." The explanation wasn't hard to figure. She remembered the time she and Ted did the tourist bit somewhere in Central Mexico and went to look at something the Mexicans had labeled with a funny, sort of obscene, name. The *Athe Holes, Ass Oles* ... something like that. Volcanic vents. A sulfur pit of bubbling mud. There had been warning signs posted about the danger of passing out.

She thought of something else that made her even more certain of her logic. The boulders, the lava rocks at the north end. Piryatuppu was the only place in the San Blas she'd seen them. Panama was a volcanic chain. There had to be some kind of vent or gas seepage on the island.

And the "ash wood" ... charcoal. Or something like charcoal. The priest used some kind of face mask with carbon in it to filter the air.

"All right!" she whispered aloud. She smiled in the half-dark. Despite the storm and losing Coconut and the soul-grinding hell on Karatuppu, her brain still worked.

So much for folklore.

But she realized that getting high on "spirit air" might make her pass out or start swimming out to sea. She got to her feet. She sniffed the air. The smell was gone. But it would probably come back, a good reason to get the Piryatuppu visit over with quickly.

She actually jogged out into the sand clearing.

She saw it. A depression in the ground. A few steps more and she saw that the depression was more than that. A pit. She stopped at the edge of it. Five feet deep. Six feet in diameter. Dark.

On the surface sand on either side of the pit were two weathered pieces of paneling or plywood. Dried stalks of flowers, trinkets and carvings, and four torn-open sacks of what looked like grain or corn were placed on the wood platforms. Much of the grain was gone. Rotted? Blown away by the wind? Eaten?

She dropped to her knees and peered into the pit. Small drifts of white sand covered the floor of the excavation. Four or five cubbyholes had been dug into the side walls. Small pots and boxes rested in the cutout chambers.

Evvie got down on her stomach, backed feet first over the edge, and dropped onto the floor of the pit.

She stood in the middle, her eyes just below the level of the top edge. She looked at some of the containers resting in the side-wall chambers. She picked one up. Shook it. Something rattled inside. She put it back. She was trying to figure out if she and the Cunas could fit in the pit, if they had to hide somewhere, when the toes of her right foot touched something hard under the sand.

She knelt down.

She dug like a dog, throwing sand beside and behind her. In minutes, the stone container of Purkwet Kala was exposed to mid-circumference. She retrieved the book of matches she had wedged into the knot of the sweat pants. By the light of a burning match, she examined the object.

It was round and half again as big as a basketball. Gray stone. Granite. The top third showed a seam like a pumpkin top would be cut. Evvie dropped the match onto the sand. She worked her fingernails into the seam and lifted off the top. The inside was hollow.

Another match.

Purkwet Kala looked up at her.

If silence could be magnified, it was magnified then. Even the constant murmur of the reef surf was gone. Not just muffled, but obliterated by the vertical walls of the pit.

The match burned her fingers, and she let it drop.

She reached into the stone.

She lifted Purkwet Kala out.

She stared at him.

The idol was carved from a single piece of stone, two six-inch uprights joined in the middle by a three-inch crosspiece. Purkwet Kala was a miniature football goal post. The two uprights and the crosspiece were all one-inch square in thickness. A small wolf-head carving topped one upright; a human hand, the other. At each base, a foot. Bird feet, claws. Both feet pointing in the same direction. All that decorated the cross-

piece were some carved letters, like letters she had seen on the corner-
stones of buildings. Greek letters. Strange.

Then Evvie did an odd thing.

She giggled.

The noise she made in the middle of the deep silence startled her.
Then she laughed out loud, as much to hear her own sound move in
that pristine quiet as to hear the woman named Evvie laugh at all.

She made a face at Purkwet Kala.

She held him up to the moon. "This god is brought to you by the
letter 'H,'" she said. And laughed again.

As her laughter died into a smile, she thought about Alecta and
what the old woman would think if she could see her there in the pit.
Religion blown away by reason. "Spirit air" and "Purkwet Kala" ...
bullshit. Gullibility riddled by reality again. If Evvie had a prejudicial
fault line, it was in her attitude toward religion. Her mother's sterile
lectures on God while hell was happening all around had seen to that.

She heard a sound. She stopped thinking and listened. Nothing.

She looked down at Purkwet Kala, now resting in her hand on her
lap.

Silence.

The sound came again.

Children laughing. Small children. Two children. But the sound
was far away. High-pitched. Barely audible. Eerie. Somehow harsh.

She set Purkwet Kala on the sand by the altar stone and stood up.
She stood on her toes and looked over the edge of the pit. Dark trees
ringed the sand plain like a black halo.

The laughter was gone.

She stayed that way for one minute. Listening.

A spine-cracking screech gutted the silence, shredded Piryatuppu's
night. Something rushed toward the pit across the sand behind her. She
whirled around to meet it, lost her balance, and lurched against the side
of the hole, her eyes still level with the earth.

A misshapen, squat apparition came low and fast and right at her.
She couldn't react, couldn't even think of ducking down. The monster
with limbs that stretched beyond each side of the pit was on her. She felt
flesh tear, her flesh. She rammed the attacker with her elbow as her arm
flew up to protect her eyes.

She tumbled back against the wall behind her, kept her feet, and tasted her own blood. Her left ear was savaged by a second hideous shriek that erupted inches from the side of her head.

"Kanir Sikwi, the demon who rides Purkwet Kala's back ..."

Religion tried to pry her fingers off reason's ledge.

"... whose screech warns of death ..."

But panic didn't have a free ticket to Evvie North.

She'd kicked hell in the balls before. Recently.

She punched and clawed and screamed right back. Her hands found solid flesh and tried to rip it. Her face ran with blood. Something hard stabbed into her cheek, almost penetrated through to her mouth. She fought back, tore the sharp spur out of her cheek and twisted it with savage strength.

The beast that was on her blotted out the moonlight, but Evvie North didn't need light. In a rush of wind and commotion, her assailant was suddenly gone.

She dropped to her hands and knees in the base of the pit. She watched blood drip from her face onto sand. She gathered her strength and forced herself to get back on her feet. She leaned forward, arms straight, both hands flat against the dirt wall.

She inhaled deeply. She rubbed her arm across her forehead and looked at the blood that painted the arm from elbow to wrist.

She straightened up. She turned around.

Six feet away, the thing that had attacked her pecked at kernels of grain.

"A bird! A fucking albatross!" Disbelieving words that bubbled red.

Or a condor. Some kind of buzzard. A goddamned fucking bird!

She stared at the animal. It was huge. One wing was obviously broken, but not by her. It was an old injury. She could tell by the way the wing flexed, a solid piece that didn't flop around, welded at a grotesque angle by invisible scar tissue.

The deformed creature was bleeding from its chest and belly. Evvie saw where she'd ripped feathers, skin, and muscle away. And the bird just stood there pecking at kernels. If anything was in shock, it wasn't her; it was that bird.

But too much blood soaked the chest of the huge animal. It wobbled sideways off the board onto the sand. It looked once at Evvie, gurgled another screech of warning to keep her away from its food supply, and began a limping wing-dragging journey back to the trees.

Evvie slid down the wall onto her backside. She wanted to laugh. But laughter seemed done for the night. What she really wanted to do was to get back to the cool waters of the channel between the islands and wash away the gore. Ted told her once that bleeding was like a car leaking oil on a garage floor: A little bit looked like a whole lot. This *was* a whole lot. The beak and claws had done a job on her. She pushed her tongue against her cheek to see if it would go through to the outside. It didn't. The beak had pinched, not penetrated flesh.

Anger came as she pictured a Cuna priest capturing and crippling a giant bird so it couldn't fly, then releasing it on Piryatuppu to perpetuate the legend of Purkwet Kala and Kanir Sikwi. How many priests over the centuries? How many birds?

Something else occurred to her. If she hadn't been able to figure out what was happening to her on Piryatuppu, if she had just turned tail and run, she'd probably be spending the rest of her life preaching Cuna folklore. Purkwet Kala? Piryatuppu's spirit air? Kanir Sikwi? The demon bit was bull, just freeloading priests working full-time to parlay the island's geology into a welfare scam. They were doing one hell of a job. The legends about Piryatuppu had to be a thousand years old. At least. She considered what Dulcie told her about Cunas using oral history instead of books. It made sense for their purposes: lots of wiggle-room.

She stopped thinking about birds and books. She was exhausted. She closed her eyes and considered bleeding to death, the easy way out. Just settle back in the nice quiet pit and go to sleep. The thought alone almost did the job.

But then she heard the voices.

Children. Two little children, again.

Not laughing, not talking baby talk. Singing.

"... *We shall gather by the river* ... "

The sound of babies barely able to ...

"... *the river, the river* ... "

Evvie got to her feet. Something about the voices ...

"... *We shall gather* ..."

She stared in the direction of the sound.

Across the pale sand, near the dark trees that separated her from the pass between Piryatuppu and Karatuppu, stood two ghostly figures. The shapes were human. Almost. Adult bodies, but with the heads of children. Young children. Something about the heads. Familiar. The voice sounds, familiar, too. But like before, the sound was eerie. Past eerie. Macabre. Evil.

"... *the beautiful, beautiful river* ... "

She crawled on hands and knees across the moonlit plain toward the shapes. The blood from her facial cuts, now mixed with tears, dripped from her chin and dotted white sand as she crawled. Her senses reeled. The earth tried to tip her over. She kept moving.

Halfway there.

The misshapen figures, standing side by side, watched her come. The singing noise was louder. A haunting leering sound. Derisive.

Twenty feet away.

Her eyes tried to see through the veil of blood coming from the cuts on her scalp and forehead. Then she saw. Then she knew for sure.

Cindy.

Bibi.

The beautiful, mean, dear, horrifying faces of the children mounted on top of mature, amorphous, adult torsos.

"... *the beautiful, beautiful river* ... "

She was on her belly and chest, dragging herself forward, clawing at the sand, inch after white inch. Crying so many red tears.

"Cindy ... Cindy ..."

She stopped. Exhausted. She turned her head sideways and rested her cheek on Piryatuppu.

The two figures danced a circle around her. Evvie's eyes, caked with sand and blood, stayed open. The face that was Cindy dripped flesh in pieces. The face that was Bibi sang through a smile that stretched gray skin beneath dark hollow eyes.

Evvie extended an arm toward Cindy, red fingers reaching.

Evvie passed out.

Back in the pit, beside the hollow stone, Purkwet Kala looked at the moon.

Chapter 21

Karatuppu. Only a few hours to daylight. Evvie wished it were more. She moved six steps farther and stopped. Sea fog rolled around the trunks of trees like slow-moving water. The air was cold.

She moved forward again. Clots of wet dirt stuck to her bare feet with every step. The silence was so complete that she could hear the material of her baggy sweat pants rub like newspaper being crumpled in a funeral parlor.

Despite the cold, sweat ran down the center of her back. The cuts on her face and scalp throbbed, but the sting of washing them clean in the channel had gone away. Her memory of what had happened on Piryatuppu was disjointed and confused. She remembered smelling the strange vapor. And that she must have passed out and fallen on the lava rocks because everything after that was a blur. Except for some stupid hallucinations, birds, ghosts …

Evvie reached the tree that Ted had been chained to. She desperately wanted to go by it, get to the gathering house, lie down in a dark corner, and sleep forever. But she was conscious enough to remember her mission, and she might not get another chance. She stood motionless in the dark, listening, looking, making sure that no one was there to see. Then she knelt down and pushed her hands into the sand.

Her fingers burrowed down to a place that still retained the heat of yesterday's sun. Fine grains sifted along the skin of her fingers like warm gloves going on. Seven inches under the surface, she felt a fibrous mesh of palm capillaries. She groped along the interface of sand and root like she was searching for something on a thick rug in a pitch-dark room. Her hands tunneled and lifted out and tunneled again for several minutes in a search that was as random as it was fruitless. She closed her eyes to concentrate her sense of touch. The feel of warm sand and the smell of ocean air let memory resurrect the child: Evvie on a beach long ago, eight years old, the fragrance of seaweed, a day simple and safe ... before other kids began to tease.

A whisper of sound jolted Evvie back to reality. Her eyes opened wide. She listened. It came again. A faint rustle. Something moving in the night.

Cold mist drifted toward her. But the white veil had changed.

She stared at a slowly spinning vortex of mist that churned as though something had passed along the beach just out of sight and disrupted the easy motion of the drifting fog.

She didn't move. She leaned forward on hands and knees. Waiting.

The swirling gap closed before it reached her, and everything was as it was before.

She listened to silence. One minute passed. Two. No more sound. No moving shadow.

What was there had passed by, if anything had been there at all.

The fog was a white silence with two faces, one friendly, one terrifying: a shroud that hid her, but at the same time a curtain that concealed danger. She began to dig again. No longer hunting at random, but in planned increments.

Something hard touched her left wrist.

She grasped the tiny transmitter and lifted it up through the sand. The sending unit. She brushed away dirt. She unwrapped the coils of aerial wire and saw that one end of the capsule was notched. She snapped the lid open and a small battery slid halfway out. The battery was the size of a cube of sugar, not colored like typical batteries, but smooth and gloss-black with a fluorescent-green letter "L" printed on one side. She pushed the battery back into the transmitter and snapped the lid shut. She placed the capsule on the sand beside her knee and dug down again. She searched to see if anything else was buried there, the receiving part, a spare battery, anything. But she found nothing else. She hadn't expected to find more.

She picked up the transmitter and put her finger on the activating switch. Who would hear her? What should she say? Her fingertip wavered on the black button. She remembered Mark's words: *"No one wants to help ... we don't count."*

She couldn't decide what to do. Logic told her to push the switch.

But something else said no.

She wiped tears with the back of her hand and tried to decide. She put the transmitter back in the hole and covered it over.

She smoothed out the signs of digging and stood up. Everything looked the same as it had before ... except for the tiny craters her tears made on the surface of the sand. She did not see those. No one else would see them either.

She started back in the direction of the gathering house. After a few steps she stopped. The quick fear was there again. She turned slowly and looked at the shadow of the tree where she had been digging.

Nothing moved. No sound.

White mist flowed from an unseen sea and folded around the mysteries of Karatuppu.

Evvie was asleep in the gathering house when she was awakened by Ile's voice close to her ear. The Indian girl was kneeling beside her. "Evvie! Wake up."

Men's voices shouted in the first light of morning.

From her sleeping mat, Evvie was able to see Nagolo standing in the door of the gathering house. He was looking out.

"Your face. What ..."

"I slipped and fell, Ile. I hit some rocks. I know it looks bad, but I'm okay. Why are the men yelling? What's happening?"

"Come."

They went to the door and looked past Nagolo.

She still couldn't see why the men were excited. Then a man moved, and Evvie saw what they were looking at. One of El Codo's men sat with his back against a palm tree. Evvie brushed past Nagolo and hurried toward the group. She stopped thirty feet from them, close enough to see what the commotion was about. The yellow handle of a screwdriver protruded from the top of the sitting man's head. The tool had been driven straight into the skull on the center line. To the hilt. The man was the one who usually slept by the motor launches because he was responsible for keeping the boat gear in order.

El Codo came out of his hut. Mark followed a few steps behind.

They stopped in front of the body. El Codo said some words to his men, then nodded at Mark and started walking toward the Cuna gathering house.

Ten minutes later, Evvie and all the Indians, including the children, were lined up side by side in the clearing.

El Codo went to the left end of the line, stopped, and stared into the eyes of the first one. Ile. Twelve inches separated the two.

Ile lowered her gaze, but El Codo put a closed fist under her chin and pushed her head up so she had to look at his face.

He moved along the line. He looked straight into each face for several seconds. When he came to Evvie, his stare was no different. Cold, eating eyes. She saw him focus for a moment on the cheek cut she got on Piryatuppu, but he didn't ask her about it. What he looked for was guilt, fear, defiance ... something to betray the murder. What he saw in Evvie said she knew nothing about the killing. And that was all he was after. Nothing else mattered.

After he reached the end of the line, he frowned, then turned to Mark. He said a few words and pointed at the ground in front of him. Mark motioned to the four remaining members of El Codo's gang. They shuffled into position and formed a ragged rank. El Codo passed down the line and looked at each in the same malignant way that he had looked at the Cunas and Evvie.

When he finished staring into the eyes of the last man, he stepped back. Evvie saw something in his face she hadn't seen before. There was the cold rage, a violence always part of his expression, but there was something else, a puzzled furrowing of the hard skin around the reptile eyes.

He walked over to Mark again and spoke a short sentence.

Mark turned and walked east under the trees. El Codo went to his hut and disappeared inside.

A few minutes later, after the Indians and the men had dispersed in silence, she saw Mark leading Ted toward El Codo's hut. The anchor hanging from Ted's neck clanked with each step he took and beat cadence like a funeral drum made out of steel.

Mark grabbed Ted's arm, pushed him into El Codo's hut, and followed him inside.

Evvie turned to face Nagolo. "What happened to that man?"

"I do not know," he replied.

"Nagolo? ..."

"I did not kill the man, Evvie. When El Codo looked into all the eyes, he did not see the killing." Nagolo turned his head toward El Codo's hut. "Do you think the man Ted did the killing?"

"I don't know."

"I do not think he did."

"Nagolo. Listen to me. Do you think you could find a gun? When you go for the water today? Could you bring back a gun so we can fight them?"

Questions that didn't have to be asked made him lower his eyes. They both knew what would happen if he brought back a gun and it was discovered. The boats were always searched after returning from the jungle rivers. And if a mainland Cuna, a friend, should wonder why those on the island of Karatuppu needed a gun and came to investigate? There would be a blood bath. For them and for anyone who came to help.

Nagolo's love for Olonaya was his life. His feelings for the others were nearly as great. El Codo had promised the Cunas that when the business on Karatuppu was finished, they'd be left in peace. And Nagolo knew that the killer wasn't one of the Cunas. What had happened to Bibi happened because they had disobeyed El Codo.

Evvie watched a brave man struggle.

"There is a gun at Ciedras. I will try," he said. He headed for the cayucos where ten empty water cans waited in a row.

Evvie went into the gathering house and sat alone on her blanket. She thought about Nagolo's question. *Do you think the man Ted did the killing?*

She remembered El Codo's stare when he lined them up to look at them. She couldn't imagine how anyone, including his own men, could have hidden from those eyes. A bead of sweat, a tremble, a held breath. No one could hold under that gaze. The body would give some sign. She had never underestimated the ability of one human being to lie to another, but that was before she had seen the horror that was El Codo.

There were only two possibilities. Ted. Or Mark. In a few minutes she'd know if it was Ted. They'd all know. She tried to picture what was going on in El Codo's hut.

"It wasn't your husband."

"How do you know?"

"Because," said Mark, "ol' Ted was drinking with his new beach buddy last night in one of the hootches. All night."

She looked hard at him. *It has to be you.*

"I know what you're thinking, Miss Evvie, but I didn't do it."

"Then the only other possibility is El Codo himself."

"No. Think about it, Evvie. We both know Carlos is psycho. If this was a normal job and he thought he had a mutiny brewing, he'd chop the whole lot of us into bait. His men and your Indians, too. He needs to hold this operation together. He needs to keep these Indians going back and forth to the mainland like nothing's wrong. And he has to keep his gang in the game so they can cover his ass and keep the Indians from pulling off a mass breakout. If his men think their boss has shifted into slaughter mode, they might panic and take the boats. Even Carlos has to sleep sometime. He's too close to the last inning to start decorating Karatuppu with guts. The last thing he needs is a stampede. He's still holding all the cards. He's collected all the weapons and buried them somewhere. He's the only one with a gun. No one can stop him as long as he doesn't screw it up himself."

"Then who? ..."

"It can't be one of the Cunas," he replied. "They've got too much to lose, unless that Indian Nagolo decided that his baby needed some kind of special send-off to that big island in the—"

"It's not Nagolo," she interrupted.

"Then it has to be one of Carlos' own guys. Someone who's a hell of an actor and has a set of balls that would make a bull blush."

"Who? Which one?"

"I don't know which one," he replied. From the look on his face, she knew that he didn't.

A familiar voice cut the air. It called Mark's name like a thrown knife. They looked toward the huts and saw El Codo signaling in their direction.

"Radio time, coach." Mark smiled a grim smile and started off. "Have a nice day."

Olonaya continued sewing the mola without looking up at Evvie. "The old woman thinks it is Purkwet Kala. She says she heard him scream last night."

"I didn't hear a scream."

"Perhaps it was in her mind," said Olonaya. "Sometimes the spirits speak only to those who believe."

"Do you believe?"

"I believed once." Olonaya stopped sewing and stared into space. "I try to believe." Evvie watched Olonaya's eyes move to the patch of fresh earth in the gathering house floor under her hammock.

The Indian began sewing on the mola again. "What I think is not important. What is important is that El Codo and his men, they were eight. Now they are six."

Evvie reached out and put a gentle hand on Olonaya's shoulder. "I think there may be only five."

"The man Mark?"

"Yes."

"I have seen how you talk to that one. Does your heart say this is true?"

"Yes."

"Then they are five."

"Will you help us fight El Codo and the others?" she asked.

"I wondered when that was coming."

"I have to know."

"There's a chance you'll all make it if you just do what you're told. There's no chance in hell if you don't."

"Look at me, Mark." His head came up. She spoke softly. "You don't believe that."

"Yes. I do believe that."

His answer came too quickly. He was trying to bring back doubt, trying to shift his indecision to her. But she was beginning to understand the other side of fear. She could change fear to fight. Fight gave her tomorrow. And it was *her* fight. There was no "handsome prince," no "shining knight" to get between her and dragons. The time had come to pray for strength, not salvation.

He looked away when he spoke. "You kill Carlos? What with? Then you'll have to kill Spider, too. Lousy odds."

"I'm not worried about your damned Spider. The one I'm worried about is El Codo. If we fight him now, we won't have to worry about

Spider later. We'll be gone before Spider gets here."

"Carlos is going to let everyone go just before Spider hits the beach. He told me that. He'll let you and the Cunas take off in the cayucos as a favor to me. He said he'd do it to pay me back for what I did for him."

"Don't believe him, damn it! He said that to keep you in line."

"I think you should wait."

"No."

He spun around and glared at her. "Look what happened the last time you tried to make a move." He rushed past the cruelty of the remark. "And what *did* happen to your face last night, anyway?"

She fired right back at him. "I'm going to try to get out of here," she said. "Don't try to stop us."

"Promise me one thing," he said. "Whatever you decide, let me know what it is first. If you go off half-cocked and screw it up, I'm not going to be able to stand by and watch him roast you. Then I'd be fucking finished, too. I'd like to maybe have a fighting chance."

"I don't make promises anymore."

"You'll get yourself killed, you and your goddamned little brown friends."

She stepped inches from his face. Her words were as definite as cracked glass. "Do yourself a favor. Help us." She turned and walked away.

Chapter 22

Late in the afternoon Evvie watched Nagolo return with the supplies. The cayuco coasted into the shallows of the coral lagoon. Sixty yards from shore he shipped his paddle and climbed over the side into three feet of water. He took a few minutes to bail out the canoe with a tin can. Then he splashed water over his face and torso to wash away the sweat of the journey. He pushed the boat across the shallows to the beach. The man guarding the other cayucos watched him come. When the boat reached the beach, he ordered Nagolo to stand aside while he examined the canoe and its cargo.

The guard gestured to the Indian to begin unloading the supplies. Nagolo transferred water containers and a few smaller items onto the beach. None of the parcels that he put on the sand was big enough to hide a rifle, and the way the guard shook the containers and looked inside convinced Evvie that Nagolo hadn't brought back a pistol either. Her spirits sank as Nagolo dragged the empty cayuco onto the beach and turned it over to dry out. She half expected that he might have attached a weapon to the bottom of the boat somehow, wrapped in plastic, hidden in a hollow in the wooden hull. But there was nothing.

As Nagolo carried the water cans past the place where she stood under the trees, he didn't look at her.

She watched him take two containers to El Codo's hut. He left them outside on the ground by the entrance. Then he hauled the rest, eight in all, to a shaded platform in the center of the island. Immediately, one of El Codo's men removed two of the biggest containers and took them toward the boats on the east beach.

Evvie didn't try to talk with Nagolo. He disappeared into the gathering house. She walked north until she could see across the pass between Karatuppu and Piryatuppu. The outgoing tidal current was strong, but she had memorized the times between tides when the water was slow enough to swim the three children and Alecta across the channel pass.

If something happened, they could try to hide there, maybe fight from the top of the beach. But how? With what? Piryatuppu offered less cover than Karatuppu and fewer things to make into weapons. The only advantage was the water barrier between the islands. Water. Not much of a weapon.

She turned and walked toward the east beach and watched for El Codo's men. She saw no one. She came to the tree that Ted had been chained to, the tree where the transmitter was buried. Something caught her eye. Half-covered by sand was the six-foot pole that El Codo had used to impale Bibi. Evvie placed a bare foot on the wood. The cutting machete had been wielded with precision. The pole's blood-tinted tip was honed to a needle-sharp spike.

She glanced north and south.

The beach was still clear.

She put her full weight on the pole and forced it flat so the pointed end no longer stuck up at an angle.

With her feet she covered the wooden shaft with sand.

As Evvie neared the gathering hut, Olonaya stepped from the shadow of a tree. "The white man, the one called Mark. He says he will meet you at the south end of the island. He must talk with you. He says it is important."

"Now? Am I to go now?"

"Yes. At once."

"Spider is on the coast."

"How long do we have?" She stood next to him and looked south toward the Gulf as day turned into night. They did not face one another. Mark tossed small pebbles one by one far out into dark shallow water. To anyone watching, their meeting would appear casual, their words unhurried, unimportant.

"No more than three days," he answered. "Maybe two. I was with Carlos when the transmission came in on the hand-held unit. They jabbered in their half-assed cover code, but I know most of it by now. Spider's call is Alpha Omega. Like I told you before, the hand-held radio is line of sight, straight-line transmission. It can't send more than twenty miles, thirty miles if conditions are perfect. Judging from the signal line, I'd say he's on a coastal island called Patmos." He threw a pebble in the direction of the mainland. "Fifteen miles. Right over there."

Evvie shut her eyes tightly. *So this is it.* "If he's that close, then why the wait?" The control in her voice surprised her. "He could be here a lot sooner than that."

"Spider could be here tonight if he wanted to, but there's talk about getting some kind of ship into position outside Panamanian waters." He bent down and scooped up another handful of pebbles. "Carlos turned away from me when they talked days, but it sounded like they were concerned about the weather. So, it's three days at the most. That's how much longer this stuff will stay sloppy. Rain, fog, overcast. They want the bad weather for cover. Karatuppu is about to get real popular."

"I've got to do something," she said.

"I still want you to tell me before you pull anything stupid."

"I'll tell you … as soon as I figure it out."

"There's something you ought to know. He's going to post a guard on your hut until tomorrow morning. That bit with the guy with the screwdriver hat has him antsy. Once the sun goes down, you and your Indians are in for the night."

"Will you help?"

"If you come up with some half-assed idea that's going to get you killed, I'll tie you to a tree."

On her way back to the gathering house, she saw that the guard Mark said would be there was there. None of El Codo's men guarded the cayucos. She had made a point to pass the canoes on the way back.

Evvie sat on her blanket with her back against the cane wall of the gathering house. She watched the Cunas bundle the children into their sleeping hammocks. One by one the women put away their sewing, finished small chores, and also slipped into hammocks. By the middle of the evening, Evvie was the only one awake.

As she sat and stared at the embers in the fire pit, she tried to rearrange the pieces of the past four months. Her life turned upside down and inside out. Ted. How could he have deceived her for so long? How in the hell could she not have seen? What did he expect would happen to them after this mission of his was over? *Kiss and make up? A bouquet of roses?* All the signs she had missed. He was more loyal to his government agency than he was to his family; the DEA was more cult than organization; Ted more a cult fanatic than a federal employee. She knew enough agents to know that they weren't all like Ted, but what caused the few to break like this? Frustration? Too much pressure? Sampling the goods? Fighting the unwinnable war?

Without answers to those questions, she put them away. Instead, she began to inventory her wounds. The gouge in her cheek hurt the most because she kept trying to push her tongue through it to the outside. What bothered her more than the actual pain was the fact that she really didn't know how she'd been cut. She might have been gouged by something that could cause an infection. She promised herself to leave it alone. *No more tongue in cheek.* The leg injured in the alley and slashed in the wreck was healed as far as function was concerned. *So what if it looks like a road map of San Francisco.* The scratches and bruises she got when pig-man went after her still hurt. But now she noticed the hurt only when she washed those cuts in the saltwater of the lagoon. *Talk about your crummy dates.* She ran it all through one more time. Colon. Piryatuppu. The boat wreck. Pig-man. El Codo's little present to Mark. *That slab of meat in the* Rocky *movie, I can do that.*

She smiled at the goofball one-liners she managed to string together out of garbage. Macabre tinsel on January's Christmas tree. Then she realized what it meant. It wasn't just her body that was toughening up.

The embers dimmed, and finally she stretched out on her pallet. Just before sleep came, she saw something move in the shadow on the far side of the hut. She kept still and watched Niki ease out of his hammock. The small naked figure, his back to her, rummaged in a dark corner. He straightened up and crept cat-like toward the front of the hut. He carried something in his left hand, some kind of stick. She couldn't make out what it was.

Evvie assumed Niki was going to relieve himself in the chamber pot left by the entry door. But something was wrong. *A stick? To go to the pot?* She sat up.

The reed arrow came off the small bow with fair speed. Aimed through a narrow gap in the cane wall of the gathering house, which served to stabilize its trajectory, the two-foot-long missile traced a shallow parabola across the clearing and impacted the guard's bare belly one inch below the navel.

And bounced off.

The arrow had no point on it, but it was moving fast and its business end was small enough in cross section so that it stung like a wasp. The guard, half-asleep, had been entertaining a vision of tarantulas. All men have a phobia. That was his.

He came up off the earth with a fearful leap, frantically slapping at his stomach and unleashing a string of expletives before calming down to search for his assailant. He couldn't find the tarantula. And the reed arrow on the ground in front of him looked like any other small stick.

When the commotion outside died down, Evvie looked back at the children's hammocks. One swung back and forth. Niki's.

Nagolo came to her in the night. He touched her arm.

Instantly awake. "Nagolo!"

"I have the rifle."

"Thank God!"

"It is in the water. Where I stepped out of the boat and washed."

"When you bailed the boat?"

"Yes. It is wrapped in a piece of cloth the color of the sand."

"Can you find it again?"

"It is in a line with the door of the gathering house and the tall tree where the dead man was. Ten meters inside the reef."

"Now we have a chance."

"We must get the gun in the night," he whispered. "Before the sun comes back. Then it could be put under the sand on the beach."

"How do we get past the guard?"

"I do not know," he said. "I thought I could go into the sea to make water in the night. I did not know they would guard the hut."

She sat up. "Nagolo, I'll distract the man. I'll make him walk to the side of the hut away from the beach. If I do that, can you get the gun?"

"The night is good for us. There will be a cloud moon. There is mist from the sea. They will not see. Yes. I can find the gun."

"How long? How long will it take you?"

"Twenty minutes. I am sure it can be done in twenty minutes."

• • •

Evvie stood in the doorway of the gathering house and looked out at the guard. He sat on the ground with his back against a tree. A small fire burned on bare ground at his feet … to keep tarantulas away. He was wrapping black friction tape around a machete handle and testing the grip every few turns.

The man looked up.

Evvie was wearing the tattered sweat pants. Nothing else.

She walked across the clearing and stopped six feet in front of him. "I would like to wash myself. May I go behind the hut? Will you let me go there to wash?"

He regarded her with disinterest. "Wash inside. Use the rain buckets to wash. Like the others."

"But I do not like to wash in front of the Indians. They always stare at me. They watch what I do."

"Go back in the hut. It will be morning in four hours. Wash then. No one goes outside tonight."

"May I use those bushes?" She nodded toward the island side of the hut where brush came up against the cane wall. "Please? I do not want them watching me." She hooked her thumbs into the waist of the sweat pants and pushed them down on her hips.

The guard said nothing, but his eyes opened more.

She pushed the waistband lower. She saw him look there. His eyes glittered in the orange light coming from the low fire in front of him.

"Wash," he growled.

"Thank you."

"Do not try to run away. Stay where I can see you."

She pulled her waistband up and went back into the gathering house. A few moments later she reappeared with a wooden bucket half-full of water. She smiled at the guard and walked into the shadows on the island side of the hut. Between low bushes and the wall, she bent forward and pushed the sweat pants down to her ankles. She stepped out of them and draped them over a clump of brush. Naked, she edged a few steps farther into the space between hut and bushes.

She didn't turn in the direction of the guard, but she knew that he was watching her. She knew he looked at the curves of her naked backside.

She squatted down and picked a wash rag out of the bucket. She washed her face and neck. She washed slowly and ladled water into her hair with cupped hands. Then she stood and carried the bucket farther into the shadows.

Her heart pounded as she waited for the guard to order her back nearer the clearing.

Get up, you bastard. Get your ass over to the corner of the wall. It was the critical moment. She had to get him to move away from the front of the hut so Nagolo could get out.

Don't call me back.

No call came.

The low light dimmed more, as though a curtain had been drawn between her and the small fire in the clearing. The man had moved. He had moved so he could see her better and had blocked some of the light. She put the bucket on the ground, picked up the washing cloth, then dropped it on purpose. As she stooped to retrieve it, her eyes flicked toward the guard.

He was standing at the corner. Past the corner. Out of sight of the door.

She began to wash. Arms, breasts, ribs.

One minute gone.

Ankles, slender legs, back, backside. Each movement slow, caressing. Bending, turning slightly. Wetting the rag in the bucket, then wringing it out. Deliberately. Unhurriedly.

Five minutes gone.

What if he should come to me? What if he tries to …

She pictured Nagolo wading through the shallow lagoon in the dark, alone and afraid, moving toward the rifle.

Come here. Come all the way if you have to. But keep watching me. Keep looking!

She moved the cloth between her legs. Her legs and all her other parts seemed to belong to somebody else. She was an actress on a stage. Performing.

Ten minutes gone.

She spread her legs farther apart and washed more thoroughly there, still with her back to him. She scooped water out of the bucket and splashed it on her thighs and belly. Wrung out the cloth and dried that place. Rubbed.

Then she repeated the sequence of bathing between her legs all over again. But this time she braced a slender leg high against the cane wall of the hut. Bending. Stretching. Trying to move so that every turn of her body gave a new angle to the man at the corner.

Washing with the cloth. Splashing handfuls of water.

Eighteen minutes gone.

She raised the bucket and poured the last of the water onto her head and neck and let the cold liquid cascade down her upraised arms and torso.

She twisted the wash rag to get out the last of the water, then leaned her right hand flat against the side of the hut to steady herself as she wiped flecks of mud and stick and leaf from the bottoms of her feet.

She stepped gingerly out of the wet area of dirt as she dried each foot, then retrieved the tattered sweat pants that were hanging from a branch of brush.

She stepped back into her single piece of torn clothing.

Twenty-five minutes.

Nagolo was safe.

An hour before dawn, a blood-freezing howl woke everyone sleeping on the island. This time, it wasn't only the Cuna grandmother who heard the call of death. This time they all heard it.

Evvie tumbled toward the door of the gathering house. Most of the Cunas cowered in hammocks, but not Nagolo. He reached the entrance at the same time she did.

"Nagolo! What's ..."

They watched in stunned silence as a ghastly apparition staggered under the trees on the far side of the island, the shape of a man engulfed in flames from head to foot. The fire reached high up toward the palm leaves. The figure seemed to be coming from the beach where the motor launches were kept. So wrapped in pain that it walked away from the lagoon where saving water was. It shrieked again. Evvie couldn't take her eyes off it.

The flame-wrapped monster seemed in no hurry. It made no more sound. It moved slowly under the trees and where it brushed against a palm trunk, the outside bark of the tree burned also.

Evvie glanced toward El Codo's hut. He was standing in front of the door, staring like the rest of them. She didn't see Mark and she didn't look for him. Her eyes were drawn back to the incredible sight of the burning shape.

The thing was slowing. Its steps were shorter. Its arms came up and formed bent curves and seemed to freeze in that up-reaching position. Then it fell forward onto the dirt. A burst of fresh flame exploded skyward as the impact with the ground released burning debris.

The heap burned brightly on the earth for almost two minutes before the flames seemed to suck down and go out. Moments later Evvie saw only a lump of man glowing on packed dirt. All the faces that watched from huts and next to trees were lost back to darkness once more.

The island of Karatuppu seemed suddenly pushed back a thousand years to a place of demons and stalking gods.

"Nagolo?" Evvie's voice cracked.

"I do not know … I do not know," he said.

Evvie watched his face as panic warred with reason behind Nagolo's eyes. He gripped a cane slat that he had partially torn out of the doorjamb.

She pried his fingers off the wood. The brave young man's hands shook. Side by side they stood and stared at the place where the glow had faded to smoke beneath the palms.

Behind them in the gathering house, the chant of the grandmother began. A low sound. Soothing.

At dawn the charred remains of El Codo's outboard mechanic were buried on the east beach between screwdriver man and the half-headed pig-man who had attacked Evvie. An empty gasoline container found near the boats was buried, too.

Twenty minutes later, Olonaya returned to the gathering house with a trance-like expression on her face. She had gone to the beach to wash clothes in the sea.

She walked past the others without speaking. She sat down on the ground next to the hammock where the old woman continued to chant softly. Olonaya's head began to sway from side to side in time with the old woman's incantation.

Evvie watched Nagolo, who was watching Olonaya. Nagolo walked over to his wife. Evvie followed.

Nagolo knelt down. Evvie stood behind him. Olonaya stared straight ahead.

"What is wrong?" asked Nagolo. "What did you see?"

Olonaya did not answer.

He reached out and touched her hand. Olonaya jerked as though burned by a hot ember. Slowly, Olonaya turned to look at him.

"My wife, what is it? What did you see?"

Olonaya stared at him for a few moments, then smiled like a child trying to comprehend an adult, a child wanting to please but not understanding words.

Evvie put a hand on Nagolo's shoulder and kneeled next to him. She looked into Olonaya's face. "She's in shock, Nagolo. Where did she just come from?"

Nagolo turned slightly toward Evvie, but kept his eyes on Olonaya. "She went to the beach to wash the …"

Evvie was on her feet at once and moving. She was one step ahead of Nagolo and going out the door when, behind them, Olonaya screamed.

The wash basket sat on the sand at the water's edge. Draped over its lip were some unwashed garments and two drying towels. A third towel lay on smooth sand some distance away, to the right of the basket. A few feet offshore, a pink Cuna skirt floated just under the water in the lagoon. Nagolo waded into the shallows while Evvie remained standing on the beach.

He picked up the skirt and twisted it in his hands to squeeze the water out. He half-turned toward the shore, then stopped. Something caught his eye farther out. He walked a few steps and bent down. She watched him reach beneath the surface. He lifted something off the bottom of the lagoon and wrapped it in the folds of the wet skirt. He came back to the beach, stood in front of her, and opened the folds of the skirt.

A machete.

She stared at it.

The grip was wrapped in friction tape.

"It was not this that made Olonaya scream," said Nagolo. He glanced left and right up the beach. His eyes stopped on the towel that lay on the sand twenty feet to the right of the clothes basket.

Holding the machete, still concealed by the skirt, Nagolo walked toward the towel.

Evvie followed.

He slipped the tip of the machete blade under one corner and lifted the towel off the sand.

Evvie gagged. Her eyes watered. She rammed her fist into her mouth, bit down on her knuckles, and fought down the stuff in her throat.

"Oh God, Nagolo." Whispered words. "Who? Who could? …"

They looked down at the face of the guard who had watched her bathe. The face was level with the surface of the smooth wet sand. Evvie watched the machete tip move again as Nagolo pushed sand away from the dead man's chin. A stump of chopped neck revealed that the head wasn't attached to a body. But the thing that made them stare without breathing was more than grisly. The eyes of the man had been gouged out, and in each socket … a round white stone.

She turned to Nagolo. What she saw brought her out of her trance. Nagolo was staring at her with an expression that hovered between disbelief and adulation.

She tried to understand what was in that look. Then she knew. "Nagolo! It was not me! I did not do this!"

He kept staring.

She extended her arm toward him, but he stepped back out of reach.

"It was not me," she said.

He did not move.

"Please, Nagolo. Don't …" She lowered her head and shut her eyes. *Don't leave me alone. Not now.*

She went to her knees.

His hand touched her cheek. He knelt in front of her. His arms went around her. They held each other.

Evvie watched one of El Codo's two remaining gang members take the severed head from the beach and carry it across the island. It was tossed into the trench on the east beach and covered over. The rest of the body, swept out to sea or submerged somewhere in the lagoon, was gone from Karatuppu. The pig-man with half a skull, the screwdriver man, the burned man, and now the severed head reposed in gruesome fraternity in white sand where black ants tunneled into meat.

Evvie wandered alone on the beach for most of the morning. *Four down, three to go. But who?* She tried to think, but the image of the face with the white stone eyes kept coming back. Finally she fell asleep with her back against a tree at the south end of the island where palms gave way to brush. She slept on and off until Mark found her.

"All hell's going to break loose. He gave me this knife, but I'm the only one." He raised the K-Bar slightly. Sun reflected off the cutting edge of the lightly greased blade. "He's got to trust somebody, but he doesn't let me get behind him. He's taken all the stuff out of the gathering hut that could be used as a weapon, even what his own men were carrying. Machetes. Knives. He hid everything. Probably buried it with the other guns. Except for the one he's got. He chained your husband to the tree like before."

She tried to understand what he was saying. His words echoed through her brain like he was speaking to her in a tunnel. She felt as though she were thirty feet in the air looking down at herself. She was acutely aware that part of her mind was trying to escape from the island. But another part kept pulling her back. She shook her head and tried to bring the two parts together. She forced herself to focus. "Ted's chained to a tree? The same tree?"

"The same one. Carlos has both keys, the one that goes to the lock on the chain around the tree and the one that fits the lock on the anchor around his neck." He glanced over his shoulder. "He's moved all the cayucos over near his own boats on the east beach. Easier to keep track of the boats if they're all in one spot." He paused. "There's something else," he said.

What? What else could there be?

"Now he doesn't have enough men to watch everything, the radios, the boats, his own back. ..." He hesitated. "Or your Indians. He can't watch it all twenty-four hours a day. Not anymore."

"What are you saying?" But she knew.

"He can't afford to keep your damned Cunas anymore."

Panic spread in her like ink poured in water.

He watched her. Then a slow smile. "Well, Miss Evvie. I think it's time to give these guys a push. What's left of them."

"You'll help us?"

"I'll help you. I'd sure appreciate it if you'd tell me who's turning these fellows into goo."

"Later. As soon as I figure it out."

"You think there's going to be a 'later'? Okay, coach. What's your plan?"

"When does Spider get here?"

"My guess is tomorrow. But that doesn't mean Carlos is going to wait that long before he ships your Indians to the spirit world. He can't handle another night like last night."

"It wasn't one of us! He has to know that!"

"He doesn't. It's the first time I've ever seen him without a clue. I think he's actually enjoying it. It's a new experience. His version of a crossword puzzle. But he won't play the game much longer."

She tried to think. He waited. "When do you two go on the radio this afternoon?" she asked.

"In two hours. Half past two."

"We're going to the island."

"What island?"

"Piryatuppu."

"Piryatuppu? When?"

"At half past two."

"In broad daylight? You're fucking nuts."

"That's why. No one will expect it."

"What about the other two? They'll be outside while we're on the radio."

"You're sure they don't have guns?"

"They don't have guns *now.*"

"We'll take our chances. You swim across later." She smiled at him.

"Just like that?"

"You're clever. Work it out."

"Jesus Christ." He shook his head.

"We don't have a choice. We have to go now. Besides …"

"Besides what?"

"We have our own gun."

"The old woman will not go." Nagolo lowered his eyes. He and Evvie were the only two in the gathering house.

"She has to come with us! If Alecta stays, El Codo will kill her."

"She will not go."

"Your brother? Your grandfather? Can they make her come?"

"I told them to try. But the old man is not strong. My brother has to help him get past the deep water. The old man cannot swim alone. The women must help the three children. I must swim with the gun."

Evvie felt sick to her stomach. If the old woman stayed behind, she knew El Codo would mutilate her. She forced the image out of her mind. There were eleven others to worry about. Nagolo would have to find a way to get the old woman across. "Where's the gun?" she asked.

"On the beach. Under the sand. There are five bullets."

She stared at him. "Five bullets? Only five?"

"I could get no more."

As much as she liked him, she wanted to scream at him. The urge passed quickly. He had done his best. "Where are the others?" she asked.

"They are in the water as you said. They make it look like they wash the children and the clothes. They are halfway toward the place where the water runs between Karatuppu and Piryatuppu."

"Get them closer to Piryatuppu."

"They are afraid. But I will make them move closer."

"The other two men, El Codo's men, where are they?"

"They are by the boats on the other side."

"And Alecta?"

"She waits in the water. But she will not go more toward Piryatuppu." He looked at Evvie. His words were soft when he spoke, almost too soft for her to hear. "She is old. She has lived her years. It is almost her time."

"Do you know how El Codo will kill her?"

"She is not afraid to die."

Evvie took his arm and steered him to the door. They looked out. Mark was standing with El Codo in front of El Codo's hut. After a few minutes, El Codo glanced at his watch and the two went inside.

"Now, Nagolo. Go now!"

"You? Where do you go?" he asked.

"Get your people moving. When you get to Piryatuppu, dig a trench in the sand close to the trees above the channel. Make a long ditch. Pile up the sand in front of it so you won't get hit by El Codo's bullets." She grabbed him by both arms and looked into his face. "As soon as the others are digging, you clean the gun. Clean it good! Put a clean bullet in it. Do you know how the gun works?"

"Yes, I know. I have shot a gun before."

"Remember, there must be no sand inside."

"I ask you again. Where do you go?"

"I'll make it across. Get moving. Be careful." She kissed him on the forehead.

He headed for the beach.

Evvie went to the back of the gathering house. She found one of Olonaya's long dresses. She ripped the material into a short skirt. She discarded the tattered sweat pants and put on the skirt. No top. She headed toward the east beach where El Codo's two remaining men guarded the boats.

Evvie jogged along the water's edge south of the two men. A light mist clouded the air, but they could see her plainly as she ran with her short skirt hiked up past the middle of her thighs. She kept her head down as she moved along, her bare feet leaving a line of scalloped impressions in wet brown sand.

Let this work. Just one more time. Give me the strength. I'm so tired.

She didn't glance up until she had closed to within sixty yards of them. They were staring at her. Evvie stopped. She waved at the men, a small tentative gesture.

They didn't wave back.

But they kept looking.

She walked out into the water far enough to cover her knees. She bent down, scooped water with her hands, and splashed it on her face and neck. She bent again and bathed her chest and arms.

She raised one arm and then the other. Water ran down her sides and sparkled into the lagoon.

She bunched the material of the short skirt with her left hand and used the right hand to ladle seawater onto her thighs.

She went through the G-rated version of the previous night's performance.

At one point, she let the skirt touch the sea. Pink cotton went from opaque to translucent.

She waded back to the shore, smoothing the skirt as the sea dropped away. On the beach, she brushed water drops from her arms. Then slowly, her toes exploring bits of shell and wood trapped in the line of seaweed, she worked her way north toward the men. A few steps. Stop to explore with toes. A few steps more. Stop again so wet cotton might tell secrets in the sunlight.

She bent three times to examine some small bit of flotsam and teased twenty minutes out of their day.

She tried to guess how much longer El Codo and Mark would take to complete the radio contacts. She had watched Mark go into the hut to work the radios before. It was never more than thirty minutes.

But each time that she made up her mind to try for Piryatuppu, she thought of the Cunas in the channel between the islands. The vision of them struggling in the water made her wait longer.

Too long.

A movement near Codo's hut caught her eye. She saw Mark step out of the door. He did not see her.

She recognized the shape of a weapon hanging from a strap that went around his neck and right shoulder. It resembled the two machine pistols Ted sold to another agent when they left San Diego.

He has a gun! El Codo gave him a gun!

El Codo hadn't come out of the hut.

She looked back at the two men who watched her. They were still standing by the boats near the tree line. Thirty yards of empty beach lay between the boats and the water's edge. An opening.

She took a deep breath and started to walk.

Be slow. Don't panic. Get past them first. Then run.

Her heart began to shovel blood.

Mark still hadn't seen her as she neared the invisible line between El Codo's men and the edge of the lagoon. When she was within ninety feet of the line, one of the men started to walk toward the water to cut her off.

She glanced left and saw Ted for the first time. He was chained to the tree and looking at her.

Sixty feet to the line.

Forty feet.

She raised one arm over her head and, with as much agitation as she could muster, waved and pointed frantically toward El Codo's shack. The man stopped, startled by what she did. He looked in that direction, confused.

Twenty feet.

Now!

Chapter 23

Evvie lowered her arm and exploded into a sprint. She was past the guard. She accelerated on the hard sand at the water's edge. Head down, elbows pumping, she forced herself to gulp air. Her body entered that free-float zone where runners coast at speed, the energy of the sprint turned off. No one could catch her. Not now. She had the traction. She had the speed. She breathed freedom. She could taste the freedom.

But the men who watched her were predators. Anything, human or animal, that ran like she ran triggered two types of reaction. One, danger. The other, pursuit.

The man who had started to walk toward her recovered. He shouted something at his companion and took off after Evvie. The second man looked north and south, then west across the island. He tried to see if there was a reason for the running. Then he started for El Codo's hut at a jog. As he ran, he saw that there were no Indians under the trees, no Indians coming and going from the gathering hut, no Indians on the beach.

Mark heard the man approaching and turned. Beyond the one jogging toward him, Mark saw El Codo's other man running fast on the beach and heading north. Mark didn't see Evvie, but there could be no other reason for the running. They didn't run for exercise. They ran to escape. Or to kill. Mark's fingers closed around the receiver of the MAC-10 on his right hip.

"Something's going on! The Indians are gone! That woman—"

Mark cut the man's words short. "Carlos! The Cunas! They're making a break!"

El Codo was at the door in an instant, pistol drawn and ready.

Mark pointed south, away from Piryatuppu. He tried to keep his voice low, reasoned. "I'll bet they're trying to get to the mainland. Another bunch might have brought a boat."

El Codo looked south, then north.

"You want me to check the north end to be sure?" asked Mark.

El Codo hesitated and looked toward the Gulf end of the island. "You! With me," he barked to his man. "Mark, check north." El Codo and his man started off at a run, heading south.

Mark watched them for a few seconds until he was sure they were going to keep going, then he turned and ran north toward Piryatuppu.

Evvie neared the place where the beach curved toward the channel. The exhilaration of speed had dissolved away. The hard sand was gone. Loose pieces of sharp coral cracked beneath her bare feet. Fear began to build. She fought off the image of the channel dotted with the heads of Indians still in the water.

She staggered around the last stand of trees. Empty. The channel was empty. On the raised slope of Piryatuppu's beach, she saw the Cunas digging furiously in white sand at the tree line.

They made it! They made it across!

Her left leg, its muscles compromised by the hard run across the angled face of the beach, cramped up. She gripped the knotted thigh muscle with the fingers of her left hand and kept moving. The muscle convulsed more, but she stayed on her feet. She scrambled over the carcass of a twenty-foot section of tree trunk washed up on the beach parallel to the shoreline. Without the leg cramp she would have vaulted over the dead tree and been into the channel, but her left leg had turned to stone. She limped toward the saving water. Her eyes stayed focused on the people in the trench on Piryatuppu.

Her pursuer's shoulder drove into the middle of her back. She never heard him coming. He plowed into her with the full force of two hundred pounds barreling downhill from the tree line.

She skidded through grit under the terrible weight of him. A mean hand grabbed her left arm and twisted her over onto her back.

Evvie tried to see past eyelids that had turned to sandpaper. The face of the man was a sneering mask against the gray backdrop of sky. He was on his knees, straddling her hips.

Then she saw something else.

Fingers crowned the man's skull like some abstract headdress hanging down over his forehead. The fingers seemed to pull the head back.

The eyes rolled up at the fingers, then went wide as something quick and bright flickered across the man's throat from left to right.

She watched a crescent of red open in the flesh. Then, as the head was jerked back farther, the carved meat of the throat opened like a second mouth.

Twin streams of blood spurted from the sides of the gaping slice. Her eyes were bathed in warm liquid. Her world turned red.

"Get across, Evvie! Get across the water!"

"Mark?" The weight tumbled off her hips. "Mark?"

"Get across! I'll cover you. Carlos is coming. Move! Get going!"

Mark turned away from her and scrambled for cover behind the beached tree trunk. He pulled the MAC-10 strap over his head as he moved. She heard the charging bolt of Mark's weapon clank as it was pulled back and released.

She rolled onto her stomach, got on hands and knees, and scurried for the channel. She started to swim before her toes left the beach. After thirty furious strokes she heard a shot explode behind her. She tried to resist the urge to look back. She couldn't. She rolled into a side stroke and looked for Mark.

What she saw made her stop swimming. From her position in the center of the channel, she watched El Codo step from the tree line onto the sand. The muzzle of the pistol in his hand poked out through a ring of dissipating smoke. He fired again, fired at Mark who crouched behind the fallen tree and fumbled with the MAC-10.

El Codo walked upright. He knew Mark had the gun, but he didn't seem to care. Mark had cover; El Codo did not. He took another step onto the beach and fired once more. Evvie saw wood splinter in front of Mark's face.

Something was horribly wrong.

It doesn't work! His gun doesn't work!

She rolled over and continued to swim hard for Piryatuppu. There was one chance. "Nagolo! Nagolo!" She screamed the words. "Shoot at El Codo! Shoot at him!"

She tried to yell again, but inhaled saltwater. She coughed out some of it and swallowed the rest. She tried to shout once more, but her voice had stopped working.

Another shot. From Karatuppu.

Then, almost in the same instant, the sharp blast of a single round from Piryatuppu.

She reached the beach.

Her blood banged at her lungs for fuel. She scratched and scrambled up the sand slope, dove into the trench, and landed on top of Olonaya.

She fought for air. Air was glue.

Mark!

She poked her head over the edge of the trench. To her right, Nagolo's rifle cracked again. Round number two. Three left.

She looked toward the far side of the channel. Nagolo's shots had driven El Codo off the beach. She saw him lying prone in the tree line with his pistol braced against the side of a palm trunk. He was aiming toward the pass.

A two-headed creature lurched backward toward the channel on four legs. Evvie shook her head to clear her vision.

Mark was holding the body of the dead man in front of him, using it as a shield as he backed into the water. His arms were under the arms of the corpse and locked across its chest. The MAC-10 was gone.

El Codo's pistol flashed again. Evvie saw Mark stagger.

No! God, no!

He kept his footing. Kept moving backward.

Another shot from El Codo bounced the lifeless head into Mark's face. Hard.

Still he kept backing. Deeper water now. Up to his waist. Chest. Neck.

Two heads in the water. Mark swam behind and slightly to the side of his shield like he was saving a drowning man.

El Codo fired. Nagolo fired. Almost in the same instant.

Water erupted in a geyser in front of the towed face.

Mark twisted and Evvie saw a slash of torn red meat in the middle of his left forearm, the arm that was around the dead man's chest.

He was hit.

Nagolo fired again. For the fourth time.

Evvie looked up in time to see a spray of sand pepper El Codo's face. He hadn't been hit, but she saw that he was rubbing his eyes with the back of his gun hand.

Mark was in the middle of the channel.

Evvie jumped to her feet.

Her voice came back. It cracked out of her throat like a dog's bark. "He can't see, Mark! Codo can't see! Swim!"

A space opened between the floating corpse and Mark. She looked quickly across at El Codo. He was still rubbing his eyes. Evvie broke for the water. She got to Mark as he crawled onto the beach.

She helped him up. He vomited saltwater. Together they started for the trench. The gentle rise of the beach seemed to tilt toward the vertical. The hideous white sand sucked at her ankles like bottomless talc. He stumbled and fell and pulled her down.

Don't kill us. Not now.

They got to their feet again but were mired in a nightmare that wouldn't let legs work. They battled for everything and gained nothing. She waited for the shot that would split Mark apart.

The explosion came, but it came from almost in front of her. Nagolo's shot. The last round. She wondered in her monstrous slow-motion dream if he'd bought them enough time.

She looked up into a Cuna face.

"Olonaya? What are you doing out here? You should be in the trench!"

Hands reached out and pulled Mark away from her.

"Evvie." Olonaya's word.

"Get him to the trench," Evvie gasped. "Get Mark off the sand!"

"He *is* off the sand," said Nagolo. "You made it."

They gave her water. After ten minutes she sat up and watched Olonaya finish dressing Mark's wound. His left forearm was horribly torn, but no splinters of bone showed. Olonaya covered the injured muscle with tight wraps of cloth ripped from her dress. Mark was in pain, but he was smiling. He looked at Evvie. "Guess what?"

"I can't handle many more 'guess whats.'" She closed her eyes.

"Do you want the good news first or the bad?"

"Bad."

"Nagolo only had five cartridges."

"I know that. What's the good news?"

"Carlos doesn't know we're out of ammo. That means he won't try to send his last man across the channel tonight. As far as he knows, we'd shoot the guy. You did it, coach."

"How does he know we won't come after *him?*"

Mark stared at her in disbelief. "We go after him? After Carlos? You're joking, right?"

"We could."

"Why? Do you think he's worried about us after seeing how hot we were to get over here? There's no reason for us to go back. He knows it and so do I … in spite of whatever the hell you've got in mind."

"What happened to your gun?" she asked. "Why didn't it work?"

He reached into his pocket and pulled out a nine-millimeter round. He placed the copper-jacketed end of the bullet between his teeth and twisted the slug out of the casing. He turned the casing over. White sand poured out. "So much for trust," he said.

Evvie turned to Nagolo. "You saved our lives."

"No," he said. "It is you who saved our lives. Your magic is big."

She turned and spoke to Mark in English. "I wish to bloody hell he'd stop saying that."

"Christ, he's probably right."

"Evvie?" Nagolo looked away as soon as he said her name. "I am sorry about the old woman. She would not come."

She'd forgotten about Alecta. "Damn it, Nagolo! You said you'd try!"

"I did try. We all tried. But she went back to the gathering house. She is there. Her gods are of Karatuppu."

Inlota began to weep, and Ile moved next to her.

"I'm sorry, Nagolo," said Evvie. "I know you tried." She glanced at Mark. What El Codo would do when he found the old woman wouldn't lack for imagination.

Mark spoke quickly to change the subject, and Evvie realized that he did it to derail any thoughts of rescue. "Tomorrow's the big day," he said. "Spider's due on Karatuppu at one in the afternoon. That's what the last radio message was about. Carlos already destroyed all the radio equipment, except for the hand-held job he carries, part of their 'scorched-earth' policy so no one can use the radio gear to complicate things." Despite the pain, he forced a smile. "When do you want us to start dog paddling for Florida?"

"Tomorrow? You're sure Spider's coming tomorrow?"

"He'll come most of the way on one of those old diesel luggers that trade for coconuts. Good cover. Once Spider hears from Carlos that things are okay on the island, he'll slip over the side and paddle the last half-mile by himself. If one of those luggers stopped at Karatuppu, it would attract too much attention. The diesels never come here. Two days after Spider gets here, he gets lifted out somehow. Boat. Chopper. Whatever."

"By who?"

"I don't know. Someone big."

"What will they do to us?"

"You can bet Carlos isn't too upset about us being over here. He doesn't have to keep an eye on this bunch, now. He's down to his last man and himself ... and your husband. And he has the island."

She didn't fall for Mark's evasion. He hadn't answered her question. She asked it again. "What will they do to us? You said Spider's killing everyone."

He looked at her. Then looked away.

At midnight she reached over and shook him out of a restless sleep. "Mark ... Mark, wake up."

He groaned softly and came awake.

She moved close to his side. "We've got to try something," she said. "We can't just wait to be killed."

"Hey, coach. One day at a time. You got us over here. That's enough for now. Give it a rest."

She glared at him.

"I'll bet you didn't know you've got a partner in crime out here," he said. "Someone with maybe as much pain-in-the-ass potential as you."

"What do you mean?"

"That kid Niki. The morning after the boat guard got himself charcoaled, I caught the little squirt putting saltwater in the outboard tanks. I was pissed. Not about the boats. Carlos is going to scuttle them anyway. But the kid could have got himself diced. I kicked him in the ass and chased him off. All I got for my trouble was a salute and a smile. You sure he's not related to you?"

She smiled at his story.

"By the way," he said. "That guy who got turned into a fireball? I poked around the boats. That was no accident. The guy was probably passed out drunk or someone put a sleeper hold on him, then doused him with gasoline. Whoever it was didn't light him up right away. Time-delay ignition. A book of matches with a lit cigarette under the heads. I found it. Whoever torched him wanted time to disappear."

She sat up. "Ted? Ted knows how to do that."

"Not Ted. He's been on a steady date."

"Then who? ..."

He cut her short. "Do me a favor, Miss Evvie? Go the fuck to sleep. Everything will turn out okay." His tone was light. He was being male. But it didn't work. She saw his face.

Chapter 24

Two hours before sunrise, Evvie rolled onto her side. In the last moments of a strange dream, she came half-awake and couldn't remember where she was. As she moved, damp sand sticking to her bare back cracked into chunks and fell away in a gritty mosaic. The chill brought her fully awake. She sat up. The trench. Piryatuppu.

In the dream, phantoms with yellow eyes had been looking down at her from somewhere high above. Human shapes. Two of them. Familiar shadows that slowly backed away and melted into the depths of a dark sea.

She stared down the slope toward the water. The others slept. Mark slept. She counted. Everyone was there who was supposed to be there.

Dream?

The shorelines of Piryatuppu and Karatuppu framed the black void where unseen water flowed. The facing beaches radiated light, a mysterious memory of sun.

A dream?

She leaned forward and squinted at the channel. But saw nothing.

A dream. Only a dream.

She stared into the night for several minutes. Then lay back down. She drifted into a restless sleep.

She awoke to a murmur of sound, a confused jumble of human voices. The first light of day was gun-metal gray.

She looked up into Mark's face. He was kneeling beside her, his hand on her shoulder. She tried to smile, but his expression stopped the smile.

"Evvie?"

"What?"

"Ile's gone."

"Ile?" She tried to understand.

"She's gone. Nagolo says she went to get the old woman."

"Ile's gone?"

"She didn't tell anyone," said Mark. "She's not here. Nagolo says he's going after her."

Evvie sat up and looked for Nagolo. He was crouched at the far right end of the ditch like an animal. He was preparing to make a run for the water.

"Nagolo!" The sound of her voice was fierce. "Wait!"

Mark's grip on her shoulder suddenly turned to iron and stopped her words. "Jesus Christ! Look!"

She looked where he was looking.

Across the channel on Karatuppu, El Codo moved in the tree line. He stood behind Ile, his deformed left hand buried in her straw-colored hair. He pushed the girl in front of him as he walked. He stopped on the top edge of the beach.

Ile was naked. A red welt ran diagonally from her right shoulder down between her small breasts to the left side of her ribs near the hip, the kind of mark that a whip would make. Except for the ugly red slash, Evvie saw no other injuries.

El Codo kept the girl positioned in front of his body as he looked across the water at them. "Mark, my good friend!" he shouted. "Did you sleep well?"

Mark started to stand up in the trench. Evvie grabbed the seat of his pants and pulled him back down. The dressing over Mark's wound dripped blood on the sand.

El Codo held a .45 pistol in his right hand.

No one on Piryatuppu made a sound.

"Mark! Let's not spend too much time on this." El Codo jerked Ile's head back hard. "This is going to be a fine day. I'd like that rifle the Indian has. Bring it over here. I'll trade it for this white Indian."

Ile had known that there weren't any more rifle rounds. She hadn't talked.

No one on Piryatuppu answered El Codo.

"I can give her to you in pieces if you like."

They watched as he angled the .45 toward the back of Ile's right knee.

"Wait!" This time Mark stood up in spite of Evvie's grasp. "I'll bring the rifle. Don't shoot her."

El Codo peered around Ile's head and squinted at Mark. "What happened to your arm, my friend? Why is it wrapped up like that? Did you hurt it?"

"I'm coming over, Carlos."

"Can you swim with one arm and the rifle too, Mark? I don't think so."

"I'll make it." Mark turned in Nagolo's direction to find the rifle. What he saw instead was Evvie stepping out onto the sand. She carried the empty weapon and was walking away from the trench toward the pass.

The rifle in her hand felt light. Like it was made of cardboard. Her pulse pounded. Not from fear. Excitement. *You can't kill me, you rat bastard. Not after what I've been through. Not now. This thing has got to end.* She had no idea what she was going to do next, but she'd get Ile back. Then she'd worry about El Codo. She almost felt sorry for him.

El Codo watched her come.

She stopped at the channel's edge. "If you let her go, I'll throw the gun in the water."

El Codo aimed the pistol at Ile's knee again.

Evvie waded into the channel. The bottom dropped away quickly. The rifle, because of its wooden stock, seemed weightless underwater. She side-stroked into the channel using one arm to swim and the other to tow the weapon on her hip. The outgoing tide wasn't running full yet, but it pulled her hard toward the sea. She kicked with her legs and tired quickly. She barely reached the beach on the other side. Exhausted and choking, she crawled out of the water on her hands and knees, dragging the rifle. She stopped moving forward and tried to get her breath back.

"Open the chamber," El Codo ordered, his pistol leveled at her.

She raised the rifle from the wet sand. After a few seconds of fumbling, she managed to pull the bolt up and back. She held the weapon in front of her and showed him what she had done.

He motioned with his pistol for her to bring the rifle to him.

As she walked up the slope, she noticed that Ile's lips were cut and saw the white splinters of broken upper front teeth. The girl's eyes were blank and staring. Evvie stopped two feet away. El Codo let go of Ile's hair.

"Now I let you go," he said to Ile. He nodded toward the trees. "Don't forget the old woman. That's what you came for." He looked at Evvie. "How does the Bible say? Do unto others? Eye for eye? Head for head?"

Ile turned and walked slowly back to the tree shadows with unblinking eyes. She bent down and picked something up with both hands. She turned back toward them, Alecta's severed head cradled against her chest.

There were no tears on Ile's face as she walked past Evvie, only the same empty expression as before. No words were said. No sounds were made. Ile walked to the channel and stopped at the edge of the water. She stood there until someone called to her from the trench on Piryatuppu. Evvie recognized Olonaya's voice. Then Ile started to go into the water.

"The current," said Evvie. "She can't swim against the current the way she is."

El Codo did not reply.

Ile was up to her chest in the churning sea with her unspeakable cargo. "I have to help her."

"No." The quiet word stopped Evvie before she completed a step. She saw Nagolo and his brother running down the opposite beach toward the channel and Ile.

El Codo started to walk away. "Come with me. Bring the rifle."

She didn't follow.

He stopped and turned around. He raised his weapon and drew down on Ile's back.

Evvie stepped into the line of sight. The pistol pointed straight at her face. She didn't blink. "I'll come with you."

He turned on his heel and started off again. "The rifle," he said. "Bring it."

She followed him through the grove of coconut palms. They headed toward the east beach where the motor boats were kept, where Ted was chained to the tree. She walked six feet behind El Codo. He didn't look around or speak. She stared at the back of his head as she trailed him through the grove.

Evvie understood once more that the cold-blooded brute who walked in front of her was beyond evil. The last twenty-four hours had started to blunt her perception of his depravity, but the vision of Alecta's severed head returned a razor edge to that perception.

I can hit him. I can hit him with the rifle.

She closed the distance between them.

She changed her grip on the rifle so that she was holding the end of the barrel with both hands. Her brain fluttered with excitement. Her chest thumped hard enough for him to hear. Something screamed inside her that this was the opening she'd been hoping for. Something else whispered that El Codo always knew when danger came.

She lifted the rifle high over her head and found herself looking into the muzzle of his pistol. She froze in that position.

El Codo didn't smile. He only nodded at the ground to his left. She looked there. Despite the overcast, she saw her shadow with the upraised rifle.

Without a word he turned and continued walking.

She followed.

He unlocked the long length of chain that secured Ted to the tree. Evvie stood alone on the beach where she had been told to stand, her back to the ocean. She watched as Ted dug someone's grave in the sand between herself and El Codo.

El Codo had positioned them like he was directing a play. He stood in the shade of the tree, his last man by his side. Ted's digging would extend the trench of dead men. The anchor on the short chain still around his neck clanged against the handle of the shovel as he worked. El Codo watched him. Snake eyes glittered.

El Codo looked across the trench at Evvie and nodded toward Ted. "For better or worse," he recited, "in sickness and health, do you take this man?" A corner of the cruel mouth twisted up.

The man standing next to El Codo was Panamanian. He shifted uneasily. He was not Colombian and had never been able to adopt the easy cruelty of the others. He wanted to be back with his family in the rain forest. Back where he could hold his small son in his arms and try to forget what he'd seen on Karatuppu. He reminded himself not to forget to buy another chick in the Punta Mansueto market on the way home. To replace the one that El Codo killed last week.

Evvie tried to think of something to say to the man standing next to

El Codo. He did not seem like the others. Words that would make him help her. … Maybe something with a look, with her eyes. But she could think of nothing.

The hole in the white sand opened steadily despite the bulky anchor. Ted did not dig slowly. Seeing him and what he was doing compounded the rage that was building in her. And rage needed at least some logic to succeed. *Not yet.* She shifted her gaze to El Codo, then to the trees at his back.

A small movement twenty yards behind El Codo caught her eye. The wind moving a flap of peeled bark? There was no wind. A climbing animal like a squirrel? She hadn't seen squirrels, rats, or anything like that on the island.

She swallowed hard. She didn't move, breathe, or blink.

She flicked her eyes back to El Codo. He no longer watched Ted. But he wasn't looking at her, either. The .45 was balanced in the crook of his bad arm, and he was using his good hand both to hold and tune the hand-held radio he had unclipped from his belt.

Her eyes went back to the trees. She saw an inch of black tube, the tip of a pistol. It drifted around the curve of the tree trunk until it pointed at El Codo.

Mark and Nagolo don't have a pistol.

The only sound in her world was the repeating swish of the shovel working the sand.

Evvie glanced quickly at El Codo's man and saw that he was staring at her. The man turned to look where she had been looking. She saw his body stiffen. He yelled, "Carlos! Behind you!"

The scene in front of her shifted to slow-motion. She saw the black radio falling toward the ground like an odd-shaped balloon slowly tumbling. With the .45 back in his good hand, pivoting as if in a dream, El Codo turned to face the shadow that had stepped from behind the tree in the grove. Both weapons spit flame and noise almost at the same time, the shot coming from the trees a split second ahead of the one from the beach. El Codo's shot actually clanked off the weapon held by the shadow figure next to the tree, the .45 slug deforming the muzzle end, rendering the weapon useless. A miss that worked. The shot fired by the man in the trees was true. But a hit that didn't work … because the killing shot did not hit El Codo. As quickly as he had whirled and fired, El Codo had stepped behind his own man. The Panamanian who had shouted the warning took the round in his forehead. Evvie watched a drifting cloud of red mist envelop both skulls. But Codo lived. Untouched. The cruel left hand moved under the left arm and across the chest of the still-standing man. El Codo held the body upright.

For a moment, Evvie didn't comprehend what she looked at next. Then it was clear. Codo's pistol was pointed at her. Not at the shadow.

"I presume you're interested in the lady?" El Codo's words. Grotesquely civil.

"Yes. I'm interested in the lady," Arthur replied.

"Then drop your weapon." El Codo knew that he'd hit the shooter's pistol, but didn't know for certain whether the pistol was disabled.

The man El Codo held, the man who had saved his life with the warning shout, pivoted suddenly and with life's last breath encircled his boss in a bear hug. Strong hands locked behind El Codo's back. The Panamanian slid toward the ground as he died, pinning both arms of the perversion that had crushed the life out of a boy's small pet. The Panamanian could not kill what he wanted to kill, but he held on with more than enough force to keep El Codo immobile until Arthur got to the weapon.

Arthur stood next to Evvie under the tree. El Codo stood on the beach where Evvie had been, disarmed, alone. The reptile eyes gleamed hate.

Without taking his eyes off his prisoner, Arthur reached down and helped Ted climb out of the trench. "Are you all right?" he asked.

"I think so," Ted replied. He had to use the shovel to support himself.

"We've got to get the Indians off the other island," Evvie said. She glanced south toward the mainland, then back at Arthur. "We have to go now!"

Arthur kept El Codo's pistol trained on its previous owner. "What's this bastard been doing to you two? Where are—"

The shovel smashed into the back of Arthur's head. He staggered, stayed on his feet, and turned partway around. The shovel blade smashed down once more and bounced off his temple above the ear.

Ted didn't have to swing the shovel a third time.

Arthur crumbled to the sand.

Evvie felt sanity lift out of her skull. She stared at Ted. He was kneeling next to Arthur, El Codo's .45 in his hand. Ted stood up and walked over to El Codo. He handed El Codo back his weapon.

She sat with her back against the palm tree. Arthur lay next to her, right on top of the spot where Ted's transmitter lay buried. He hadn't moved since he hit the ground. The body of the dead Panamanian, face down, was an inert lump at Arthur's feet. El Codo, in control again, squatted ten yards away on the ocean side of the trench, the .45 in his right hand, the hand-held radio resting on his thigh. He waited for Spider's call.

Ted sat next to the grave he had been digging. His forehead rested on his knees. His eyes were closed. His arms wrapped around his shins.

"What do you know of this man?" El Codo's words were directed at Evvie.

"I don't know anything about him. I don't know why he's here."

"He spoke to you. He knows you."

"I met him in Colon. When we bought the boat."

"Did he kill my men? Is he the one?"

"I don't know," she answered. But she knew. Now, she knew.

El Codo turned to Ted. "You!" Ted's head jerked up; his eyes opened. "Why did you hit him?"

Ted hesitated. He glanced at Evvie, then back at El Codo. He straightened up a bit and curled his fingers around the anchor chain to keep it from cutting deeper into the skin of his neck. "Me and her, we're flat busted," Ted answered. "We put our last bucks into that boat. We were going to move some product from Mulatos to Providencia. Cocaine. Some emeralds. You're the only one around here who can bail us out. I thought you might pay me to ... might let me work for you. Your men are dead. I can help."

El Codo continued to stare at him. Ted's offer wasn't rejected; it was ignored. "Do you know if this man killed my men?"

"I think he did."

"I will wait until he wakes up. I will make him tell me. I must know. I will kill him then, but first I must know."

El Codo went silent. He was in no hurry. He would finish the three people after the question of the killings had been answered. The Indians on the other island could be slaughtered if Spider wanted them slaughtered.

There was nothing more to do. Nothing but wait.

Two minutes later the radio crackled and the sound of rushing air came out of the speaker. A thin reedy voice talked in Spanish. El Codo keyed the sending switch and talked back.

The critical word was spoken, a code word, but the way it was framed, the way it hung in the air with silence on either side … Evvie knew the signal had been sent. El Codo turned off the unit.

Spider was on his way. Close by.

El Codo looked at Evvie. "Try to wake him."

"So you can kill him?"

"I will not kill him. Even if he tries to run away, I will not shoot to kill him. I will catch him. It is a small island. I will shoot pieces of him until he tells me about the killing of my men."

Evvie refused to move. *Rot in hell, asshole.* If defiance was to be her last shot, defy she would.

El Codo formed a dead grin. He glanced down for a moment to refasten the hand-held radio to his belt.

In that split second, like a rabbit bolting cover, Arthur was on his feet and heading into the palm grove.

Evvie raised her left hand instinctively to protect her eyes from the shot she knew would come from El Codo's pistol. But her right hand remained where it had been for the last five minutes.

El Codo howled. That fearsome sound was punctuated by a three-shot volley. The reptile face burned with rage in swirls of gunsmoke. El Codo exploded forward from his crouched position. Despite the soft sand, in the space of three strides he was moving like a jungle cat. He cleared the grave in a flat charging leap. Eyes on fire. Eyes on Arthur.

He moved with unreal speed in Evvie's direction. He would pass close to her. He saw only Arthur. Her right hand tightened on the wooden shaft beneath the sand. She raised the forward end of the mean pole that had killed Bibi. The rear of the shaft remained wedged against a hump of palm tree root. Evvie's world went to quarter speed. She watched the needle-sharp point of the pole drifting up. Sand poured off the top of the shaft like water slipping off the back of a surfacing whale. El Codo seemed to float toward her.

In that magic place where seconds turn to minutes, she refined the point of impact. She centered his stomach.

His own momentum carried him halfway down the shaft.

When Evvie was young, a month short of seven years, a neighbor boy speared a snake behind her house one summer afternoon. The boy used a thin metal rod and stuck it into the snake's middle. Other than feeling sorry for the reptile, the most vivid memory she retained from the killing was of watching the incredible contortions of the creature as it twisted powerfully to get off the spear. The snake was only two feet long. It tied in knots. It rattled the silver shank. It squeezed so mightily and thrashed so hard at the ground that the boy lost his grip on the metal rod. The reptile wrapped around the shaft with such wild strength that Evvie saw metal bend.

Now, right in front of her, El Codo was reacting in exactly the same way.

That surprised her. She'd seen a lot of movies where people were impaled by arrows or spears. They always dropped to the ground after a few stunned seconds, then passed away with subdued resignation. That was how humans died. They had minds. Logic, memory, shock, and the perception of reality combined to create an acceptance of death based on what the senses were reporting; the escape from pain enabled one to depart life with mute grace.

Not El Codo. Not him.

He grasped the spear with his good hand and tried to push his body backward off the shaft. He could not. He emitted a strange shriek, then fell on his side and thrashed with an uncoordinated violence so furious that twelve inches of the bloody pole sticking out of his back broke off against the ground. He twisted and squirmed and coiled around the shaft like living rope, then uncoiled and repeated the sequence with hideous variations. It seemed as if pain didn't exist for that body, and without pain, the brain was free to explore every contortion and combination of savage force to escape the shaft.

El Codo took a long time to die.

Up until the moment the point drove into, through, and out of his middle, Evvie had assumed that, despite the monstrous evil, El Codo was still a human.

She sat with her back against the tree. She was painted with his blood and fluids. Small sticky things that somehow came out of him were drying on her skin. What had been El Codo lay on its back, the yellow light gone from the flat eyes.

She tried to look at the sea. She tried to look at her own hands. She tried to focus on the trees, on the shovel lying on the sand, on El Codo's broken radio that lay in the sun. Anything. Anything except what she kept coming back to.

She couldn't stop staring at the grotesque face.

El Codo's face.

Its frozen features, its expression, even more savage in death than in life.

Chapter 25

Evvie closed her eyes and rested the back of her head against the trunk of the palm tree. When she was a little girl, she used to play a game all children play … stare at something bright, a light, a picture, then close the eyes and watch the reverse image linger. As she sat there, eyes shut tightly, the gaunt visage of El Codo lingered in the same way, whites gone to black, blacks to white, a spectral negative. The afterimage fragmented and dissolved. She was too tired to think, too tired to move, too tired to sleep. She was so tired that, even not asleep, she began to dream anyway. She was alone in a small boat at night on a wild ocean, where each dark wave hid the next, and to windward, moving toward her, the rogue sea that climbed higher and blacker than all the rest.

Spider!

She shuddered out of her reverie and saw Ted on the beach, limping and stumbling south, holding the anchor, and looking toward the mainland. Looking for Spider. The sky had grown dark. Cat's-paws scurried over the surface of the lagoon. Palm branches slapped and sawed at one another. She looked down at El Codo one more time. Delicate wind-driven sand had already begun to fill the hollows of his upturned face.

She averted her gaze from El Codo. Back to Ted. He was almost out of sight in his haste to scan the Gulf approaches to Karatuppu. She was alone with two corpses. Ted gone. Arthur somewhere on the other side of the island and probably unaware that El Codo wasn't a threat to anyone at all.

I killed him. I killed El Codo.

Surprisingly, she felt dissatisfied more than relieved. For several seconds she couldn't figure out why. Then it came to her.

Wait a minute. What the hell's wrong with me? It's not over.

A slight smile animated the flesh of her right cheek and lip, just enough of a smile to crack the gritty scab of El Codo's blood and Karatuppu sand that covered her face. Some of her war paint flaked off and fluttered away on the wind. But not too much. She scooted four feet to the right on her rear and dug up Ted's transmitter. She looked around to be certain no one was watching, then crawled ten feet up the beach on her hands and knees and reburied the transmitter in a new place. And marked it with a piece of driftwood.

She smoothed out the sand and got to her feet. That's when she thought of Arthur again. *Damn it all! He was hurt!*

She hurried toward the center of the island.

"I've had better days." He tapped at his left thigh.

She tore the pants leg up to his groin and discovered a blossom of red muscle above the knee. "Anywhere else?"

"The second one scratched my skull. Not one of my vulnerable places." But the words were slurred.

She saw the horizontal tear in his scalp. "You ought to wear a helmet."

"Funny girl."

He saw the concern on her face and tried to put her at ease. "The leg is through and through, lady. No bone. Looks worse than it is. Where's the bad guy?"

"Which one?"

He smiled at that. "The one without the big necktie."

"In hell."

"Dead? How? ..."

His question was interrupted by the clank of metal on metal. Ted struggled toward them beneath the palms. It appeared that a pair of testicles, bruised blue-purple and swollen, were giving him as much trouble as the anchor he wore. Matched streams of blood ran down either side of his chest from the abrasions cut into his neck by the short chain. "The bastard doesn't have the key on him. I couldn't find it in his hut, either. I gotta get this thing off."

"You'll wear that thing for the rest of your life, which won't be long!" As Arthur yelled the last word, he tried to lunge at Ted, but Evvie put both hands on his chest and forced him back down. She was startled by how little pressure it took to stop him. "Not now!" she snarled. She bent forward and used her teeth to start a parallel rip in Arthur's pants leg. She tore away a long strip of material and wrapped the wound while Arthur continued to glare at the man who almost got him killed. She finished knotting the bandage. She stood up. She looked at each of them and shook her head.

Men. So much macho bullshit. "You two figure it out."

She turned on her heel without saying another word and started for Piryatuppu. She didn't run. She was too tired to run. She only walked.

"Codo is dead! Come get the boats!" She splashed into the channel up to her waist and yelled again. "Nagolo! Codo is dead. They're all dead!"

She dunked her head under the water and used her fingers to comb through her hair. She rubbed at the congealed chunks of El Codo stuck to her face. She tried to rinse the blood off her hands, El Codo's blood, Arthur's blood. When she looked up, she saw Nagolo and his brother standing on the beach across the pass. The current, well past full ebb and now flowing gently back into the gulf, was not strong enough to prevent some of those on Piryatuppu from swimming across. She went back to scrubbing at the gore. All she could think of was removing El Codo's filth before she threw up in disgust. When she looked up again, Nagolo was standing next to her. "Get all the cayucos over to Piryatuppu," she said. "And move one of El Codo's boats over here. I might need it later." She saw three more Cunas swimming the pass toward her, but she didn't wait for them. She turned away and headed back to Arthur.

As she trudged through the grove, exhausted and confused, she tried to figure out what to do next.

Spider's on his way. But Mark said he won't be here for another three hours. Time. We've got some time.

With El Codo out of the way, she realized there was a good chance that the U.S. government, not Spider, was the greatest threat. At least for now. She envisioned black planes strafing Karatuppu. Then pictured a score of khaki-clad military types storming the beach and shooting at everything that moved. She knew her imagination was in free fall, but then remembered Waco. And Spider was a much greater threat than two dozen Texas children and a Bible-spouting hermit.

But I moved the transmitter. Ted can't call them in.

265

She decided that the Cunas had to come first. She had to figure out what to do with them.

But she was so tired.

When she was fifty yards away, she saw Arthur and Ted facing each other, inches apart. One of Arthur's elbows was jammed under Ted's chin, pinning Ted against the trunk of a palm tree. Arthur seemed to be aiming the black bulk of El Codo's .45 at Ted's face.

"No!" But just as she shouted, Arthur fired. Ted's head jerked back and rebounded off the tree trunk.

She ran toward them, then saw Ted slap Arthur's elbow from under his chin. "You dumb son of a bitch. You'll bounce a round into my damned neck."

Why is Arthur helping him?

She realized that Arthur was trying to get the anchor off. Some sort of deal had been struck.

Arthur lowered the pistol and looked at Evvie. "The lock is tempered. We can't shoot it off." He smiled.

"There's got to be a way," said Ted. He had one finger stuck in his ear and was wriggling it to stop the ringing caused by the noise of the shot. "You idiots don't know how important this is."

Arthur cocked his head toward Evvie. "Idiots? I think it looks good on him. I say we leave it the way it is."

"I'll show you how important!" A stare, a nod, then a grin more sneer than smile. "I want you two to see something," Ted said. He clanked over to the palm tree, dropped to his knees, and started digging in the sand. "This is what it's all about." He was digging faster. Throwing sand now. "This is more important than a few inbred Indians. You two almost fucked the dog on this one." He glared at Evvie. "Yeah, it's important. Like I told your pal here, if you don't help me do this, you're both looking at fifteen to twenty on obstruction."

That's why Arthur's helping.

Arthur raised his eyebrows at Evvie. "He's threatening us." Another smile. But despite his nonchalance, Arthur wobbled on his feet. His gun hand went to his forehead and he almost fell.

When Ted hit him with the shovel. Concussion.

She glanced quickly up the beach. Four Cuna adults, two males and two females, were wrestling one of the black hulls down the skids into the lagoon.

Ted was frantic. The hole he made was deep. Wide. He kept clawing at the sand.

Once more Evvie looked at the Cunas. The two women were pushing the motor launch quickly to the north through the shallows. The Cuna men, with their small armada of cayucos tied bow to stern, trailed behind.

"Where is it? Where the fuck is it?" Desperation. Fear. Ted looked over his shoulder at them, then his eyes found El Codo's body several feet away on the far side of the tree. He scrambled on his hands and knees toward the corpse. With his back to Evvie and Arthur, he began to rifle El Codo's pockets. Then each seam of clothing.

Arthur stared at him. Fascinated. Unsteady. Not understanding.

While Arthur watched Ted, Evvie walked ten feet to the driftwood stick that marked the place where she'd buried the transmitter. She went to her knees. Shielding her movements from them with her body, she dug up the little radio. She brushed off the sand and pried open the lid to the battery compartment. Unsnapped the terminals. Took out the battery. Picked up a small rock next to her knee that felt as though it weighed about the same as the battery and put it into the terminal compartment. She snapped the lid back on. She pushed the small lithium battery several inches into the sand and covered it over, then tossed the transmitter next to the tree where he had been digging. She got to her feet and went back to stand next to Arthur. Retrieving the radio and removing the battery had taken thirty-five seconds.

Ted had stripped El Codo of his shirt and was in the process of trying to pull the pants off the corpse. His expression alternated between panic and rage. Oddly regular intervals. Like the intermittent loom of a lighthouse.

"Ted."

He paid no attention.

She spoke louder. "Ted!"

He turned.

She pointed to the transmitter capsule. "Is that what you're looking for?"

He looked where she was pointing and pounced on the capsule from his position next to El Codo. A distance of twelve feet. One scrambling leap. Like the anchor was papier-mâché.

Evvie stared at him as he brushed off sand and caressed and fondled and fingered the radio as though it were delicate crystal. He stood up and faced her. His face went to cruel in a storm of scowls. He shook the radio at her. "These are the big leagues, you simple fuck. This isn't kid stuff. This is billion-dollar big-time. This is revenge and power and law and winning and everything that's right. ... That's what this is about." He lowered the arm that waved the transmitter in her face. "Some day maybe you'll grow up."

She didn't reply.

"And when you do, maybe you'll get that tit cut off. See, that's the difference between us. When I find something wrong, I fix it. That's what I'm paid to do. Fouled-up people need fixing. And the guy we're after is about as fouled up as they come."

She nodded in the direction of Piryatuppu. "You sure as hell did a great job fixing things around here. And as far as tits go, I'm doing okay. Maybe I'm lucky. Maybe being a little less than perfect keeps me from treating people like you treat people."

He pushed between them heading toward the south end of Karatuppu. As he did so, he snatched the .45 away from Arthur with his free hand. Arthur made no move to resist; his head hung down and he was alternately opening and squeezing his eyes shut in an attempt to fight off the effects of the concussion.

Ted moved away. Oblivious. No more words. Cradling the precious radio.

Evvie stood there staring after him.

Arthur turned to look at her. What he saw dissipated some of the fog that twisted through his brain. The emptiness in her eyes and the way her face suddenly seemed frozen made him blink some more, and he touched the side of his skull where the shovel had bounced off his temple. He hobbled over to the tree, sat down in the shade, and tried to force the dizziness away.

He sat there and watched Evvie drag El Codo's body into the grave meant for her. She mumbled some words about the Cunas not having to look at the monster's carcass, but she made no attempt to pull the wooden pole out of El Codo, and the shaft-tip protruded above the level of the beach.

Fighting confusion, Arthur stared at the woman he thought wouldn't touch a body like that. He was reminded of the detached efficiency he'd seen on the faces of burial teams in Nam thirty years earlier. Resigned. Exhausted. Somehow frightening.

That's how Evvie looked in those moments. She used the shovel Ted had used, and began to fill the grave with sand. As she worked, Arthur tried, with monumental effort, to explain what he'd learned from Dulcie. That Davis, Ted, and Dulcie herself were working together on the DEA sting. That the alley mugging was Dulcie's desperate attempt to keep Evvie out of the San Blas operation without blowing the government's cover.

Evvie kept working. She didn't seem to hear what Arthur was saying. Or didn't care. Then it came to him. What he was seeing and where he'd seen it. She was two personalities. Sane, but two. The insert teams coming out of Laos. The unwilled, unremembered temporary madness that a normal brain used to defend itself against insanity. Evvie was transferring easily. Too easily. When had it started?

Arthur staggered and fell to his knees twice as Evvie walked him to the north end of Karatuppu. Nagolo helped put Arthur into one of the cayucos, then the three of them crossed the slow-moving flood current to the Piryatuppu beach. Cold wind rattled palm fronds high in the bending trees. Curtains of blue rain from a steel sky moved toward the Holandes Channel.

The rest of the Cunas clustered around Evvie on Piryatuppu's shore. Mark looked at Arthur passed out in the cayuco, wanted questions answered, but didn't ask them. It wasn't a time for questions. It was a time for goodbyes.

Evvie put her arms around Nagolo. "You were very brave these last days, my friend," she said.

"Sometimes being brave is not enough." There were tears in his eyes.

"You'll be all right?" she asked.

"We will be all right." He turned and pointed at the approaching squall. "The spirits have sent the storm to hide us. We will go to Icacos and wait for a few days. It is only four miles. Mark and the one in the cayuco will rest there with us. They will be safe." He looked at her. His expression was serious. "I told you that you have great magic." He reached over and took something wrapped in white cloth from Inlota. He handed it to Evvie.

"For me?"

"For you. Inlota made it. She made two, but we must keep one."

Evvie unwound the cloth. She held the wooden *uchu* in her hand and smiled. The foot-long icon was a woman. With three breasts. Evvie looked at Inlota in silence for a long moment. "Thank you." Then she kissed Inlota on the cheek. "Thank you so much."

Nagolo spoke again. "You know why we must keep the other. It has great magic." He paused. "Evvie, the storm will let us go to Icacos. But it will not let us come back. Not for two days. If you can't …"

"Nagolo," she scolded, "you know I can work magic." A smile.

He tried to smile back, but it wasn't his nature to smile about such things.

Evvie glanced across the channel and saw Ted moving in the tree line. He was looking at the motor launch that Nagolo had positioned on the Karatuppu shore. She saw Ted turn and disappear back into the grove.

She looked again at Nagolo. Olonaya had stepped forward and was standing a short distance behind her husband. The rain began to fall. Evvie walked over to her. They looked into each other's eyes. She was about to speak to Olonaya when Mark practically shouted at her. "You're just goddamned crazy! You've got a ticket out of here and you're not going to take it? What's wrong with you?"

"Mark. Listen to me. El Codo's dead. They're all dead. It's over. Ted's going to call down hell on Spider. You were right. Ted's DEA."

Mark's expression showed that the revelation came as no surprise. "And you? Are you DEA? Are you bullshit, too?"

"No. I'm not DEA. And you know it."

"And you're going to stick around? You'd take a chance like that? Get between Spider and the narcs? If you're nuts enough to stay, I'm staying, too."

"Mark." She smiled. "Don't give me a hard time. You saved my tail when you sliced that guy's throat over there." She nodded toward the Karatuppu beach. "I appreciate what you did. But I'll be out of here by tonight on one of Ted's helicopters. When I get to the States, I'll check to see if your record is clear. If you stay here, you'll screw everything up. You're a wanted man—don't forget that. These guys are DEA. I'm not going to let you get yourself—"

A thick shank of lightning lanced into the sea beyond the reef. The air exploded. Mark jumped. Evvie did not. The light deep in her eyes was easily as intense as the light that had just flared across the islands. "And take care of that guy in the cayuco. He's special. We owe him. We all owe him."

She turned back to Olonaya. They shared the indescribable loss, the loss of the little ones. Centuries seemed to shift and, for a brief moment, Evvie remembered the book Arthur had given her that showed the picture of the murderous conquistadors and described how they killed the babies of this land so long ago. A mother's ageless sorrow. What passed between Evvie and Olonaya as they stood face to face on the sands of Piryatuppu was too deep for tears.

"Will time help us?" Evvie asked.

Olonaya waited a long moment before answering. Her eyes were not as soft as the moment. "There are some who will not let the lost ones go. Some who would trade the future to stay with the lost ones. That way is the way of madness. Time does not help those."

"Olonaya, sweet Olonaya. I ..."

"You will come again to sit with me someday?"

Evvie swallowed so hard that the muscles of her throat ached. "I will come back to sit with you."

"I will send a gift to your Cindy in the next spirit boat if you wish."

"I would like that."

"I will do this for you."

"Thank you." She started to reach for Olonaya, a slight beginning motion, but something in Olonaya's look stopped her.

Olonaya nodded once. "Goodbye," she said.

After the boats were loaded, Evvie walked up to the line of palm trees above the beach to watch them go. From the top of the rise, she looked down at the small band of people moving in cayucos through the rain. The boats stayed close to the edge of Piryatuppu, moved slowly in the eerily calm water of slack tide, then headed out into the wide gulf. A rolling mist drifted in from the ocean and began to fill the space between them and her. The cayucos, shrouded by sea fog, faded before her eyes. Shapes ... then shadows ... then nothing at all. An empty wall of white.

"What the hell are you doing here?"

"Why, Ted?" she asked. "Why did you do this to me? Why have you done this to them? Bibi? The old woman? Ile? What in hell were you thinking of?"

"This is important. If—"

"Important? Bibi was important. Cindy was important, too. But what happened to Cindy was an accident. A damned accident. What you're doing here is worse than murder."

"You still don't have the slightest fucking idea of what's going on, do you?"

"Spider? The air cover? The way you stuck that transmitter under your balls?"

Ted's face went slack with disbelief.

"Tell me," she said. "Why did you do this to me? I want to hear it in your own words."

The shocked expression on his face betrayed what he was thinking: Spider? Air cap? If she knew, who else knew? Was the cover blown? If it was, then everything ... "We're going to nail Spider. That's why I did it. He'll be ice by tonight. The biggest fish in the pond. It doesn't matter chasing down the little shits. We've got to nail the—"

"Why? Why wait around? Why not call it in now?"

"Because it could be a straw man. A diversion. These bastards aren't as stupid as they look. I have to confirm Spider in the flesh before we scramble the Black Hawks. Someone has to see him to be sure. Otherwise, we spook our man, lose him, maybe forever. That's my job. Confirm him. That's what I have to do."

"You had to keep El Codo alive, didn't you? You needed him to give Spider the last green light. You traded everything for Spider. Me, these poor people, your conscience, even your damned ... all for Spider."

He didn't answer.

"My husband. My lover." Her face went flat-rock hard. "Does the Agency teach anything about human beings? Real ones? Or is it only about people like Spider? Do you know when you've stepped over the line? When the rot sets in? Is it contagious? Tell me what it feels like when you're no different from the garbage you're collecting."

A crash of thunder jolted the island. Ted flinched.

Evvie smiled a strange, almost coy, smile. But the eyes blazed with an odd chained violence. "Do you think you'll make it?"

"I'll make it," he snarled.

"And if Spider gets here before your people get here?"

"I'll hole up somewhere. Maybe on the other island. Maybe I'll just grab one of those motor boats and head out to sea if there's too many of them. I've got this." He shook the transmitter in her face. "I can call in our SAR with this baby. They lock on the RDF azimuth and pick me up. It won't take them more than an hour to find me out there, less than that."

"You sure that thing works?"

"They run these senders over with tanks, stow them underwater, boil them in oil. They work."

"I'll let you in on a little secret," she whispered. "There won't be 'too many' of them. Spider's coming the last leg by himself. By cayuco. So he won't be spotted."

"There's no fucking way you can know that." Despite his sunburned skin, she watched him go pale.

She smiled. "Have your ... people ... told you that Spider's killing everybody? Even the guys helping him? Spider's not a nice man, Ted. Maybe the guys running that diesel lugger aren't going to see tomorrow, either. It probably takes only two or three of them to crew one of those boats. Shouldn't be too tough for someone like Spider to—"

"Diesel lugger? What lugger?"

"We've got some time to kill. Maybe an hour. Spider's due here at one."

Ted blinked rapidly. He'd blinked a lot since the start of the conversation. "One o'clock? Thirteen hundred?"

"Give or take a few minutes."

His face went past pale to white. What had been doubt was fear. And fear tiptoed toward panic.

"Gee, Agent North, look at that sky. Now that's a storm. Even Black Hawks might not be able to get far in that."

He looked up.

On Icacos Island Arthur lay bundled in a blanket beneath a tarp that Nagolo had strung between palm trunks. Mark crouched next to him. The Cunas huddled together beneath a larger tarp twenty feet away.

"You're lucky," said Mark. "Carlos is a crack shot."

"Was a crack shot," Arthur replied. He had just regained consciousness, but was fighting double vision and a grinding headache. The pain from the bullet hole in his left leg had faded to nothing in the brighter pain of the raging migraine.

"I've got to hand it to you," said Mark. "No telling where I'd be if you hadn't showed up."

"I almost didn't show up. Couldn't find out which island they were on. No float plan. Then I ran into a Cuna who said Nagolo over there had been asking around for a gun. I had to pay twenty bills for the info. Then that weasel charged me another seventy bucks to get me out to Karatuppu. I couldn't just sail up in my own boat. I'd have got my ass handed to me by that bunch that was giving Evvie a hard time."

"She's a hell of a gal."

Arthur glanced at Mark, then stared up at the underside of the tarp again. "I figured you thought as much. Yeah. You've got that right, kid. She's sneaky tough."

"You did one hell of a job picking those bastards off. Where in hell did you hide out all week? Underwater?"

"Picking who off? I got dropped on the south end of the island two hours before I tried to shoot it out with that psycho El Codo. Hide out? I didn't hide out anywhere." Arthur sat up like he'd been bit by a scorpion. "Wait a minute, partner. Where the hell's Evvie?"

"That's him! That's him!" Ted's hands trembled on the barrels of the binoculars he'd found in El Codo's hut.

Evvie watched the distant figure working against the storm, slowly paddling a cayuco toward the south tip of Karatuppu. "You're sure?"

"Every few seconds the wind blows a hole in the rain. It's him! No way it's not him!"

"You can't be sure. Like you said, it could be a decoy."

"That's no decoy. I've studied film on that son of a bitch for weeks. What he looks like, what he eats, how he moves. It's him!"

"You should let him get closer."

She saw the fear in Ted's face then. A bravado-dissolving fear that undercut resolve because it came slowly and had time to eat the kind of courage that depended on reflex. "I don't understand," she said. "You've got the pistol. He doesn't know you're here. Why don't you hide in a bush, get him up close, and shoot him in the back?"

"Close my ass! That guy's got a reputation. One time he put a pressure hose down a guy's throat and blew him up till he split."

"You ought to be able to handle that."

She watched him shifting his feet. Like he was getting ready to run a race.

"It'll take him another twenty or thirty minutes against this wind. There's a boat on the beach on the north end. I checked it out when you were talking to your little fucking Indian friends. Let's get out of here."

He turned quickly and started clanking toward the channel. Evvie trudged behind him.

They reached the motor launch beached on the Karatuppu side of the pass between the islands. The channel boiled in the violence of a full ebb tide. The rushing water churned with debris that washed seaward from the rainswept beaches of the San Blas. Anything afloat in that slice of hell would pass over the remains of Coconut and be expelled far out to sea.

Ted stood on the north beach in the rain and clutched the radio capsule with both hands, held the transmitter like an exorcist holds a cross. Even the cutting weight of the chain and anchor around his neck couldn't claim one of those hands at that moment.

She watched him trigger the sender.

"Striker, Striker, Striker. Jesus Six. Jesus Six. Jesus Six. Go on Holandes number one. Go on Holandes number one. I repeat. Striker, Striker, Striker. Jesus Six. Jesus Six. Jesus Six. Go on Holandes number one. Go on Holandes number one. Out."

He bent forward and pushed the transmitter into a dry place beneath the bow seat. He jammed the .45 into a slot between two strakes in the boat's side. "Three Black Hawks are going to be pouring hot white into this place in thirty minutes. Hurry up!"

She knew there would be no Black Hawks and grinned.

Together they pushed the launch off the beach into the water. The current wrenched the hull parallel to the shore and almost tore the gunnel out of her hand. She helped him turn the boat a quarter turn more so that the bow pointed away from the beach. She gripped the transom edge, dug her feet into wet sand, and hung on while he clambered over the side and fell hard into the bilge.

It took him a while to get onto a seat and to twist Coconut's anchor back to the front of his body. One of the flukes had torn a patch of skin from his shoulder.

"Get your ass in the boat, Evvie."

"... *the river, the river ...*"

She looked at him and smiled.

"... *We shall gather by the river ...*"

She let go of the transom. The current sucked the boat away. Six feet from shore. Twenty feet. Forty. The boat spun sideways and moved faster toward the ocean.

"Evvie! You stupid bitch!"

"... *the beautiful, beautiful river ...*"

She waved.

"You stupid little bitch!"

She watched him stumble back to the outboard. He was doing well for someone with an anchor around his neck.

Three times he tried to start the motor before she saw him look down at the rainwater covering his feet in the bilge.

But it wasn't all rainwater.

When Niki had poured seawater into the outboard tanks, the pint-sized superhero had also pulled both bilge plugs out of the transom holes and thrown them into the lagoon, a trick that wasn't in the comic books. Niki figured that one out by himself. No one knew the plugs were missing because the boat was beached. When the Cuna women pushed the launch north to the pass, it was done fast enough to keep the water draining out, not into the bilge.

A curtain of heavy rain closed over the metal hull and Evvie couldn't see Ted anymore.

So long, Ted.

She knew that the next time she saw him, if she ever did, they'd both have a lawyer nearby.

She heard the starter rope spin the motor two more times.

Then only the rain.

She was glad she wasn't out there with him. She preferred to be where she was. She straightened up, put her hands on her hips, and arched her back. It felt good to stretch; holding the boat had taken real effort.

Ted shouldn't have called her names in front of Arthur. People shouldn't call people names or order them around. Arthur had tried to help him get the anchor off. But all those silly orders. Do this, do that. Go get the gun. Find the key. Get your breast cut off. Get in the boat. Well, people could decide what they wanted to do. Arthur told her that.

"Yoo hoo, Mr. Spider!"

She waved from the beach, then waded out and helped him by pulling the cayuco ashore. She knew that El Codo didn't like to be called El Codo, but Mark told her that Spider actually liked to be called Spider.

She had changed out of the torn skirt and put on Ile's most beautiful mola dress. "I'm sorry that Carlos left in the boat before you got here. It's been a hard week for him and his men. I think he was a bit nervous. You must admit, Mr. Spider, you do have a reputation. ..."

"Carlos said you should sleep here. The Cunas call it the gathering house. It's the only place that stays dry when it rains like this."

"That? That's where the Cunas buried some prayer sticks in the floor."

"Oh, these are just a couple of white stones. Lucky stones. I want you to have them when you leave."

"... *the beautiful, beautiful river ...*"

Chapter 26

He was tired. Close to exhaustion. Many miles. Many men. Many graves. If the white woman in the Cuna dress hadn't helped him across the beach and into the Cuna gathering house, he would have curled up and slept in the low brush as soon as his feet touched the south tip of Karatuppu. But she said that she knew Carlos, and that was enough to let her stay alive for at least a few hours. He needed a pair of eyes and there was no one else. Only two days until the pickup. She could be controlled. Carlos wasn't there and he didn't like that, but he had to sleep. It wouldn't be a problem. ... She was only a woman.

She answered his few questions in an odd and disconnected way that made him think her simple or mad. But harmless. Like a child. So he didn't protest when she led him to one of the sleeping hammocks. One of those without wooden cross braces in the strings so the sleeper could nestle down securely between the high sides. Like a cocoon.

Because it was his nature, he ordered her to retrieve one of the balls of heavy fishing twine common to every Cuna gathering hut and, with a steel fishing knife still drying human heart, he cut off an eight-foot length of line and fashioned an ingenious knot around her wrist, doubling the bitter ends to his own wrist. The resulting four-foot tether tied her to him, and she could not untie it without waking him. He frisked every inch of dress and fold of female flesh, a violation she endured with a quizzical smile. Then he put both the black pistol he carried and the steel knife into the space between the hammock and the small of his back. He stared at her for a while, then closed his eyes. She sat on the bottom of an overturned reed basket next to him, as instructed, and gently swayed the hammock with her tethered hand and hummed soft sounds.

Spider slept.

High in a dark corner of the hut, up where thatch roof and cane wall joined, a gray spider spun silver strands around a fly. A silk casket.

Evvie studied Spider's face in the light of a candle that flickered in a dish on the floor where he had placed it ... too far away for her to reach without pulling hard on the line that bound them together. She liked his mustache. One of those full, Spanish, upper-lip mats without curled-up ends or wax on the hairs. Mahogany skin nicely weathered and quite dignified. The face, like the man, was small and narrow, small bones that looked like they had stopped growing when he was very young. Except for the nose. That was an old man's nose. Blunt. Flabby. Too big for the head. His body, what she could see of it, wasn't muscular at all. And the fingers, rather delicate, ladylike. But messy, of course; all the fingernails capped by dirty little crescent moons. Not his fault. The jungle. She looked more closely at the hands and fingers. He slept with his fingers splayed apart and bent like claws. She remembered seeing them that way when he was awake, now that she thought about it. Not so much like claws, but more like the limbs on a daddy-longlegs spider. She smiled. Of course! Spider.

As she watched him sleep, she tried to decide something. Could Spider, this nice-looking man, really have been the one who sold the drugs that had reached far enough to touch the man responsible for Cindy's death? It was a thought she'd been turning over in her mind for the last few days. Ted said it was the big guys you had to get. The big fish who always got away. It was very important to get the big ones. Mark said Spider was the biggest.

She decided that Spider was a big one.

She looked down at the ball of twine that Spider had used to make the tether that tied her wrist to his. A few days earlier she had seen Nagolo test a single piece of that same line by standing on it and trying to break it by pulling up with both hands. The line stretched just a fraction, but he hadn't been able to snap it. That made Nagolo smile and nod his head. Good, sweet Nagolo.

Being careful not to interrupt the gentle motion of the swaying hammock, she picked up the ball of heavy fishing twine from the dirt floor. By resting the ball in her lap, she managed to tie the loose end of the line into a frayed opening halfway along the top edge of the hammock. It was a stupid-looking knot and she smiled at it. But it held. Evvie sat quietly for several minutes after that. Humming. Gently rocking the Spider that snored. Waiting until he shifted to a position where both arms rested across his chest.

And Evvie began to spin.

The spinning was easy to do. When the hammock swung toward her, she simply dropped the ball over the far side. It plopped softly onto the dirt floor and made a little "poof" sound when it hit ... much too small a sound to hear. With her foot she slid the ball of line back to her side.

Poof.

Slide.

Poof.

Slide.

Poof.

Slide.

The first twenty turns she made were made with a light touch so as not to wake him, but each wrap was a tiny bit tighter than the previous one.

He looked so peaceful.

Twenty more turns. The sides of the hammock began to wrap snugly around the center line. Spider was the center line. She worked the next ten turns quickly because he tried to move one of his arms and she was afraid he'd wake up. All tight turns. Turns that captured Spider's chest and arms and pressed in on his stomach.

Twenty more turns, this time around his hips and upper thighs. Back to his middle with twenty more. Real tight now.

She stopped the spinning and the humming and the hammock swaying and leaned forward and looked into Spider's face from a distance of six inches. His eyes were wide open now. They had been for the last ten turns. In fact, the eyes were more than wide open. They sort of bulged like frog eyes. The Spider was trying to be a frog.

He could breathe, but just barely. He couldn't make words. He could only make wheezes.

She knew it would be impolite to tell him about Cindy when he couldn't answer back. But she thought he should know.

"My name is Evvie. I had a little girl. Her name was Cindy."

She waited a moment just in case he really could speak and wanted to say something nice about Cindy. He didn't.

"Cindy was shot when a man who needed drugs tried to rob a store. You know, the little stores with all the lights? That stay open all night? The kind that sell cigarettes and sodas and those cups of ice slush?"

No response.

"Well, she was killed and my husband ..." Evvie smiled " ... who's really a big jerk and used to work, oops, still works for the DEA, well we, me and him, we bought Coconut? A really nice boat? ... And we came down here with Arthur in his boat?"

She paused and tapped herself on the forehead with a finger.

"You don't know Arthur. He's pretty special. He takes these pills. ... Well, we came to Karatuppu and met Olonaya and Nagolo and all the Cunas. ... This is their house. ... And El Codo, Carlos? ... He was here. I guess waiting for you."

She leaned close to his face. She whispered. "It was really terrible. The worse thing was Bibi got killed. And then a lot of Carlos' friends got killed."

She sat back and spoke in normal tones and volume. "So, guess what happened. I took Ted's battery so he can't call the DEA and tell them to come get you. And all the Indians got away and I killed El Codo with a big stick."

She smiled and rocked the hammock a little bit.

"And that's about all there is to it."

She stared at him for a long time and listened to the wheezes and watched the eyes bulge. Then she jammed the ball of line between Spider's knees so it wouldn't get loose and stood up.

She ducked under the hammock and moved to the other side. By pulling hard on the tether line she could reach the candle dish with her toes. She herded the candle close and held the tether line in the flame for a few seconds until it burned through. She untied the tight turns around her wrist and stretched. It felt good to be free.

She went back and sat next to Spider again. She picked up the ball of fish line and saw that she had used less than a quarter of the roll.

With her wrist now free of the tether, she began to rock the hammock again and hum the soft sounds ... and spin. She tried to neaten her effort by making symmetrical and spaced turns starting at his thighs and working steadily toward his head. At the level of his sternum she paused because the wheezing stopped. She moved close to his face again. No, there was a barely audible wheeze still going on. She smiled. She spent several minutes looking at his eyes, which seemed as though they were being forced out of his skull by some sort of pump that was pumping him up from the inside. And she looked at and touched the side of his neck where a big vessel swelled like a balloon every few seconds before shrinking back beneath its cover of bright red skin.

The red skin reminded her of the times when she was a little girl and she wrapped sewing thread around and around her finger and was always surprised at the funny feeling it got, at how a delicate thing like thin thread could cause so much pressure. Her mother had scolded her about that and told her that her finger would fall off if she didn't stop. Her mother really did scold too much. Evvie promised herself that she wouldn't scold her baby about every little bother.

If she ever had another baby.

The fish line ran out right at the level of his throat. She was hoping it would last until she had covered his face, which she didn't want to see anymore. But she'd underestimated how wide the shoulders were and how much twine it would take. She did gain some extra slack right after something made a loud crack in his chest and shoulder area, but the slack wasn't enough. And she didn't want to unwrap and rewrap him from the stomach up. Besides, when whatever it was cracked, Spider had done a very ungentlemanly thing by breaking wind for an uninterrupted five full seconds, and a bad smell was all over the hut.

She thought for a moment about her friends, Olonaya and Nagolo and the others, coming back and having to look at Spider's Halloween face.

She picked up the candle and began to burn away the hammock's end ties where they hitched onto the support poles.

Chapter 27

Mark stood on Susurro's foredeck and scanned the south and west beaches of Karatuppu. He turned once more to look back at Arthur. "Nothing's moving!" he shouted. "I don't see a damned thing!"

"She might be inside one of the huts. Can you make out any boats or cayucos on the beach?" Arthur feathered Susurro along the west reef. The gathering hut was visible and two of the smaller huts.

"No boats. Nothing. Shit!"

"Give a yell."

"Evvie! Evvie, it's Mark! Answer up!"

No answer came.

After Arthur and Mark had talked in the rain under the ponchos, Arthur asked Nagolo to get them off Icacos Island and take them to El Tigre Island where Susurro was moored. They had to go back for Evvie, but there was no way the frail cayuco could make it upwind to Karatuppu in the storm. Nagolo heard the urgency in Arthur's words and understood the concern on Mark's face. Without hesitating, Nagolo told Olonaya that he was taking the two men to El Tigre Island.

El Tigre was thirty miles southeast and just off the mainland. The storms rolling over the archipelago were strong, and the trip in the frail cayuco, even running downwind, had taken all night and part of the next day. Finally, they said goodbye to Nagolo. Twenty-six hours had elapsed since they'd last seen Evvie. But Susurro beat to windward quickly and they made it to Karatuppu with three hours of daylight left.

"Evvie! Where are you?"

Still no answer.

"The other Indians couldn't have come back to get her. Too much weather," said Arthur. "And there's no sign of druggies or feds. I'm going to tack back to the south end. We should be able to hold an anchor there. It's a lee shore."

Compromised by the bullet wound in his left leg, Arthur stumbled up the south beach holding on to Mark's shoulder for support. "Check the east shore!" he ordered. "Look in the huts. I'll take the west side."

Halfway up the island Arthur came abreast of the gathering house and left the west shoreline to check inside. Empty. No sign of life. He began to examine the interior. He needed to find something, anything, that might explain what happened to Evvie. Signs of a struggle. A shell casing. Blood. Even some kind of message scratched into the dirt. But all he saw that was out of place was a burned-down candle wick in a dish of cold wax in the middle of the bare floor.

The light dimmed behind him as a figure filled the doorway. He whirled to meet the threat. Mark. Only Mark.

"She's not in any of the huts. She's gone." Mark slid down into a sitting position, his back against the cane doorframe, and tried to catch his breath.

"Wait a minute, partner." Arthur was staring at the cleared ground outside the gathering house. "Look. There."

Bisecting the dirt and storm debris of the clearing was a smooth track. It curved toward the beach, as obvious as a knife slash in a painting.

The two men followed the track. "This isn't a cayuco drag, is it?" Mark asked.

"There's no skeg mark. It's not a cayuco." Arthur didn't say more. They both knew what they were looking at. Something, or more likely someone, had been dragged out of the gathering house.

The trail led out of the trees and onto the beach, then angled to the north. The rainstorm had smoothed the sand and the drag was even easier to follow. It snaked like a country road to the water's edge and disappeared.

Arthur stood in the shallows up to his knees and looked for some kind of sign beneath the surface. "It must have been loaded into a boat here. Or ..." His eyes snapped up in the direction of Piryatuppu. "Come on!"

They saw it at the same time. Across the channel pass, on Piryatuppu's shore, the drag trail led up from the water's edge and into the tree line. Even from where they stood, they could see it had been a struggle for the one who had done the dragging … and it had been one. Deep gouges in the sand next to the track showed that. Footprints. One person.

Arthur grabbed Mark's arm to keep him from going into the water. "Hold it. Not in that current. We need Susurro."

They used Piryatuppu's lee as they had Karatuppu's. After anchoring at the edge of the coral shelf, they waded ashore. Arthur carried a pistol-grip Mossberg 20-gauge shotgun taken from Susurro's rope locker in the forepeak. Something about the strange island seemed to make him unsure. Mark wanted to ask him what it was, but did not.

They picked up the trail on Piryatuppu's beach. They followed it through the tall palms to a white sand clearing in the center of the island. The trail ended at a pit in the sand plain. They looked into the pit.

The morning sun littered the gray ocean with scraps of gold foil. Susurro was twenty miles off the coast and under way for the Canal Zone. They had found Evvie sitting on a small wooden pier on the north end of Piryatuppu wearing Ile's mola dress, scrubbed and calm and sunny as if she were waiting for the tender to take her back to the cruise ship. She greeted Arthur and Mark like they'd gone off to pick up a case of beer and were just returning.

Arthur moved to the windward side of the tiller and settled back against the cockpit rail. He looked through the open hatch at them as they slept, Evvie on the bunk in the soft angle between cabin berth and lee bulkhead, Mark on a pad on the cabin sole.

A few hours earlier, before Evvie had gone into the cabin to sleep, Arthur told her that the reason he had sailed back to the San Blas was because he had been the one, unaware, who had escorted her right into the middle of a nightmare. "I didn't know what I was getting you into at the time, but when I found out … well, I don't want to get a bad reputation as a tour guide." She kissed him on the cheek when he said that.

Arthur trimmed the jib and headed up a few degrees to clear Manzanillo Point. Susurro heeled to port and whispered her approval. Arthur sailed while Evvie and Mark slept.

Thirty minutes later Evvie awoke and rummaged through a cedar box where she found some of Arthur's old sailing clothes. She put together a sorry mismatch of oversized pants and shirt. She made coffee, brought it out into the cockpit, and sat beside Arthur as he guided the boat over gentle swells that heaved up slowly from astern.

He answered a few more of her questions, details she wanted to know. They sipped hot coffee. Minutes passed in silence. When Arthur turned and looked at Evvie, he saw tears.

He put an arm around her shoulders and pulled her gently so that her head lay against his cheek. "What's going on?" he asked.

"It's been horrible," she said. Her voice was breaking. "These last two weeks. One nightmare after another. Hell, my whole damned life's been horrible." She grabbed a fistful of his shirt and held on. "It's like a book with pain on every page. I'm so tired."

He squeezed her shoulder. "You should look closer at some of those pages."

"I don't want to look at pages. They hurt too much."

"You're missing something," he said.

"Missing something? I wish I'd missed it all!"

"Think of some of the little things. Good things. Good stuff in the middle of all the bad stuff."

"Like what?"

"Like in the last two weeks. Do me a favor. Make an old man feel good. Tell me some good things. Say them out loud. No matter how small they seem. Even if they're in the middle of a pile of bad stuff. Maybe start back in Colon."

She waited long moments, soft hair against rough skin. Then she started to talk. "When I first sailed Coconut? In the bay? That was good."

"More."

"When the big ships went out. They made me cry. But it was a good kind of cry. They were so beautiful." Her words were stronger. "When Dulcie and I laughed. When I was stupid and talked to her like she was Tonto."

Arthur felt her smile move against his chest.

"When I spilled water on you in the restaurant that first day." She twisted the material of his shirt. "That was good ... maybe not good, but it was funny. You looked so, so deadpan." She took a deep breath. "And the storm ... I did good there, didn't I?"

"You did good."

"When I was sailing Coconut way out on the ocean, a little bird came and sat next to me. I think it would have drowned if I wasn't there."

He nodded.

She let go of the fistful of shirt and wiped away a tear. She straightened up and touched her cheek to Arthur's hand that rested on her shoulder. "I helped Ile get out of the sun. I sat on the beach with Bibi on my lap." She wiped a tear on the back of Arthur's hand. "And I said goodbye to my Cindy. I did. I said goodbye."

She closed her eyes. "And Niki, my little guy. He never stopped thinking he could help. Always trying, always a big smile."

Arthur mussed her hair. "Some people press flowers between the pages, even in sad books," he said. "Get the picture, kid? Life's a bucketful of twenty-dollar losses, but there's a few ten-cent wins stuck in. Nobody's got a right to much more than that. Nothing wrong with ten-cent wins."

"We got the gun, me and Nagolo. We beat them, didn't we?"

"Yes, you beat them. You beat them all. Fair and square."

"And I helped you, Arthur. When El Codo started chasing you and you didn't have a gun. I helped you."

"Now we're getting out of the ten-cent category."

"Maybe fifty cents?"

"Let's go a buck on that one," he said.

"And when—"

He rapped her on the head. Not hard. "Okay, okay." He put his arm around her shoulder and pulled her close again. "You're special, Evvie. You're the kind of person who makes other people want to keep trying. You don't quit. You care. You're real." He shook his head. The old voice became a softer voice. "Someone like you can put together a whole bouquet of ten-centers."

"Arthur? Can I sail Susurro?"

Without speaking they changed positions.

Evvie took the tiller and folded herself into Susurro's needs. After a few minutes, when the sailing needed only touch and not eyes, Evvie turned and looked astern in the direction of the San Blas horizon. "What do you think is happening back there?" she asked.

Arthur didn't look where she was looking. "Does it matter?"

"Shouldn't it matter?" she asked.

He looked at her. "On the way out from El Tigre, Mark told me some of what happened. I can figure out the rest." He paused for a moment, then shifted position to face her.

"Most people never have to do what you had to do," he continued, "never even come close. Those Indians back there are toast if you don't step up, but that's not an option, is it? Not for you. Good people don't really have much of a choice. Sometimes they just get picked up by the ankles and dipped in shit."

She made a small smile.

"You've got hard nights coming, Evvie. You'll have bad dreams and you'll wake up and find your mind on the floor next to your bed. Deal with it. Combat ribbons don't come cheap. Do what you have to with the memories. That's your business. Whatever works. And don't go thinking you're crazy, 'cause that don't apply to you. Maybe to your daddy, but not to you. You don't get off that easy. Some pretty strange things happen to a normal healthy person when she's pushed past hell. I've done my share of reading on it. Had to." He tapped the tin of pills he carried in his pocket. "Go put Evvie back together. There's always something left. And don't give her a hard time. She did good."

Mark came out of the cabin. He was wrapped in a wool blanket. He sat down on the lee side across from them and watched Evvie tend to Susurro as though Susurro were a child.

"How's the arm?" she asked.

He raised the sling. "Hurts like hell." He grinned at them. "Nothing that four weeks in bed with a kilo of penicillin won't cure." Mark looked around. He wasn't a sailor, but the expression on his face told Evvie that he was looking at morning in a way he hadn't looked at morning before. He leaned back and watched Susurro's white sails slip past dawn-pink clouds.

A small sparrow fluttered into the luff of the sail and settled onto Susurro's boom track. It cocked its head and looked at Evvie. The tiny flier bobbed up and down a few times, then jumped into the air and flew back the way it had come. Toward the land. Evvie and Mark watched it go.

Arthur didn't pay any attention to the bird, just shook his head and rubbed the back of his neck. He glanced down at Susurro's compass, then looked back at Evvie. "Watch your course, sailor," he said. "She's heading up on you. She'll do that."

Back on Piryatuppu, in the sand pit in the center of the island, a still and silent body, bound tightly in its shroud, stared up at drifting clouds through white stone eyes. Spider. Dead. On his chest sat Purkwet Kala, who waited for the moon.